TARZAN TRILOGY

*The ape man wheeled around to catch him with a left cross
followed by a solid knee into the abdomen.*

THE WILD ADVENTURES OF EDGAR RICE BURROUGHS® SERIES

TARZAN®
TRILOGY

THOMAS ZACHEK

ILLUSTRATIONS BY DOUGLAS KLAUBA

COVER BY JOE JUSKO

EDGAR RICE BURROUGHS, Inc.
Publishers
TARZANA   CALIFORNIA

Tarzan Trilogy
First Edition

Trademarks including Edgar Rice Burroughs® and
Tarzan® owned by Edgar Rice Burroughs, Inc.
Front cover by Joe Jusko
Interior illustrations by Douglas Klauba
© 2016 Edgar Rice Burroughs, Inc.

Special thanks to Bob Garcia, Jim Gerlach, John Gerlach and Gary
Buckingham for their valuable assistance in producing this novel

Trade Paperback ISBN: 978-1-945462-05-4
Hardcover ISBN: 978-1-945462-04-7

TABLE OF CONTENTS

TARZAN TRILOGY

1936

---

*Tarzan and the
"Fountain of Youth"*

Chapter One

THE BOTANIST

"Isn't it beautiful?" asked Professor Alistair Winslow. The rumpled botanist with the tousled graying hair, mustache and stubbly growth of beard stared through his large magnifying glass. "The Ghana daylily," he said. He pronounced the Latin scientific name, which the man next to him could not fathom, and then added, "A simple, unassuming flower in many ways. It grows in a variety of climates and soils, though all tropical."

Holding the stem between the fingers of his left hand, he slowly turned the flower, steadying the glass with his right hand to focus on one petal, then another surface detail. "Look at it," he continued, "its elegant curved petals, yellow as the sun when they are mature, with lovely striations along the inner surface, the anther and filament bright orange, so attractive to insects...."

The man standing over him, a tanned fellow with squared face and graying brown hair, dressed in a dusty brown shirt and khaki pants, and wearing a holstered sidearm, was less impressed. "But what have you found out about it?"

"Well, that's even more interesting. It's not the lovely flower, but its stem. The secretions of its stem apparently have a degree of curative power. They improve muscle tone, lower the blood pressure, and even—apparently—enhance the natural healing and regenerative powers of the body. We discovered it almost by accident. It isn't in any of the journals. In fact, one of the native bearers put us on to it."

"So what does that mean exactly?"

"Well, we can't be sure yet, you understand," Winslow answered. "It must be tested much more thoroughly, and we need greater quantities of it. But it may help people heal more quickly, feel more vigorous, resist disease better. The one problem we've discovered so far is that it doesn't last long. It needs a stabilizer to extend its useful potency."

"And that's where the bark comes in?"

"Yes. The bark of the jakaba tree. It might be possible to make an extract from it which, when processed and powdered, and blended with the stem secretions, will allow the mixture to have a longer shelf life, so that it can be put in pill or potion form and taken as needed."

"And that grows here, too?"

"Yes, both of these species thrive in this tropical climate. They grow wild, but you could cultivate them both, together," said the botanist.

"So that's what we need, then, Winslow?" the man asked, his brow furrowing. "We can begin production? These will do the trick?"

The botanist put down his glass and gently returned the flower sample to its container. "Well, yes, provided you can harvest them in sufficient quantity and in good condition."

"I'll have the manpower for that."

"I don't know about the type of men I've seen arriving here lately." Winslow nodded toward the window, where he had been hearing the sounds of trucks, shouts of arriving men, and increasing commotion in the yard of the compound for days. "They don't seem exactly like botany assistants to me."

"You let me worry about that. Just tell me if we're getting what we need. Do your part, Professor, and you and your college boys'll come out all right. You will all be safe and protected."

The professor looked up at him, hesitantly. "From what?"

"From whatever misfortune might happen to befall you...at the hands of those men."

Winslow turned back to examining the flower samples. "But you do realize that you'll need considerable quantities of both the plant root and the tree bark to process."

"Again, you let me take care of that. We'll get enough. You just make sure that it's the right stuff."

"That's the point. We can't know whether it's the 'right stuff' unless it's processed properly, and tested, and the results will have to be replicated, and you will need the approval of government drug agencies."

The other man held up his hand in a dismissive gesture. "My company can deal with all of that. I just need to know what we have the makings of here."

"Well," Winslow said tentatively, "what we have is the possibility of a medicine which can make people feel, at best…"—the botanist chose his words carefully, despite the apparent impatience with which the other man waited for him to say what he wanted to hear—"…more vigorous, more energized, healthier."

"No, Professor." The other man allowed a cynical smile to cross his face. "What we have here is the Fountain of Youth!"

Chapter Two
GEORGE FREDRICKSON

J ohn Clayton, Lord Greystoke, pulled open the leaded glass door of the London pub and stepped in. As he strode past the long mahogany bar with the tap handles of painted wood and gleaming brass, he turned more than a few patrons' heads. Though he was impeccably dressed with a waistcoat, topcoat, conservative tie and even a long umbrella, his tall frame, his elegant stride, his bronzed skin and his rather long shock of black hair suggested that this was no ordinary British peer.

Passing through the elongated bar area, he paused in the dark wooden archway trimmed with stained glass and looked around the back parlor until he spotted the familiar balding, ruddy face and graying temples.

"John!" said the man in the corner booth.

Clayton grinned at the sight of his friend George Fredrickson, then strolled over and slid in across the supple leather upholstery. It had been a while since he had seen George, who was an official in the Ministry and one of the few Europeans who knew his secret. Clayton did not normally frequent pubs, but he knew that George, never one to stick to social conventions, liked to get away from the office in mid-day, and this meeting was at George's request. That also told Clayton that the reason for this meeting was personal, not business.

"Let me get you an ale. Boddingtons?" Clayton nodded. Fredrickson eased out of the booth and ambled over to the bar.

Though he was impeccably dressed with a waistcoat, topcoat, conservative tie...his bronzed skin and his rather long shock of black hair suggested that this was no ordinary British peer.

Clayton took a moment to enjoy the early afternoon sunlight illuminating the coat of arms on the stained glass window before Fredrickson returned with two pints of amber ale.

"Ah, here we are." They raised their glasses to each other and took a sip. Fredrickson wiped a bit of foam from his lip, almost in a smack, and ventured, "Good, isn't it?" Clayton acknowledged with a neutral nod, though he was reminded of how he preferred the hearty brew that his African friends made.

"So," Fredrickson began. "How've you been?"

"Good."

"Well, a lot's been going on since you last visited…a new king in Edward VIII, Olympic Games in Berlin, Spain's Civil War…."

"Yes," Clayton acknowledged neutrally.

"Are you going back to Africa soon?"

"Yes, soon. Why?"

Fredrickson put down his pint, looked down, and hesitantly pursed his lips before saying, "It's about my son."

"Jack? How is he?" Clayton asked. "I haven't seen him since he graduated from Oxford two years ago."

"He's missing. At least I think he is."

"What happened?"

Fredrickson took another sip of ale, as if to fortify himself. "My son is in the Belgian Congo, and I haven't heard a word from him. He used to send me letters regularly, almost weekly, but I haven't heard a thing for seven weeks, almost eight now."

"What would you like me to do?" asked Clayton, suspecting the answer.

"Well, the site where he was working is about fifty miles from your"—he hesitated, realizing that "home" wasn't the right word—"… your area…."

"Yes," ventured Clayton, filling in the space where Fredrickson searched for words. Fredrickson had put on a jolly expression to greet him, but Clayton, a perceptive judge of character, felt that his friend seemed to be uncharacteristically hesitant, as if he was not sure how to bring up what he wanted to discuss. "You wish me to find him?"

"I don't want to put you at risk. I just wonder whether you could… make inquiries…."

"You want me to ask whether anyone has seen him?" Clayton had not meant it to sound as dense as it apparently came out.

"Well, you do have certain…acquaintances down there who might have sources of information. Perhaps they have heard something…word gets around…." The expression in Fredrickson's eyes widened hopefully. Clayton wondered why Fredrickson felt he needed to be so indirect in asking a favor.

Then Fredrickson extended his hands palm upward on the table and said, more directly, "I'm worried. His mother's worried. Can you help us?" The bit of perspiration on Fredrickson's head and the growing restlessness with which he sat in the booth suggested increasing anxiety.

"I'll look for him," Clayton stated.

"He might not even be there. I…I don't know," Fredrickson went on.

"I'll do what I can," Clayton assured him.

"Oh, thank you," Fredrickson replied, relieved. "I hoped I could count on you. I am in your debt. Can I buy you lunch? They have a terrific beef pie under pastry here."

"No, thank you. I'm not really hungry," said Clayton, almost the truth. He was indeed a little hungry, but British chefs cooked their meat too much for his tastes. He would later get some fruit and stop by a little shop whose trusted proprietor would provide him with meat he preferred, which he would then enjoy his usual way.

"What was Jack working on?" Clayton asked.

"He went down there with a contingent of botanists and other scientists to study and catalogue species of plant and herbs. When he was doing his postgraduate work he told me he had become fascinated with some new developments in medicine coming out of the Belgian Congo region, something about herbs or some such that were powerful against certain strains of disease. When an opportunity to go down there came along, he signed on with Professor Alistair Winslow, who was apparently in charge of a research team investigating these new developments. As I say, he wrote me every week. His letters didn't say much about this professor's research, just that Jack was enthusiastic about all the work of Winslow's team. Most of his letters were filled with personal matters about how he was getting along…you know, the kind of thing his mother would want to know about. Here are his last two.…"

From the breast pocket of his coat he produced two envelopes and handed them to Clayton. Inside were handwritten letters on cream-colored stationery, their corners and creases supple from having been opened and read and refolded repeatedly. "They don't give you much to go on, but I'm afraid that's all I've got. That's why I'm worried. He should have been back by now, or I should have heard something."

"Have you contacted the university?" Clayton asked, skimming over the letters.

"None of the party has returned or been heard from in the last month. The Botany Department says that is not a long time to go without word. They are not worried, because they say these things happen. Letters out of the Congo are often delayed, phone lines fail, and so on. Seems frightfully casual of them. But I'm not satisfied."

"Have you tried the Foreign Office?"

"They are involved with larger matters. Plus they need some proof, and that's the point—I haven't any, have I?" His brow furrowed a little and his face became more flushed with worry. "This is not like Jack," he continued. "I don't want to wait any longer and that's why I thought I'd ask you… you know…whether you will be going back soon."

"May I study the letters?"

"Of course. Take them with you." Fredrickson sipped his ale, feigning a casual reserve, and then after a moment said, "When might you be leaving?"

Clayton had intended to remain in London for at least another two weeks, but he knew that Fredrickson was trying to ask him to leave as soon as possible, without saying as much.

"I have a few details to wrap up here. I can leave in two days."

George Fredrickson's bushy brow relaxed and the corners of his mouth turned upward in relief that was almost palpable. He proffered, "I know that you will not accept money, but let me get you a plane ticket. It's the least I can do".

"Thank you."

"And let me give you a rifle and ammunition. I think it'd be a lot better than that bow you use."

"George, you know that the way I travel, a rifle is too heavy and cumbersome," Clayton began with a smile, not wishing to be condescending to his concerned friend. "And if the rifle breaks or I run out of cartridges, I cannot fashion more from the materials around me." He need not have added what Fredrickson already realized: "You have chosen to ask me to do this. Let me do it my way."

Clayton finished his pint and rose to take his leave.

Fredrickson added, "Any information…anything you could tell me…would be appreciated."

Looking his old friend in the eye, Clayton assured him, "I'll find him."

Chapter Three

THE CHGALA

The village of the Chgala tribe lay deep in the interior of central Africa. It was a small village, primitive and isolated even from many other tribes. The Chgala were a simple people who had hunted, fished, and lived off the land for generations.

The village bustled with activity much the way it did every day, but this day brought something new. It started as a great rumble off in the distance. The heads of villagers bent over their midday chores began to pop up one after another as they turned to look off into the jungle toward the main trail approaching the village. They all stood up, still and silent, watching two dusty brown trucks come to a stop at the outskirts of the village.

No one in the village had ever seen the great elephant-sized vehicles before, nor heard the roar of engines and the squeal of brakes. Their hands that a moment ago had been weaving baskets or skinning pelts or tending cooking fires now hung at their sides as they all stared at the strangers emerging from the vehicles.

Into their camp walked a half-dozen white men, a motley assortment of Europeans, their brows grim and their faces stubbly with several days' growth of beard. Some wore field jackets, mostly stained, and others wore remnants of various military uniforms, rifles slung on their shoulders, hunting knives and machetes hanging from their belts. The white men stared steely-eyed at the African village, some of them smoking cigarettes and some chewing tobacco.

From among this lot an African man, dressed in garb similar to that of the strangers, stepped forward and spoke in a dialect the Chgala understood. He identified himself as Matu. This man the Chgala knew. Indeed, their chief approached and, with a grin, extended the traditional tribal greeting to him. The two conversed for several moments, with considerable nodding and gesticulating.

Matu turned to the leader of the white men, who advanced to meet the chief. He had a more clean-shaven, squared face and graying brown hair. His clothing was cleaner and crisper than the others, his pith helmet unstained. Matu spoke to the leader in English, and the leader responded. Most of the Chgala had never heard English before, and they all, even the children, watched the strangers intently.

"These are the representatives of the white tribe who contacted you," Matu then said to the chief in his language. The chief nodded and smiled.

The white leader said, "Greetings to you and your people. We have come to visit with your old ones. Are they ready, as promised?"

Upon hearing Matu's translation, the Chgala chief turned to call to some of the villagers. Four men and two women emerged from one of the grass huts and were presented to the white strangers. They were all very old, gray-headed and gaunt, their faces sallow, the flesh hanging loosely around their necks and torsos. Their posture was stooped. They walked unsteadily on spindly legs, and two limped. They wore breechcloths or tunics of grimy, coarsely woven fabric.

The leader asked, "And these are your oldest villagers?" The chief produced the tribal healer, who attested that they were indeed the oldest people in the village. They certainly look old, the leader of the visitors thought, looking at the wrinkly skin and the thin, gangly arms and legs.

The leader looked at one of them, a stooped and wizened man and asked, "How old are you?" The question was translated. The tribesman looked at the white leader with heavy-lidded, milky eyes and said, "I have seen a hundred rainy seasons."

"And you?" he asked of the next man.

"I have seen more."

"And you?" he asked of a frail woman.

"I have seen ninety-six."

"That's amazing," the leader said. "They're just what we want. Get them onto the truck."

Several of the white men escorted the old villagers to the trucks and assisted them in getting up and inside the canopied cargo areas in the rear.

At the same time, the white leader produced a pair of new, gleaming, finely honed hunting knives and a small box containing some bejeweled metal bracelets and necklaces and presented them to the Chgala chief. "There will be more when we finish," he said. "We will return them in three days." The chief smiled, nodding, and accepted the gifts graciously.

The trucks roared to life, turned around, and drove off down the road. The villagers watched them disappear, the young ones waving and expecting to see their grandparents and great-grandparents back again in three days.

The white men drove the Chgala elders many miles in the trucks over rough jungle roads and trails, beyond territories familiar to the elders. The four men and two women jostled back and forth in the rear of the truck, their frail bones stiffening from sitting in an uncomfortable position for what seemed to them a long time. They grew increasingly uneasy. No one spoke to them. Most of the white men riding with them did not even look at them, or only cast sidelong glances in their direction.

At length, the vehicles rumbled to a halt near a clearing where an encampment had been set up with tents, a generator, and lab tables. Several burly, sweating men tended cooking fires. Others cleaned and loaded weapons and sharpened knives. They looked up as the trucks arrived, more with a passing sense of curiosity than of welcome.

Anxiously, the Chgala elders looked at each other. This was not what their chief explained would happen to them.

"Bring 'em over here," the leader called. His henchmen gestured for the Chgala elders to get out of the truck, roughly tugging them along when they evidently did not move fast enough. They were herded into an open central area and lined up, facing the leader. He then gestured as if to indicate, "This one."

Two grimy, tattooed men grabbed one of the old black men, one taking either arm. A third drew his hunting knife and in one swift stroke, slit the old man's throat and let the frail body crumple to the ground.

One old woman opened her mouth to let out a scream, but before she could give vent to it, another white man slit her throat. A third white man, grinning, stabbed one of the old men in the back. "Not in the back, you idiot! The throat!" shouted the leader. "We have to keep the organs intact!"

A third Chgala man wriggled free from his captor and began to run clumsily for the jungle. The leader quickly drew his sidearm, sighted down the hobbling figure, and fired, sending the old man tumbling to the ground, his head burst open. "Jesus, you dumb bastards, hang onto them!" he barked. "Is it that hard?"

The remaining Chgala were dispatched in short order. The white men then picked up the frail bodies and hauled them over to the working area that had been set up and swung them up onto the tabletops.

The leader turned to a man who had been standing near the working area, a bespectacled figure with tousled gray hair and rumpled tweed jacket, whose appearance and manner did not seem to belong with the rest. This man tried to conceal his trembling lower lip or any other visible agitation he might have shown at the speed and ferocity of what had just happened. The leader turned to this man and said, "All right, Winslow. Here they are. Tell us everything you can.

Chapter Four
ARRIVAL

John Clayton was rarely nervous, but he could not get comfortable in the seat of the AW.15 Atlanta that carried him south from London to Rome and over North Africa to end with a night stop in Cairo. He did not particularly trust the craft. The plane jostled frequently, its huge propellers were loud, and the long, narrow cabin offered hardly any room to walk or move about. Normally, he would have taken a steamship for this journey, but George Fredrickson had been kind enough to provide him with an airline ticket (indeed, rather insisted upon it), so that he found himself strapped into the seat of this noisy, jouncy airliner for hours with little to do but look out the window, sip the tea the stewardess had given him, and anticipate landing.

He finished the last of the magazines available on board. He took out Jack Fredrickson's letters and read them again. The first one, dated nearly three months ago, dealt mainly with his enthusiasm at the new venture. He read:

> *We have arrived in the Belgian Congo and set up a base camp a few miles from the Bolongo River. Living in a jungle camp is quite a change from university life, but we are learning fast. The others are all in jolly good spirits and eager to begin our work.*
>
> *As for Prof Winslow, well, you know his dedication to duty. He set to work almost immediately organizing expeditions to gather samples. And when we brought them back*

24

to study, his dogged perseverance often resulted in his working well into the night. He never seemed to tire as long as there was one more species to study, one more log entry to make. He is an inspiration to us all.

It is quite beautiful here. Though the jungle can be dense and treacherous in some ways, it holds a real fascination for me, and indeed for the rest of us. The air is always clean and refreshing and although the weather is hot, the nights are cool.

No, we have not encountered any elephants or big cats or other such creatures yet, but we have firearms and are well protected. We have seen some extraordinary birds, beautiful plumage. Mosquito netting keeps out nearly all the bugs.

And, mother, rest assured that I am eating properly. Cedric is our cook and with the help of our native bearers who obtain provisions, he has managed to come up with some rather tasty dishes day after day.

I hope you are all well. I'll write again when I can. All my love.

Your son,
Jack

He should consider himself fortunate indeed, Clayton mused, for many jungle expeditions fared much less favorably. The second one, the last one his father had received, was rather different:

We have apparently found a new benefactor. The university has provided us with a new mission. We have found a new area of research to pursue. We will shortly be breaking camp and setting off further to the south. I'll write you again when we have established at our new location and I have more details.

Clayton wondered whether Jack's vagueness at the new enterprise was really all he knew or whether he was simply avoiding giving worrisome details to his parents.

*   *   *

In the morning, Clayton resumed the flight which after an in-
terminable numbers of stops reached Nairobi. Though this second
leg of the journey was no smoother, it had the advantage of taking
him that much closer to his destination. At least when he gazed
out the window, rather than seeing oceans and desert, he could look
down upon grasslands, mountains, and eventually dense jungle,
each mile looking more and more familiar and welcoming. After
landing, he caught a bus to Nyumba.

The final leg of Clayton's journey was aboard a riverboat along
the Bolongo River. From its worn wooden decks he could survey
the vast expanse of African landscape passing by. He could drink
in the sunshine and the air, and even the occasional whiffs of diesel
fumes from the engines and smoke from the stack did not diminish his eagerness to return to this land.

His destination was Point Station, a major way station on the
highway that was the Bolongo River. The river snaked through
miles and miles of the central part of the Belgian Congo, sometimes broad and deep, other times narrowing to treacherous rapids
or dropping in spectacular waterfalls. It was plied by all manner of
river craft, everything from large wide-bottomed passenger boats
to fishing scows and native canoes.

When at last the clearing and the old pier that identified Point
Station slowly appeared, Clayton smiled a bit. Standing on the top
deck, he felt the lumbering old riverboat slowly ease its way in toward the pier. A small gaggle of people watched it from the landing,
some of them clearly anticipating arriving visitors. Soon he heard
the calls of the crewmen as they tossed out the mooring ropes,
docked the boat, and extended the creaking gangplank. Putting on
his khaki jacket and seizing his brown valise, he made his way down
the white painted metal stairs, his step so balanced that he had no
need to grasp the pipe railing, narrow though the staircase was.

Only a few other passengers disembarked at this spot, so that
it was but a few moments before he was advancing down the

rickety gangplank onto the graying wooden pier boards.

Before he could step onto the well-packed earth of the shore, a resonant voice shouted, "Well, you're back!" Ambling forward from the knot of people on the landing was his old comrade Captain Reynolds, hand extended in greeting. The two men shook hands, nodding at each other's renewed acquaintance.

William Reynolds, not much shorter than Clayton, was a man with a trimmed mustache and an expression both stern and engaging. He was the provost marshal of this outpost, the provisional authority that passed for the law in this remote area. His dapper blue uniform edged with brass trim was surprisingly neat for this weather, almost starched. From his boots brushed nearly free of dust, to his holstered sidearm, to the polished brass trim, buttons and badge, he presented a portrait of order and colonial authority to the locals. Only his pith helmet and the few sweat stains on his collar belied the concessions a uniformed man must make to the African climate.

"Good to see you back, my friend," exclaimed Reynolds jovially. "Aren't you a little early?"

"Well, yes. I cut my visit a bit short," replied Clayton, glancing around at the grounds of the station. The two walked off to the side a bit, away from the calls of the sailors tending the boat and the conversations of the passengers embarking and disembarking. "How are things? Quiet?"

"As a matter of fact, they are. Nothing much seems to be in the wind. Or does your return sooner than expected mean that things are going to suddenly get more interesting?"

"Well, I don't know that I'd put it that way," Clayton allowed. "I am on an errand, though, looking for the son of a friend. A scientist by the name of Jack Fredrickson. He would have come down here with a party of botanists from England, studying plants. Seems he hasn't been heard from in a while. Heard anything?"

Reynolds thought for a moment. "Fredrickson? Botanists? No, but I'll ask around and keep a look out. Will you be staying for some lunch and a bit of a chat to catch up, or will you be going on straight away?"

"I'll be going," Clayton said.

"I imagined so," Reynolds replied, knowing that this was as much of a good-bye as he was going to get. From his breast pocket he handed Clayton a key, which Clayton took, then turned and jogged across the compound past the main office and past the barracks and supply hut, around the back to a small, dingy, little-used storage shed. Unlocking the door, Clayton entered and crossed to the end of the room, where there stood a series of locked cabinets and footlockers. He moved to the far corner to unlock one paint-spattered and rusty cabinet, inside of which lay an unassuming cache of objects that added up to a secret many men would have paid dearly for.

Clayton began to remove his clothing and pack it up into a footlocker kept in the cabinet. From within he first pulled out and donned an animal-skin loincloth, modest by African tribal standards. He then strapped on a large, sheathed hunting knife and slung around his shoulder a leather quiver of arrows and a lengthy coil of rope. Lastly, he took out an elegantly hand-fashioned long bow and proceeded to bend it against his propped ankle to attach the string, then slung the bow around his shoulder.

Thus attired, he stowed his travel valise in the locker, leaving the letters from Jack Fredrickson safely inside, locked the cabinet, concealed the key in the prearranged hiding place, and made his way out of the shed and the compound without calling any attention to his departure.

The jungle in this part of the continent was ancient and primeval. Huge trees, many a century old, grew closely together, with massive trunks and great networks of intertwining limbs that stretched to the height of multi-story city buildings. The floor of the jungle was so thickly matted with weeds and undergrowth and decaying leaves that walking through it was often virtually impossible. This man Clayton, however, needed no path through the jungle entanglements. With the dexterity of a chimpanzee, he scaled a tree and climbed—indeed, scampered—to the uppermost terraces. From there he moved like an ape, swinging and leaping from limb to limb, traveling faster than nearly any creature on the ground could manage. This lofty height not only provided him safety from other denizens of the jungle, but moreover allowed him to survey the surrounding terrain and the breathtaking vistas that this land afforded. The only creatures who shared this level were the tribes of monkeys with whom he had long ago established a kinship, and who feared him not.

In this fashion he traveled on for many miles. To offset the afternoon heat, he sought out a secluded lagoon. As he approached it, he dropped down onto a boulder extending out over the placid blue waters. He removed his weapons, stood over the edge of the rock, and dived in. The cool water was as refreshing as it had been so many times before.

He swam swiftly, effortlessly, the water almost second nature to him. He dove below the surface to cruise downward, then up again. His head broke the surface and he shook the drops off his dark locks. His gaze fell on the opposite side of the lagoon, where from the brush emerged a visitor wishing to drink—a leopard. He called out loudly and splashed, taunting the leopard, who looked, then turned and scampered off. He laughed at the small triumph.

He emerged from the water refreshed. He took up his weapons again and set off into the jungle, now hungry from his exertion. Attaining a suitable height in the trees, he paused and listened, sniffed the air, listened again. His keen nostrils picked up a scent he recognized, and he waited to hear the sounds to which it corresponded. In a moment, they reached him—the sounds of a wild boar. In another moment he saw it. He quietly moved through the limbs to a spot nearly above it and watched as it rooted around below, searching for grubs.

He pondered his choices. He could take the boar down with an arrow, or make a noose with his rope, but he chose to rely on the elemental method with which he had first learned to kill game. He removed the weapons on his shoulder and cautiously moved over the beast's spot, intensely focusing on its every move. It stopped to look up once, and he froze on his branch, soundless. It promptly returned to its task of rooting in the brush, and he positioned himself precisely above it, whereupon he instantly dropped down upon its back and circled his left arm tightly around its neck. The beast bolted, thrashed and squealed, but the man held his grip firmly and with his right hand plunged his hunting knife repeatedly into its loins. A crimson blood stain spread and spattered the beast's haunches, the man's arm, and the jungle floor. As the boar's thrashing began to diminish, the man repositioned his sinewy left arm to allow him one quick, decisive slash across the throat. The beast growled and wailed in its death agony—and so did the man, in triumph.

At length the boar's writhing ceased, and the man let it sink limply to the ground. He stood over it, and then there followed a sight which would have sent shudders of shock though the halls of Parliament had any of this man's noble peers gazed upon it. For the man crouched down on his haunches and commenced to tear at the boar's flesh and devour it there on the spot, looking in every way a jungle animal save for his loin cloth and nearly hairless skin.

Wiping his face, he rose and stood proudly, straight and tall, slowly surveying his surroundings, listening, sniffing, watching, becoming one with the primitive jungle. The afternoon sun played on the curves of his rippling muscles, and the breeze tousled his black hair. The last veneer of civilization was now stripped away. As he stood there, a half naked bronzed demi-god of the forest, the transformation was so complete as to be startling. Gone was any semblance of the British peer who could stroll the hallways of Parliament in bowler hat and frock coat. Instead there stood, in primitive glory, Tarzan of the Apes, Lord of the Jungle.

*   *   *

His hunger sated, his longing to reconnect with the jungle satisfied, Tarzan returned his attention to the task at hand. He left
the remains of the boar's carcass, knowing that he had done the
scavengers of the jungle a favor. Taking to the trees, he swung at a
smooth, efficient pace, traveling many miles to the west roughly
paralleling the route of the river, though inland from it.

He lighted down in a small clearing where the trees were still
tall giants towering over the earth, but where the grass and underbrush had been trampled from time to time by passing feet. He
stood still, raised his head, and uttered a cry—not loud or obvious,
but one blending in with the surrounding jungle noises yet distinct
enough to be interpreted by any who were listening.

In a moment he heard a response.

He strode forward and, contrary to his usual manner, walked
slowly in a relatively open area, so that he could be easily seen. And
seen he was. From a few dozen yards away in the brush he heard a
call in the Waziri language, which he answered. In a moment there
emerged from the brush a tall, ebony Waziri warrior brandishing a
long spear and a broad shield of okapi hide. He noticed another
and another poking out from the bush, staring grimly at first, and
then, upon recognition, smiling broadly. At that moment a drum
pounded in the distance. It was a message. It announced, "Ape Man
arrives. Welcome."

Chapter Five

THE WAZIRI VILLAGE

The Waziri scouts joined Tarzan and escorted him to their village, which sat behind a wall of tall wooden poles, a sturdy fortification. He was admitted through the great gate and proceeded into the central compound, where the dulcet sounds of a thumb piano wafted through the air and where tribesman after tribesman greeted him with grins and acclamations. Tarzan felt gratified to be welcomed by such friends.

Perhaps the heartiest grin was found on the countenance of M'Bala, chief of the Waziri. Short and stocky, wearing a leopard skin pelt which mostly covered a slight paunch growing over what must have once been taut muscles, the chief presented an imposing figure. In addition to bearing his ceremonial scepter, he wore an intricate string of copper medallions and animal teeth and an elaborate headdress of ostrich plumes, fur and beadwork that conveyed his status to friend and foe alike.

M'Bala immediately bade him in and began to rattle on animatedly about the news of the village before Tarzan even inquired about it. They walked past cooking fires, scampering children, women bearing water pots, woodworking areas, and curved rows of grass huts and tended garden plots.

As they (mostly M'Bala) chatted, Tarzan looked around the busy compound and felt that it was good to be back at one of his favorite places. The European world considered tribes such as the Waziri to be "primitive," yet every time he came, Tarzan was struck by the level and complexity of activity that made up Waziri life. The Waziri village was a model of interconnected enterprises, a small universe of artisans and craftspeople.

At their core, they were warriors, skilled in jungle lore and survival. That meant that they were, of course, hunters who provided the game and fowl and fish for the village, and from which the tribe gained not only sustenance but hides, pelts, and feathers for clothing and adornment. But they were skilled at a great deal more.

Some Waziri were woodworkers, not only cutting and keeping in repair the long poles which formed the village's protective barricade and the ribs for their huts, but also fashioning the finely crafted bows, arrows, spears, and utensils needed for daily life. There were those who skillfully gathered and grew herbs, roots, and seeds to season their food and prepare their medicines. The Waziri women wove and sewed elegantly beautiful robes, loincloths, and headdresses, as well as tending to the more mundane garments always in need of repair.

Others were metalworkers who melted down local ores to fashion tools and blades. It was from one of these that Tarzan had been presented with a hunting dagger, its handle wrapped in finely crafted hide, its long solid blade tempered to steely hardness and its edge razor keen. He would also in this visit be given a new supply of sharp arrowheads that he kept in the bottom of his quiver, to be affixed to arrows later as he needed them.

And everyone, it seemed, was a storyteller, a singer, a musician. Tarzan marveled at the extraordinary music that seemed always to be part of Waziri village life. The tones of the thumb piano that echoed from one part of the village or another for the balance of the day were only a prelude. Tarzan looked forward to the glorious music that he would hear later, for M'Bala had commanded that a feast be prepared for the evening. Tarzan was never quite sure whether they feasted every night, whether they feasted in honor of his visit, or whether perhaps they simply used his presence as an excuse to feast.

At any rate, he eagerly awaited the festivities as he watched the Waziri assemble a massive bonfire in the pit in the center of the compound. They erected a large, sturdy spit and cooking grates and proceeded to rub huge slabs of meat with herbs as they waited for the fire to burn down to its proper level.

By nightfall, when the fire had been leveled and the meat put on to cook, the villagers, arrayed in their feathered and beaded finery, assembled in the central compound area.

A drum line of Waziri men and women formed a half circle around the fire pits. They set up an impressive array of drums, from the round-bellied ones to tall, imposing congas to the squat, symmetrical ones, their top and bottom rings wrapped in colorful cloth, to carved drums covered with taut antelope hide. The players began with a basic rhythm established by a simple cadence from one voluminous bass drum, then a second and third, pounded by the open palms of skilled hands. It began slowly, methodically, and then the higher-pitched, assertive congas introduced a counter-rhythm, which was picked up and complemented by the other smaller hand-played drums and hourglass-shaped drums played with sticks.

As the pounding rhythm continued, the percussion began, with seemingly every villager holding a beaded gourd, a rattle, or a string of seeds, shaking and rattling to the tempo. Even the children shook their little rattles or struck their sticks together. The rhythms grew, palpitating, intoxicating.

Then the voices rose. The rich baritones sang a Waziri chant, whose melody line was then harmonized by higher voices, and then a different chant with a counter melody burst forth to interweave around and through the main chant, so that the blended voices, complex harmonies, and the powerful rhythms soared and filled the night air with such an intensity that Tarzan thought the very trees would shake and the creatures of the night would stop to listen in awe. It was hypnotic.

The chanting and drumming were followed by the dancing. Dozens of Waziri men and women, gaily clad, brandishing spears or gourd shakers, leaped and gyrated to the still-frenzied percussion and chanting.

London had nothing like this, Tarzan could not help but think.

The Waziri feast was as splendid as the musical prelude. Joints of roast antelope, wild boar and fowl were pulled from the roasting pits and passed around, accompanied by earthenware platters of fruits, seeds, nuts and warm flat bread made from local grains with rich, red dipping sauce in clay pots.

Tarzan, sitting cross-legged before the fire among a group of tribal elders, took a particularly rare segment of antelope loin. Between bites, he turned to M'Bala next to him and said in the Waziri tongue, a dialect of Swahili, "This is all magnificent. I thank you, my friend."

M'Bala nodded and smiled in acknowledgment, his mouth too full to talk, boar grease dripping on his chin. He turned to gesticulate to a serving woman bearing a large hide bag, who ambled over and poured into their drinking gourds the Waziri native beer that Tarzan had hoped would be part of the evening. Tarzan took a modest portion, because he preferred to be clear-headed, but he relished the heady, fragrant blend of herbs and the smooth body with which the Waziri brewers had long ago learned to infuse their brew. It was why he dismissed the hoppier, more bitter London beers, much to George Fredrickson's dismay. "British brewers have been making beer for hundreds of years," he would sniff.

Ah, yes, Tarzan thought, but my jungle friends have been making it for a thousand.

The flames of the bonfire continued to illuminate the night, as villagers continued to feast, sing and carouse.

Finishing his ample portion, M'Bala tossed his gnawed bones into the fire, turned to Tarzan, and asked, "And so my friend, what brings you to our village this time?"

"Do I need a reason to visit my old friends and allies?" Tarzan asked, savoring his beverage.

"No, but you have one. What is it?"

Tarzan put down his drinking gourd and turned to his comrade. "I seek the son of a friend. His name is Jack Fredrickson. He is an Englishman, a scientist. He has come here to study plants."

"The friend of Tarzan is a friend of M'Bala, and his quest is our quest. How can we help?"

"He arrived here with a party of Englishmen about three months ago. They would have a small expedition, or perhaps would have set up a camp. They would be studying plants and wildlife. Have you heard anything?"

M'Bala thought for a moment. "No. We have had no reports of such white men. The only thing we have heard is a brief report of a village attacked many miles from here, but our report was vague with no details. I do not think that is the son of your friend. Do you wish to take a party of warriors to go look for him?"

"Thank you. I may need a party of warriors, but I am uncertain what I shall do next," Tarzan replied as he contemplatively finished the last drops of his beer.

The flames of the bonfire were ebbing into embers as Tarzan exchanged a few more pleasantries with members of the tribe and subsequently excused himself to retire to the hut that had been provided for him. Its clean, freshly plumped grass mat was comfortable and inviting, so that he spent little time considering the course of action he would take tomorrow before he drifted off into sleep.

Chapter Six

ASSAULT

Dawn crept slowly but steadily upon the Waziri village as the light through the trees began to dapple the ground of the central compound. Tarzan of the Apes stirred with the first light, as was his custom, and rose refreshed and rested. He looked out the entranceway of his hut at the women beginning to move about, gathering water, starting a fire here and there, beginning the rituals of the day. Off toward the south wall he heard the murmur of soft conversation and, beneath that, a protesting infant.

Because he had turned back to fetch his knife, Tarzan did not see the huge flash of orange directly, but felt in the next instant the entire compound rocked with thunder. One of the huts had exploded and was being consumed in a fireball. He looked quickly around to see another on the far end burst into flame.

Scattered portions of the fence splintered with the crack of rifle fire—five, six, seven shots, then a volley, echoed through the morning air.

Women screamed. Men dashed out of their huts, brandishing their shields. Some, seeing the futility of that gesture, dove for the ground. One warrior, then another caught bullets in the back and tumbled to the dirt, writhing in pain. Orders were shouted as M'Bala, dashing from his hut, attempted to regroup some men to begin a defense, though as yet they had but the vaguest idea of what was attacking them.

The assault continued for several more minutes. Smoke roiled
up from the burning huts, clouding the eyes and the nose. Cries of
anguish mingled with thunderous cracks and confused commands
as the villagers scrambled for cover. Blood began to spatter the
ground.

Tarzan, like many of the veteran warriors, quickly attempted
to regain his composure, to observe, and to ascertain the nature and
the location of this enemy. No visible force was attacking; no warriors were scaling the walls. They were only being fired upon.
Tarzan wondered whether this was the first phase or, inexplicably,
the entire assault.

One thing was certain. He could not see the attackers from
behind the village's wall.

Fetching his bow and quiver of arrows from within, he
crouched down and scurried past the smoking remains of a hut,
headed for the west wall, bounded up the wall and, leaping up,
grasped the low-hanging branch of a large tree. He raised himself
up and quickly climbed to the higher terraces of one tree and with
catlike balance leaped to the branches of another and another. In
this manner, he moved almost effortlessly along, high above the
ground, and reconnoitered. It was an easy matter to follow the
sound, the smell, and the smoke to its origin many yards out from
the compound's perimeter.

He saw at least three nests from which the firing came, scattered in a half circle from the southern end of the compound
around to the western, each located close enough to the wall to lay
down effective fire, yet far enough away so that the assailants could
retreat into the jungle. Their positions showed they had expected
only retaliation from warriors on the ground, who would unavoid-
ably run into their machine guns' lines of fire. They did not imagine
anyone at Tarzan's lofty height reaching them without even being
seen.

In a moment, Tarzan assessed the situation. Below him he saw
a nest of four men, roughly dressed as soldiers, two snipers with

*Smoke roiled up from the burning huts... [Tarzan] quickly attempted to
regain his composure, to observe, and to ascertain the nature and the location
of this enemy.*

rifles firing upon the village, and two manning a mortar. He assumed the other nests were similarly manned.

It was another moment to nock an arrow into his bow, take aim, and let fly. The arrow sailed downward to pierce the back of a man about to launch another mortar round. He let out half a yell of pain and dropped lifeless to the ground. His astonished comrades paused, looking around frantically, shouting, unable to gauge where the arrow had come from.

Fools, Tarzan thought, *the last thing you want to do is stand still,* as he fired another arrow—*thunk*—into a second attacker.

The remaining two panicked and ran off into the jungle, separating.

Tarzan dropped down into the nest and went to the mortar, which he noticed was still loaded. He looked over to see the next sniper nest fifty yards to the west, where a second group of men was still assailing the village with fire. He crudely aimed the mortar and fired. Its missile exploded in a fireball on the edge of the sniper nest, sending at least two figures flying aloft and the remaining men dead and smoldering in the brush. The commotion, now noticed by the third nest, was sufficient to break off the attack.

The Waziri mustered their forces quickly and began to charge from the village, brandishing spears, scattering and pursuing the assailants from the third nest in a rout.

Meanwhile, Tarzan ran after the two escaping snipers. Swinging into the trees, he decided to track the closer one. This man had considerable difficulty running at any sort of pace because he had no path, just thick vegetation to hack through with his small hunting knife. He stumbled twice over gnarled tree roots, getting up and looking back to see whether he was being followed. Dozens of yards above him, Tarzan easily kept up with him, swinging and leaping from branch to branch, watching undetected.

When the runner reached a somewhat open area, Tarzan chose to end the pursuit and dropped down, effortlessly, a few yards in front of him. "Chri…," the man blurted, half in fear and half in amazement. "You're…you're a white man!" He stared for a moment at the ape man, naked but for his loin cloth, who crouched and returned his gaze with steely gray eyes. "Who the hell are you….*what are you…?*" Then the man realized that he still held his hunting knife, and made a few ineffectual passes at Tarzan, who dodged them. Waiting until the moment his adversary was clumsily off guard after a lunge, Tarzan swiftly kicked the knife out of his hand. It sailed into the bush. The man tried to turn and run, but Tarzan overtook him instantly, spun him around, and hit him with one cross to the chin. Stunned, the man stumbled backward. Tarzan reached out and almost had him in his grasp when he heard "Hold it" followed by the sound of a rifle bolt being pulled back.

He turned to face another of the assailants—the second one who had run away—pointing a rifle at his chest.

"Charlie, am Oi glad to see ya. 'Ow'd ya find me?" asked the first, in a broad Cockney accent.

"Whattya got here, Reg?" asked Charlie, looking at Reg for a moment but nodding toward Tarzan. "He ain't exactly a native."

"Oi dunno. Oi thought the camp was Waziri. Then 'e showed up. Dropped from the trees like a bleedin' ape."

"I guess 'e's the one that killed Mike and Jake."

"Yeah, an' 'e almos' killed me."

Tarzan carefully watched the eyes of the two men, noting the moments when they looked at him and when they glanced at each other. As they briefly conversed about their situation, he slowly, in a series of careful steps, moved his right hand unnoticed toward the handle of his knife and gauged the distance between him and Charlie. He waited for the moment when Charlie would be looking away, just long enough. And it came.

In an instant the knife shot across the few feet to solidly pierce Charlie's neck. His choking, gurgling gasps lasted only for a moment as he slumped down. Startled, the one called Reg tried to run. Tarzan quickly caught him by the shoulder and threw him down onto his back, holding his neck tightly against the ground with his powerful hand. "If I kill all of you, it will be a lot more difficult to get the information I need," he said. "Perhaps you would like to live today?"

The Waziri village was in disarray. Smoking and charred ruins from several burning huts clouded the morning air. The cries of the wounded mingled with angered shouts and harsh commands. Men and women scurried about picking up debris, assessing injuries, tending to the repairs.

Tarzan entered the village gate carrying Reg over his shoulder like a side of antelope. He strode to the central area, where M'Bala was holding council over the damages to the wall, and flung the Cockney to the ground.

"It seems that once again I must thank Tarzan of the Apes for helping my village!" M'Bala exclaimed. "We found some of our sentries killed, which may explain why they managed to get so close. Our warriors are pursuing the others who have run off." Looking contemptuously down on the Cockney, the chief added, "Who is this"—he used the Waziri word for "garbage"—"you bring to us?"

"I do not know," said Tarzan. "I will find out." He looked down at Reg and asked in English, "Who are you? Why did you attack the village?"

Reg, afraid to rise from the dust but looking a bit puzzled, thought he recognized some speech patterns in Tarzan's voice, and replied, "Say, you're English! 'Ow is it you're with them?"

"Why did you attack the village? What were you after?"

"Dunno. We wasn't told. Just 'ired to do a job."

"Who hired you?"

"Somebody who paid well. 'E'd pay you, too, t' let me go."

Tarzan nodded toward the grim Waziri faces. "They want to kill you before you see another hour."

"You wouldn't let 'em do that, would ya?" Reg implored. "How about givin' a break to a fellow countryman?"

"We have nothing in common," Tarzan said flatly. "Who hired you?"

"'E'll kill me if Oi tell you."

Tarzan said, nodding toward the tribesmen, "They will kill you if you don't. I am the only thing standing between you and their vengeance."

Reg, beginning to grasp the gravity of his situation, conceded, "Awright. 'Is name is DeKelm. Peter DeKelm. 'E's got a lotta money and a lotta interest in this 'ere area, though Oi don't know why. 'E didn't explain and us blokes don't ask a lotta questions if da money's good."

"Where can I find him?"

Sweat began to form on Reg's grimy forehead as he contemplated the various possible scenarios for his future, none of them very promising. Then he confessed, "'E's got an operation abaaht six'y miles nor'west from 'ere, but Oi don't know what it's for, honest Oi don't. He only tells us what 'e wants us t' know, and dat's de God's truth." He looked back and forth between Tarzan and the angry Waziri faces and added, "What's gonna 'app'n t' me?"

It was that very point that Tarzan, M'Bala and the Waziri subchiefs began to debate in the Waziri dialect. Reg feared that the animated gestures and increasingly raised voices of the tribesmen did not bode well for him. He began to put his faith in the more calm, reasoned tones of this white man. As it turned out, he was perceptive, for Tarzan persuaded a reluctant M'Bala to allow the Cockney mercenary to be taken to Point Station to be turned in to the authorities. Tarzan, however, was obliged to pledge to M'Bala his personal assurance that Reg would be brought to justice.

Tarzan asked for a canoe and some provisions, which were supplied. Reg, his arms bound strongly with hide thongs, was escorted to the Waziri river landing.

"Where ya takin' me?" he asked.

"To the authorities," Tarzan replied.

"What? You're turnin' me in!?" he cried incredulously.

"I could leave you here with them," noted the ape man, which silenced the grizzled Cockney for some time.

And thus it was that Tarzan of the Apes set off in a canoe from the Waziri territory along a western tributary of the Bolongo river, with a tense and anxious Reg sitting in the bow.

Chapter Seven

THE MERCENARIES

"**B**loody hell!" Willie Hudson cried out, after the third overhanging branch in ten minutes smacked him in the forehead. "Damn jungle! I shoulda never come here. I shoulda took something in the desert!"

"Shaddup," his comrade Liam Jameson snapped. "Yeh came for the money like the rest of us. And yeh knew that only this kinda work paid that kinda money with no questions to be asked."

Hudson and Jameson had been trudging their way through the jungle undergrowth for several hours, taking turns hacking away at the dense undergrowth with the one machete they possessed. In addition, they possessed two rifles, one handgun, one hunting knife, one empty canteen, six cigarettes, no compass, and no sense of direction. Though they did not fully realize it at the moment, these two were the only remaining attackers of the Waziri village who had not been captured or killed. Nor did they realize that they were quite lost.

They had seen their two comrades blown into the air and had needed little more time to assess their situation before abandoning their nest and escaping into the jungle.

Jameson, the older, was a wizened mercenary soldier who had served many masters in many campaigns. He fancied himself an independent, self-made man, skilled at tactics and survival. Among a generally unruly lot, he was boisterous, opinionated, and loud, unless he needed to be focused on a target or a maneuver. He took

45

orders when he agreed with them, and he generally agreed with them when they served his self-interest. This had made him unsuitable for most military organizations, but gave him the personality and bent of mind needed for mercenary missions.

Hudson, his unwilling comrade in arms, was on his first expedition as a hired soldier. His hair, though equally unkempt, was darker and his jungle gear of newer vintage, less stained and soiled. He gave vent to his complaints even more than his outspoken comrade, because this turn of events was not what he had expected, as he reminded anyone within earshot at every opportunity.

"Where's the truck? Why don't we go back to the truck?"

"We don't know where the bloody truck is, remember?" Jameson answered, annoyed. "We got separated and we had to run for it. If we go back the way we came, we'll likely run into those damn savages."

"What are we supposed to do? The radio was in the truck," said the increasingly agitated Hudson.

"Well, we don't have any bloody radio, do we? So we have to make it on our own. Our best bet is to find the river and hope for the boat to come along. If we don't meet that, we can at least work our way back to the landing point for the boat, where maybe somebody from the compound will meet us."

"And supposin' they don't?" Hudson asked.

"It's our best chance. You got a better idea? Maybe askin' them villagers to take us in or somethin'?"

"Well, do you know where you're goin'? 'Cause I don't."

"I told ya. I think the river is this way," Jameson said with increasing irritation.

"What do we do in the meantime? I mean, it's a jungle here."

"We survive, ya idiot. We have weapons. We're not hurt. We use our instincts and our resources. We make it through. Quit yer bitchin' already."

Stewing on that thought, Hudson followed Jameson a bit further through a thick grove of trees and underbrush heavily entangled with palm fronds and vines. Though Hudson believed they were hopelessly isolated, they were far from alone. A great many ears heard them curse and hack their way through the jungle, and a great many pairs of eyes watched them stumble and plod along. Some of those eyes belonged to little creatures who scampered away at their approach. Some eyes surveyed them with a passing interest. Some stared intently at their every move.

At length, Willie Hudson became weary of the oppressive thicket and declared, "I need a rest."

They stopped. Hudson set down his rifle and immediately plopped down in the shade of the closest tree, leaned against its great trunk, and unlaced and removed one worn and cracked leather boot. Massaging his sore calf and ankles, he let out a moan of relaxation and began to undo the other.

"You can rest a bit, I guess," Jameson allowed, standing over him and unslinging his rifle from his shoulder. "I'm gonna see if there's any water around. I'm damn dry."

"Don't leave me!" a suddenly nervous Hudson cried out.

"I ain't gonna leave ya. I'm just lookin' around." Jameson walked slowly a few feet away, poking his rifle barrel into bushes and spreading branches apart.

"You need yer gun to find water?"

"I never leave me gun behind. You watch yours, too." Jameson disappeared behind a thicket.

Hudson massaged his other foot, savoring the moment of relaxation. He had not yet learned that one relaxes in the jungle at his peril.

For he was not alone. A pair of amber eyes that had discovered the two of them some moments ago now stared fixedly at the reclining Hudson, some thirty feet away, concealed by undergrowth. The eyes belonged to a fully mature—and quite hungry—leopard. Without breaking its gaze, it stepped out from the brush. From its throat there emerged a low rumble as it crouched down, muscles tensing and hide bristling eagerly.

When the great she-cat made eye contact with Hudson, his blood chilled. This was the moment he had feared since he came to the jungle. He had heard stories about men's lives flashing before them at the moment of death. Hudson did not know whether his life flashed before him. His mind stopped. His body froze. He could not utter a sound to summon his comrade.

The leopard charged. Its great maw was open and its sharp talons extended. Hudson did not know how many moments passed before the great beast leaped in midair and flew at him, because he had no sense of time, or anything else. His eyes could only glare intently at the huge beast bearing down on him, a scream caught in his throat.

A rifle shot blasted, and then another. The leopard flopped down from its midair arc and rolled onto its side. Blood oozed from the wounds in its side as it writhed, breathed its last, and succumbed, scarcely three feet from Hudson's boot.

It took a moment for Hudson, still wide-eyed and staring, to regain his wits. Twenty yards off to the side, Jameson plugged a third bullet into the carcass for good measure and lowered his rifle, its barrel still smoking.

"Jesus Christ! You killed it!" Hudson exclaimed. "You saved my life!"

"Yeah, well, remember that. And don't tell me I don't need me gun."

The crack of the rifle, so loud and discordant, echoed and rippled through the forest byways and blended with the tapestry of many other sounds, some shrill, some subtle. It was picked up by some ears, unrecognized, and dismissed as mere noise. Other ears, more attuned, perked up at it, focused on it, sought it out.

Thus as Hudson and Jameson moved on, hacking away, cursing the jungle and their situation, their presence was easily detectable to anyone wishing to find them. Unbeknownst to them, they were the object of continuous scrutiny by other denizens of the jungle, even more interested in them than the big cat.

Chapter Eight
THE RIVER

Tarzan of the Apes paddled the Waziri canoe down the main trunk of the Bolongo River with smooth, even strokes. He gazed up at the overhanging limbs which stretched out over the river in a high arc from either side. The morning mist, which had earlier hovered over the river and swathed many of the trees on both sides, had lifted, and now the light from the late morning sun high in the sky filtered down through the leafy canopy. Scarcely a breeze disturbed the water or the leaves of the overhanging boughs. The sunlight reflected brightly off the gentle ripples undulating from the bow of the smooth-sided canoe.

Though the river was wide in this part, Tarzan kept the canoe in the center channel, many yards from the shore on either side. Tarzan would just as soon have stopped and fished here for the day, had it not been for the burden of his cargo that sat restively in the bow.

Reg, his arms still bound tightly to his sides, twisted around to look back at Tarzan, and then around to face the front again, as he had been doing repeatedly for the balance of the journey.

To Reg, Tarzan appeared to be merely admiring the scenery, but the ape man's keen senses were attuned to the messages his surroundings continually sent him. A distant sound, a sudden flight of birds, a disturbance in the water—any of these might signal a situation which he ignored at his peril.

Indeed, at that moment he would have heard an unfamiliar,

discordant sound echoing through the jungle, a sound which would have troubled him—and which he would have done well to heed—except that his captive piped up, "How much farther?"

"About an hour past the waterfall."

"Waterfall? How far is that?"

"Up ahead."

"Is there anything to eat?"

Tarzan nodded toward a pouch in the front of the canoe. Reg could see the contents inside as it lay partially open.

"What's 'at?" he inquired with a certain disdain.

"Antelope," Tarzan replied, continuing to scan the banks and the waters ahead.

"You expec' a bloke to eat that?"

"It is of no matter to me whether you eat. You will not starve before we reach Point Station."

Tarzan resumed his customary silence while Reg muttered under his breath and then retreated into sullen disdain.

"So what was the point?" a sweaty, grimy Willie Hudson said at length, after a protracted period of silence where the only sounds had been the occasional swatting of insects on their necks and the continuous swish of Liam Jameson's machete as it crudely cut their path.

"What point?" a weary Jameson indulged him.

"The point of that raid back there. On the village."

"He told ya," Jameson answered with some irritation. "To scare 'em off. Keep 'em spooked and at a safe distance so they don't interfere with the operation."

"Scare 'em off? They don't seem to scare so easy. In case you didn't notice, they didn't exactly run away from us. They came after us."

"Yeah, we shoulda had more backup. When we get back to the compound, DeKelm'll send a bunch more of us, and we'll wipe the black bastards out. Ain't hardly human anyway."

"Wipe 'em out? Since when did we come here to start a jungle war?"

"It would hardly be a war. They got spears and we got guns and explosives. We could take out a village a day. Clean the whole place out in a coupla weeks. DeKelm doesn't wanna do that, but he'll see soon enough that that's the way to go. Then we can come in and take what we want, whenever we want." Jameson took a particularly vicious swipe at some vines entangled before his path.

Hudson went on, "Say, did you notice that one of 'em was white?"

"Yeah. I swear the one that broke up Reg and Charlie's nest was white. I don't know who he is, but I wish I could get my hands on him."

This exchange had been watched by several pairs of eyes from a proximity that would have surprised Jameson, who fancied himself observant in the field.

Willie Hudson came to a halt for a moment and stood to wipe his brow. At that instant a large spear cleared his head by an inch and lodged—*thunk*—in the trunk of the tree next to him.

"Wha—?" Hudson sputtered.

"Get down!" Jameson shouted. An arrow whizzed past his head and lodged in the next tree, an arrow that he just ducked in time to avoid.

They crouched low behind broad fronds, rifles ready, and carefully looked around, studying the brush and foliage from left to right and back. Then they saw him about twenty yards away— a warrior moving quickly from behind one tree to another. Too quickly for a good shot. From near the spot where the first one darted, a second one emerged. This one, visible from the waist up, stood to draw his bow back. Had the white men been observant, they would have recognized his markings as Waziri.

Jameson took quick aim and fired his rifle, dropping the warrior where he stood, before he could release the missile.

Arrows flew above the mercenaries' heads and past their shoulders. Another Waziri man emerged from the bush, spear cocked, about ten yards to Hudson's right. Hudson wheeled around and fired again and again, pumping bullets into the Waziri man long after he had fallen. He screamed, rage in his eyes and veins throbbing in his neck. All his anger and frustration at being here in this miserable jungle, at being the target of one jungle denizen after another, at being on this bizarre mission gone badly awry, was vented in that outburst.

"All right! Christ! Let's go!" Jameson intervened. "We don't know how many more there are!"

They plunged through the thick jungle as swiftly as they could, believing instinctively that the more distance they put between them and the Waziri party, the better. They ran. They ran for their lives. They ran until their hearts pounded and their legs ached. Perhaps they ran a half mile, perhaps a mile. They could not say.

At length, thoroughly winded, they came to a halt, propping themselves up against a giant of a tree to catch their breath. Red-faced and sweating profusely, they looked around for signs of their pursuers.

"Did we lose 'em?" Hudson asked.

"Yeah," Jameson said, panting. "I think so." Looking around, he added, "Where are we? Are we closer to the river or farther away from it?"

As his composure returned, Jameson raised his head to listen. No sound of pursuing warriors. No sound of animals. But yet… what was it…?

"Listen," he said, holding his hand up.

"What?"

"Shhh." He listened again. Water? "Yes. Over that way. It's the river."

This time they made their way slowly and deliberately through the lush green bushes and shrubs, because they possessed enough sense of the jungle to know that all manner of creatures—including unfriendly tribesmen—might be approaching the river to drink. The fewer of those they had to deal with, the better.

From a vantage point concealed by large fronds near the rock-encrusted shoreline, under the shadows of overhanging trees, the two mercenaries stopped to reconnoiter the river.

It was not long before they spotted a canoe—bearing markings which they again did not recognize as Waziri—approaching from their left. They most certainly did, however, recognize its passengers.

"Look!" Hudson whispered excitedly. "That's Reg tied up. But the guy paddling…is that…?"

"Yeah," Jameson acknowledged. "The white guy. I don't think there are too many guys around here that look like him. He's the one. It's his fault we're in this predicament instead of back at the compound."

"Well, I've got a little thank-you message for him." Hudson sighted down his rifle, following the movement of the canoe, waiting for the moment when a clear shot unobstructed by the overgrowth in front of him presented itself. Thinking he had one, he fired.

In the instant that Tarzan heard the rifle's report and felt the bullet whizzing past him, he rolled over the gunwale of the far side of the canoe and in one swift move dropped into the water.

"Hey! Who's shootin'!?" Reg yelled.

"Reg! It's me, Hudson! Did I get him?"

"No! I don't think so! He jumped in the water. He's tryin' to take me in! He's the white man from the village—the one that busted us up! Get him! And get me outta here!"

Tarzan did not hear most of this exchange as he swam swiftly and powerfully under the water toward the shore. He had estimated well the distance he needed to cover to reach the shoreline, though he had not ascertained where the shot came from.

His head and shoulders surfaced silently, unseen by Reg or the attackers, amid a massive cluster of rocks and bushes hugging the shoreline. He waited there for a moment, listening for words or other noises that would give away their position. He wished he had his bow, which was in the canoe. Ironically, he could have used that rifle George Fredrickson had offered him. That passing thought reminded him that in three days he had made no progress toward finding Jack.

"Ya idiot!" The voice of Liam Jameson echoed in the forest. "Why are ya tryin' to shoot him in the boat? There's a waterfall up ahead. All we hadda do was wait till they came ashore to portage, and we coulda had a clean shot easy enough."

"Damn."

"Yeah, right. Now if the white man's hit, how can we get Reg out of that drifting canoe? And if he's not hit, where is he?"

"Let's split up and look around," ventured Hudson.

"Smartest thing you said today," Jameson muttered, and added, "Be careful."

This conversation revealed to the ape man's trained ears their approximate location and distance from him. He heard the bushes rustle and twigs crack as they parted to search for him. One set of noises drifted further away from him, and one got louder, signaling an approaching man. Tarzan could not risk raising his head up to look over the rocks on the hillock concealing his presence. He waited a moment, and the rustling of the approaching man stopped. Cautiously he peered above the rock to where the foliage was sparse enough to see through. In the distance, partially concealed by undergrowth, he saw the figure of Willie Hudson, crouched, looking around rather carefully, his rifle cradled in his hands.

From even that brief glance, Tarzan's jungle instincts told him many things about Willie Hudson. They told him that this man did not know where his quarry was, that he was nervous and uneasy in this situation, and that he did not know how to proceed.

Tarzan reached down to pick up a stone from the muddy bank, took aim, and flung it off in the distance away from him and away from Hudson. Hearing the stone land with a thump and rustle of branches, Hudson turned and instinctively fired two shots toward it. *An old trick, yes,* Tarzan thought, *but how these types fell for it.*

"Hey, I think he's over here," Hudson yelled, and began to dash off through the undergrowth and around the trees to the area where he thought the sound had come from. Tarzan used that distraction to leap up onto the shore, run to the nearest large tree, and scale it to the middle terrace. Undetected, he swung through the branches to follow Hudson.

Hudson came to a stop where he thought the noise had originated, searching carefully, but puzzled that no sign of the ape man was to be seen. Many feet above him, the ape man positioned himself noiselessly on a limb and dropped down, nearly on top of the startled mercenary.

Hudson let out a curse and tried to struggle to free himself from Tarzan's grip, but his efforts were futile, and did not handle surprise well. From behind, Tarzan held his left arm around Hudson's neck and with his right drew his hunting knife, whose point he held at Hudson's throat. "Hold still," he commanded. "Drop your weapon or I will kill you."

The man dropped the weapon.

"Now, who are you? Why are you shooting at me?—Where do you come from?" Tarzan asked.

Hudson, instead of answering, uttered a string of disjointed responses: "Did you come from the village? You're the one who killed my mates? Do you have more of them with you?" In a moment he managed to work up a bit more bravado, given his precarious position, and essayed, "There are more where I came from. I am not alone. Let me go!"

By this time, Liam Jameson had heard the struggle and had covered much of the distance between him and Hudson. He stopped several yards from the two and raised his rifle. "Hold it," he called out. He stared at the strange figure of the white ape man for a moment, then added, "Let him go."

Tarzan turned to demonstrate to Jameson that he clearly had

the knife at Hudson's throat, and answered, "No, you drop your rifle or your partner will die."

Jameson considered the options. Hudson, for whom the moment was much too tense, cried out, "Do it! Do what he says!"

Jameson stared at the ape man as he hesitantly bent down a bit, extended his arm, and dropped the rifle.

Hudson relaxed and let out a breath in relief. Tarzan, still restraining him, moved to advance toward Jameson. At that instant, the older mercenary reached back to his side, drew his pistol from its holster, and fired straight ahead once, then again.

Hudson gasped. A crimson spot deepened in the breast of his field jacket and, wide-eyed in shock and confusion, he slumped forward. Equally taken aback for an instant, Tarzan regained his wits and quickly dropped Hudson and dashed off behind the nearest large tree, whose bark was splintered by Jameson's next two shots.

The tree's trunk was massive enough to conceal Tarzan, but he was pinned there. Jameson, however, could move, and did. Tarzan could just peer around the edge of the tree enough to see him holstering his sidearm and moving to pick up his rifle. Then Jameson began to advance in a military manner toward Tarzan's position, ducking behind tree trunks, palm fronds, or anything that would afford him cover, keeping his rifle trained forward.

Tarzan could see the dropped rifle in the grass near Hudson's body only a few yards away. Though Jameson was many more yards away at this point, Hudson's rifle was too far for Tarzan to reach without exposing himself to Jameson's view. He needed to somehow get that weapon or move from this position. He stood motionless, trying to glimpse Jameson as best he could from behind the trunk. The adversary was advancing on his position, perhaps trying to also reach the rifle. He thought of trying to scale the tree, but even the swiftness of the ape man might not be sufficient to escape the fire that that movement might draw.

"'Ey, what's goin' on!" Both men heard the voice of Reg yell in the distance. "What about me?"

Jameson turned to look in the direction of the river. It caught him off guard.

Tarzan seized upon that. *Thank you, Reg.* With instincts bred of years of jungle confrontations, where split-second actions have literally meant life or death, Tarzan dashed out from behind the tree to reach down and scoop up Hudson's dropped rifle and roll to the ground with it. Taking a quick aim, he fired toward Jameson. He missed, but Jameson reacted by running off for cover. During this moment, Tarzan bolted back to the same large tree which had just sheltered him, rifle now in hand. By the time Jameson noticed, Tarzan had scaled the tree to its first level of massive limbs.

Jameson caught the movement, and as the ape man leaped from one limb up to the next, Jameson began to fire again. He was a fair distance away, but some of his shots hit limbs as Tarzan's foot left them; others whizzed by his legs as he climbed.

Tarzan reached a level where dense foliage concealed him for the most part, so that Jameson was essentially shooting blindly toward where he thought his quarry might be. The ape man nestled himself in the crotch of two large limbs and took a moment to seek out his adversary's location. When he caught a wisp of floating rifle smoke, Tarzan leveled Hudson's rifle and began to return fire. Jameson had skillfully moved away, however.

Tarzan paused. He watched. His keen ears and eyes waited for the snap of twig or rustle of leaves or other telltale sign of where his adversary had moved. Jameson had paused, too, undoubtedly clever enough to know that at this point firing again would be more likely to reveal his position than achieve his goal.

Then Tarzan spotted the bit of color he needed to see—Jameson's head and part of his upper torso became exposed. He proceeded to carefully sight down Hudson's rifle and squeeze.

Click. Empty.

Hearing the distinctive sound, Jameson called, "Hah! That moron Hudson shoulda known he was runnin' short of ammo.

Well, I've got a full belt. Whattya gonna do now, jungle man? It's only a matter of time!"

Jameson's boastful challenge was complemented with another burst of rifle fire. Bullets whizzed by Tarzan's head, tearing leaves, splintering branches.

Emboldened by the knowledge that his quarry could not fire back, Jameson broke off his fire and began advancing.

Tarzan saw him move strategically from one point of concealment to another, rarely exposing himself for more than an instant. He had skills, this mercenary.

Tarzan knew he needed to put further distance between them, so he leaped to the closest strong limb of the neighboring tree, timing his leap to coincide with a move of his adversary's. While Jameson repositioned himself to get a better shot at the tree he thought Tarzan was hiding in, the ape man observed him from a spot further off. The limbs of the tree he was in did not allow him to situate himself above Jameson in such a way that he could drop onto him. He would land to one side or another, and Jameson might be able to turn and fire before Tarzan could get to him. He needed Jameson to move into position or be distracted. The ape man had no bow, no rope, and he could not risk a knife throw at this distance. He had only an empty rifle.

Tarzan held up the rifle in his right hand. He positioned it carefully, like a spear, gauging its weight and balance. He moved his hand forward and back to get the right feel, sighting it. Cocking his arm back, he cast the rifle with a powerful forward thrust straight down at Jameson. Its barrel struck him between the shoulder blades, knocking him forward and off balance enough for Tarzan to drop down and leap on top of him.

Tarzan's arms encircled Jameson from the back and sought to grab his rifle. Jameson was startled, but only for a moment, as he reacted by twisting and flailing violently to keep possession of his weapon. Tarzan held his grip around him while they thrashed and tugged.

Jameson gripped the rifle mightily, but Tarzan's stronger grip pried the fingers of one hand loose, and as the rifle stock popped free from Jameson's hand, Tarzan twisted the weapon around to wrench it free from the other hand. The rifle fell onto the ground.

Jameson instantly began in a fury of curses to scrabble for his pistol or sheathed hunting knife or whatever he could grasp. Tarzan grabbed his right wrist to keep him from drawing a weapon while circling Jameson's neck with the other arm. As Jameson continued to thrash and twist, Tarzan tightened his grip on the man's neck until first his face reddened, and then he thrust himself up and down to try to break free, and then he struggled just to breathe. Tarzan squeezed his grip even more, pressing in with his shoulder, until he heard the characteristic crack which told him what he needed to know. In an instant Jameson's body grew limp, and Tarzan let it slide to the ground.

Panting for breath, Tarzan bent to pick up the empty rifle he had thrown at Jameson. Staring at it a moment, he wondered, *How shall I tell this one to George?*

"Somebody! 'Eeelllp!" Reg's cry broke his thought. The canoe!

Tarzan turned to run toward the river, dashing around trees, angling in a diagonal to meet the shore upriver from his position.

"'Ey!" Reg screamed. "'Elp! A waterfall! 'Elp, somebody!"

Tarzan came to a stop at the water's edge and looked out at the river. The canoe carrying Reg had continued to float downstream and now approached the waterfall drop-off whose roar he could hear not far ahead. Keeping an eye on the canoe retreating into the distance, Tarzan ran along the bank to get closer to it. He sprinted to the top of a rock outcropping that extended over the river and launched himself into a dive that arced over the water and down into it at considerable speed. The momentum propelled him underwater like a bullet for several yards. He then surfaced and with powerful strokes swam rapidly toward the canoe, which was beginning to swirl around from the eddying crosscurrents that marked the approach of the falls.

"I can't stop! I'm gonna go over!" Reg continued to yell.

Tarzan reached the stern of the canoe and grasped it with a sinewy arm, halting its forward progress. The roar of the waterfall drop-off was audible ahead, and the force of the current rushing toward it became stronger by the moment. He battled the powerful force of the water, straining and kicking mightily, pulling the canoe against the current and away from the precipice that loomed ahead. He managed to turn the stern of the canoe toward the shore and with great effort forced it out of the path of the strongest central current and closer to the riverbank, where the water was shallower and outcroppings of rock slowed and diffused the flow of the current somewhat. His muscles aching, he towed the canoe several more yards toward the bank until the river became shallow enough to gain a foothold where he could then walk the canoe in and beach it.

Tarzan secured the front half of the canoe on the muddy shoreline. He then sat down on one of the rocks at the river's edge to catch his breath and rub his sore arms. Reg climbed unsteadily out of the canoe and onto the shore, breathing as heavily as the ape man. He was uncharacteristically speechless at the thought of all the deeds that he had seen this jungle demi-god perform today. He ventured a question to the seated ape man, "Hudson and Jameson…are they dead? Did you kill them both?"

"Not both," answered Tarzan. "I killed one after he killed the other. Not that it matters. The Waziri or the beasts of the jungle would have claimed them soon enough. I would have preferred that. I am weary of having to deal with men like them—like you— today."

"Well," Reg asserted hesitantly, "You coulda easily just let me go down. But…you saved me life."

"I did not want to lose the canoe."

After a brief rest, Tarzan portaged the canoe along the riverside past the waterfall. This waterfall, which went by many native names but as yet no English of French one, marked the dividing point between the upper Bolongo River, whose tributaries extended into the Waziri territory, and the lower Bolongo, a broader, more traveled avenue that flowed past Point Station and other ports farther downriver.

Even the grizzled mercenary thought it a spectacular falls, with torrents of foaming white cascading forty feet down to the boulders below, sending up clouds of mist that sparkled as they reflected the midday sun. Indeed, as they made their way down the hilly embankment, Reg pondered what his fate might have been had he gone over these falls in that canoe.

They proceeded along the vestiges of a path that had been worn by repeated visits from animals and natives, until they reached level ground beyond the point where the raging water would swirl a canoe into the rocks. There Tarzan launched the canoe again and continued downriver, all the while steadfastly refusing to untie Reg, even when he offered to help paddle.

Chapter Nine
THE RIVERBOAT

Tarzan steered the canoe gently in toward the pier of Point Station until it nudged the edge of the graying wood and came to a stop. "We're here," he said, tying up the canoe. He retrieved his weapons and stepped out onto the pier, then turned and assisted Reg by coarsely grabbing the neck of his shirt and helping to hoist him out.

Still grasping his collar, Tarzan escorted Reg down the pier and across the well-trodden earth of the Point Station compound until Captain Reynolds and some of his guards came out to greet them.

"Well, what have we got here?" Reynolds inquired, eyeing Reg, then Tarzan. "I didn't expect to see you back quite so soon, and certainly not bearing gifts."

Tarzan pushed Reg in Reynolds' direction. "Something for you to keep. There was a raid on the Waziri village this morning. This is one of the ones who did it. Most of the others are dead or, I expect, captured by now."

"Yes, we've been getting reports of a few other villages attacked, as well. What's this all about?"

"He can tell you. Take him."

"I'll put him in a holding cell, and we'll have a little question-and-answer session. But you look tired. Come into my office."

"I am. Thank you."

Reg was taken away under guard and confined. Captain Reynolds ushered Tarzan into his office and offered him tea. In truth, the good captain preferred to chat with Tarzan or other visitors than tend to his duties, as evidenced by the neglected folders and documents piled haphazardly on the desktop, which Reynolds pushed aside to make room for his tea. The rickety ceiling fan stirred up as much dust as air in the crowded office space.

Reynolds settled into his creaky desk chair and said, "Raids by mercenaries on villages. I don't like the sound of this."

Tarzan had scarcely begun to share the details of what he had seen at the Waziri village when one of Reynolds' men came rushing up to the door with the news that a riverboat had arrived, and that a man from the boat was requesting to see Reynolds immediately in regard to the prisoner.

Tarzan looked at Reynolds, curious. A moment later, Reynolds' sergeant ushered into the office a bespectacled, officious-looking little man with a small mustache and wearing a trim but somewhat worn brown suit and bearing a leather-bound folder.

"Captain Reynolds?" he inquired. "I am Nigel Vanden Avond. I represent Consolidated Pharmaceutical and their agent in this area, a Mr. Peter DeKelm. Pleased to meet you. I understand that you have in custody one of our operatives." He produced from the folder a document bearing elaborate scrollwork and an official seal at the bottom. "This is a royal certificate of immunity granted to us and duly executed by your government. It orders that you release your prisoner—and any other of our employees—into our custody."

"What!?" exclaimed Reynolds, grabbing the paper and examining it. "You can't do this."

"I'm afraid we can. It supercedes your jurisdiction, as you can see. It's quite legal and proper."

Tarzan rose to his feet and said through clenched teeth, "That man participated in a raid on a native village! People were killed, including some of my friends. He must be brought to justice!"

"And he will," Vanden Avond said to him with an unctuous smile. "Any untoward actions carried out by any agent of Consolidated Pharmaceutical will be appropriately dealt with, I assure you.

But you must release him into our custody. And as we are in a bit of a hurry, I'd like to take him forthwith."

Tarzan stared—indeed, glared—at Captain Reynolds. Reynolds looked down at the document, then up at Vanden Avond's thin façade of a smile, then down at the paper again, and then up at Tarzan, saying, "I'm afraid there's nothing I can do, old boy. In this I am powerless."

Reg was fetched and released into the custody of Vanden Avond. Tarzan stood in the center of the compound and watched as Vanden Avond led the mercenary away toward the dock and aboard the riverboat. He thought he saw a bit of an arrogant smile light up the dirty Cockney's face. His jaw clenched and his fists alternately closed and opened at his sides.

Reynolds approached him and said, "I know how you feel. I wish there was something I could do. My hands are tied."

"Mine are not."

"What do you mean? What are you going to do?"

Tarzan replied, "That piece of paper does not prevent me from following them, learning who they are and what they are doing here."

"Well, no, it doesn't, but look here—don't you go doing something rash. I don't want the jungle littered with more bodies."

Tarzan turned and looked at his old friend and half smiled. "Would I do that?"

Tarzan packed his weapons into the Waziri canoe and set out after the riverboat. Paddling slowly and deliberately, keeping a sufficient distance behind it to avoid detection, he followed the vessel for many miles as it headed east, away from Waziri territory.

At times the river was broad and open, which meant that he needed to keep back considerably, too far away to see or hear anything transpiring on the decks. At other times, when the river narrowed, he could ease up close to the boat by hugging the shoreline concealed behind outgrowths, and overhear snatches of conversation. It was a large boat for this river, newer and longer than the passenger ferry he had come in on. Perhaps forty feet in length, it rose two full decks above the water, with metal railings encircling on each level. On both its bow and stern was emblazoned the name *Consolidated Pharmaceutical.*

Tarzan guessed that the boat carried at least a dozen men, in addition to the small crew, because they spent a lot of time walking about and mingling. Most were dressed in variations of khaki jackets or remnants of assorted uniforms, and most were armed with pistol belts or rifles slung on their shoulders. They were a loud, raucous lot and not at all reserved about their opinions or their wishes. Tarzan heard many talk about the villages. Apparently others had been attacked, too, and by some of the men on this boat. They expressed fear and outrage at the failed Waziri attack. Some grumbled that they didn't like to ambush and murder innocent women and children. "That's not what I signed on for," Tarzan heard one particularly loud voice say.

Another chimed in, "Now I hear he wants us to move on to some kind of goddamn logging operation or something."

A third added, "There'll be more money for more work."

"I'll believe it when I see it," replied the second.

Tarzan also heard them mention the Chgala tribe.

Several times on its journey the boat stopped and put ashore. Some of the men got off the boat and walked around through the jungle for a while, then returned and moved on. *What are they looking for?* Tarzan wondered.

The third time they pulled over and men spilled ashore, Tarzan concealed the canoe a few hundred yards back from their position and took to the trees to spy. He observed several of the men walking through the jungle, looking down and around. He thought they might be looking for food, but they did not adopt hunting stances. Those who had rifles kept them slung on their backs instead of holding them, and some had no rifles. Tarzan wished he could hear them better, but they did not seem to be saying much. Odd behavior for mercenaries, he thought.

Even more odd was what they did out in the jungle. Tarzan saw that they were stopping from time to time to gather flowers—apparently a particular variety of yellow-petaled flowers. He saw several of the men pull such flowers up by their roots, then congratulate themselves on having found some, gather a collection in trays, and return to the boat, pleased.

As darkness approached, the riverboat made for the bank and appeared to stop for the night. Its starboard side eased in to hug the shore as mooring lines were fastened to a few protruding branches and roots. An anchor was dropped.

Tarzan glided the canoe toward the shore, coming to rest behind overhanging boughs and grassy hillock outcroppings along the irregular bank. He listened and waited patiently until most of them seemed to have finished supper and stopped strolling the deck and went inside for the night. When the deck seemed deserted, he silently paddled up behind the rear of the riverboat and tied his canoe to the aft railing of the lower deck.

Removing his coil of rope, quiver and bow and leaving them in the canoe, he climbed aboard over the aft railing and crept a few feet forward on the deck, which ran around the circumference of the cabins located in the center of the craft. He could see the light of lamps coming from windows along the corridor on both sides of the deck, and he could hear men inside. Satisfying himself that they were oblivious to his presence, he cautiously advanced along the port side, hidden by the cloak of night, careful to stay away from or below any windows casting out illuminating light. He listened. He heard perhaps a half dozen voices, mostly from one or two larger central rooms, joking, cursing, and playing cards. Strands of conversation were about the day's haul and how much money this operation would bring.

"Don't worry," one voice seemed to reassure some grumblers. "When this operation is over, you'll be well paid for your efforts. The company pays top dollar for running a little interference and picking plants the rest of the day."

"It's not the picking flowers—it's the murderin' the natives."

"Ah, lousy black scum. They're no-good savages anyway."

"They ain't done nothin' to us."

"You want 'em to get in our way?"

"How are we doin', Mr. DeKelm?" one voice said to change the subject.

"Yeah, how much longer?"

The calmer, more modulated voice, a product of more education, said, "Mr. Vanden Avond assures me that two or three more weeks' worth of operations will guarantee us a tidy nest egg. The company will be pleased."

"Yeah, I'll be glad when we gets our money," groused another voice.

"Now gentlemen, you already got your advance, and a tidy sum it was. You know you'll get the rest in full when we're finished here. Just see that everything goes smoothly."

"But it ain't goin' smoothly. The damn natives fight back. We lost men!"

"Yes, that was regrettable. But the other raids we've conducted have been successful. We need to be more careful about our strategy, but that does not deter our mission."

"Well, it doesn't seem like anybody's around here to stop us," another added.

"Just see that no one does. That's why you're here."

The man addressed as DeKelm left the crew's room and walked through a doorway into the adjoining smaller, lounge-like room. Tarzan strained to get a look at this man DeKelm, but the room's windows, shaded with Venetian blinds, allowed him to listen in but see little. Among the fragmentary comments of several other men within, he picked up the unmistakable Cockney tones of Reg, now regaling the men with his tale.

"Oi tell ya, 'e's a devil!"

"Oh, come on—a white man?"

"Yeah, a white man! Swings through the trees like a bloody ape! 'E cut Charlie down in the blink of an eye. Made short work of Jameson, too. Killed at least six of us that Oi know of. And 'e's still out there. Mark my word, if you see 'im, drop 'im in an instant before 'e gets you, too!"

Tarzan's lip curved in a hint of a smile. *At least he isn't claiming that he slipped away from me,* he thought.

His curiosity piqued, Tarzan crept forward to the foredeck, where there was little light or sign of life, and clambered to the upper level. Hunkering close to the wall, under the cloak of darkness, he cautiously advanced along the upper deck and listened. He came upon another cabin with audible voices inside. He took a chance to peer in to see what appeared to be a lab table upon which were scattered examining tools such as forceps and probes. The table also bore a microscope along with bins of plants, other trays of soil, and casually discarded leather gloves crusted with dirt. One of the men, his back to Tarzan, was standing over another, who was seated. He could see neither face. The man standing was giving orders or instructions to the seated one. Then he asked, "How's the day's run doing?"

"Some of these are not bad," was the seated man's answer, "but you'll have to tell your men to pull them up more carefully. I'm getting too many roots ripped and torn to shreds. You need the roots intact, remember? Use the spades and trowels."

"I'll see to it. Are we close to our quota?"

"Another week or two at least, at this rate, before Professor Winslow will have enough to process."

"Another week or two? We have to have a shipment to the company before then. They have to have enough to make an initial run. They are eager to see some results."

"What about the fields that you've started cultivating next to the compound? How are they coming?"

"They won't be ready for weeks. In the meantime, we have a quota. Mr. DeKelm has to answer to others."

"Well, as I said, tell your men to be more careful."

"Ach," the standing man grumbled, "it's always something," and turned to leave. As he walked away, exiting on the opposite side of the room, Tarzan could now see the face of the man seated at the examining table.

It was Jack Fredrickson.

Chapter Ten

INTO THE JUNGLE

Tarzan waited until the other man had definitely left the corridor and gone below to the still-noisy crew quarters. Silently he nudged open the latch on the door at the end of the central corridor, eased the door slowly open, and entered the corridor. Gliding quickly down the hall to the laboratory room, he opened its door and stepped in.

Still focused on the exam table, Jack muttered, "Now what do you—"but then, as he looked up to see who had entered, his mouth dropped half open at the sight of the intruder whose face was familiar but whom he had never seen clad in a loin cloth and hunting knife.

"Lord Greystoke…?" Jack stammered.

Tarzan raised a finger to motion him to silence, then whispered, "Are you all right?"

"Yes. Well, no. I am being held here by these brigands. Did you come"— he was not sure how to assess this—"…to rescue me?"

"Are you working for these men?"

"They are holding me. I have knowledge which they can use, and as long as I help them, I am kept alive. "

"Do you want to leave?"

"I didn't think it was possible."

"It is now."

Tarzan cautiously peered out of the lab room door and into the outer corridor and ascertained that no one was nearby in either direction. Swiftly he led Jack down the corridor and opened the door leading out into the night on the rear upper deck. They stopped at the railing overlooking the rear of the boat, where Tarzan was about to point out his moored canoe, when one of the mercenaries came around from the left and exclaimed, "Hey! What? Who are—" His words were stifled as Tarzan swiftly hit him with a hard right and knocked him down. The movement alerted a man on the port side who had just stopped to light a cigarette, and he came jogging aft to investigate. Jack was amazed to see Tarzan grab this man by his shoulder and belt, hoist him up and toss him, wriggling, over the side, so that he landed in the water below with a loud splash. This splash and his cry of outrage stirred several more men on the decks, who came out, some looking around, some seizing their guns.

Tarzan said quickly to Jack, "You get down to the canoe and fetch my bow, arrows, rope, and the food bags and head for the jungle. I'll fend them off from here."

Having no time to ponder how a British Peer of the Realm was going to do this, Jack scurried down the ladder to the lower deck and off the boat. He had scarcely gotten to the canoe when another soldier appeared around the corner of the cabin to Tarzan's left and managed to raise a rifle and fire. In the semi-darkness, the shot missed Jack but startled him, so that he hastily seized Tarzan's weapons but left the provisions and dashed off into the jungle. The bullet was not entirely off the mark, however—it put a hole into the bottom of that finely-crafted Waziri canoe.

It was but an instant after the shot rang out that Tarzan wrenched the rifle from the mercenary's grip and slammed it pile-driver style into his face, sending him tumbling. At that moment another assailant came around from the port side. In almost one single motion, Tarzan jammed the rifle into his abdomen, then swung it up to slam his jaw and thus dispatched him.

Other voices stirred at the commotion, and Tarzan knew it would be only a moment before several more men would descend upon him. Seizing the deck railing palms down, he pitched his body forward and swung it over the railing to flip around like a gymnast and land on his feet on the lower deck. From there he turned and ran down the narrow wooden gangplank and off into the jungle. He heard more crewmen shouting and scrambling to the deck, and one fired two more shots whose bright flashes split the night.

Tarzan soon caught up with Jack and told him to follow him into the jungle. Though they had already traversed a considerable distance, they could hear the shots and the resultant commotion of voices and the scrambling of footfalls as a handful of DeKelm's men tramped down the gangplank and into the undergrowth in loud, clumsy pursuit.

Tarzan veered off from the direct line they had been moving in, and worked his way through the brush, taking advantage of what pale illumination the moon provided, making sure Jack was just behind him. Abruptly he stopped in front of a huge tree and, with the agility of a monkey, swung up to the lowest limb, where he perched himself and then extended his arm down to invite Jack to do the same. After two tries, with the assistance of Tarzan's strong arm, Jack was able to scramble up to the limb. They made their way up to the higher terraces.

"What are we doing here?" Jack wondered anxiously. "Why aren't we trying to run away from them?"

"How many reasons do you need?" Tarzan replied in a considerably softer voice. "Even with the moon, it is dark and we will not see where we are going. Moreover, making our way through the underbrush will be noisy, which will alert them to our presence. It will also alert the big cats who prowl at night. If we remain here, we will be safe from most predators, and our pursuers will not think to look for us up here, even if they pass directly beneath us. They are not that clever. Believe me, I have dealt with such men. Settle in, get as comfortable as you can, and keep silent until dawn."

Though he had a hundred questions about what he had just seen transpire, Jack heeded the advice.

Jack spent the remainder of that night in some trepidation, not sure whether he had managed to drift off fitfully into sleep. Dawn came soon enough and with it, the light to assess their situation. Tarzan rose from the branch above Jack and clambered to the highest limbs of the tree that would bear his weight. From his lofty perch, he could survey his surroundings and see a view of the river hardly obscured at all by leafy branches.

"The boat is gone," he observed. "They must have given up on us, at least for now. We can get down."

When they alighted on solid ground, Jack hastened to ask, "Now what do we do?"

"I will take you to Point Station, where you may remain in protective custody until transportation home can be arranged. I assume you would like to go home?"

"Well," Jack essayed, "there is the matter of Professor Winslow."

"What about him?"

"He's still with them. He's being held, too. I mean, I can't just leave him if there's a chance to rescue him." Jack was not quite sure at this point what he was getting himself into.

"Where is he?"

"At DeKelm's main compound. DeKelm keeps him there to advise him—against his will. And he's all alone. He can't get out by himself. I don't know what they will do to him when they don't need him any more."

"Where is DeKelm's compound?"

"Let's see, we drove north from it in trucks to the river, I'd say thirty miles overland. Where we left the riverboat last night was about halfway between Point Station and where we boarded. DeKelm's compound is in a relatively open area, where the jungle breaks and begins to merge into grassland, before a series of large hills form a few miles further on."

Jack was not sure his description was helpful, but Tarzan, mentally calculating the distances, ventured, "I think I know where this place is. Traveling through the jungle I could reach it in a day, but

I expect that with you the trip might require two, if you can keep a fairly constant pace. I could use your knowledge of the place. Are you up to it?"

"You mean…rescue him? Just the two of us?"

"Or at least learn what is going on enough to alert the authorities. Do you think he will still be there a few days from now?"

"I don't expect any of this will change his status. My God, if there's any chance of getting him out…I can't just leave him there. It seems that this expedition is going to be one new experience after another. Let's have a go at it then, Lord Greystoke."

"Tarzan. Here I am called Tarzan of the Apes. Come, let us move. We will travel quietly. Talk may pass the time, but it also drains energy and announces our location to others. Save the conversation until later."

Once again, Jack would have to withhold his many questions for the moment, as they set off toward the southeast.

The jungle they traversed was thick, with tall trees, outstretched leafy branches, and considerable layers of tangled underbrush. Jack struggled frequently to keep up with the steady pace of the ape man, who strode sure-footed through sometimes nearly impenetrable tangles as if he could see a path. For his part, Tarzan wished that he could take to the tree boughs and swing freely above all this undergrowth, but his sense of obligation to the Waziri and to George Fredrickson and by extension to Jack and his professor convinced him that this was the course he needed to take.

The day grew late, and heat and brilliance of the African sun began to wane. Tarzan would have preferred to keep going, but he knew that his intrepid and thus far uncomplaining trail mate would need rest and sustenance to withstand the remainder of the journey. Soon enough they happened upon a bit of a clearing in the dense thicket of forest, where Tarzan declared, "We'll stop here for the night." Looking around a bit, he added, "There is plenty of dry wood in the brush. Gather a supply of firewood. We'll also need flint and tinder."

"Even better—I have matches." Jack indicated the breast pocket of his safari jacket.

"Good. Build a fire. I'll get supper."

Jack noted the casualness of this remark, as if Tarzan were merely stepping into the next room to pull something from the fridge. Then he turned to the task of assembling dry grass, small twigs, and a few larger branches into a campfire, which he soon had ablaze and crackling. Though Jack barely heard any rustling in the bushes, it was not long before Tarzan returned, gripping by the legs the carcass of a guinea fowl about the size of a wild turkey, its multicolored wings flopping outward and its head bobbing as Tarzan walked. "I thought you might like something that tastes like chicken," he said. "See if you can rig up a spit to hold this on."

While Jack began assembling a primitive rotisserie out of branches, Tarzan expertly stripped the bird of its feathers and with his knife slit the carcass to remove the innards. In short order, the bird was roasting to a golden brown over the coals, and, as darkness settled in, the two men feasted on its flesh.

"You know, this is actually quite good," Jack said, wiping his chin. He continued to chew on a piece of breast meat, and then wondered aloud, "So, is this the kind of food you live on here?"

Swallowing his piece, Tarzan replied, "I prefer antelope or gazelle or wild boar, occasionally lion."

Jack was a handsome young man, well spoken as befitted an Oxford degree. Tarzan thought that with his brown hair and firm but slightly rounded chin, he looked the way George Fredrickson must have looked in his youth. And, as a scientist, he was curious about everything.

"How do you kill a lion?" Jack asked.

"Well, the easiest way is to dig a trap, bait it, and then when the lion falls in, finish him with an arrow. But sometimes if I surprise him or he surprises me, I have to take him down with my knife."

Jack's eyebrows raised. "You've wrestled a lion?"

"When I've had to." Jack observed Tarzan's strong hands and firm biceps, and felt no doubt that they could break the neck of a beast—or a man.

"How does grilled lion steak taste?"

"I prefer it raw."

Jack pondered this silently awhile, munching. As he eyed this imposing figure whose bronzed muscles reflected the firelight, his mind was abuzz with such curiosity about the things he had witnessed this ape man say and do, and he scarcely knew which question to give voice to first.

"But you…you're English. A Peer of the Realm. I've seen you in London society. How did you…come to be here?"

"I was born here," Tarzan answered. "My parents were English, Lord Clayton and Lady Alice. They were shipwrecked in this country, then died shortly after I was born. I was raised, improbable as it seems, by a pack of great apes. I learned to swing through the trees, hunt, forage, and do whatever else was necessary to survive in the jungle. During my childhood, I knew no other life, though it became increasingly obvious to me that I was different. As an adolescent I happened to discover my parents' abandoned cabin, and from the books and other documents there, I gradually learned to decipher those printed characters which I later learned were English. I was also able to piece together some sense of my true identity and heritage. I first learned to speak English from a French naval officer named D'Arnot, who befriended me."

He paused a moment to pull off a leg from the roasting carcass. "Eventually I made the journey to England to reestablish my Peerage ties. That is where I met your father. My affairs draw me to London more often than I care, but I try to return here yearly, usually during the dry season, to live as you see me."

"And you came looking for me? My father asked you to find me?"

"Well, yes, he wanted me to find you and, if alive, rescue you, but he did not quite put it that way. You know his reserved manner.

He asked me to 'make inquiries.' But I knew that he was worried about you and I was only too happy to oblige. He has done me favors and I consider it an obligation to help him, and you."

Tossing some bones into the embers, Tarzan concluded, "So that is what brought me here. But what of you? How did you come to be in this place with these men? I read your letters, but they do not explain all this."

"It started simply enough. I studied botany at Oxford, and I decided to pursue graduate work after one of my professors made a fascinating comment. He said that many, if not most, of the species in the world have never been identified or catalogued. Imagine that—all the scientific texts that fill our libraries listing all those species, yet they are quite incomplete. Species of plants, insects, and even larger animals have yet to be found and named, let alone studied and understood. We may be unaware of species that have gone extinct, or are about to go extinct, in our lifetime. And it seems that the most remarkable area in need of further study is right where we are, in the heart of equatorial Africa. Half the species of plants on earth are found in these forests. This area has an incredible diversity of flora and fauna, and a complex interrelationship of life cycles that we are only beginning to understand.

"Take, for instance," Jack continued, finishing the last of his piece, "the cacao tree, which produces chocolate. Now the world loves chocolate. I sure do. But the tree grows only in tropical jungles where it thrives in a moist, shady climate. When they tried to cultivate the tree in groves, they grew all right, but few cacao flowers were pollinated to produce beans—not because the tree was not thriving, mind you, but because the tiny midge that pollinates the flower prefers the shade and does not like to venture out into the open sun of a plantation. It is this type of complex interrelationship which we are only beginning to study. What seems clear is that the more man tries to cut down and strip the jungle in search of commodities, the more he threatens to destroy the very environment that produces what he seeks.

"At any rate," he continued, looking alternately at the stars and at his listener, "I became interested in learning more about this rich land. I decided that I wanted to contribute to that effort and possibly even help discover a new species or two. Professor Winslow said that there simply haven't been enough people to do this work. It seems that not everyone in the scientific community wants to leave their comfortable European laboratories."

"And so you came here with Winslow?" Tarzan inquired.

"Yes. Professor Winslow was organizing a research expedition and I was able to secure a position. We left about three months ago. We established a research camp in a relatively uncharted area. Within weeks we not only had catalogued what we believed were some new species of tropical plants and some bizarre insects, but we began to discover some truly remarkable properties of some of these plants."

"Like what?" Tarzan added a few branches to the dying fire, whose mass first sent up a shower of sparks, then reinvigorated the flames.

"The leaves of one plant seemed to affect the growth of certain types of tissue. The stem secretions of another, the Ghana daylily, had a remarkable capacity to hasten the body's healing power. Of course, our findings were quite premature."

"Then what happened?"

"It was about two months after we set up our field camp and about a month after we began sending reports of our findings back to the university. I had at this point been writing my father fairly regularly. We got a wire from the university saying that we would be contacted by agents from Consolidated Pharmaceutical and that we were to provide them with the materials and data that they requested."

"How was your university persuaded to go along with this?"

"Oh, I suspect that someone showed up at a Council meeting nattily dressed, well spoken, expressing the proper admiration for the rigors of academic research and inquiry—and wrote them out a check. It wouldn't be the first time companies have drafted universities to further their goals. I rather imagine that it didn't occur to the Council members to ask a lot of questions about their methods or the type of people they hired."

"How did you get involved with DeKelm?"

"He was their representative. DeKelm and a small party showed up one day with credentials from the company. He told us that his company was interested in research and development of new medicines and drugs and that they thought our findings were promising. They had heard from the university about our discoveries. He was particularly keen on the Ghana daylily. We told him that what we had could hardly be called a discovery, just some findings which had to be subjected to further study before any conclusions could be drawn.

"He agreed that our findings were premature, but said that we were onto something nevertheless and that his firm had offered to fund our efforts for at least a year, with the blessing of the university. They hoped that if they could grease our wheels a little, the likelihood of our finding something would increase."

"What did they expect you to find?"

"Something that they could turn into a medicine and sell," Jack answered, poking the fire with a stick.

"But then would not the company be directing your efforts?" Tarzan wondered. "What would happen to your scientific cataloguing of species? Surely the company had no economic interest in that?"

"Precisely. I raised that point with Professor Winslow, but I was overruled. He felt we could do both, and the additional financing would allow the expedition to be better equipped to do both. He believed that the interests of science would be served either way."

"It did not strike you as strange," Tarzan queried, "that their agent would be this type of man?"

"I didn't know what type of man he was. He seemed very businesslike, earnest, somewhat charming, and genuinely interested in our efforts. That changed soon enough. In the months between then and now his true colors came out. It became clear that he had hired a small army of mercenaries and that we were to serve at his pleasure. I don't know what became of the other two students in our original party. Our native bearers were sent off. Professor Winslow was compelled to work in DeKelm's central processing facility night and day supervising the preparation of the extracts, and I was dragged along on the expeditions, as you saw, to oversee the daylily gathering operation. DeKelm essentially told us that we were alone out here and expendable and he held all the cards and that if we did not cooperate he would find someone who did. It was made quite clear to us that if we did not go along, our lives were in danger."

Jack reached over to pick up another branch, break it apart, and add it to the flames as he added, "But what I don't understand is why he had the villages attacked."

Tarzan asked, "How many of these flowers would he need to have to return a profitable shipment to his company?"

"The more the better. Dozens, maybe hundreds of pounds, I suspect."

"And how many acres of jungle growth would have to be combed through to find such an amount?"

"Well, you can imagine, quite a lot."

"And does this plant," Tarzan continued, "grow only in certain concentrated areas, or is it spread out over the country?"

"It is not thickly concentrated in any one area. One would have to range far and wide to find a lot of it. He plans to clear a field to plant and cultivate it, but he hasn't gotten far on that project yet."

"So that is perhaps why he attacked the villages."

"I don't follow you," Jack replied.

"The area he intended to search must overlap the lands of several tribes," Tarzan speculated. "Some tribes in this country are territorial. Anyone who enters their territory for any purpose without their consent is an enemy. I suspect that DeKelm has heard that much about the natives. DeKelm is apparently ruthless, a mercenary himself, who will accomplish his goals by whatever means necessary. He must have believed that if he attacked them, they would be frightened and leave his operations alone, or perhaps move their encampments further away. But he does not know much about the African peoples, the fool. What he did not realize is that tribes like the Waziri are great warriors, afraid of no one, and they will defend their territory to the death. He also apparently does not know that many of the tribes whose territory includes these flowers would have been content to trade with him for access, had he approached them peacefully."

Tarzan's tone became increasingly acrid as he added, "Like so many meddling white men, he chose to exploit the native peoples using force and intimidation to accomplish his ends."

Jack sat silently, staring at the flames licking a twig, wondering just how foolish his own actions might seem at this point.

Tarzan thought for a moment, then went on, "What perplexes me is the motive for doing such things. Is there really such a profit to be gained from this plant extract that justifies the taking of lives?"

"I've been trying to piece this picture together, Tarzan," replied Jack. "We reported to the university that we had discovered the restorative powers of the Ghana daylily, and we also at a different point reported that we had discovered that the bark of the jakaba tree yielded an excellent buffer which could bind divergent compounds and extend the shelf life of medicines. And then this DeKelm shows up, very fascinated with those two developments. We actually thought we were on the verge of several other significant breakthroughs, but that's what he was focused on. And the next thing we know he has us in his compound, under guard, supervising his company's operation to produce the extract and the buffer."

"So why then is his company so interested in just these discoveries, to the point of financing such an undertaking?" Tarzan asked.

"Pharmaceutical companies are interested in selling medicines," Jack replied. "They are willing to invest vast sums if they can get in return something that the public will buy in droves."

"So they must seek what the public needs to cure its ills?"

"No, that is naïve. They must ask themselves what the public *wants*."

"How are this bark extract and these flower stems what they want?"

"They want to sell a Fountain of Youth," Jack declared.

"You mean…" Tarzan wondered aloud, "is that what you have discovered?"

"No. There is no Fountain of Youth. But that is what they want people to believe they have. I suspect that they will create a clever marketing campaign and perhaps make millions by selling this potion to gullible Americans and Europeans."

"You mean people will believe this? Lots of people?"

"It is an ancient dream, Tarzan, that they will be trying to cash in on. Civilizations throughout recorded history have sought magic potions for easy shortcuts to youth, vitality, longevity. And they are extraordinary in their tenacity. It's like the widespread belief that ground rhinoceros horn is an aphrodisiac. Now there is no scientific evidence whatsoever to support that, yet people believe it, simply because someone said it. And on the strength of that belief, they have hunted the rhinoceros nearly to extinction."

Jack watched the smoke curl up through the leaves to the stars a moment, and continued, "We fall prey to a form of this illusion ourselves, with the way we embrace some of these newly developed wonder drugs. Swallow a pill, all your pains and troubles are gone. It's very attractive. Who can blame people for wanting to believe in such a thing?"

"But don't these pain medicines work? Are we not able to inoculate against diseases that used to be deadly?"

"But you see, that is just the danger. Because we can now inoculate people against diseases that used to kill millions, or fight infection with an antibiotic pill, the public believes that science can do anything. It's true that modern civilized man tends to live longer than his tribal brothers in the wilderness, but that is due more to lifestyle than wonder drugs and vaccines. Most of the improvements in longevity and health in the last sixty years or so have come from improvements in living conditions. Roofs to keep out the rain, window glass to keep out the disease-bearing insects, refrigeration to prevent food spoilage, indoor plumbing to allow hands to be washed and toilets to be flushed—these are the 'magic' discoveries that have done more to ward off disease and prolong life than any herb, potion, or jungle spring."

"You are saying," Tarzan retorted, "that life in the civilized world is superior to life in the wild? I do not think so. I have seen more dirt and grime and smoke and sick people in London than I ever saw here. I live healthy and content here, and so do the natives I know. The air is fresh and clean and the jungle provides great bounty."

"Of course. You are correct," Jack said, stirring the last of the dying embers, releasing a cloud of orange sparks and puffs of smoke. "That is the other side of the coin. You get exercise and fresh air and your diet is free of chemicals. You have probably developed immunities through long exposure. On the other hand, people in London may have immunities which someone from the jungle would fall easy prey to."

"Indeed," Tarzan replied, "I never had a head cold until I went to London."

"You could live your whole life in this jungle and die a natural death at a ripe old age. Or you could fall victim tomorrow to an infection you are powerless to combat. One must never be complacent about nature. She is not simple, nor does she yield her secrets easily. As time goes on and the influences on people's lives become more complex with environmental changes, new diseases and strains of microbes develop. Who knows but that even now some new strain of disease is evolving, in a monkey perhaps, which will someday spread to humans and be so complex and virulent that in fifty years it may constitute the plague of the Twentieth Century."

The last whiffs of wood smoke curled up from the few remaining ashy embers as Tarzan and Jack retired for the night, again ensconced in tree limbs a safe distance from the ground.

The next day they continued southeast. About midday, Tarzan noticed an unusual number of vultures circling around above a spot about a mile to their right. Curious, he told Jack that he was going to depart from their route to investigate. The two of them approached the spot where the birds favored a somewhat more open area, where more tall grass rather than thick underbrush grew. They observed several vultures swooping down and rising up again, some carrying pieces of carrion in their beaks. As they neared the spot which apparently was the target of the scavengers, an area where the grass had been matted and trampled upon, they heard, and a moment later saw, several hyenas rooting around in the ground, pulling out sections of flesh and snarling at each other for possession. Tarzan yelled out and flailed his arms, and the cowardly hyenas, startled, bolted into the forest.

The two men approached the spot which had attracted these grave robbers of the jungle. Expecting to find the remnants of some slain beast, they found instead the corpses of five native men and women. Some had been buried in crude shallow graves. Others were in the process of being uprooted and hauled out of their graves by the scavenging hyenas and vultures.

"My God, what happened?" exclaimed Jack. "Who are they?"

"I do not know what happened, but they are Chgala," Tarzan said, upon examining their raiment and markings. "This is puzzling," he added. "We must be thirty miles from their grounds. The tribe would not bury its own here. And they would not leave their kinsmen in such shallow graves, which appear to have been dug in haste. But no other tribe, even an attacking enemy, would leave them like this. They would either leave them where they lay after battle, or, if a cannibal tribe, carry them off. I heard some of DeKelm's men mention the Chgala tribe. Could this be his handiwork?"

Jack knelt and closely inspected a few of the corpses, then said, "There's something peculiar about these bodies. They are all elderly, for one thing. And they died elsewhere and were left here, obviously. But look at what else." He turned a few over, then poked and prodded into the stiff flesh. "Their throats have been cut. Except this one over here." He turned to indicate another sprawled a few feet away. "He got a bullet in the back." He took a few steps over toward two more protruding from their shallow makeshift graves in grisly postures of death. "Notice how their torsos have been cut open, then partially sewn together in the case of this one, and not at all in this one." He indicated slits in their abdomens, several inches long, the edges of the cut flesh now swollen, discolored, and grotesque, revealing blackened and oozing internal organs.

"These bodies have been autopsied. Organs have been removed." Jack paused for a moment, studying the condition of the flesh, considering what it meant. He continued, "DeKelm must have taken the step of examining them for something, though I don't know what, then left them here to conceal the evidence."

"What could he have been looking for?" mused Tarzan.

"Is there anything unusual about the members of this tribe?" Jack asked.

Tarzan pondered. "There was a legend which had received some attention even in Europe, that the members of this tribe lived unusually long lives. It was attributed to their primitive diet and simple life style and the presence of many old ones among their members. But my friends in other tribes tell me that they live life spans no longer than other tribes, who also have elders."

"Perhaps that's it, then," Jack said. "This talk may have started as idle rumor, unsupported gossip, but these things have a way of getting around and taking on a life of their own. It reminds me of the stories of the Russian people who supposedly lived to be over a hundred. But when researchers studied them, they found that, yes, they had a simple, healthy diet with few diseases, but their claims of advanced age were taken mostly from their word, based on their memories of numbers of events, not calendar years."

Jack was finding it difficult to continue to stare at the swollen tissue, the ghastly faces, and in some cases the open, staring eyes of these victims. He began to halfheartedly replace some of the corpses into their graves, then was struck with the futility of the gesture and turned away, sickened. Tarzan's visage was more stolid, his gaze intent in thought. Both were silent for a moment.

Jack ventured, "I wonder whether DeKelm's people are interested in some kind of research into genetic makeup? Rather like that Hitler fellow in Germany?"

"I suspect that a man like him was looking for some simple answer, and did not find what he was looking for," Tarzan suggested. He then stood up and looked around, surveying the carnage, and declared, "This man must be stopped."

Chapter Eleven

THE COMPOUND

T
hey proceeded southeast through the jungle for the balance of the day. As they walked, the ape man questioned
the young botany student more extensively about their
destination.

"What are we going to find in this compound? How is it laid
out?"

"Well, it is intended as a central processing facility for both the
stem secretion and the bark extract," Jack explained. "DeKelm has
found this location near a jakaba forest, but yet with enough open
land nearby to clear and cultivate fields for the daylilies. The secretion must be extracted from the stems and processed. And the
trees must be cut and hauled into the compound, where bark must
be stripped from trees and pulverized, then refined. And he needs
to do all that on a large scale."

"He must need quite a bit of equipment to do all that," Tarzan
commented.

"He will need cultivation and harvesting equipment, logging
equipment, machinery to strip the bark, plus a laboratory, plus
everything needed to maintain a crew and equipment—barracks,
cook shack, generators, machine shed, and trucks to bring everything in and out. It's a major operation."

"How many men?" Tarzan asked.

"I don't know. When I was there, more kept arriving weekly. Native workers, company representatives like Vanden Avond, and of

course, plenty of mercenary soldiers to keep the native population in line. There may be twenty men at the complex, maybe forty."

Tarzan pondered all of this.

As they advanced through the jungle, the tangled vegetation became sparser, and the ancient forest began to give way to more patches of open or nearly open ground, progressing toward more grassy plains intermingled with rocky hills. A more mountainous region rose in the distance.

At length, Tarzan stopped to listen. Off in the distance he could hear a rumbling, muffled roaring sound. Trucks. Several of them.

"We must be near the road, perhaps a mile or two," he said.

They continued their way toward the sounds of the trucks. Soon they emerged from a cluster of trees and found themselves within sight of a dirt road snaking through the wilderness. The area through which the road had been constructed was relatively open, but it wound through sections of denser forest and around large hills and rock formations. Tarzan and Jack scaled one of these hills overlooking the road. The top of the hill was encrusted with rock outcroppings, several of which were large enough to conceal the two from view. Tarzan surveyed the road and its environs. To their left, the road emerged from the jungle about a mile and a half away. To their right, they could see that further down, the road ended in a cluster of buildings.

"That's it," Jack indicated.

A tract of forest had been cleared away to make room for a complex of buildings. On the far side of the complex lay open fields recently tilled and cultivated. "Over there are the fields where they are starting to grow a crop of Ghana daylilies. It's already planted," Jack explained. "And over there on the other side of the compound is the edge of a forest particularly rich in jakaba trees. Raiding the jungle to find the flowers and bark was just preliminary. He expects to have the entire operation centered here—so that he can ship out the extract and the buffer in sufficient quantities to market."

Tarzan studied the complex. The buildings were constructed

mostly of wood or sheet metal, mixed with some huts and shacks, apparently thrown together quickly. Smoke belched out of two smokestacks. Trucks drove through the gate and pulled up to loading docks. Workers, both black and white, scurried about, tending to tasks.

"That building is the lumber mill and bark processing center," Jack indicated. "Over there next to the greenhouse is the lab, and over there the barracks, and the office next to it off to the left. That big building on the far right, with the big doors, is the garage with the generator shed."

They remained and observed the traffic on the jungle road below for some time. Trucks came at irregular intervals bouncing along the dusty, bumpy road. Some were small pickups with open beds; some were larger cargo trucks with canvas tarpaulins over ribbed cargo frames. A few jeeps passed by, driven by native blacks, and bearing what appeared to be more mercenary soldiers.

"Do the trucks come through all the time?" Tarzan asked.

"No. They come and go a few at a time. They come in from the river, mostly."

"What do they carry?"

"Everything the complex needs," Jack explained. "Supplies, sacks of grain and boxes of canned goods, equipment and parts... even fuel—that one's a tanker."

Tarzan studied the layout further and at length asked, "If we got into the compound, could you find Professor Winslow?"

"Probably. They gave him a room. There or the lab, I'd say."

"It's getting late in the day. We'll need the cover of darkness."

Jack wondered what his companion had in mind. "I want to find the Professor, but what are we going to do?"

"Is there a security checkpoint at the gate?"

"Yes. But the man at the gate at this time is probably Byron. He's an easygoing sort. I know him. He might let me pass, if he believes I am returning from being lost. But the two of us can't very well just walk in."

"Can we drive in?"

"What?"

"I have an idea."

Tarzan and Jack concealed themselves near the edge of a section of the road about a mile from the compound. They crouched
behind boulders a few yards from the shoulder and waited for the
next truck to come along. And it was not long before a rusty brown
cargo truck, muddy and pocked from considerable jungle driving,
lumbered from their left out of the forest.

Jack stepped out from the concealing shrubbery at the roadside
and waved at the driver, who pulled over to the side and parked
along the grassy shoulder, the engine still rumbling.

The grizzled driver, his leathery skin a deep tan, recognized
him. "Fredrickson! What are you doing here? Heard you left the
boat or something. DeKelm's been looking for you."

"I was taken from the boat. By this wild jungle man. But I got
away from him. And I've got something DeKelm needs. Can you
help me? Over here." He gestured off the roadway. The driver, even
more gullible than Jack expected, promptly got out of the vehicle
and followed Jack a few paces until they moved into an area of
thick, leafy brush. The driver began to ask, "What could you have—
" but never finished his query before Tarzan knocked him cold.

Jack quickly turned and headed back to the truck and slid in
behind the wheel. Tarzan disappeared into the back end through
the canvas flaps of the canopy covering the cargo bed. Inside, he
noticed a miscellany of cargo, including an assembly of shovels and
gardening implements, boxes of canned food, a few medical supplies stenciled with red crosses—and two more mortar assemblies.
He could not investigate the inventory further because the truck
lurched ahead, moving back onto the road again, and then jerked
a few more times as Jack shifted gears and bounced in and out of
ruts in the dirt road.

It was, mercifully, not long before they reached the gate of the compound. The fence surrounding the compound was about eight feet high, fashioned of interlaced wire and framed with metal poles. As Jack had predicted, Byron was manning the gate and admitted Jack in the truck without question. He had not even heard that Jack had left the boat and did not question his arriving in a truck. Tarzan, overhearing their brief exchange and the bravado with which young Fredrickson essayed it, marveled at the level of poor communication this company tolerated. Even the primitive jungle tribes he knew would have quicker and more reliable information about their members' whereabouts than these white men.

Nightfall was fast approaching. They parked the truck in a row of other parked vehicles at the far end of the compound from most of the buildings and waited until the cloak of darkness descended.

At length, Jack asked tentatively, "Now what?"

"We find Professor Winslow," Tarzan answered. "And I need to find a drum."

"A drum? Whatever for?"

"I need to send a wire."

They sneaked through the fleet of parked trucks, keeping between the backs of the trucks and the fence. The lengthening shadows provided excellent cover to conceal their movements as they worked their way along the perimeter of the fence and around to the side of the compound that contained most of the buildings.

They carefully emerged from the shadows behind the utility shed and made their way around to the other side. Tarzan stopped to survey the surroundings. He was faced with several sheds and buildings ahead and to his right. Trying to remain in the lengthening shadows, he gingerly stepped along the wall of one utility shed and approached the next one. Jack dutifully followed, unsure of where they were going.

Tarzan soon reached an alley-like area between two sheds. It was filled with stinking garbage cans, discarded cartons, and several fifty-gallon oil barrels. Tarzan approached one of the metal barrels and tilted it back and forth a little to determine that it was nearly empty. He cast cautious glances back and forth for several moments, making sure that no one was nearby. He then opened his palms and began to pound on the metal top, a short rhythmic palpitation, and then a longer one.

He paused and listened. The night air was still. Nothing.

Ascertaining once more that no one was nearby, Tarzan repeated the ritual. After the second attempt, the ape man cocked his head and listened again to the jungle night, this time satisfied at his effort, though Jack heard nothing different. Jack resisted the temptation to ask the obvious question.

They advanced along the walls, concealed by the shadows of night, making their way toward the building which Jack had identified as the place Professor Winslow was likely to be quartered. Several office windows were lighted, and conversation filtered out. They edged closer to one set of windows.

Jack Fredrickson heard his name. He nudged Tarzan and gestured toward the corner window where two familiar voices were conversing. They crouched, motionless, and listened. The soft, rounded tones of Nigel Vanden Avond's voice was asking about the loss of Fredrickson. The sterner voice of Peter DeKelm said, "He's not important. I have what I need from him. He is expendable at this point. He probably got lost in the jungle and is lion shit by now."

"But what about that fellow who snatched him? That ape man?"

"Ape man?"

"Yes. The native boys talk about him," Vanden Avond responded. "He is called Tarzan, I think they said. Tarzan the Ape Man."

"Are you serious? A white man who lives in the jungle like an ape? What would he want with Fredrickson anyway?"

"Who knows? But he needs to be reckoned with. The men who tangled with him on the boat said he was fast and strong."

DeKelm's tone became irritated. "Nonsense. They were all drinking too much."

"Well, I doubt Fredrickson beat up four men by himself."

DeKelm paused a moment and stared out the window that Tarzan and Jack crouched under. "I've been too lax with these men. Too much has gone wrong. This interference isn't going to sit well with the company."

"They have given you free reign. You said it yourself."

"Yes, they have given me a great deal of latitude in this operation. I insisted on the right to do it my way, and they know—or should have known—what that meant. Personally I don't give a damn if we have to wipe out a few ignorant blacks to make progress," DeKelm muttered.

"But the firm hardly expected half their hired soldiers to get killed tangling with some jungle fellow and a few natives, now did they?" Vanden Avond said. "There are going to be questions. They will want an accounting. You have gone to a lot of trouble to organize this operation and hire all these men. But you cannot continue to dismiss the amount of difficulty we have had. You have made some bad calls. Like that tribe. You cut them open and just left them there."

"The company told me to investigate the stories about that tribe. So I did. They wanted to explore all different angles of longevity. We took a shot. Can I help it if that Winslow couldn't tell me anything from autopsying them? All he knows about is goddamn plants."

Vanden Avond's tone turned unctuous. "Well, he has been useful. And the most important accounting is that which comes after we begin to ship back quantities of the extract and the compounds. The first plantings in the lily fields are beginning to flower, and the lumbering operation is beginning to produce significant quantities of bark extract. The natives are leaving us alone. Things are proceeding...."

Tarzan and Jack did not hear the rest of Vanden Avond's

glowing report. Tarzan thought he heard footsteps and swerved to react, but everything went black.

They both awakened with headaches and found themselves in an office, slumped on the floor, their hands securely bound behind them. The room was furnished with some shelving and a desk, apparently unused, and some chairs. A small naked light bulb burned from a ceiling fixture. From one of the chairs rose a tall, imposing figure in a khaki field jacket and leather cap, brandishing a submachine gun. He smiled maliciously and spoke in a vaguely Austrian accent: "Ve have security, you fools. Did you sink ve have no guards in zis place?"

He waved the barrel of the machine gun toward the door. "Nap time is over. Ve go now. *Mach schnell.*"

They rose and stiffly shuffled out the door. Another armed guard who had stood outside the door led them down the corridor, followed by Jack, Tarzan, and the Austrian guard, who took delight in pushing Tarzan forward down the hall with the barrel of his gun.

Jack was certain they were in the building with the office and lab. As they walked down the narrow corridor, he attempted to observe the contents of each room. He noticed a laboratory, and beyond that a bedroom, in which sat a figure whose unruly gray hair he thought he recognized, but he could not be certain after only the brief glimpse he had.

They were ushered into a larger office with brighter lights and a large wooden desk cluttered with maps and documents. From the chair behind the desk, Peter DeKelm looked up. His squarish face, tanned and a bit reddened from recent outdoor work, smiled sardonically. "Jack. How good of you to come back. We missed you. And you've brought a friend."

He gazed up and down at the tall bronzed figure who also stood before him, naked except for a loincloth. "So this is the ape man who is responsible for the deaths of at least seven of my operatives at last count." His grin faded and his eyes narrowed. "You have cost me a lot of trouble. Who the hell are you? And what are you doing here?"

"I am Tarzan of the Apes, Lord of the Jungle."

DeKelm chuckled through smiling yellow teeth and graying mustache. "Am I supposed to be impressed?"

"You hired men to attack villages. You have killed innocent people, including Waziri, the Chgala, and other tribes who have done you no harm."

"You can't prove any of that."

"I have seen it. The whole jungle knows it."

"Well, you see," DeKelm said, scratching his chin in mock seriousness, "my men will deny everything. My company has high-priced lawyers to defend me, and no civilized court would convict me on your word or the word of black savages."

As if oblivious to what he had just said, Tarzan stated, "You have violated the law of the jungle."

"The only law of the jungle that I know of is survival of the strongest. And that, my naked friend, is me, not you. You can't stop me."

Tarzan's steel gray eyes stared directly at DeKelm's as he slowly, through nearly clenched teeth, snarled, "You will stop, or you will be stopped."

"A threat? Well, then, it seems we do share a common view of jungle law. We both believe that the strong prevail. But you are one man. And if you look around, you'll see that I have the distinct advantage."

"I have more allies than you imagine."

DeKelm smirked. "Bring them on. I have machine guns and grenades. I'm not going to let any self-important tree swinger like you get in my way." He gestured contemptuously with his hand, as if brushing away an irritating fly. "Take them away. Tie them together in the shed until I figure out what I want to do with them."

The two guards pushed Tarzan and Jack toward the door and escorted them down the corridor, one in front and one behind at a cautious distance, weapons leveled.

Chapter Twelve
THE CLASH

Tarzan and Jack sat bound together, backs toward each other, on a dirt floor in the center of a small, dingy storage room. It smelled of must, oil and diesel fumes. A small, greasy skylight window was propped open, admitting a bit of night air and a glimpse of the stars.

The only contents of the room were a solid old metal table stuck in the corner, and a cardboard box or two scattered about. Tarzan had searched repeatedly for some object or surface to cut their bonds or help them break out, but to no avail. Tarzan wondered how often this room had been used as a holding cell.

He reckoned that they had been here at least three hours. The dead weight against his back and the sound of regular breathing told Tarzan that his young friend had fallen asleep, despite the uncomfortable posture. Just as well, he thought. The ape man, however, had been devoting his attention to methods of escape. When DeKelm's men had bound his upper body to Jack's, he had held his breath in and tensed his arm and shoulder muscles, in the hope of creating slack when they were relaxed. The pull of Jack's weight, however, offset any advantage this might have gained for the ape man, and his efforts were for naught. Likewise, he had been working at the thongs that bound his wrists behind his back, but they too proved formidable, and he had been unable to loosen them. DeKelm's men were experts at this.

Thus Tarzan sat as the time dragged on, wondering whether

perhaps an opportunity to break free might present itself in an awkward moment when they came to get him. He wondered where his weapons were. He wondered other things, too. He wondered whether he had chosen the right course in bringing Jack here. He wondered whether he had taken unnecessary risks which would result in tragic consequences. He wondered how he would ever face George Fredrickson if things turned out for the worst. Tarzan had been in situations like this before—indeed, graver—and survived, but there was always that moment of nagging doubt that this time might be the time when his skills and his fortune failed him.

His deliverance came in a most unexpected form. From the doorknob came the sound of a key unlocking it, and then the door creaked open, and the voice of none other than Reg said softy, "Jungle man! You awake?"

The grizzled Cockney entered the room carrying Tarzan's bow, quiver of arrows, rope and knife and set them down. He cautiously but quickly moved to Tarzan and Jack. Jack stirred awake as Reg crouched down and said, looking at Tarzan, "The way DeKelm figgers, 'e can't just kill yeh outright and leave yeh, though 'e'd just as soon, becuz 'e knows enough about these jungles to know that the natives'll foind out and avenge yeh. And you (he nodded to Jack), you can't just be left dead either, becuz you'll be missed. Someone'll come searchin' for yeh and ask a lotta questions. So there 'as to be an accident. Oi dunno know what 'e's got planned, but it's prob'ly gonna be tomorrow."

As he explained this, he moved around to position himself within reach of Tarzan's wrist bonds, which he began working on. "What are you doing?" asked the ape man.

Reg replied, "Yeh coulda killed me back there on the river. Yeh coulda left me, but yeh din't. Yeh saved me life. Well, Oi want to go on with no obligation, so Oi'm repaying me debt 'ere and now. Oi figger we're square. And if anythin' 'appens later on, well, this ain't got no bearin' on what Oi might need to do to save me situation." He untied Tarzan's bonds, and then loosed the straps that bound the two of them together, and finally untied Jack.

"It has to look like yeh freed yehself, not like somebody cut 'em," he explained. The two prisoners stood, stretching their leg muscles and massaging their wrists. "Gimme five minutes to make sure Oi'm long gone before you take off, so's they won't go suspectin' me," he said to Tarzan, and then added, "If Oi wuz you, Oi'd take off, get away from 'ere."

I am not you, Tarzan thought, but said aloud, "Thank you for freeing us."

His task completed, Reg was only too happy to quit the room. Standing legs apart, in the middle of the room, Tarzan donned his weapons, allowing Reg all of the time he asked for to get away.

Tarzan and Jack found their way out of the building and into the main compound, where the night sky was gradually giving way to a sliver of dawn in the east. Tarzan looked around cautiously, not wanting to be surprised by a guard again. His circumspection paid off, because, sure enough, a guard with a rifle walked back and forth in the yard not ten paces from their spot. Tarzan sneaked up on him from the rear and knocked him unconscious with the hilt of his hunting knife. They took his rifle.

They sought out the area where most of the fleet of trucks and jeeps were parked, along the outer fence on the northern end of the compound. There they could feel comfortable discussing their strategy out of earshot of anyone in the compound. Jack began by reminding Tarzan that they had to get Professor Winslow out.

"Where is he?" Tarzan inquired.

"I believe all the staff and mercenary soldiers are quartered over there," Jack said, indicating the dormitory building off to the right of the cluster of buildings far across the compound, a wooden two-story building with many windows and one double-door main entrance. "But I believe the professor has his own room back there in the building we were just in"—he indicated to his left—"and I believe I saw the Professor briefly tonight. At least it looked like him, and I can't imagine too many other people in this camp looking like him. He's in the same area where the lab is and where DeKelm has his rooms."

"We need to get in to find him and quickly get out. We can take one of these trucks and head down the road for the river."

Jack wondered, "How are we going to stop them from chasing us?"

"That's the problem," Tarzan replied. "We need to create a diversion, to occupy their attention. Better yet, we need to prevent them from following us."

"I know how," Jack essayed. "That truck parked over there" — he gestured off to their right toward the middle of the cluster of parked trucks—"is a fuel truck. It arrived earlier today, but hasn't been emptied yet. It's full of diesel for the generators."

Tarzan noted the large gray-green tanker parked among the jeeps and cargo trucks. "What are you saying?" he wondered.

"We can drive it into the building and it will blow up. That'll occupy their attention, don't you think?"

"But we can't just drive it in all the way. We'll have to get out first, but keep it moving."

Jack looked around the yard. A few feet off toward the fence lay a pile of construction debris. He walked over and, from among the pieces of lumber and scrap metal, pulled out a brick. "This will do. Drop this down on the accelerator pedal, and jump out before it hits."

Tarzan looked at the brick. "I'll have to get up enough speed to—"

"No, I'll do it." Jack cut him off. "I have to do this."

Tarzan considered for a moment the boldness of this young man's offer. He realized that George Fredrickson would go apoplectic over this, but he also realized that he could not do everything himself, and assented. "Take the rifle," he said.

The keys for the vehicles were all still in the ignitions. Jack explained that no one bothered to take them out, since the assumption was that no one in the jungle would be aware of or interested enough in a vehicle to want to steal it out of a camp full of mercenary soldiers.

They reached the diesel tanker, and Jack climbed into the driver's seat. Tarzan looked up at him and said, "You will have to roll out of the truck and quickly move to find the professor and get back here, so that we can take advantage of the confusion and take a truck out of here right away."

"I'll try," Jack responded. "You'll cover me?"

"Yes. Give me a moment to set myself up behind that truck." He indicated a canopied cargo truck parked at an angle a bit in front of the others, closer to the center of the compound. "Good luck."

Tarzan moved over to secure himself behind the cargo truck. He crouched down, pulled an arrow out of his quiver, notched it in his bow, and waited. Jack started the diesel tanker and slowly pulled out of the parking space, driving it out and turning to aim it directly at the barracks building, which sat a few hundred yards across the compound. The guard's rifle and the brick lay on the passenger seat. He mentally rehearsed what he needed to go through, practicing opening and closing his door. Then he dropped the gearshift lever into first, revved the engine, and took off across the compound.

The truck lumbered along, its acceleration sluggish with its full load. Jack nudged it into second gear and tried to speed up. He quickly tried to guess how fast it might approach the building and how much farther he could manage to drive it. He pushed down on the rusty clutch pedal and jammed the gearshift lever into third. He was picking up speed, and the front wall of the dormitory building was approaching. *Now!* he thought. He reached over to grasp the dirty brick and dropped it down full on the accelerator pedal. The truck lurched ahead faster. Jack let go of the steering wheel and with as smooth a motion as he could manage, he grabbed the rifle, pulled up the door latch to open his door, and leaped out. He hit the ground and rolled in the dirt as the tanker careened toward the dormitory.

One of the emerging soldiers saw him and halted to raise his rifle. Tarzan let loose an arrow which stopped the soldier before he could fire.

He stopped rolling and looked back in time to see the impact. He heard the sound of crashing, creaking metal as the truck slammed into the wall of the barracks. An instant later the explosion was bigger and louder than he imagined it could be. A huge fireball rocked the compound with a prodigious roar that shook the jungle for a mile around. The entire compound was illuminated. Flames were consuming fully half of the two-story dormitory and rose high above the roofline. The blast sent flaming sections of roof and siding spinning off yards away to land on adjoining buildings and shacks, setting them ablaze. The generator shed, fed by diesel fuel tanks, exploded in a second blinding fireball that sent a mushroom cloud of black smoke churning high into the dawn sky.

Men from the blazing dormitory began to run or stumble out in a chorus of yells and screams. Some, badly burned, collapsed and fell in the yard. Others had been lucky enough to escape injury. Jack saw that the first few ran out, panicked, in undershorts, but the next several had managed to grab shirts and pants. And their rifles and pistols.

Jack rose and began to run off toward the office/lab complex, which was as yet far enough from the explosions to be undamaged. One of the emerging soldiers saw him and halted to raise his rifle. Tarzan let loose an arrow which stopped the soldier before he could fire.

In the time it took Tarzan to secure a second arrow, another mercenary had spotted the slain comrade and looked around to see whence the arrow had come. Hoping to prevent being spotted, Tarzan unleashed a second arrow, which also struck home.

Meanwhile, Jack arrived at the door of the lab and made his way in and through to the corridor leading to Winslow's quarters. "Professor Winslow!" he shouted. He continued down the corridor until he found Winslow's room. The professor was in bed, sitting up, dazed.

"Jack, what are you doing here?"

"I've come to rescue you and get you out of here."

"Wha…Now? Just you? You're with them, too. How do you propose to rescue me?"

"No, not just me. I have….a friend outside helping me. Tell me, are there any others from our expedition here? Clarke? Cedric?"

The professor, still drowsy, gathered his thoughts for a moment. "No…Cedric left. Clarke went back to England earlier. All our native boys have scattered. You and I are the only ones left in this compound from the original expedition."

"Good," Jack replied hurriedly. "Then let's go."

The professor raised his hand and shook his head. "I can't go. They'll kill me. I have to stay here and do what they want. It's the only way I'll be safe."

"You can't stay. You don't know you'll be safe. Look at how far underway this operation is. Soon they won't need you, and then they'll get rid of you. These men are butchers. They are a perversion of everything you stand for and have worked for. Why ally yourself with them? We have a chance to get out, right now. I'm taking it. Are you with me?"

Winslow's eyes nervously glanced around the room and out the partially shaded window. He listened to the din outside. He rose to dress in rumpled trousers and waistcoat. He hastened to grab his valise and stuff a few personal items into it.

"Let's go," he said.

They ambled out of Winslow's room and down the short corridor to the large laboratory room, where rows of tables were filled with microscopes, glassware, earth-lined specimen trays and examination tools. One portion of the room contained a collection of potted Ghana daylilies in various stages of growth. Out from behind a cluster of these plants stepped Nigel Vanden Avond.

"Where are you gentlemen going?" He drew a Luger from the leather holster at his side and pointed it at Jack. "You're not thinking of leaving us, are you?"

"There's no point in trying to stop me," Jack retorted. "You'll gain nothing. Your operation is over. It's burning up, or haven't you noticed?"

"What I've noticed," Vanden Avond said, beginning to circulate around the tables and approach Jack, "is your jungle man out there trying to hold off our men. I don't know how long he can continue that, but with you as my hostage, he'll quit." Vanden Avond had advanced to the point where he was the width of a lab table away from the two men. "You're not getting away."

Professor Winslow seized a specimen tray filled with earth and young daylily sprouts and threw it at Vanden Avond's face. His hand holding the Luger went up and fired wildly at the ceiling. Then he stepped back to shake some of the dirt out, tried to wipe his eyes, and leveled the pistol at Jack again. Jack could not hesitate. He fired his rifle. Vanden Avond fell.

"Come on!" Jack urged Winslow, who was both still groggy and stunned by the suddenness of Jack's move.

Jack opened the door to the outside yard carefully, looking to see what was happening. The entire area was hellish chaos. Smoke roiled up from the roofs of several buildings, and everything in the central compound was reflected in brilliant firelight. Men screamed and shouted. Random bursts of rifle fire filled the air.

Jack noted that Tarzan was still ensconced in his position. They exchanged glances and nods to indicate that each was all right. Jack and Winslow crouched down and headed for the closest group of trucks to afford cover.

Though some men had gotten out of the blazing dormitory burned or maimed, at least a dozen were unscathed, and it was these who presented an increasing menace for Tarzan. In the initial confusion, none of the soldiers had known who their attackers were or how many they numbered, but after some observation they began to realize that Jack and Tarzan may be the only two as-sailants—and Jack had been seen heading inside.

By now they had all seized rifles and pistols and had begun to regroup and plan a strategy for reaching Tarzan's position. Some, not knowing for sure which vehicle concealed Tarzan, and reluctant to shoot trucks they depended upon for supplies and transport, peppered the ground around the parking area.

Tarzan regretted that he thought too late of moving around to change his position and keep them off guard, for now he was pinned down.

One of the bolder mercenaries reached an open rover parked near a supply hut which had not yet been touched by the flames. He leaped into the driver's seat, started it up, and, keeping his head low, whirled the vehicle across the compound toward Tarzan. Perhaps he thought the ape man would cower in fear and become vulnerable to capture, or perhaps he thought the ape man would run in fear and become an easy target. On the contrary, Tarzan coolly sighted down his bow, tautly drawn, and waited, tensed, for the right moment. It came when the driver turned and the left front tire came fully into view. The arrow flew across the distance and solidly punctured the tire. The nearly-instantaneous blowout caused the swerving vehicle to spin out and tumble over, spilling the driver onto the dirt. The driver rose hastily and tried to run away, but Tarzan's next arrow caught him, and he tumbled back to the ground. This display of marksmanship deterred some of the hired soldiers, but others, perhaps more arrogant or simply foolhardy, felt challenged by it.

Two of the soldiers worked their way to one of the canopied utility trucks and climbed in. One started the engine and drove the truck out of its parking stall, around several other trucks, and out into the main compound area. The other clambered into the rear cargo area and flopped back the canvas canopy—revealing a mounted machine gun. The driver whirled the truck around and stopped it to face Tarzan some fifty feet away. The second man leveled the machine gun, fed a supply of ammunition into the magazine, and opened fire on the vehicle which they were now certain Tarzan hid behind. A spray of bullets churned up dust around the truck and spattered the body with holes and dents. One tire popped and hissed flat, shaking the vehicle.

Unable to escape or to stand up for a clear shot with his bow, Tarzan crouched low behind the vehicle as the metal body panels afforded him increasingly frail protection against the hail of lead.

The gunner paused to adjust his sights and consider whether to tell the driver to move in closer to Tarzan. He stood for a moment, silhouetted against the brilliant light of the blazing compound, when suddenly a spear shot through him. He had but a moment to look down in shock at the bloody spear point protruding out from his chest, and clutch at the handle of the machine gun, before a second spear tore through his body. He crumbled to the ground.

The driver, astonished, looked to where the spears had come from. Other mercenaries in the compound began to stop in their tracks and look.

From off in the distance they heard a low, rhythmic chant rippling through the dawn sky. One by one the mercenaries looked over to the west, and one by one their eyes stared agape and their jaws dropped. Standing at the edge of the forest, shoulder to shoulder in a line that stretched like a great wall fronted with shields, was an assembly of fifty Waziri warriors in full battle regalia, their spears leveled and their bows drawn.

Chapter Thirteen
THE CHARGE

The low, ominous, Waziri war song broke off, and for a moment silence reigned as the ragged band of mercenaries stared at the magnificent foe.

Then with one note there came a piercing war cry, and a volley of spears and arrows was unleashed upon the compound, picking out with uncanny accuracy a half dozen of the soldiers and sending the remaining ones scattering to seek cover and regroup.

The Waziri charged.

The speed and ferocity with which the Waziri mount a full charge is a matter of jungle legend. The fifty tall, muscled, ebony warriors ran toward the central compound, leaping over rock and log and bush. They drove forward in one line over the fence and into the compound like a wave of locusts, letting nothing deter their progress.

With ferocious yells they clashed with every resisting soldier they met. A few of DeKelm's men fired and dropped warriors, but one after another they were set upon and beaten or impaled before they could fire again.

The driver of the truck that had pinned Tarzan down got out and climbed up to the machine gun mount. He whirled the weapon around to face the oncoming Waziri and fired a burst which picked off two of them. He did not fire a second burst, because Tarzan's arrow silenced him. He collapsed on top of the machine gun.

The charge advanced through the compound. Jack, having

taken cover behind one of the vehicles near the fence, had been about to raise his rifle to assist Tarzan, but he promptly saw that he did not need to.

Clusters of four or five warriors at a time converged on every spot of concealment or refuge one of DeKelm's men took—behind barrels and crates, along the fences, around corners of buildings. The cracks of rifle and pistol shots mingled in the air with the chants of the natives and the shouts and cries of the soldiers. Even with firearms, the soldiers were no match for the Waziri because the soldiers could hardly shoot fast enough before being overwhelmed by the warriors' charge. The loss of an occasional man did not deter Waziri for one moment. They would have time to mourn their dead later. They pursued their mission single-mindedly. Their attack was ruthless, and their victory was swift.

Tarzan watched in amazement, as the Waziri routed the last of the mercenaries who resisted. *How fitting,* he thought. *A dawn raid for a dawn raid.*

The smoke continued to cloud the emerging morning light. The main dormitory had been reduced nearly to a charred and glowing shell, but the fire still burned, advancing to engulf other buildings.

Scattered across the central compound, the bodies of black-skinned warriors and khaki-clad mercenaries lay dead or writhing in pain, their figures outlined by the inferno behind them. Moans of the burned or the wounded mingled with the crackling of the blazing walls and collapsing roof beams. The horrific stench of burning wood and diesel and flesh permeated the air.

Some Waziri began gathering their spears and arrows and tending to their dead and wounded, while others rounded up the few mercenaries who had surrendered. Tarzan approached the chief, and the two clasped arms in greeting. "You got my message," said the ape man. "Thank you for coming to help."

Jack and Winslow ambled to the central area where Tarzan and M'Bala stood with several other Waziri. As they approached, they were taken aback by the spectacle of destruction. Winslow allowed, "Yes, Jack, I think that we might be able to leave now without them objecting too much."

"Professor Winslow?" inquired Tarzan, looking at the rumpled and rather distraught old scientist.

Jack said, "This is John—uh, Tarzan. He is a friend of my father's."

"Your father has…interesting friends, Jack," Winslow replied.

Tarzan explained to M'Bala who these two were. M'Bala grinned and expressed how gratified he was that Tarzan had found that for which he searched. Then his ebullience faded as he wondered to Tarzan, "Where is their leader?"

"I have not seen him," Tarzan said in the Waziri tongue, then asked Jack, "Have you seen DeKelm?"

"No," Jack replied. "Vanden Avond is dead, but I don't know where DeKelm went."

Tarzan turned and said, "Look over there." They all looked toward the remains of the office building and lab, the last portion to have caught fire, and saw DeKelm walking toward them, hands clasped over his head, clothing and face smudged. He was being urged from behind by a man with a rifle. The man was none other than Reg.

"'Ere!" Reg cried out. "Oi've got 'im! Take 'im!"

They stopped before the group. DeKelm looked at the Waziri, and at Tarzan, and then at Jack and Winslow, and cried defiantly, "You fools!" His blackened face twisted into a foul sneer. "You don't know what you're doing! You'll pay for this!"

"Shaddup," Reg said to him, and then said to Tarzan, "You want to take 'im?"

"You disloyal turncoat!" DeKelm shouted, red-faced and infuriated. "I paid you! Your allegiance is to me! What kind of a man are you?"

Reg sneered sardonically. "Oi've seen what a man is. An' it's not you, you scum. You're gonna answer for all the things you made us do!"

"You yellow bastard!" DeKelm shouted, and in a sudden move he spun around and shoved Reg roughly away. DeKelm made a break for a discarded rifle that he had spotted on the ground a few feet away. In one motion, he reached down to grab the rifle, whirled around, and fired at Reg.

Reg dropped his weapon and clutched at his chest. His face grimaced, then sunk as his eyes widened in shock. He began to slump. But before he fell, and before DeKelm could fire again, a half dozen Waziri spears from as many angles instantly sliced into DeKelm's chest, neck, and abdomen, ripping flesh and cracking bone. A brief flash of consternation, then horror passed across DeKelm's countenance as he looked toward Tarzan and the Waziri, but then his eyes glazed over and he sank to the ground. He landed roughly, breaking off some of the Waziri spears while others protruded from him like so many giant pins in a cushion.

M'Bala looked down at DeKelm writhing in agony in the dirt, then falling still. "I wish he had not made that move," said the chief. "I would like to have taken him back to the village and roasted him over my ceremonial fire."

Tarzan translated the comment for Jack, who emitted a low whistle. Then Jack asked, through the ape man, how the warriors had been able to find this place.

M'Bala chuckled and replied, "The beacon you sent up was rather easy to follow, my friend."

Chapter Fourteen

AT THE STATION

The ceiling fan whirled lazily in Captain Reynolds' office as the attending corporal in the starched navy blue poured tea into Tarzan's cup. Steaming English Breakfast Tea was hardly the most appropriate beverage for this time and place, but Tarzan accepted Reynolds' traditional hospitality with gratitude. He held up the cup appreciatively to sample the aroma, then placed it down on the table to cool a bit and leaned back in his chair. This was the first time he felt he could relax since the night in the Waziri camp. The corporal moved ceremoniously around the table to Jack, to Winslow, then to Reynolds, and served them. A plate of English biscuits and local fruit was passed around.

"So," Reynolds spoke up to Jack, "your first trip to Africa was a bit more than you expected, eh?"

"I rather enjoyed it," Jack replied. "Well, the exploration part, I mean. Apart from the gunfire and explosions and nearly getting killed."

"Yes, well, it does tend to get a bit dodgy when our friend here comes around," Reynolds added, nodding to Tarzan.

Tarzan took the jape with an amused half smile. "I do not look for trouble. It finds me."

"Indeed it does. We almost had the makings of an international incident here."

Reynolds took a sip of his tea and declared, "The remaining mercenaries have been rounded up and taken into custody. The governments of France, Belgium, England, and the United States have all lodged official protests about the conduct of Consolidated Pharmaceutical, which, according to George Fredrickson, are being acted upon at the highest levels. It'll be a relief to have their kind out of the jungle."

Professor Winslow, who had been quiet and pensive since his rescue, stared vacantly at his teacup and said, "It was an incredibly stupid, blundering choice to make." He looked up at Jack and added, almost defensively, "I didn't know what I was getting into."

"But how could you, professor?" Jack hastened to reply. "You couldn't have known what the company really wanted. You couldn't have known what DeKelm and his men were going to do."

"Still, I should have used better judgment. I was naïve. And I shouldn't have gotten you mixed up in it, either. I thought I was doing some good."

"You were. And you will again," Jack said.

"It just seems that we can hardly do any sort of research these days for the betterment of humanity without some company or other trying to get their hands on our work to exploit it," said Winslow.

"The jungle and its people have always been used by men for their profit," Tarzan commented.

"It's enough to make me want to abandon field work and stay home and write my memoirs," Winslow added.

Reynolds said, "What's amazing is how far they'd gotten along in their schemes. The audacity of this company. If our friend Tarzan here had not acted so quickly, we might have had a full scale jungle war on our hands in a matter of weeks."

"Even so, I grieve for the loss of my Waziri friends," said Tarzan. Turning to Jack to change the topic, he asked, "Well, then, what will you do now? Continue plant study in the jungle?"

"No, I think not."

"What?" Winslow reacted. "Abandon botany after all this?"

"Too much excitement," Jack smiled. "I think I might switch

over to physics. I hear there is some fascinating new work being done with nuclear fission. That sounds much quieter."

1937

*Tarzan and the
Cross of Vengeance*

Chapter 1
IDENTITY

The rain tumbled down in sheets, a cold hard rain that chilled to the bone, the kind of rain that even seasoned Londoners cursed.

A taxi, sleek from water sheeting off it, pulled up to the curb, throwing runoff from the gutter onto the sidewalk. The taxi door swung open and a man in a fedora and raincoat stepped out and dashed across the sidewalk from the cab to the doorway of the brick-fronted building facing the street.

He stepped briskly from the street into the foyer, closed the door behind him, and stomped his wet oxfords on the worn, dirty wooden floor to shake off some of the rain. He looked up at the long flight of wooden stairs and then grasped the mahogany railing, worn smooth and yellowed over the years, and started up, the steps creaking as he ascended.

At the top of the stairs, he turned to the right and walked down the narrow corridor to the second door. He paused to look at the pebbled opaque glass panel in the upper half of the molded wooden door, where the stenciling read:

205
Raymond Wilson
Confidential
Private Investigations

He turned the knob and entered the reception area of a weathered office whose rug and furniture had seen better days. To one side sat the old wooden desk. On its surface lay a black Remington typewriter, an office-model black dial phone, and stacks of papers loosely scattered about. Behind the desk stood an empty wooden swivel desk chair. Apparently Wilson had respected his request to meet alone. Good.

The visitor removed his topcoat and began to shake more of the rain from it onto the floor. He was five-feet-ten, with a stocky build and a ruddy complexion, punctuated by piercing brown eyes and thinning brown hair and mustache.

A man in a rumpled brown suit stepped into the arched doorway from the next room.

"Maximilian. You're late."

"It was impossible to get a cab in the rain. This better be good, Wilson. What have you got for me?"

Wilson smiled. "You'll find this interesting." He led the rain-drenched visitor into the next room. Atop a desk in the center of the room sat a dusty Bell & Howell sixteen-millimeter film projector aimed at a small wrinkled screen which stood on a rickety tripod stand at the opposite end of the room. A reel of film about six inches in diameter was threaded onto the projector.

"What is this—show time? I didn't bring my popcorn."

"Watch," said Wilson. He pushed the button on the wall to turn off the ceiling light, then turned a switch on the projector, which started up with a clatter. As the film began to wind through the sprockets and onto the take-up reel, he spoke over the racket: "This was taken by a Pathé news crew three years ago, filming some documentary on Africa. They were shooting footage of African tribal rituals, like dances and so on. This was culled from hours of outtakes that they never used, but lay gathering dust in their vault. I managed through great effort and considerable expense—"

"I'm sure," Maximilian said.

"—to get and convert these shots."

Projected on the small screen were grainy black-and-white images of what appeared to be African natives jumping or dancing around a fire, waving their arms and brandishing spears. The film image jiggled and jostled as if the camera man did not know how to hold it still, or did not care. No sound. Very repetitive. The images continued with little variety for several minutes.

"And why am I looking at this?"

"You'll see. There. See in the corner of the frame? Left side?" Maximilian had to look carefully, but there it was—the face of a white man sitting along the sidelines.

"I've spliced these together from hours of shots like this, from various tribes, to highlight what I think you're looking for. This is the...let me see...the Waziri tribe, I believe (he mispronounced it WAH-zi-ree)."

Wilson continued, "The next series of shots was apparently filmed by a cameraman whose camera was running, apparently unintentionally, while he held it. You'll see here that it's very wiggly and the angle is down low. It shows a lot of ground, and part of the fire, and a lot of feet running around, but then off in the distance... you'll see it...there! Right at that moment."

From upstage of the bonfire smoke and between blurry images of dancers cavorting, there appeared a figure leaping up into a tree. It was the white man.

Maximilian stood up, suddenly aware that he had been leaning forward to stare at the screen, and said, "Well, then, that's my man. Except all I have is this film. Three years old. How does that help me?"

"There's more," said Wilson, with the confidence of a man who knows that what he is about to say will please. With a bit of a flair, he switched off the projector, switched on the lights, and continued, "Because, y'see, I took a print of one frame of that shot around the campfire, the one where we got a pretty good look at his face, and I had it blown up." He reached over to a pile of papers on the corner of the table and retrieved one. "Here it is."

He handed Maximilian a photograph. It was fuzzy, having been enlarged from the film image that was none too sharp to begin with, but it showed a white man with black hair, straight nose, and a strong chiseled jaw line, staring at the revelry.

"Now look at this." Wilson handed him last week's *The Observer*.

"*The Observer?*" the visitor scoffed. "That rag?"

"Don't judge it before you've seen whether it serves your purpose. Look here, on page six." He flipped through the pages until he found what he was looking for and spread out the paper on the table. "An article about a debate in the House of Lords. And an accompanying photograph. It shows a photo of members of the House of Lords, sitting in chambers listening to a speaker." The visitor stared at the photo. "Have a closer look," said Wilson, picking up a magnifying glass and handing it over. He allowed the visitor a moment to study the face, then placed the grainy photo of the white face witnessing the African tribal dances down on the desk next to the newspaper photo. The visitor leaned over to look back and forth from one to the other and noted the distinctive features: the straight nose, the firm jaw line, the dark hair.

He straightened and said, more to the newspaper than to Wilson, "They are the same man."

"Is this the man you are looking for?" Wilson inquired, somewhat eagerly. When he observed the visitor's expression of sobering surprise, he added, "Not only is he right here in London—he's a Peer of the Realm!"

Chapter 2
CHOICES

More than three thousand miles away in rural Massachusetts, in a small white church dwarfed by oaks, the voices of some twenty children floated out from the church basement, struggling to hit the high notes as best they could as they sang:

Just a few more weary days and then
I'll fly away
To a land where joys will never end
I'll fly away.

They sat on wooden benches or folding chairs on the uneven concrete floor of the basement, which had been painted gray a long time ago. They were led by a woman clamping the chords on an old pump organ at the front of the room. Her cotton print frock fell nearly to the floor as she pumped the foot bellows. Her buttoned-up collar was trimmed in rather frayed white lace. Her wispy brown hair, gathered at the sides with a few bobby pins, framed her face, which was unadorned by makeup. She heartily sang out the notes in an effort to keep the children on key.

The song finished as she softened and let up on the last chord. She turned to the group and proclaimed with a smile, "And that's the message for today, children. We will fly away. We will see that land where joys never end, truly we will."

She closed and set down her music book, rose, and, picking up her shawl and wrapping it around her shoulders, faced them. "Now boys and girls, if you remember last week we were discussing heaven and hell and the things we must do in our lives to earn our reward in heaven."

A small, white-sleeved hand shot up. "Missy Ruth?" In the Church of the Evangelical Brotherhood, the children used the first names of their teachers, and the adult members all addressed each other as Brother or Sister, in the spirit of communality.

"Yes, Robert?"

"You know how you said last week that we must belong to our religion and have faith so that we can die in a state of grace?"

"Yes."

"Well, I was talking with my friends, and they said that they didn't think God would punish people who died without knowing about our faith, like little babies."

"Now, Robert, I'm sure God will not subject innocent babies to eternal fire. Some people believe in a place called Limbo where innocent souls are sent. But remember that God also gives us eyes to see and ears to hear, and the Word of God is out there for people to see and hear. Those who ignore this message do so at their peril."

Another girl raised her hand. "Yes, Missy Ruth, but what about people who don't live where they can hear about our faith? Like natives in Africa and so on? How can they get to heaven if they have not been saved?"

"Well, Frances, we must all support those who do missionary work so that these pagans can be saved. It's good that you ask that question, because as you may remember, Brother Adamson and others from our church are about to undertake the perilous journey to Africa to join in this missionary work. We must all pray for his success in converting the heathen. And we will be taking up the collection this Sunday for this important work. Be sure to remind your parents to be generous."

The lesson came to its end after a few questions about the Gospels and a final prayer and hymn. As the children picked up their books and filed out, they passed the imposing figure of

Brother Walter Adamson standing in the back doorway of the room. They greeted him politely and then dutifully walked up the stairs, waiting to put a respectful distance between themselves and the church elder before they picked up speed to scurry the remaining distance out the rear door of the church and into the sunshine. Their whoops of exuberance echoed down the stairwell.

Walter Adamson was tall, with distinguished features and ample brown hair that had begun to gray at the temples when he turned fifty three years before. His brown suit and striped tie had evidently been worn many times. Though his brow was quite capable of being stern, his eyes could sparkle and his features could soften, as they did now when he looked down at Ruth as she gathered up her papers from the organ and stopped for a moment, noticing him standing there.

"Brother Adamson!" she exclaimed, not expecting him to have been observing her lesson.

"Hello, Sister Ruth," he smiled. "You know, you really are quite good with the children."

"Thank you." She brushed a strand of hair out of her face and looked at the floor in mild embarrassment. Even though he was scarcely ten years older, Ruth always felt that Walter Adamson was more of a father or mentor figure to her.

"I just happened to be passing by. I heard your comments about the missionary work. I want to thank you for the support."

"You're welcome. I wasn't sure that I answered all the children's questions adequately. They are so curious, and they ask clever ones. Sometimes I think they are trying to trap me."

"You did fine. God's work is never easy. But you are up to the challenge."

"I do wonder about those children in Africa, Brother Adamson. Frances is right. How will they be saved?"

"You answered her question, Sister Ruth. By our missionary work."

"But surely the missionaries can't get to them all..." Ruth's brow furrowed. "And they are such pagan savages. Cannibals, head-hunters…." She shuddered.

He grasped her shoulder and said, "Sister Ruth, if you are concerned that there are not enough people to do the missionary work, why don't you join us? We leave next month. We could always use more help."

"Me?" The thought gave her pause. "What about my work here? What about these children?"

"The children here are important, but they will be saved," he replied. "They have already heard the Word. You have a gift. Perhaps God is calling you to use it in new ways."

"But how…I don't know the first thing about missionary work. I don't know the language. I don't know the land. Or how to build huts…."

Walter Adamson's weathered face smiled the benign, paternal smile she always found endearing. "We have people with those skills. You don't have to know it all. We begin in small steps. We have done some preliminary fieldwork. We have a translator and a place to set up a field mission. But we always need people to work with the children. The children are the heart of this endeavor."

Ruth pondered this question for the next day and a half. Then, in the middle of the night, she reached her conclusion with startling clarity. At age forty-three, with silvery gray threads in her mousy brown hair, with creases beginning to line her face, with no husband or family to keep her here, and with little prospect of that ever changing, she realized that she would have to go to Africa.

* * *

Franklin Granger, Professor of Archaeology, sat at his desk in his cramped university office in upstate New York and stared at the pile of student papers he had just collected. He already knew they were going to be dismal. Blake over in the English Department had joked only last week that this would be a great job if it weren't for the paperwork, but Granger knew it to be true.

He stared out the open window at the courtyard bordering his office building. It was a bright day in early spring. Huge oaks and maples sprouting new green leaves stood tall around the courtyard. Butter-colored daffodils and flaming tulips bloomed in patches arranged about the massive green quadrangle.

The well-manicured look of the grounds contrasted, as it always did, with the disarray of his office. Papers lay askew on his desk and poked out from several volumes on his shelves. His 1937 calendar hung conspicuously on the wall, well marked with notations reminding him of the various events and deadlines that obligated him.

His gaze moved from the window to the shelves of books that lined the walls floor to ceiling on three sides of the cramped office. Actual science texts, he thought. Volumes documenting genuine research and real knowledge. He wondered whether he could get any of his students to touch a single one.

He had just concluded his lecture on the *Australopithecus africanus* and the early Pliocene era. He might as well have been speaking in Martian, for all the attention he felt from the students. He had tried not to make his lectures dull and academic. He had joked about things like opposable thumbs and walking upright and tried to stir their interest with what he considered startling statistics about the similarities between apes and humans. He always tried to impress upon them that we must understand where we came from if we are ever to understand who we are. That is, after all, the basis for what education is all about, he thought, but apparently that idea failed to seize the imaginations of more than a scant few students. How could they not be curious, he wondered.

He removed his tweed jacket, undid his bow tie, wiped his palm over his balding pate, took a breath, and tried to work up some enthusiasm for plowing through the looming pile of student papers. He braced himself for the sloppy measurements, the hasty conclusions, the shallow analysis.

"Come on, get cracking on those lab reports!" He turned to see his jovial colleague, Edgar Thryson, poking his head in from the hall.

"Do I have to?" Granger returned in mocking whine.

"Oh, come, come, they can't all be that dreadful, can they?"

"Don't be too sure. Sometimes I think there isn't a scientific mind among them. Just kids who want to get the credit and get out."

"Rather be digging in the dirt, eh?"

"Hell, yes. That's where we find things out. I'm a scientist. I was hired by the university as a scientist. The credibility of my body of work rests on my status as a scientist. So why am I required to teach Archaeology 101 to effete freshmen whose concept of their history extends about as far back as their parents' home town?"

"Well, we do have promising graduate students, don't we?"

"Yes. I believe we had one two years ago," Granger said, only half kidding.

"What about Abrams' dig? Aren't you supposed to join him?"

"But I can't get leave unless they have something significant. That's the catch—I can't go looking for it until it's already been found."

"Well, this might cheer you up." He handed Granger a folded and sealed manila envelope.

"What's that?" Granger took it.

"Telegram for you. Came just now. Maybe it's what you've been waiting for?"

Telegram? That's odd. He knew no one who would be sending him a telegram. No, wait—he did know at least one place a telegram might come from. And sure enough—he looked at the address on the inside and confirmed that it was from his colleagues at the dig. He tore open the paper and read:

HAVE SOMETHING YOU MIGHT LIKE TO SEE

Abrams

The wording was coded. Deliberately vague. He knew what Abrams' expedition had been looking for, and that they had found something that he was definitely more than a little likely to want to see.

He knew what it meant, all right. It meant that he would have to go to Africa.

Chapter 3
QUARRY

When he first embarked upon this enterprise, Maximilian had never imagined that it might take him into the marbled and gilded halls of the Palace of Westminster. Yet that was where he found himself, striding down the corridor near the antechamber of the House of Lords. He approached the polished mahogany reception desk. The pert brunette with pearl earrings and ruby lipstick who sat behind it smiled at him and asked, "May I help you, sir?"

"Yes," he said with his best upper-class accent and aristocratic bearing. "I wonder if I might find Lord Greystoke here?"

"Well, sir, the Lords are in session, and Lord Greystoke has indicated that he shall be going home directly afterwards. Do you wish to leave a message? May I make an appointment for you for tomorrow?"

"No, thank you, that won't be necessary. Is the gallery open?"

"Yes, it is, sir. Right that way." She pointed her manicured finger toward the doorway that led up to the Strangers' Gallery.

"Thank you. Good day."

He ascended the carpeted staircase to the balcony surrounding the floor of the House of Lords on three sides and joined the scattered numbers of tourists and guests filling the seats here and there.

On the floor below he could see the array of black-suited Lords sitting at their polished wooden desks and red benches, the ornate chamber echoing with speakers' voices. He stared intently, scanning back and forth along the rows. Often he could only see the tops of heads, but occasionally one turned or looked up so that he could see the face. Time after time, it was not his quarry.

At length, after some minutes of patiently and intently scrutinizing row upon row of the faces of the Lords, he found what he sought. The shock of black hair, the complexion more bronzed than the other pasty or ruddy faces, the firm jaw line and straight nose—there he was! John Clayton, Lord Greystoke, in the flesh.

Now there was little to do but wait for the session to be over. And wait he did, through the dry speeches and mumblings and endless procedures. Six o'clock. Seven o'clock. He could hear Big Ben outside bonging away the hour. How easy it would be to take his target at any time, he thought more than once, but he would never get away with it here. No, he reminded himself, he must be patient.

Finally they finished. As the Lord Chancellor was about to gavel the session to a close, Maximilian rose and moved quickly toward the door and down the stairway.

He knew that if he had done his research correctly, Clayton would be stopping at his office briefly and then leaving by the Members' Entrance off Bridge Street. Darkness was falling as he left through St. Stephen's entrance and turned right to jog up St. Margaret Street to the north side of the Parliament building, whose carved walls and spires shimmered golden in the last rays of the setting sun. He mingled with the crowds at the carriage gates, watching intently as one after another of the members of Parliament left the building to catch waiting cars and taxis.

Once again, his patience paid off. Clayton emerged, chatting briefly with a few older, portlier gentlemen, and then parted company and hailed a cab. Maximilian procured the next available cab and slipped the driver a handsome sum to follow Clayton's discreetly.

Their route took them across Westminster Bridge and down several of London's wide thoroughfares lined with granite facades of banks and stores. Maximilian admired the driver's skill as he wove his way through the gnarled traffic, maintaining a distance from Clayton's cab yet always keeping it in sight. The curved streets were particularly challenging. Maximilian wondered whether any side streets in London were straight for more than a block or two.

They entered a section of residential areas filled with more modest blocks of flats. When he saw Clayton's cab stop at one corner about a block ahead, he bade his driver to pull over quickly and got out.

His quarry walked down one of the narrow alleys dimly lit by lights from the street at either end. Three hundred years ago this passageway might have been a street flocked with people from residences or shops, but now it was merely a narrow bricked walkway between two tall stone buildings, populated by garbage cans, fire escape gratings, and the occasional rodent.

As he observed his target stroll down the alley, swinging his folded umbrella, Maximilian kept himself concealed by moving cautiously from one corner or doorway molding to the next. He paused to pull out a revolver from his jacket and proceeded to draw a bead upon his target. But Clayton was in the shadows. It was too dark to get a clean shot. Patience. He had waited too long and gone through too much to risk a miss.

When Clayton stepped just barely into better light, Maximilian held his breath and tightened his grip, but he had to hesitate—two scruffily-dressed figures stepped out of the shadows. They appeared to be brandishing knives. Maximilian was far enough away to avoid being seen but close enough to hear.

"Well, what have we 'ere?" said the first one, a grizzled, scrawny runt of a man with a crooked nose. "Judgin' by the looks of 'im, Oi'd say 'e's got a fat purse, don't yeh think, 'Arry?" With a bit of a swagger, he began to circle around Clayton, who had come to a stop in the middle of the alley.

"Drop the umbrella," said the other man, a taller, more burly man wearing a particularly tattered coat.

Clayton stood there in the half light, looking back and forth from one to the other. They were about ten feet away from him, the one called Harry just to his left and the runt circling to his right.

Maximilian, watching this scene unfold, came to the ironic realization that he might have to bring down all three of these men, that he might have to save his quarry's life to take it. Then he heard Clayton say firmly, "Leave me alone. Walk away and you will be unharmed."

"Hah!" the burly, tattered Harry exclaimed. "Listen t' that! We're the ones wi' the knives, squire." He waved his knife in the air. "Now go on," he continued. "Drop it nice an' easy. And then you're gonna give us yer fat wallet and *then* no one'll get 'urt."

Clayton slowly began to extend his right hand, which held the umbrella, as if he were going to drop it, all the while glaring at the ragged street thief called Harry. But at that moment there issued from the throat of the tall, stately British Peer a low rumble that grew into a growl that even Maximilian could hear from his vantage point.

"Wha' the 'ell?" exclaimed the scrawny one, his voice becoming more agitated. "You tryin' to be some kinda freak? Come on. We ain't got all night! Drop the bloody umbrella!"

What happened next was so swift that Maximilian was barely able to follow it. Clayton flung the umbrella into the chest of the weaselly one on his right, who staggered backward from the impact. The tall lord took advantage of the brief moment of surprise to leap toward Harry on his left and grab his raised arm that held the knife and bend it upward. Harry struggled. As solid as the thief's arm was, his strength was no match for Lord Clayton, who forced the arm down and around behind Harry's back and wrenched it upward. Maximilian was certain he heard it crack. The would-be robber cried out in pain. Clayton released the man's arm, then swiftly bent down and picked him up bodily with both arms and flung him toward the scrawny man with the upraised knife. They both tumbled to the ground.

Harry struggled. As solid as the thief's arm was, his strength was no match for Lord Clayton, who forced the arm down and around behind Harry's back and wrenched it upward.

Clayton stood there, hunched down, arms stretched out, poised to check their next move. They quickly but clumsily rolled apart and separated. The scrawny one still had his knife and, as he raised it, Clayton swiftly kicked it out of his hand.

"You bastard!" the man said. He rose and ran toward his intended victim, attempting to tackle him. Clayton clamped an iron hand on each side of the weaselly little man's head and yanked him upright. From his throat there came a roar of rage as he shook the assailant back and forth like some great rag doll, then cast him against the nearby wall of the building so forcefully that his head cracked on the brick. Both thieves now lay crumpled on the pavement, moaning in pain.

Clayton turned and ambled off.

Maximilian stared, eyes agape. He thought about sighting down his pistol and firing at his quarry, but before he could aim, this Peer of the Realm leaped up to grasp a fire escape grate extending out from the side of the building above his head. In an instant Clayton swung himself up to the level of the grate, then continued to scale up several more flights of grid work as agilely as a monkey climbing a tree. He vanished into the night.

Maximilian considered what he had just witnessed. Another hunter may have been disappointed that his prey got away, or intimidated by such a demonstration of its prowess. But this hunter was calculating and deliberate, capable of learning from his experience. He realized that he needed an entirely different strategy to get close to this one. Today's effort had been a failure, but he learned three things from it. One, that John Clayton and Tarzan of the Apes were one and the same. Two, that this Clayton/Tarzan was a formidable opponent not to be taken lightly. And three, that he would have to go to Africa.

Chapter 4
A F R I C A

Six months later, Ruth Cheever could scarcely believe that she was standing in front of another class of some twenty children, singing hymns and praising God, but in such an altogether different setting. These children were not well-scrubbed white New Englanders in their Sunday best, but rather, dark-eyed African children of the Urulu tribe, dressed for the most part in loincloths of animal skin or coarsely woven fabric with a bone necklace or spray of feathers as the only adornment on their glistening ebony skin. Over her head was not the ductwork and plastered ceiling of a seventy-year-old clapboard church, but a recently-constructed network of interwoven branches and palm fronds supported by poles of skinned tree limbs, a shelter whose open sides admitted the occasional breeze, the only remedy against the midday sun of the tropical African village in which she now found herself. Indeed, as she pushed back the strands of her wispy brown hair and wiped her brow of the sweat that trickled in the creases of her face, she lamented that her modesty did not permit her to wear something less than a cotton print dress gathered at the waist with a trim belt.

The route that took her here had not been easy. Had she had the leisure to take a moment's pause from her busy schedule, she would have been amazed at how far things had come. Brother Adamson's missionary group had made preliminary contact with this Urulu tribe before she arrived and had ascertained that they were at least willing to listen to the Word of the Gospel and not shrink the missionaries' heads, as she had imagined.

The missionaries lived in an encampment of huts and tents constructed only a few dozen yards from the edge of the Urulu village. The tribe had granted them an area of jungle and even helped them clear it. With regular shipments of goods and supplies from America and Europe, life was comfortable, if rather primitive, in the missionary community.

Ruth benefited from the services of a translator named Juma, a jovial twenty-five-year-old son of a tribal elder who had studied in Boston for a while and had sung the praises of modern civilization he saw there. She was never quite certain, however, what Juma was telling them. From time to time, she got the impression that he was promising them that this missionary group would bring them all the conveniences of life in the 1930's, instead of the word of God.

She learned quickly that she had to recast her thinking and had to present the catechism in simple terms that the children could understand (and, indeed, that Juma could translate). She always hoped that the message of her faith would be impressed upon the children accurately.

"Who made me?" the children repeated after her.

"God made me," they replied.

"And why did God make us?" she asked them.

"To serve Him in this world and be happy with Him in the next," they responded in unison.

Simple rote catechism went only so far, Ruth discovered, as she fielded the daily barrage of questions, well-meaning but at times exasperating.

"Where is He?" inquired one bright-eyed ten-year-old, whose endearing cheekiness reminded her of a few of the boys back in Massachusetts. "Why does He have no other servants, that we must serve Him?"

"Yes," piped up another. "If we cannot see Him, how can we bring Him water and food?"

"He does not need water and food," Ruth smiled. "He desires your love and your loyalty. You serve him by keeping his commandments and having love in your heart."

"Is that not the same message as that of the God of the Forest?"

This part, though it came often enough, always gave Ruth Cheever pause. She was, after all, expecting these people to essentially transform the religious beliefs they had held for generations. She soon realized that, certain as she was of the rightness of her faith, she had to move in cautious steps. She had to find points of comparison between her beliefs and theirs, which meant that she had to have some understanding of their beliefs (which she did only marginally). Adamson had told her that most African tribes believed in multiple gods, often patterned after animals or elements in nature. Her goal was to try to replace, step by step, the tribe's faith in their sun god and water god and animal gods with her vision of the Almighty, and do it in a way that did not diminish their beliefs, but rather showed that hers were more correct and complete. It was a fine line to walk. But she ventured on, convinced of the absolute necessity of bringing every wayward soul to the ways of Christ.

Fortunately, she had a great mentor in Walter Adamson. His ebullience and personal charm endeared him to the missionary volunteers and to many in the Urulu tribe, from the elders on down to the children. Besides being a man of strong faith, he was an impressive manager, able to co-ordinate efforts and get done the tasks that needed doing in the challenging business of running a jungle mission. He had assembled a team of volunteers whose efforts made sizable contributions to the missionary effort. Their party included several college-age missionary students, fresh-faced and eager, including some studying for the ministry.

There were a great many practical needs to be satisfied as well. Adamson had not wanted to rely upon the hospitality of the Urulu alone and preferred that his missionary compound become self-sufficient. Life at the missionary camp became easier with the addition of four men whose services Adamson had secured.

Adamson was rather vague about where he had found these men, but they seemed knowledgeable in the ways of the jungle and proved themselves very handy with the myriad construction and maintenance tasks warranted by life in a jungle camp.

The youngest of them was Bingham, blue-eyed, sandy-haired, not much older than the missionary students. Hayes was short and wiry, with a sallow complexion and full lips, veins prominent in his neck and forehead. The most menacing of the group was Wolfe, tall, hatchet-faced, with black hair rimming dark eyes set behind a prominent hooked nose. His dress was the most disheveled, often a rolled-up flannel work shirt or khaki undershirt and canvas dungarees. The fourth, their leader, a stocky, ruddy-faced outdoorsman, had piercing brown eyes and brown, thinning hair and mustache, and went by the name of Hunter. Maximilian Hunter.

About a day's journey from the Urulu camp, Tarzan of the Apes stretched his legs and leaned back in a wicker chair. "So how is London these days?" asked his longtime friend, Captain William Reynolds, the provost marshal of Point Station. They sat in Reynolds' modest office, which provided a touch of comfort and civilization amid the jungle that encroached at the edge of the compound.

"Large. Noisy. Cold," answered Tarzan. "And it smells. The air is foul. The women wear too much perfume, and the men reek of tobacco. Or, often, whiskey."

"So, you're in no hurry to go back, I take it?" Reynolds rose from behind his scuffed desk, cluttered with documents, logs, and a black Remington typewriter, and poured Tarzan a drink from a native gourd. "But surely you enjoy the comforts and conveniences there, don't you?"

The appearance of the man who sat and chatted with Reynolds about London was even more removed from that city than his location was. His London clothing had been stowed away in a remote part of the compound, and he was clad only in an antelope skin loincloth and a large hunting knife in a hide sheath strapped to his hip. The well-muscled limbs that may have been concealed by the frock coats of Parliament now lay exposed and unencumbered, bronzed from the sun. Even when he took a sip of the fruit juice from his cup, his biceps bulged at that small movement.

"Life is complex there," the ape man went on. "I wish I had fewer peerage affairs to take care of. The power of the House of Lords is becoming more and more negligible. I don't need to be there. My presence makes no difference. If I didn't feel a certain sense of obligation to my father's legacy, I'd just as soon chuck it all. Maybe I will anyway."

Captain Reynolds had removed the smart, brass-trimmed blue coat of his uniform and placed it on the back of his wooden chair, so that his white shirt, together with the ceiling fan, made the heat of the day a little more tolerable. His often-stern eyes softened as he mused, "I miss England. I wouldn't mind going back there when my tour is through."

"Yes," Tarzan replied, "but you were born and raised there, weren't you?

"Point taken, I suppose," Reynolds said, stroking his black mustache. "Still, it *is* civilization, you know."

"I was attacked by two men with knives on my way home from Parliament. It's a jungle there, too."

A uniformed soldier, a young lieutenant, marched in, stood stiffly at attention while saluting, and handed Reynolds a piece of paper, intoning, "Tomorrow's duty roster, sah." He then saluted stiffly again, spun on his heel, and strode out.

Reynolds allowed an amused smile to curl up. "Chapman. New man. Eager beaver."

After a moment of stroking the rim of his handmade cup as it sat on the desktop. Tarzan allowed, "I've been thinking of building a tree house."

"A what?" Reynolds almost spit up a bit of his drink, struck by the notion that his jungle friend might settle down anywhere.

"A shelter. High in a tree. I'd have to find the right tree, something tall and strong for security. Near water and game. Someplace I could keep my things."

"Your things are secure here, my friend. We haven't had a security breach."

"This would be a place I could, well, call home."

"Thinking of settling down in your old age, then, are you, old boy?"

Tarzan stared out at the central compound and the pier beyond it, where a river boat full of passengers had just docked at Point Station's landing. "The jungle is becoming too crowded. I need to get farther away."

He shifted his posture and changed the subject. "So how are things here? It seems quiet."

"I'd love to tell you that it is," Reynolds said, "but it seems that every time I do, things get dodgy rather quickly. Like last year. A few scientists come down here to study flowers, and the next thing I know the place is blowing up. No small thanks to you."

Tarzan let the jape pass. "So do we have any interesting visitors this year?"

"A group of missionaries from America. Massachusetts, I believe. They arrived here about six months ago. It seems they have taken it upon themselves to convert the heathen tribes."

The ape man raised an eyebrow. "All the tribes?"

"Well, they've taken up with the Urulu. Living with the tribe and everything. Led by a minister named Adamson. His assistant, a woman named Cheever, seems to be quite the zealot. She seems to think that she can sweep the old tribal beliefs right out of their heads, and replace them with Christianity. And won't take no for an answer."

"How many tribes are they working with?"

"Just the Urulu so far. Why? You wondering whether they want to take a crack at the Waziri?"

Tarzan smiled. "I wonder what old M'Bala would say if she tried to sweep away the beliefs they've held for a thousand years."

Reynolds chuckled at the thought of their mutual friend, the proud, strong-willed warrior chieftain of the Waziri tribe, being told what to believe by a white woman, however well-intentioned. "I just hope that she doesn't stir up any trouble. I'd rather not have dead missionaries." The captain uncrossed his legs to adjust his posture in his chair and poured a bit more. "And then there's the expedition."

"What expedition is that?"

"Archaeologists digging for fossils in the caves and rocks near the hills of Khataam. Well, at least archaeologists are a quiet sort."

"What do they search for?"

"Rocks, bones…whatever archaeologists look for. I haven't really talked to them yet. Why don't we find out? I've been invited to see their digs. I'm going out tomorrow morning. Want to come?"

Captain Reynolds, Tarzan, and two of Reynolds' men, Chapman and Harris, set out the next morning in a dusty, khaki-colored Crossley 20/25 Tender heading north from the Point Station compound. What they drove along could hardly be called a road. It was a path originally hacked through the jungle by early explorers decades ago, widened only slightly and sporadically over the years, and maintained only by those travelers who took the trouble to move fallen limbs or hack away at encroaching undergrowth. The path snaked around boulders too formidable to remove, and, as tree roots grew bigger, it wound around them too, thus forming a route with mile after mile of rough riding in anything with wheels.

Tarzan, though he preferred a largely solitary life in the jungle, enjoyed the company of Reynolds, one of the few Europeans who ever came to this land whose presence had generally meant less rather than more trouble for him. After miles of this bone-jarring ride, however, he began to question the advisability of having gone along. More than once he wondered whether it would have been better to make the journey himself on foot. It would certainly have been easier on his kidneys.

The journey was at least fifty miles from the Station, which meant that the drive took the better part of the morning. As they approached the Khataam hills, the rich, dark green of the thick jungle gradually gave way to the more dusty browns of scrub grass until they reached a vast, broad plain marked with only an occasional large tree. Reynolds gestured toward the area a few miles ahead at the base of the hills that rose gradually from the plains, pointing their rounded summits to the sky.

"This area has been the site of diggings for several years now," he said. "Artifacts were found in some caves at the foot of the hills a few years ago, and one scientific party or another has always been poking around since."

Tarzan saw an encampment at the base of the hills, near a number of caves. It consisted of several yellowed canvas tents and a few lean-tos sheltering supplies. He saw the expected cooking area with tables and utensils near a fire pit and a central sitting area nearby with a wooden table and several folding camp chairs arranged haphazardly in the sun. But farther on toward the cave was something not typical of jungle campsites—a large canopy erected over several tables cluttered with boxes, trays and storage cabinets, suggesting a work area.

Reynolds brought the vehicle to a bouncy halt about thirty yards from the camp, parked in one of the relatively scarce flat areas not encrusted with rocks, and shut off the engine. The four men got out and walked along the rocky, dusty trail toward the canopy, where they saw two young men, who looked like graduate students, bent over and rapt in their work.

"Hello," Reynolds hailed. "Franklin Granger?"

The two young men looked up, shielding their eyes from the sun high in the sky, and saw that they were being approached by three figures in smart blue uniforms trimmed with buttons and epaulets and holstered sidearms and, rather incongruously, one tall, tanned figure clothed only in a loincloth and armed only with a large hunting knife in a leather sheath. The young men eyed the approaching party for a moment, especially the ape man. "Over there," one of them said, pointing toward the closest cave beyond the canopy.

As they walked past, Tarzan noticed what the two men were attending to. Arranged on top of the work table were several objects that looked like ancient, primitive tools or weapons, including two fragments of sticks with chipped stones at one end, resembling hatchets, and a long, thinner piece of stone tapering at one end, like a knife or cutting tool.

Many yards in the distance, three figures were at work hunched down inside a cave opening. "Doctor Granger?" Reynolds called again. One of the men looked and stood up. He was much older than the others, his face grizzled by a week-old growth of graying beard and his tousled hair streaked with gray.

"Yes?" His pants and boots were sepia with dust, so that their original color could barely be distinguished. He wore a cotton shirt, sleeves rolled up, and a faded leather vest stitched with utility pockets on both sides. His ill-fitting, nondescript cloth hat completed a picture of a man who has been working in the dust for a long time and wouldn't have wanted it any other way.

"Good morning! I'm Captain William Reynolds, the provost marshal for the province. I got your message."

"Ah, yes. I'm so glad you came." He shook Reynolds' extended hand. "This is my colleague, Professor Abrams, and Moore, one of our interns."

Reynolds turned to gesture to his three companions. "This is Lieutenant Chapman and Sergeant Harris. And my old friend Tarzan."

"Well, you're obviously not in the Captain's outfit," Granger said to Tarzan. "And you're not a native…" his voice trailed off in search of the proper characterization.

"I'm not a native, but I do live here," Tarzan said.

"British, with an undercurrent of French?" said Granger.

Tarzan smiled, impressed with the observation, but Reynolds dutifully said, "Well, then, what have we here, Doctor Granger?"

"What we have here, Captain, is what may be the scientific discovery of the decade. Let me show you." He turned and walked toward the entrance to the cave, continuing, "You see, Africa is really the cradle of civilization. People have been living here longer than most anywhere. Millions of years, in fact. And we've suspected for a long time that this area was rich in archaeological deposits. The problem is finding them. They don't exactly leave markers. So we start with places where the remains and artifacts are likely to lie, places where the soil and climate are right for preserving material. Sparsely populated places where encroaching civilization is not likely to have disturbed them. And we dig. And dig. Patiently. For a long time. And if we're very lucky, we find a little something. One party or another has been in this area for over two years."

"And you've found something here?" Reynolds asked.

"Have we!" Granger exclaimed.

He bent down over an area about eight feet square that had been sectioned off with a boundary of two-by-sixes set on their edges in the dirt. The archaeologists had been working away at this spot with forceps, brushes, small picks and other implements that lay scattered around the site. Visible within the boundary was the yellowed relief form of a skeleton, curled up, lying on its side. The visitors could see a skull, a portion of rib cage, a portion of arm, and a section of hip bone and leg emerging from the dusty soil.

"It's a skeleton," Chapman said.

"Not just any skeleton, lieutenant," Granger said, as he picked up a small brush and began to whisk away some of the dirt around the protruding skull. "What we have here is an early ancestor of man. It might even be related to a *Homo erectus*."

"A what?" said Chapman.

"A primitive man. Your early ancestor. By about a million years, I'd say."

"Well, it looks like a skeleton, all right, but how do you know how old it is? It could be a hundred years old."

"Well, we won't know for certain until we have it dated," Granger said, looking from the visitors back to the bones. "But for one thing, we look at the fossilized texture and condition of the bones. For another, the shape and construction of the bones, particularly the skull. You see its size?" He picked up a set of calipers and spread it to the breadth of the exposed cranium, then, holding it steady, moved it up next to Chapman's head. "About three-fourths of yours. That, plus the shape of the brow and the jaw line and teeth, indicates that it is your ancestor from long ago, Lieutenant."

Granger set down the calipers and continued, "Recent discoveries in Africa and elsewhere have begun to give us a much more detailed picture of how life began and developed on this planet. This may be a nearly intact skeleton, and who knows what other implements or artifacts, or for that matter, other skeletons, may be lurking around here under our feet, waiting to be uncovered? This is indeed quite a find, gentlemen, for science and for mankind."

Reynolds said, "I'm glad you showed me this, Doctor Granger. It's fascinating, to be sure. But your message said that you required my assistance? How can I help you?"

Granger stood up to his full height and licked his dusty lip, as if to buy himself a moment to phrase what he would say next. "Captain," he began. "You have a compound maintained in a military manner, under guard, don't you?"

"Well, yes, to the extent necessary."

"I am concerned about the security of these artifacts. I wonder…could you keep them for us? Under guard and lock and key?"

"You think someone might steal them?" Reynolds asked.

"It's possible. They aren't really secure here. Some people in the scientific community are quite competitive, and a find like this can mean a great deal to the institution that brings it back. For that matter, the camp could be attacked by animals in the night. I want to take no chances. Can you hold them? Until I can make arrangements to send them to the university? You would be doing science—indeed, the world—a great service."

"Well, when you put it like that," Reynolds half-smiled self-consciously and looked at Tarzan, "one can hardly refuse."

"Excellent!" Granger replied. "Thank you so much."

"When would you want to transfer them? Right away?"

"Hardly, Captain. It will take us quite a while, perhaps weeks, to unearth the rest of this skeleton."

"Weeks?" Chapman said. "Just to dig that up?"

Professor Abrams looked at him with something of a scoff. "Well, son, we don't dig it out with a shovel. We dig it out with these." He held up a small pick of the type a dentist might use. "It's quite delicate work," Granger added. "We have to separate the bone from the dirt it's bonded with for a million years. We work away at it a little at a time. It took two weeks to remove this much. And as we work away at the layers of accumulated sediment, we never know what else we will find. So we have to work carefully."

"So then," Reynolds began, "when shall we expect to make arrangements?"

"As soon as we're ready, Captain. I'll send a message. Thank you again."

It was settled. The excavated artifacts were to be packed and transported to Point Station.

Weeks passed. The arrangements for the transfer were made. The carefully-crated skeletal remains were secured under lock and key in a remote corner of Point Station, and a regular guard was posted.

Franklin Granger and his team continued to dig, having found pieces of other skeletons as well as traces of what might have been implements or weapons on the site. He began to write his reports and make arrangements for the ultimate transfer of the materials back to New York, a great coup for his university. He and Abrams had even permitted themselves to imagine, in the quiet of the night over a dram of whiskey in their camp, how it would feel to win the International Archaeological Association Award of Merit.

Walter Adamson and Ruth Cheever continued to make inroads with the Urulu tribe, who were gradually but decidedly coming to accept the God of the missionaries with more certainty. Even some of the adults who had early on been skeptical of these white strangers, Adamson noticed, were now speaking openly of God's grace, God's word, God's law, and other phrases, which brought joy and gratification to the hearts of the missionaries. They even made preparations for the first baptisms among the tribe, though they had to assure certain older members of the tribe that, no, the ceremony was not homage to the water god.

Among other signs of the Urulu's growing acceptance of the God of the Old and New Testaments, Adamson began to observe a certain pride in the Urulu's bearing, almost a feeling of superiority. More than once around the tribal campfires, some of them were heard to mutter disparaging remarks about those who had not seen the light. They began to take on a certain disdain toward other tribes who foolishly clung to the old beliefs. The Urulu not only began to feel gratified that they were now possessed of true understanding and insight into the Divine, but began to remark that other tribes like the Waziri were inferior because they were not privy to the truth and preferred to live in the darkness of ignorance and superstition. For his part, Juma, the missionaries' translator, having heard such mutterings and whisperings from time to time, was uncertain of how they would be regarded by Adamson and Ruth, and thus did not often report them or translate them fully, preferring to let them pass lest they offend the good minister and kind lady who had been so beneficent to him.

Tarzan of the Apes went off on his own to the forest to hunt, to fish, to visit his friends the Waziri, and to renew acquaintances with other denizens of the jungle.

And Maximilian Hunter made arrangements for, among other things, an important shipment from Europe and a day trip to the east with his associates.

Chapter 5
THE BAZAAR

The sun shone brightly upon the bazaar at Mansa, an unclouded day, auspicious for attracting crowds to buy and sell and trade goods.

Held monthly on the days of the full moon, the bazaar at Mansa was as much a festival as a marketplace. Tribes came from many miles, often traveling days, to trade their wares, to acquire provisions and possessions, to share jungle lore, and to catch up on news and gossip.

The bazaar grounds, a wide, spacious clearing next to the Bolongo River, were like a patchwork village that had been assembled from the tents and huts of many tradesmen from many tribes, with materials and construction techniques as varied and heterogeneous as the tribes were. The dusty streets of the bazaar were lined on either side with row upon row of sellers, some hawking their wares from rickety tables, others from solidly constructed booths with awnings, tent poles and sturdy racks.

Farming tribes had brought their crops of fruits and vegetables, stacking them high in a dozen shades of red and yellow and green. Hunters displayed impressive hides and pelts from trophy kills. Weavers laid out stacks of intricately woven garments of carefully stitched fabrics dyed in glorious hues. Jewelers presented their rings and necklaces and medallions, glinting in the sun, spread out upon strips of cloth or dangling from small racks. Potters offered their bowls and jugs. Some artisans exhibited carvings or weapons, including long and straight arrows, tall and sturdy spears, and a wide variety of knives and daggers, honed keen and smooth to catch the eye and tempt the touch. The smell of stewed meat and *chapati*, a type of fried dough made from local grains, and other tribal treats wafted throughout.

Hundreds of onlookers meandered through the streets, stopping to browse at the tables, to examine merchandise, to haggle, to greet friends. The merchants gesticulated and cajoled and sometimes shouted to urge browsers to buy. Women hefted gourds and sniffed fruit. Men scrutinized pelts and eyed up arrows. Children whined impatiently at the sluggish pace or grinned to receive a sweet treat.

And above all the clamor of buyers and sellers and the chatter of gossip rose the sounds of jungle music. Off to one end, a trilling thumb piano and breathy pan pipes blended with dulcet flute notes. From another area, thrumming drums and rattling percussion instruments wove in and out and around the general drone of talk. From time to time, singing voices rose in impromptu chants to the accompaniment of the percussion.

Among the hundreds of onlookers, Tarzan of the Apes and Captain Reynolds strolled the grounds, enjoying the sun and eyeing the merchandise. The ape man strode without his customary bow, quiver of arrows, and rope, having left them in Reynolds' vehicle, an acknowledgment of the peaceful atmosphere this bazaar usually presented.

Drawn to the music, the ape man stopped to look at a display of handmade instruments. He picked up a gourd banjo and examined it for a moment. It was made from a yellow-brown gourd which had been sliced lengthwise. The resulting opening had been fitted with animal skin. A fingerboard about two feet long had been fashioned from wood and attached to the gourd, and animal-gut strings had been strung across the top. Tarzan plunked the strings absent-mindedly, smiling at the pleasing sound.

"You like?" said the gray-headed craftsman behind the counter, in broken English. "I trade you for your beautiful knife!"

"The knife was a gift from a friend whose life I saved," said Tarzan, smiling. "The banjo won't help me against the beasts of the jungle."

"It may scare them away," Reynolds japed.

Tarzan set the instrument back down, and the two of them continued on. Not that he would buy anything, however. Having minimal needs, Tarzan bought little on his market trips, but nonetheless took interest in browsing the crafts, the weapons, and the food. The bazaar also provided an opportunity for him to visit with friends from many tribes. Chief among these were the Waziri, his longtime allies.

It was, in fact, not long before he heard the gregarious bellow of M'Bala, chief of the Waziri. "Tarzan!" he yelled, and Tarzan and Reynolds turned to look.

M'Bala strode toward them and waved, his toothy grin like piano keys. He was decked out in a ceremonial dashiki and necklace of elaborate beadwork. He sported polished wrist bands and gleaming rings. He was indeed dressed for the bazaar. He was accompanied by a half dozen Waziri men, tall, muscled ebony warriors holding spears, impressive splays of feathers gracing their heads and loincloths of lion or leopard skin their only other garments.

"M'Bala!" Tarzan greeted the chief. "Are you trading today?"

"Always, my friend, always," M'Bala replied with a laugh. "Come and have a drink with us. I know you relish our beer. We have a fresh batch today, and in this heat it will go fast!"

Tarzan did indeed relish it, and a modest portion was one of the indulgences he allowed himself when M'Bala's hospitality offered it. He and Reynolds followed M'Bala and his men down the street to the Waziri booths where, amid the stacks of weavings and hides and glistening metalwork and weaponry on display, two Waziri women scooped their foamy native beer out of a large ceramic crock. Upon a word and a gesture from M'Bala, they cheerfully ladled some into drinking gourds, passing one to Tarzan, one to Reynolds, and, of course, one to their chief.

Tarzan savored his sip of the hearty, aromatic brew. "How do you like it?" he asked of Reynolds.

"It's not Boddingtons, but it's quite all right," Reynolds allowed with a smile.

Tarzan took the opportunity to catch up on the news with M'Bala, whom he hadn't seen in some time. M'Bala dutifully chastised the ape man for not visiting his village more often. "We need a reason for a feast! Things have been quiet in the jungle."

"Be careful about saying it's quiet. You know what usually happens after that," said Reynolds, only half in jest.

"But the tournament is coming up," noted the ape man. "You must be preparing for that." He referred to the Tournament at Khanja, the upcoming intertribal contest of skill.

"We are indeed! That will be exciting, as it is every year."

"I don't care for excitement all that much," Reynolds groused. "It usually means trouble for me."

"Captain Reynolds!" The group looked up the street to see Ruth Cheever, Walter Adamson, and a few of the other missionary workers in the company of a party of Urulu warriors, a few children, and Mabuto, their chief, all strolling toward the Waziri booth.

"Miss...Cheever, isn't it?" Reynolds responded. "How nice to see you." Reynolds walked out to greet them, Tarzan, M'Bala and two Waziri tribesmen following. They met near the center of the street, gathering around in a cluster.

Reynolds gestured and said, "Tarzan, this is Walter Adamson, who is heading the mission among the Urulu that I told you about. This is his enthusiastic assistant, Ruth Cheever. This is my friend Tarzan." He gestured toward the ape man, who nodded an acknowledgement. "I believe the Waziri and the Urulu know each other?"

Adamson extended his hand and reciprocated, "A pleasure to see you again, Captain. Allow me to present my assistant." He indicated a man who stood behind Ruth and two Urulu men. He was far enough back that he could not readily shake hands, so that a nod sufficed, which suited him.

"Hunter," said the man. "Maximilian Hunter."

Maximilian stared at the ape man. There he stood, in the flesh. He could not believe his fortune. After months of research and planning, after his efforts to track down this man with his dual lifestyle, his efforts to ingratiate himself with the missionary people, to establish a credible and innocuous reason for being here, all now seemed to have paid off.

He tried to relax his facial muscles to keep his countenance pleasant but reserved and his eyes neutral, as if he were meeting Tarzan for the first time. He was quite certain the ape man did not recognize him and gave him only passing notice. It was better, Maximilian thought, to be able to confront him here in his native environment. So much more delicious.

"And what do you do for the mission, Mr. Hunter?" Reynolds asked. "You don't quite look like a man of the cloth."

Indeed, Reynolds and Tarzan observed that Hunter dressed in garb more befitting a hunter or explorer fresh from safari. One almost expected him to be carrying a rifle, though he was not. He wore a rumpled khaki hunting jacket, complete with (empty) cartridge pockets. A thick leather belt gathered the jacket at the waist—again, something one would expect a holster attached to, though there was none. He sported worn and creased trousers, heavy-duty hunting boots, and a khaki field hat, battered and creased as if it had been used a great deal. His skin was cracked and rough and his beard was grizzled, as if he had lived out in the jungle and expected to go back again.

"Whatever needs to be done," he answered flatly, and then, somewhat awkwardly, broke into a bit of a smile.

"We need all sorts of people in our calling, Captain," Adamson chimed in, clapping Maximilian on the shoulder. "Mr. Hunter here is very useful in assisting us with the rigors of jungle life. Everything from construction and repair to, well, hunting. We are lucky to have him."

"So then, how is your missionary work going?" Reynolds asked.

Walter Adamson turned toward one of the two children with them, an impish girl of about ten, with radiant white eyes set against her gleaming black skin. He bent down to look at her and asked, "Well, Nayla, how do you like mission class?"

Nayla piped up, "We like Missy Ruth! She teaches us good things!"

"Apparently she teaches you good English, for one thing," Reynolds allowed. "What have you learned lately?" he added, leaning down toward her and smiling.

"We learned about Noah!" the other child, a boy of about nine, chimed in.

"And what did Noah do, Keon?" asked Adamson, priming the pump.

"It was a time when all the people were being bad, disobeying God," said the boy Keon.

Nayla added, "Yes, and God told Noah that He was going to make it rain, and He commanded Noah to build a huge boat and gather all the animals, two of every kind, to protect them!"

M'Bala let loose his hearty laugh, saying, "How can that be? How can you gather two of every animal? Birds, too? Bugs, too? Have you seen all the animals in this jungle, Sister? How can one man gather them all up?"

The other Waziri tribesman added, "If your God wanted to destroy all the bad people, why did he not just make them die? Why bring all the rain and make it so hard for this man Noah? What did this man Noah do to displease God so much that he had to do all that work?"

The Urulu men next to Walter glared at the Waziri. Ruth sighed and said to Reynolds with a resigned smile, "It's not easy. There will be better days."

Reynolds said, "If you ask me, these tribes need more medicine and health care than prayers."

"Come, come, Captain," Adamson said, with a hint of umbrage. "Nourishment for the soul is at least as important as nourishment for the body. Why don't you come to the village sometime and see how our classes go? I think you'll be impressed."

"Perhaps I will," Reynolds replied, turning away and continuing with Tarzan down the rows.

They strolled further along, away from the Waziri booth and toward the displays of the Urulu and Wahali tribes. Reynolds and Tarzan were in no particular hurry, so that the Adamson party from the mission lagged only a few paces behind them most of the way.

About two dozen paces down from the Waziri area, amid some elaborate weavings and hangings of Wahali craftsmen, Reynolds heard a voice hail him above the thumping of a togo drum.

"Doctor Granger!" Reynolds called and smiled as the senior archaeologist, still dusty in his khaki fatigues and worn boots, waved from several feet away and then walked toward them. Granger was accompanied by Professor Abrams and one of their assistants, who was just finishing a piece of jerky and who had apparently purchased a fine metalwork necklace for someone back home.

"Taking a day off from your labors?" Reynolds said as they approached.

"Not quite," Granger shook his head. "The others are still working. We needed some provisions. And a bit of a break, I confess. They'll get theirs next time."

"I haven't seen you here before."

"This is my first bazaar at Mansa. I confess to having been very focused on the dig."

"Well, what do you think of our little jungle marketplace?"

"I'm quite impressed. I had no idea of the richness and variety of African tribal life so close to our site, relatively. I see a great deal of the dirt in Africa, but little of the people, I'm afraid."

Reynolds saw that Adamson's missionary party and the Urulu were not far behind them. "Speaking of a variety of people," he said, beckoning to them, "you should meet our missionaries. Mr. Adamson, Miss Cheever?"

Reynolds introduced the missionaries and the archaeologists, so that all the white faces in the place were now standing in a rough circle together.

"Where are you from, Dr. Granger? We're Americans," asked Ruth Cheever.

"I'd say by your accent you're from New England," Granger suggested.

"Massachusetts," Ruth said cheerily. "And you, Doctor?"

"Upstate New York. I'm a professor of archaeology at a small university."

"What brings an archeologist all the way to Africa?" Adamson asked.

"Africa is the cradle of mankind." Granger said. "There is more to find here than any other continent, I daresay."

"And have you found anything yet?" Ruth inquired.

"Indeed we have. We have found what may turn out to be one of the most complete sets of bones of early man ever discovered in this area. And there may be more. And other artifacts that go along with them."

"Early man?" Ruth asked.

"An ancestor of ours. He lived a million years ago, possibly even a million and a half," Granger explained.

"These bones cannot be that old," Ruth said.

Granger raised an eyebrow at her declaration. "Oh? What makes you so sure?"

"My Bible. Archbishop Ussher, a very meticulous and thorough scholar, has calculated that, according to the Bible, the Earth is no more than six thousand years old."

"And you accept this calculation above all other evidence?" Granger asked.

"My Bible is the Word of God," Ruth Cheever declared.

"And suppose you encounter some evidence, such as these

bones, which contradicts your Bible?"

"Your evidence is wrong," Ruth declared. "The bones are not that old. You will discover your error."

"Well," Granger scratched his stubbly beard, "If I am wrong, I am open to looking at and considering new evidence, wherever it leads. In fact, some years ago there was a discovery of remains called the Piltdown Man in East Sussex, whose authenticity has been the subject of considerable skepticism."

"Well, there you have it," Ruth declared, a bit smugly. "Mankind's understanding is limited and feeble compared to Almighty God."

"No, you don't quite see, madam," Granger said. "If these bones prove to be not what they seem, we in the scientific community are quite prepared to accept that and carry on. But suppose this evidence is correct. Can you not admit even the possibility that your Bible is wrong?"

Tarzan noticed a bit of a flush in the cheeks of Ruth Cheever. "One does not question the Word of God. My faith is unshakeable," she said with firm lips.

Franklin Granger turned, adjusting his hat, and began to feel as if he were back in the lecture hall addressing students. "There is nothing to be gained by constructing a system of belief based on error and presumption with no credence given to empirical evidence."

Ruth declared, "It is based on faith, something you would do well to investigate, Mr. Granger!"

This exchange might have continued, except for a dispute that sprang up a few yards away at one of the exhibit booths. A young Urulu warrior named Gamba held a necklace in his outstretched fist a few inches from the face of the wrinkled, gray-headed craftsman selling medallions and jewelry.

"You will not trade me for this!?" Gamba cried out, his jaw clenching. "You would trade the Waziri for it. I have seen you do that."

"Your necklace is not that good," the old man sputtered. "It is not a fair trade."

"What do you know?" Gamba shouted. "My people are ancient metalworkers, every bit as good as you." He looked around angrily at the old merchant's displayed wares. He seized a small case of rings and threw it down, declaring, "Better than this! And this necklace is not better than mine!" He knocked over a small wooden stand displaying a necklace.

"Please...don't..." the old man pleaded, trying to right the display and secretively moving aside the three or four decorative daggers he also had on display.

Gamba yanked down a chain hanging from a raised wooden bar and threw it to the ground. "All you want to do is trade with the Waziri. Only their wares are good enough for you. Thief!"

Tarzan strode vigorously over to the Waziri-frequented booth just as Gamba was about to grab the old man by the collar. Tarzan seized the young man's wrist, making Gamba turn to face him. He stared at the tall, black-haired lord for a moment, grimacing, and then quickly grabbed a handcrafted dagger from the counter and stepped back, brandishing it at waist level and glaring at Tarzan.

"Put down the knife," the ape man said, his gray eyes staring coldly.

"Stay out of this," Gamba said, his lip beginning to curl in a snarl.

"Would you stab an old man? Put the knife on the counter and walk away."

Gamba swung the knife once in an arc from his right to his left, then back again, menacingly. Tarzan deftly stepped backward to avoid the swings, moving out into the street, crouched, hands raised and open. Both stared, alternately at each other and the knife blade, and slowly began to circle each other.

Tarzan did not pull out his own knife. He did not wish to draw blood. Instead, he lunged toward Gamba in a feint, and Gamba whirled the knife again. As Gamba completed the arc, Tarzan stepped to the side to avoid the blade, and Gamba clumsily raised his arm to strike while Tarzan was close. Tarzan grabbed the youth's wrist with both hands and forced it down and around to his back, twisting it until the youth had no recourse but to drop the knife. Tarzan thrust him away, thinking it was finished.

Gamba did not resign. He stepped backward several paces to regain his balance, then lunged toward Tarzan. The ape man, lithe as a chimpanzee, rolled himself backward on the ground and thrust his legs out to catch the charging Urulu warrior in the midsection and fling him high overhead and back so that he landed hard and rolled in the dust.

Rising to his feet, Gamba heard laughter from several people in the gathering crowd. He spotted the knife on the ground between him and the ape man. Gritting his teeth, he charged, only to be met by a crushing blow to the jaw from Tarzan. He reeled a moment from the punch, then swung madly at the ape man, who nimbly dodged his attack and then connected again with another roundhouse to Gamba's face, which now began to bleed.

Enraged, Gamba threw himself at Tarzan, encircling one arm around his neck to try to pull him down. Tarzan blocked and resisted, their arms entangled, and they began to wrestle. Tarzan worked his way into position to grasp Gamba with one arm around a shoulder and the other around a leg, raised him bodily off the ground, and hurled him several feet, so that he landed on his back with a thud.

"Now leave him alone," the ape man told him. "Walk away. Unless you want to die today."

Several onlookers chuckled and snickered. Some of them offered comments.

"Give it up."

"You are beat!"

"Had enough?"

Gamba was chagrined to note that some of the hecklers were his fellow Urulu. He then noticed one prominent member of the

He stared at the tall, black-haired lord for a moment, grimacing, and then quickly grabbed a handcrafted dagger from the counter and stepped back, brandishing it at waist level and glaring at Tarzan.

crowd approach him and stand over him. It was M'Bala, with his garish dress, glaring grin and raucous laugh. M'Bala spat out the Waziri word for *young fool*, which Gamba understood full well, and laughed, "You think you can take Tarzan? Ha! Why do you think they call him Lord of the Jungle?"

Gamba rose from the ground, stood as tall and dignified as he could manage, and brushed himself off. He glared at Tarzan, then at M'Bala and the rest of the Waziri in the crowd, and gruffly turned and made his way off toward the Urulu area. Some of the Waziri in the crowd chuckled as he left. Some of the Urulu men began to clench their jaws and stared at the Waziri.

"How foolish," Ruth Cheever commented, watching the scene disperse. "Why would he pick a fight over something like that?"

"These tribesmen are fiercely proud warriors," Captain Reynolds answered. "They will quarrel over the smallest thing. A wrong look, an imagined insult. Wars have started over such matters."

Maximilian, too, watched the defeated hothead retreat and reflected upon what he had witnessed. It was the second time he had seen this ape man take on some foolhardy ruffian. If he were to succeed in his goal, he realized, he would need to make certain that the odds were decidedly in his favor.

Chapter 6
PREPARATIONS

The talk at the missionary supper table that night was filled with the recollections of the day at the market. Although the men in the mission had traded for a number of things, Ruth Cheever in particular was delighted at what she had been able to acquire. She hadn't been on a proper shopping trip in a long time and confessed that perhaps she had indulged too much. When Walter Adamson joked that she could have gotten more, she said that she had run out of things to trade.

The conversation turned briefly to the Gamba incident. Juma the translator said that some of the Urulu were embarrassed by his behavior, yet others believed that the white ape man had pushed him around. Juma said some of the tribesmen were hoping to defeat Tarzan's tribe, the Waziri, in the tournament.

"Tournament?" Walter Adamson asked.

"The annual Inter-Tribal Tournament," Juma said. "In three weeks. There will be contests in archery, spear throwing, combat, everything. Tribes come from all over!"

"Well, there is certainly no end to interesting things going on in this province," Adamson commented.

Juma added that some of the men had approached him to ask Maximilian whether he would help them set up targets for the upcoming tournament.

"All right," Maximilian said. "When do they want to start?"

"Tomorrow!" Juma replied with his typical exuberance. "They

want to be ready!"

"Very well, then, Juma. Tell them I'll see them in the morning."

Juma left to return to the village and retire. Most of the rest of the group left the table in the next few moments, too, since the hour was getting late. Ruth was just finishing up when Maximilian lit up a cigarette and relaxed, resting on his elbows on the table.

"Quite an interesting day at the market, eh?" Ruth said to Maximilian, to make conversation.

"Yes. Educational. A bit more than usual, I'd say," Maximilian said, somewhat cryptically.

"I cannot believe that we have that scientist Granger digging in the same region as our mission," Ruth said. "Those bones are an abomination."

Maximilian turned to her. "Why?"

"They will be dusted off and shown in some museum and people will come to see them and believe the falsehood they represent."

"And why is that such a problem?"

"Mr. Hunter," she said, extending her hand to gesture, "I give of my life to do missionary work to bring the Gospel to these heathens, and the devil's work of evolution slips right in under our fingers. And now our flock is confused, and it will be just that much harder to bring the word of God to them."

Maximilian crushed out his cigarette. "Is it such a threat, Miss Cheever?"

"It undermines our missionary work, and the work of saints like Walter Adamson, the world over," she declared, firmly. "Something should be done about them."

"How do you mean?"

"I don't know. I just wish the bones would disappear. It would make things a lot easier."

Maximilian nodded his head, scratched his unshaven chin with his coarse hand, and pondered her words.

*   *   *

Eagerness to begin training for the Inter-Tribal Tournament was by no means confined to the Urulu. The Waziri, like many other tribes, prepared extensively. Their training area at the outskirts of their village was particularly busy the following week when M'Bala invited Tarzan to visit, observing the progress. In one section, spear-throwers practiced for distance and accuracy, their sinewy arms heaving the solid shafts at distant tree trunks, muttering and enduring their colleagues' laughter whenever the spears fell out instead of lodging solidly into the wood.

In an adjacent area, archers lined up and fired at trees or grass targets, spaced at varying distances from them. The air sizzled with the *whoosh* and *thunk* of arrows flying and hitting targets.

"Tarzan!" called out a voice whom the ape man recognized as Baka, a young man of the village. "May I see your bow?"

Tarzan smiled and unshouldered his great bow to pass it to Baka, who ran his finger along the smooth carved recurve. "It is handsome!" he said.

"Your uncle wove the bowstring," Tarzan said. "And he made arrows for me, too. His handiwork has saved my life and the lives of others more than once."

"Yes," said Baka. "I miss him."

"So do I," said Tarzan.

"Can you show me?" the youth beamed.

"You seek help from the best!" M'Bala said.

Obliging, Tarzan took up a position at the archery practice line and reached back with his right hand to pull an arrow out from his leather quiver. Nocking his arrow, he looked down at the target in the distance, a crudely-made grass figure resembling a man.

As he drew back on the bowstring and raised his arms to sight down the target, his bronzed right bicep bulging from the pull, he said, "Grasp the arrow firmly, draw back smoothly and solidly. Sight the target carefully. Do not be in a hurry. Speed comes with practice, but only if you practice properly." He let fly the shaft, which whizzed off and slammed into the target in the distance, hitting it in the center piercing the heart.

"Aww!" Baka exclaimed. "You killed him!"

"I hit a target," Tarzan smiled. "Now you try."

Baka stepped into position and nocked his arrow. He raised the bow and drew back the string, trembling a bit, as he sighted the target. "Steady," Tarzan said. "Wait for it."

Baka released. The arrow sailed out and lodged in the dummy's shoulder about a foot from Tarzan's arrow.

"I didn't kill him," Baka lamented.

"You hit him. You stopped him. You may have saved your life, or the life of your friend," Tarzan said. "Keep practicing." Baka smiled at the ape man's encouragement and began to fix another arrow in place.

Tarzan retrieved his arrow, and he and M'Bala strolled on to the next area, where warriors practiced hand-to-hand combat. A circular area with a roughly fifteen-foot diameter had been set up for practice. Warriors had been paired off, usually an older with a younger, for lessons in hand-to-hand combat with a wooden knife or blunt spear. As each pair dueled, the knot of Waziri warriors on the sidelines cheered or jeered them on.

Currently, an older warrior was battling a youth Tarzan recognized as Dajan, a strapping young warrior who was training for his first tournament. Tarzan watched the two in the ring swirling and lunging at each other with wooden daggers. Dajan's opponent feinted, Dajan jerked back clumsily, and his opponent followed through with a hit, though injuring only the young man's pride.

They halted, and Dajan turned to Tarzan to ask, "Tarzan! What am I doing wrong?"

"You are watching his feet," Tarzan replied. "Or his blade."

"What should I be watching?"

"His eyes. They will tell you what he is thinking and what he will do, a split second before he does it. That split second is your advantage."

One of the tribesmen in the crowd said, "Show him!"

"You are popular today, my friend," teased M'Bala.

"Have you no other trainers?" Tarzan returned the ribbing.

Tarzan obliged by setting aside his weapons and stepping into the ring as Dajan stepped aside to watch. Tarzan whispered an instruction into the ear of the opponent, and they separated to take combat stances. Slightly crouched, they circled, each to his left, brandishing their wooden daggers menacingly.

The opponent swung a backhand toward Tarzan's midsection. Tarzan instantly leaped back with the agility of a cat to dodge the swing. In the next instant, the opponent followed with a forehand swipe. Tarzan grabbed the man's knife arm in midair, spun around and, using the opponent's momentum, flung him forward over his shoulder and down onto the ground. Tarzan quickly stepped on the wrist holding the knife, causing him to release it. He helped the man up, and they shook hands.

"I cannot do that!" Dajan exclaimed.

"You have three weeks. Practice!" the ape man said with a hearty laugh.

As Tarzan donned his quiver again and the tribesmen returned to their drills, Dajan asked, "Have you killed many men?"

Tarzan said, "I kill only for food, or defense, or when there is no other way to thwart an enemy."

"What is it like to kill a man?"

Tarzan smiled at him. "Why do you ask such questions?"

"I want to be a warrior! I have killed a lion, but I do not think it is the same thing as killing a man."

"Be glad that it is not. Sometimes it takes courage and strength to kill. Sometimes it takes more not to kill."

Chapter 7
SHIPMENT

In the week before the tournament, excitement was not quite in the air everywhere. Captain Reynolds was enjoying a quiet afternoon at Point Station—his favorite kind. He had spent some time hunkering over records and documents and was nearly finished with his paperwork for the week. He ran his fingers through his thinning black hair and looked at the last of the batch. He thought he might even be able to relax with a bit of brandy if things continued to go this quietly.

The Point Station compound was relatively small, a cluster of buildings in a large clearing pushing out the edge of the forest all around, but it was often busy because of its docks on the Bolongo River. The daily traffic could include anything from dilapidated fishing trawlers to great riverboats dropping off or picking up cargo and passengers of all sorts.

Reynolds had paused to look out the door at the lone riverboat currently at the docks, unloading the last of its cargo, when in walked Lieutenant Chapman to hand him the manifest from the boat. Reynolds thanked him, and as Chapman turned to leave, he paused.

"Something else, Lieutenant?"

Chapman looked straight ahead, then down at Reynolds' desk, and began, "Well, sah, I was wondering if…well…if I could be one of the men assigned to go to the tournament. You will be sending a detachment, won't you?"

"You want to see the tournament, do you?"

"Yes, sah. The men say it's quite the thing. But it seems I've got guard duty the first night. Simms said he would take it for me, and I could do the second."

Reynolds smiled. "I'll see what I can do."

"Thank you, sah!" Chapman grinned, turned smartly, and left.

As Reynolds watched Chapman disappear through the office doorway, he could see beyond across the compound to the riverfront and recognized four men at the cargo dock, one in jungle fatigues and three others more scruffily dressed.

As Reynolds continued to watch, Maximilian and his men unloaded cargo from the boat. Most of the cargo was recognizable as basic necessities—canned goods, sacks of flour and beans—the kinds of cargo he had seen unloaded at the pier hundreds of times. But hold on…what was that? He spotted Maximilian's two assistants hefting down a nondescript but unusual wooden crate of a certain proportion.

Reynolds' instinct was to stop them then and there. To order the crate be opened. But he had no actual authority to inspect private cargo. On the other hand, the law was vague and out here, and subject to little overview. He was often compelled to exercise his individual judgment.

He wanted to know what was in that crate.

He got up from his desk and walked into the doorway of his office, shouting, "I say, Hunter!"

Maximilian turned from the task of loading a crate onto their boat and looked up as Reynolds strode toward the dock. At that same moment, Hayes, the short, wiry one, said to Maximilian, "I need to use the privy." Maximilian nodded for him to go, and he took off for the side of the administrative building.

By that time, Reynolds had arrived at their loading site and said, "What have you got there?"

"What do you mean?"

"In the crates. What is your cargo?"

Maximilian stood tall as he bristled a bit, his mustached lip firm. "Supplies," he said flatly.

Reynolds looked down at the crates, noting more closely their size and proportion, and said, "It doesn't look like food or medicine."

"Does it matter? Am I breaking some law?"

"That depends on what's inside. Let's have a look. Open that one."

"Look here, Captain, I don't think you have the authority...."

"My dear Mr. Hunter, I can have the entire shipment impounded if I choose," Reynolds lied, and added with a wry smile, "Have you got something to hide?"

Maximilian moved to reply, then thought better of it and replied calmly, "No. Bingham, open this crate. Show the captain."

The sandy-haired Bingham produced a small pry bar and pried open the wooden lid and lifted it off to reveal the contents—neatly folded trousers, khaki vests, work gloves, and leather boots. All quite suitable for jungle life. Reynolds leaned over and briefly rummaged through the clothing, probing beneath the first layer. He then stood up and took a breath, his jaw clenched a bit.

Maximilian allowed the trace of a smile at the Captain's apparent hint of indignation. "Adamson needs clothing for his people. Satisfied?"

"Not quite," Reynolds said, looking at the next one, which was narrower and longer. "Open that one as well."

Maximilian pursed his lips and nodded to Bingham to open the indicated crate, which he did. As Bingham pried off the lid, making the last nail squeal, Reynolds saw bush jackets, shirts, socks, and mosquito netting all tightly and carefully tucked in place. Resting atop the well-packed clothing were three brand-new Bibles bound in black leather with shiny gold crosses embossed on the front covers.

Maximilian allowed Reynolds to stare at the cargo a brief moment before asking, "May we go now, Captain?"

"Yes, of course," Reynolds muttered and turned to leave.

Hayes returned from using the privy, and the four of them boarded their boat and shoved off. When they got several yards downstream from the dock and saw that Reynolds had walked away in the direction of his office, Bingham said, "That was close."

"Not to worry," Maximilian said. "I had a cover story ready." He then turned to Hayes and said, "Well?"

"Yes, it looks like something important's being held there. They have a storage building or shed at the back of the camp. Guards are patrolling it back and forth. Three, with sidearms."

"That's definitely it. Good work," Maximilian said smugly.

"Now—what about the crates? Did we get the merchandise?" Hayes asked.

"Let's see." Maximilian pulled off the lid from the first crate that Reynolds had examined, set it aside, and began to rummage through the clothing within, removing several pieces. When he reached what appeared to be the bottom of the crate, he gestured for Bingham to hand him the pry bar, and it was but a moment's work until he had pried loose the false bottom of the wooden crate to reveal the rest of the shipment lying underneath—brand new Lee-Enfield rifles, their barrels gleaming gunmetal blue in the noonday sun. In the bottom of the second crate, they confirmed that the unassembled sections of a Thompson submachine gun had arrived intact.

"Looks like they made it just fine," Maximilian said.

"The Bibles were a nice touch," commented Bingham.

"If he had opened the third crate, with the ammunition, he would have found boxes of English tea and biscuits." They had a good chuckle.

Maximilian felt gratified that Reynolds had been so inquisitive about the crates, because it had allowed him to embarrass the imperious meddler. It was a source of no small amusement to him that his plan continued to turn out better than he had hoped because of moments like this that proved so fortuitous.

They came to shore and unloaded their cargo from the boat onto their waiting vehicle and climbed in. The moment had now come for Maximilian to show something to his cohorts which he had heretofore never mentioned. They were not expected back at the mission until much later, and they were already closer to this destination than to the village, so he took the opportunity to drive them further to the east and then to the south along a well-worn road leading from the river.

They drove for more than an hour, passing through heavy jungle into areas of sparser bush growth, approaching the plains and mountains of the east. At length they came to the edge of a forest of jakaba trees, one section of which had been partially burned out, new growth just emerging from between the charred stumps. In the distance just beyond the forest lay the remains of a cultivated field, largely overgrown with weeds, where a few scattered yellow flowers bloomed. Between the grove of trees and the field lay the burned-out ruins of a complex of buildings.

Maximilian drove the vehicle up the dirt road into the central compound, parked, and stepped out for a moment to survey the ruins in more detail. On their right they saw the blackened and charred foundations of several buildings, including a generator shed and dormitory. On their left lay the half-burned remains of what appeared to be offices and laboratories. What was not charred was grown over, particularly the mesh fencing that had once encircled the compound, which weeds had now begun to choke. Tracks revealed that the only visitors for some time had been animals, who apparently found nothing enticing.

After looking around for a moment, less interested than Maximilian was, Wolfe, Hayes, and Bingham wondered what this place had been and why he had brought them here. He sat back down in the vehicle and proceeded to tell them. He told them who had been here. He told them a story of the company that had set up a research and development station here, of a battle that had been fought, of explosions and fire and a merciless attack. He told them who was behind that attack, and what he now intended to do about that. He told them why he had come here to Africa and why he had hired them, and why he had made efforts to gain the confidence of the tribe and missionaries.

"So that's what it's all about," said Hayes.

"Do you see my purpose now?" asked Maximilian. "Are you with me?"

They all nodded.

They drove back to the Urulu village, where they all by mutual agreement spoke not a word about what they had seen today or what lay in the bottom of the shipping crates.

Chapter 8
TOURNAMENT

The Inter-Tribal Tournament at Khanja, an annual celebration of skill, was the most festive, most widely-anticipated event in the year. It was held in a specially constructed area like the bazaar grounds, but much larger. Thousands attended from a dozen tribes, living in camps arranged in a huge arc around the central tournament grounds. Colorful banners and feather sprays flew over the encampments, and tribal shields and insignia identified each tribe. Music from drums, pipes and voices arose and mingled from camp to camp.

"So how intense is this competition?" Ruth Cheever asked Captain Reynolds, whom she had run into on the grounds. "The Urulu seem to be quite worked up over it."

"Well, the rivalry is usually good-natured, but the tribes are very competitive," Reynolds told her. "They are proud of their combat skills and marksmanship. This event allows them to show off to everybody. It probably defuses a certain amount of intertribal hostility."

"So this prevents the tribes from making war on each other?"

"Not entirely. They have warred with each other off and on over the years. But we haven't had a war for quite some time."

"And how many events are there?"

"About eight, spanning at least two days, or until winners emerge. Let's see, there's running and archery and spear throwing and feats of strength, like log hurling. And hand-to-hand, of course.

There's an overall tribe winner, and winners in the individual events. And the tribes have a big celebration afterwards, especially if they win anything."

"Gamba says the Waziri have won three years in a row. But he says the judges favor them."

"See what I mean about hostility?" Reynolds commented. Glancing at his pocket watch, he added, "I see it's almost time for the first event. Archery, I believe."

"Well, thank you for the explanation and the tour, Captain. I must go to the Urulu area now and lead the prayer circle."

"The what?"

"We'll be having a group prayer before the contest. Would you like to join us?"

"Uh, thank you, no," Reynolds stammered. "I need to, uh, see that my men are posted."

They parted. Reynolds watched Ruth Cheever walk over to the Urulu camp and join Walter Adamson and the other missionaries who had gathered with the tribal athletes and their supporters.

Reynolds could hear Ruth's raised voice ask for divine guidance in this contest, for the men to be strong of hand and sure of foot, and other such sentiments. When the tribesmen chanted their responses, Reynolds couldn't help but notice that many of them prayed rather loudly, clearly audible in the neighboring camps, such as the Waziri. He wondered whether at least some of the Urulu competitors made a show of this prayer because they wanted the other tribes to think they had something special going for them.

Reynolds dismissed the thought and resumed his duties. The circle began to sing a Christian hymn which he did not recognize, and their voices faded away as he moved on. He sought out his friend Tarzan, whom he guessed would be in the Waziri camp.

The competition the first day moved through archery, foot racing, and spear throwing. At the end of the day, many tribes were nearly evenly matched. The Urulu were behind, though they had made a strong showing in archery.

As the second day progressed, several tribes felt they had a competitive edge. The Waziri had superiority in the spear-throwing, but the results in the next level of races, hurdles and archery were mixed.

The hand-to-hand combat contest, saved for last, would establish the real winners. It was the only event where members of the tribes actually faced each other, and thus was the closest the tournament came to simulating actual combat.

It was held in a marked-off circle about twenty feet in diameter. The rules for the hand-to-hand combat were quite specific. Two combatants at a time faced each other. Each combatant had a wooden dagger which had been fashioned with a flat blade which could not cut, but was solid, so that it made a noise when it was slapped against the skin.

The judge, a respected tribal elder named Amaad, held a ceremonial rattle made of a small gourd decorated with feathers and strips of cloth, mounted on a bone handle. When a hit was scored, he gave the rattle a sharp flick of the wrist, so that the dried seeds inside clacked almost like a snare drum. A tally was kept of how many slaps each combatant was awarded. Each bout was timed with a device similar to an hourglass, but using gourds and running water. The winner was the one who scored the most hits before time was called. Points were awarded for disarming the opponent, and the match was lost if a combatant stabbed his opponent or struck him with anything other than the wooden blade.

Enthusiasm mounted, and the large crowd grew more fervent and more vocal as one after another of the hand-to-hand events finished. The Urulu had pinned their hopes for this contest on the proud Gamba, whose vigor and fierceness were well known. He had outscored his first three opponents and in the final round was paired with the Waziri Dajan.

Gamba was tall and strapping, eighteen years old, with a stern brow and a visage that scowled more often than smiled. He strutted into the circle, swelling with the confidence that his tribe placed in him. He usually sported gaudy jewelry, though for the contest he removed all but a beaded necklace, so that he was naked except for an ostentatious leopard-hide loincloth. He looked around at his fellow tribesmen and the others in the crowd with a ghost of a smirk. And then he glared at Dajan.

Dajan was nearly two years younger and three inches shorter, leaner and wiry. A more ordinary antelope hide girded his waist. He had expected neither to get this far in the contest, nor to be paired with the fearsome Gamba. As he felt a bit of apprehension looking at his opponent's bulging, well-formed leg, chest, and arm muscles, he recalled Tarzan's words: "It is not about muscles. It is about brains and swiftness."

Gamba and Dajan stood about twenty paces apart and squared off, crouching and facing each other. At the starting signal, they began their match with a series of feints and parries, testing each other, striking only the air.

The brawny Urulu moved in and made a more ferocious pass with his dagger, this time nearly hitting Dajan, who veered away just in time. The audience shouted encouragement.

Dajan watched his opponent's icy eyes carefully, as Tarzan had taught him. He saw that Gamba looked where he would strike just before he attacked. That was the edge he needed. He watched Gamba's eyes dart to his forearm, so that he was able to swiftly block the swing and strike a slap to his arm, scoring a point.

The audience roared. The Waziri cheered Dajan on.

The two circled around each other, watching and feinting, for several moments more. The wiry youth looked Gamba in the eye and simultaneously swung, slapping his upper arm so that he scored another point. Cheers.

The proud Urulu clenched his jaw, visibly irritated at his Waziri opponent. Dajan sensed his resentment and tried to use it. With several feints in a row, he taunted his aggravated foe. Gamba tried to swing back or block, but he only swung at air. Then he clumsily tried to block a swing, but Dajan nimbly avoided the block and slapped his dagger hard against Gamba's chest and then sprung back away. Another hit.

"Come on, you can do it!" Ruth Cheever cheered Gamba on, much as if she were at a basketball game back home.

Some Waziri in the crowd, mostly to goad Gamba, derided her shouting:

"You have been listening to the white woman!"

"You need a stronger faith!"

"Pray to our gods and you might win something!"

At this, several Urulu were heard to mutter, "They insulted our beliefs! They insulted the teacher of our children!"

"This is not good," Tarzan said to Reynolds. "Gamba has a temper and does not like to be mocked."

Dajan continued to feint and dance, avoiding blows. Time was running out. Beads of sweat formed on Gamba's broad brow, and his jaw clenched. He needed to score some hits. The Waziri crowd continued to jeer and taunt him, more loudly. Others in the audience added their insults and shouts, their enthusiasm for a blood fight easily aroused.

Gamba became more distracted by the crowd, his dark eyes darting nervously.

Dajan, who kept more focused, hit again. "You will lose!" he taunted. "Go back to fighting old men in the market!"

Louder catcalls came from the crowd. Gamba gritted his teeth, visibly incensed. He whirled around to glower at the crowd. Even some children were laughing. Then suddenly, with a loud cry, he threw down his wooden dagger and charged Dajan, going for his throat. They tumbled to the ground and wrestled.

The crowd erupted. Several Urulu men tried to pull them apart, and then several Waziri men leaped into the fray and tried to yank the Urulu men away and protect Dajan. A melee ensued, with shouts and curses, punching and kicking.

A tangle of a dozen bodies rolled around on the ground, stirring up dust. At one point, Gamba managed to free himself. He spotted a knife in a sheath on the waist of the man next to him, and he seized the handle and pulled it out. At that same instant, he saw Dajan roll out from underneath another man, and he lunged, slashing Dajan in the left side. The Waziri youth cried out, grasping the wound, and struggled to stand.

Gamba sprang to his feet and raised the knife to strike again, but Tarzan leaped in from the sidelines and grabbed Gamba's wrist and forced the knife from it. The incensed Urulu turned to swing at him with his left, but Tarzan was quicker, slamming him full in the face with his fist, knocking him back. Several men from the sideline grabbed Gamba and restrained him as he tried to lunge forward toward Tarzan, spitting oaths at the ape man.

The melee broke apart. The wounded Dajan was carried over to a cot along the sidelines, where a crowd of onlookers gathered. The youth gnashed his teeth and winced, crying out when the pain of any movement stung him. He gripped his side, which continued to bleed profusely. Walter Adamson kneeled down next to him, but was gently nudged out of the way by Mabuto, the Urulu chief. Mabuto called for his tribal healer, but Uba, the tribal healer of the Waziri, shouldered his way in, saying, "Here. Let me look at him." Some of the Urulu muttered, but made way.

Ruth Cheever immediately moved in and said, "Let me pray over him," which Juma translated to them for her.

Uba said, "You do not need to be next to him to pray, but I need to be next to him to heal." His assistant handed him a bowl containing some type of liquid which he had heated. From a pouch in his shoulder bag, Uba produced a handful of what looked to be herb leaves and dried roots. He mixed and crumbled them with his fingers, then blended them into a poultice with some of the sappy liquid and other ingredients provided by his assistant, and began applying them to Dajan's injuries.

"What are you going to do, spread herbs over him?" Ruth said. "Let the power of God heal him!"

Uba looked directly at her. "I do not know what your prayers will do, but this mixture will draw out infection and ease his pain."

Juma translated this, then added, "Missy, he does not know about the power of your prayer."

M'Bala, looking on, said, "Let him do his work. He is using methods that have been used for centuries."

Captain Reynolds said to Ruth, "Some of his remedies do help with pain and infections, though I must say what this place needs is a good hospital."

Ruth watched the skilled hands of Uba the healer clean and dress the wound. She noticed that Dajan grew calmer, wincing less in pain, though she nevertheless continued her prayers for his recovery, urging Adamson and the Urulu to do the same. She did not accept that the Waziri healer had more power than her prayers. It occurred to her that perhaps this poultice was simply the way God had chosen to channel His healing graces.

Gamba's flagrant violation of the rules lost him the match and forfeited all his previous matches that day. The Waziri were declared the winners of the Inter-Tribal Tournament, amid great cheering, back slapping, and M'Bala's beaming smile and hearty laugh.

"We will feast tonight!" M'Bala exclaimed, to no one's great surprise. He invited Tarzan and Reynolds to join his victory celebration in the Waziri village. He almost invited the Urulu, but this was simply not done. Besides, most of the Urulu slipped away from the grounds rather quietly, since, with the penalty for Gamba's outburst, they had lost badly.

That night, Tarzan and Reynolds sat around the huge bonfire in the center of the Waziri village, feasting on their roast meats and fruits and spicy sauces while being uplifted by the interweaving rhythms of their throbbing drums and the soaring harmonies of their voices.

By contrast, the dejection in the Urulu village was such that the feast that had been planned to celebrate their victory was called

off, and the various families sat down to their evening meals on
their own in their huts. The village was sadly quiet. In the adjacent
missionary camp, supper was rather subdued as well.

Finishing her greens, Ruth Cheever said, "I didn't pray that
they would win, you know. I prayed that they would do their best,
serve God's will, compete honorably. But now I'm told that many
in the tribe had prayed for an Urulu victory. Little Keon wanted to
know how it could be that God would deny their prayers."

Ruth looked at Walter Adamson, who returned her gaze and
smiled. "Time for a talk about God's larger plan, Ruth."

"Yes, but they are so disappointed, Walter," she answered ruefully.
"Nayla wanted to know whether we had not prayed hard enough."

Adamson said, "It's not just the children. Juma reported a conversation he had heard in the village where their fathers started
echoing such feelings. Then the next thing they said was that we
did not teach them how to pray properly. Some said that the Waziri
are stronger because their gods are stronger, and he heard voices
mutter in agreement."

Ruth put down her fork and stared wide-eyed for a moment.
"Are you suggesting that our missionary work here is becoming un-
done because of one tournament? Is that all that God means to
them, a victory in a contest?"

Adamson said, "I'm suggesting, I think, that these people are
complex and motivated by many feelings, including pride. Our next
challenge is to get them to see that God's word is about more than
just earthly victories. The Waziri may have been physically superior
in some ways today, but that does not mean their religion is superior. In truth, I don't think the Lord takes side in contests." He
tossed his bones into the nearby campfire and began to stack the
tin dinner plates on the table, adding, "We need to begin thinking
of ways to convey the message about how God's grace truly works."

He looked at the two young missionary interns across from
him. "This could be what you two should do. Let that be your next
challenge. See if you can come up with some suggestions for a

sermon or lesson on that subject." Adamson finished his beverage, wiped his mouth, and rose to leave. He retired early, as did Ruth.

Having heard this conversation, Maximilian walked over to the main tribal fire in the center of the village, around which several tribesmen had gathered after supper. He was bidden to sit, and he began to speak to the Urulu men in their own language, at which he had become increasingly skillful (another bit of information about him that Ruth and Adamson did not know). He did not trust the obsequious Juma to witness this.

He listened for some time to their comments about the tournament. They minimized the impropriety of Gamba's outburst and had a lot to say about the officiating and about the Waziri's taunting. Maximilian began to carefully steer the discussion around to their attitudes about the Waziri. He asked the men how they felt about the Waziri winning the contest again. He asked them whether they liked the grinning M'Bala and the way he laughs at them. He asked them why the white men Tarzan and Reynolds were always in the Waziri company. Were they just friends? And if a dispute arose between the tribes, which side would the authority of Captain Reynolds take?

Again and again, Maximilian let the strands of their conversation weave their way around to the Waziri's superiority, which before long began to be perceived as arrogance. As the dialogue progressed, Maximilian realized that he did not even have to suggest what the Urulu men began to say for themselves—that the Waziri needed to be brought down, taught a lesson.

The Urulu men groused about the contest and the Waziri for some time, until well after Maximilian made his excuses and left to retire.

He let no one see that he did not head for his tent, but instead went to the outskirts of the village, where he rendezvoused with Hayes, Bingham and Wolfe at a pre-arranged place and time. For his night was far from over.

Chapter 9
RAID

The pre-dawn African moonlight bathed the jungle with an eerie sheen. Its pale luminescence splayed out over the open areas of the Point Station compound and cast long, irregular shadows over the rest. The river bank was particularly shrouded in blackness, concealing even the movements of a small craft landing almost noiselessly up onto the bank.

Lieutenant Chapman stood in the middle of the Point Station compound and gazed up at the moonlit sky. It was a warm, clear night. Dawn would arrive soon, and he could look forward to his bunk at the end of his shift, but for the moment, he felt gratified.

Since his recent arrival, Chapman had rarely had time to actually appreciate the beauty of the post he had been assigned to, particularly at night. He noticed how surprisingly quiet it was—just the humming sounds of insects and occasionally, far off, the cry of an animal. He resumed his pace back and forth, in a stiffly formal stride. He performed his sentry duty properly and fully even though no one would see him but Harris and Wills, who were standing guard at the building in the rear some twenty yards away. Captain Reynolds had left him not only with command of the camp but in charge of security for its precious newly-arrived cache. Not everyone on the base knew all the contents of the modest, nondescript storage shed now under lock and key, but Chapman felt gratified that Captain Reynolds had entrusted him with its secrets.

183

As he paced, he surveyed the quiet compound left and right. A few leaves rustled in the breeze. The river lapped against the shore. Then he heard…something in the shadows? He turned to look.

What he saw no one would ever know, because at that instant an arrow whizzed through the night air and pierced his back with a nearly silent *thunk*. He curled up and fell to the earth.

Four crouched figures cautiously crept forward from the darkness around the perimeter, four figures bearing native bows and spears, but dressed in European jungle wear. They made their way from the river bank toward the administrative building, carefully steering around the more brightly lit areas and clinging to the shadows. They moved to the corner of the main office building, then carefully crept around to the back, keeping concealed in the dark.

One of them came forward to lean down and verify that Chapman was dead. He looked up and nodded to the others, then moved to rejoin them in the shadows. At that instant, Sergeant Harris, hearing some movement, came around from the rear of the building to see Chapman lying in the moonlight. Harris reached for his sidearm, but before he could pull it out, an arrow struck him—*thwack*—in the side. He turned to look at the intruders, but one of them unleashed a second arrow, which pierced his chest. He was dead before he could utter more than a brief gasp.

The four intruders advanced from the shadow of the office building around to the rear of the complex, toward the storage areas. As they rounded the corner Harris had come from, they encountered Private Wills. Having heard the disturbance, Wills had headed their way from his position. He drew his pistol and began to level it when one of the intruders lunged forward with a huge spear and struck Wills powerfully in the stomach, full on. Another intruder rushed to seize Wills' revolver from his hand before the soldier's muscle contractions fired it. He grabbed the revolver and struck Wills on the head to prevent him from crying out in his death throes. Wills fell silently, his hand briefly gripping the spear lodged in his body before becoming still.

"That was close," one of the intruders said. The others bade him to silence. They looked around to make certain that there were no more guards, then moved to the dingy storage building. They made short work of breaking the locks, gaining entrance, and retrieving what they had come for. They worked efficiently and silently, lest they wake any of the other men in the barracks. With two of them bearing their cargo and the other two carefully looking out, they made their way back through the compound and to the river, avoiding the African moon whose pale light was just beginning to wane in the first slivers of dawn.

As the early morning mist began to give way to midmorning brightness, Captain Reynolds, sated from the Waziri hospitality of the night before and groggy from too much of their beer, sat rather still in the canoe and let Tarzan paddle it from the Waziri village to Point Station. The Waziri feast had been bountiful, and their victory celebration had gone far longer into the night than he, as a man whose duty called the next day, should have indulged in.

Their canoe had just begun to glide inward toward the docking area at Point Station when they saw one of Reynolds' men running toward the wooden pier and, by waving, urging them to hurry. When they were within shouting distance, he cried, "Captain! Captain! Come quick!"

Tarzan steered the canoe smoothly up next to the pier while Reynolds looked up and said, "What is it, Simms?"

"It's terrible, sah! You've got to come look! Hurry!"

Quickly tying up the canoe, Tarzan and Reynolds followed Simms down the pier and onto the shore, where he broke into a run. They all raced across the yard past the administrative buildings and around the corner of the barracks to the far end. They came across the body of Chapman lying in the yard where it had been left. Reynolds stopped, taken aback, and looked at the body of his loyal lieutenant. Reynolds kneeled down and, grasping the stiffened face, turned it slightly into the light. "It's Chapman," he said. "He's dead." A bloody arrow point protruded through his chest.

"They came in the night, sah. Before dawn. We didn't even hear them," Simms said plaintively, his lip trembling.

At Simms' beckoning, they hurried the rest of the way around toward the little-used, nondescript utility and storage building, where two more of Reynolds' men were standing, awaiting them. They found the bodies of the two other guards.

Reynolds hesitated a moment, loath to face what he was dealing with. He saw Tarzan lean down and examine the second body. It was Harris. Blood had pooled in the dirt from the arrows in his side and breast. Tarzan looked up at Reynolds and shook his head slowly. Reynolds clenched his jaw. He looked over a few yards to see the body of Wills and then made eye contact with Simms, whose shake of the head indicated that Wills, too, did not survive.

The ape man studied the scene before him. Still crouched, he noticed an object on the ground near Harris's body, and he knelt and reached to pick it up. It was a cluster of feathers joined with an ornamented ring. He then returned to Harris's body. He firmly grasped the shaft of the arrow near the point where it protruded from the chest and forcefully yanked it out. He held up and examined the shaft, red with gore.

"There's more, sah," Simms said. He gestured to the storage building. The door was open.

Tarzan continued examining the bodies for a moment while Reynolds, at Simms' urging, proceeded inside. He found that several locker and cabinet doors had been broken. Crates had been forced open and the various supplies stored in them had been pored through.

"Your locker has been broken into," Reynolds said when Tarzan entered the room a moment later.

The ape man looked over the items strewn around the room. He saw his valise open, his London clothing askew on the floor, and the few personal possessions he kept here for his travels scattered about. "They certainly did rummage through them, though they do not appear to have taken anything," he said. "Just threw them around."

"What the bloody hell is this about!?" Reynolds cried, swerving about to look at one section of the room and then another. His teeth clenched and his face began to redden. "Who could have done this?"

Tarzan held up the cluster of feathers he had found and bloody arrow he had withdrawn from Harris. "These are Waziri markings," he said to Reynolds. "These and the spear, too. I recognize the workmanship."

"They are?" Reynolds asked, puzzled. Tarzan showed him the distinctive feather patterns that he had seen the Waziri craftsmen so often make in their village. The feather patterns identified their kills in hunting—and in war.

Tarzan's brow narrowed as he pondered the meaning of this. Silently, he commenced picking up and arranging his belongings, when Reynolds, off to the side, let out, "My God."

"What?"

"They've taken the skeleton!"

They both stared at the vacant cabinet where the crated skeleton had been stored. The lock had been broken. It was empty inside. They hastily looked around the room.

"Why would the Waziri kill my men? And what would they want with those bones?" Reynolds asked.

Tarzan said, "I do not believe the Waziri would do this. I will not believe it until I see the box of bones in M'Bala's possession."

"Well, then, come along, and let's pay them a little visit."

Tarzan looked at him. "My friend, you do not want to go marching into the Waziri village making unfounded accusations. They do not take kindly to them."

"I can simply have a talk with M'Bala. He won't be on his guard against me, will he? And they'll be more receptive if you come along, old boy."

"No. I will not go there," Tarzan said grimly. "Because the Waziri did not do this."

"Oh? How can you be so sure?"

"First, it does not make sense. The Waziri are not interested in the bones. And if they wanted to take something by stealth, they would not have left things to be so easily identified. They would have used plain arrows, or picked everything up." He held up the arrow and feathers. "No, this was done by someone who wanted us to think it was the Waziri, to throw us off. Someone who knew the bones were here."

"Well, then, we're back to the question of who, as well as why. And how do we find them?"

"We can follow their trail, before it gets too cold."

"Their trail!? They took off into the jungle. You think you can track them through that? It's been several hours, at least."

"I will try," replied Tarzan, shouldering his bow. "With their burden, I do not think they will be difficult to follow."

"I hope you can find them."

"Granger will have to be told at some point. And he will need to identify the bones when we find them."

Reynolds shook his head slightly. "There's a duty I won't relish. I promised him those bones would be safe."

Tarzan let a smile cross one side of his mouth. "You promised me my things would be safe, too."

"Perhaps you should have built that tree house for the bones!"

The ape man adjusted his quiver strap and his rope and began to amble across the compound to the shore, but then turned and said, "I'll need to borrow one of your boats to cross the river. I will return it."

"You mean like last time?" But he was gone.

Reynolds was relieved to see the jungle lord take off in pursuit. He knew that his tall friend could track these raiders like no other. If anyone could swiftly locate them and bring them to justice, it was he. Reynolds also knew that he did not need to send accompanying soldiers along with him, because, as the ape man had said before, they would only be "in the way."

Now it was a matter of overcoming his grief and rage and dealing with the aftermath of this brutal crime.

Tarzan crossed the Bolongo River on one of Point Station's small crafts fashioned for that purpose. As he approached the far shore, his jungle-honed eyesight easily noticed the kinks and indentations in the marsh grasses bordering the river, and beyond them, in the drier field grasses. Several men had come through here, in a hurry, with a fairly heavy burden. They obviously made no attempt to conceal their trail, and thus they left behind a manuscript of their movements which could be read by anyone who had tracked quarry in the jungle. To the ape man, detecting their trail was as simple as the reading exercises in a child's school primer.

He set off on a trot, then on a run, heeding the signs along the trail as rapidly as he could. At length, he saw that his quarry appeared to have stopped their hurried progress, because the trail widened and the markings of footsteps clustered, as if they had halted for a while and milled about in one spot. But when the trail began again a few feet later, Tarzan recognized unmistakable signs: the imprints of twin ruts in the soft jungle earth, the particular width of the trail of flattened grasses and brush. He did not even need the confirming smell of fumes his nostrils detected on the moist, broken fronds. They had gotten into a vehicle.

Tarzan took off in a run, pounding the ground along the raiders' trail as it coursed through the thickening forest, snaking around larger trees and plowing over younger ones. At times he was even able to take to the trees and thus propel himself along as fast as, if not faster than, their cumbersome vehicle would have been able to move, so that the journey that took the raiders perhaps half a day or more, Tarzan could traverse in much less time. If only they had not had such a head start.

Chapter 10
SAVIOR

In the Urulu village, Ruth Cheever was just finishing up her morning catechism class when Maximilian approached her and said, "I've got something to show you." He led her to the camp truck and bade her to get in. A bit hesitantly, she climbed into the passenger seat, and Maximilian roared the engine to life and took off.

"What are you going to show me?" she shouted over the roar of the winding engine as they bounced down the trail.

"Something I'll bet you never expected to see," he replied, somewhat cryptically.

They came upon a spot where the navigable trail ended, overgrown from disuse. Maximilian got out and said, "We'll have to walk. It's just a little farther." He led the way through a fairly thick entanglement of branches and vines, hacking with his machete as needed. About the time Ruth began to get weary of the persistent vegetation, they came upon a somewhat more open area, a glade that struck her as quite picturesque, even charming. Small, undulating hillocks, marked with outcroppings of rock or boulder, encircled a grassy central area several yards in diameter. As Maximilian led her into the area and approached one small hill, she noticed that it presented an opening, rather like a small cave, and that the opening had been concealed somewhat with brush and leaves, so that one had to know where to look to find it.

Maximilian bent down on one knee and pushed aside the

concealing vegetation. He reached inside the recess and partially pulled out a strong wooden packing crate several feet square.

"Do you recognize this?" he asked.

Ruth glanced at the nondescript wooden sides. "No."

Maximilian used the edge of his machete to pry open one side and lift it up enough so that light penetrated and Ruth could peer in to see beneath the packing excelsior a segment of dusty, yellowed skeletal remains.

"My God!" Ruth started upright. "The bones!"

"Yes," Maximilian smiled.

"You've stolen them!" She looked him in the eye, then looked back to the box.

"Now they don't really belong to anyone, so they can't really be stolen, can they?" he replied. "We simply obtained them."

"They were not yours to take!" Ruth said indignantly.

"Miss Cheever, not long ago you said that these bones were an abomination to the Lord, and that Granger had no business digging them up and that we'd all be better off if they disappeared. Well, now they have. This is what you wanted."

"I certainly did not want theft! I cannot condone this!"

"You will say nothing," Maximilian said flatly.

"I cannot remain silent, and I cannot lie. We will all be in trouble for this!"

"No one will know." Maximilian smiled sardonically. "They will believe the Waziri stole them. For all you know, they did."

"Why...why would they?" Ruth sputtered. "Why would anyone think that?"

"You just let events take their course and stay out of it. Don't interfere with my mission and I won't interfere with yours. We'll just call it my contribution to God's plan."

"You are not an agent of God! You will be exposed and brought to justice!"

Maximilian looked at her sternly. "No one will connect this to me unless you say something. You see, I have never said anything about these bones one way or another. But you, Miss Cheever, bad-mouthed the bones and Granger's work loud and clear in the marketplace for everyone to hear. So if you say one word to connect me to this, I assure you they will be reminded of that, and you will be blamed for giving the order."

"They will not believe that! Walter Adamson will not believe that!"

"Can you take that chance?" He looked at her condescendingly. "Don't worry. It will all work out. You'll see. Now let's go back."

"I'll have nothing to do with this!" Ruth Cheever declared. "I'll find my way back to the camp myself, thank you." She turned and proceeded to stomp off through the brush, not quite precisely in the direction of the camp or the vehicle.

She tried to run, but stumbled again and again, attempting to put distance between herself and the bones, both mentally and physically. The branches at her face and the weeds and roots underfoot were too thick to allow her to run, so that she had to slow to an ambling walk. She thought she knew where the vehicle had been parked, and she believed she could retrace her steps to the missionary camp if she found the road. She passed by a tree that she thought she recognized on the walk in, but the two next to it were unfamiliar. She plodded on, looking left and right as she advanced. She was certain she was on the right path. Yet she did not see any of the brush Maximilian had hacked when they approached.

At length Ruth grew weary of pushing aside branches and stepping over gnarled roots. She was hot and sweaty and sore. She sat down upon a fallen trunk to get her bearings and wipe her brow. She took a moment to look up at the tree branches high above, arching over her at a height of at least three stories, dense and tangled, allowing only patches of light to reach the forest floor. She looked down and around for any sign of the road or the vehicle. None. Just thick jungle in every direction. She was apparently far away from Maximilian and he was not pursuing her, not that she expected him to. In fact, she did not know what to expect now.

Absorbed as she was in her discomfort, she least expected what she heard next—a low, throaty, rumbling sound. Her ears perked up. She did not know what it was. Slowly, she looked around. She heard it again. About thirty yards away, she saw the bushes rustle.

What she saw next froze her blood. The fierce head of a full-grown lion peered out from the dense shrubbery, its large green eyes fixed firmly upon her.

Ruth Cheever gasped, open-mouthed, and then stared back at the lion, stiff and still. She could barely breathe. She watched as it emerged from the brush, first the forepaws, then the torso, then the haunches and rear legs. She could never imagine a creature being that big, even from that distance. Its paws were massive and its body a block of muscled fur.

The lion looked back and forth for a moment and sniffed the air. In that instant Ruth believed that it might ignore her, though she had absolutely no reason to think so. It turned to look back at her. She feared it might hear her heart pounding.

Almost instinctively, she began to mouth in a whisper, "The Lord is my shepherd; I shall not want."

As the cat slowly moved closer, staring at her, she continued to whisper, louder, as if the words themselves could defy the beast, "Though I walk through the valley of the shadow of death, I will fear no evil: for Thou art with me...."

The lion growled and stared at her.

"Surely goodness and mercy shall follow me all the days of my life, and I will dwell in the house of the Lord forever."

Her eyes widened, her brow sweating. The beast opened its huge maw, revealing spiked yellow fangs.

Her paralyzing fear gave way to numbness as the lion halted about twenty yards from her and crouched down on its haunches. Those brown eyes glared hypnotically at her as the great cat bristled...tensed...and leaped!

In the instant before Ruth Cheever closed her eyes to accept death, she saw a naked bronze figure with black hair drop as if from the sky onto the back of the leaping beast and immediately wrap one arm around the great spotted neck. The mighty beast reared up in mid-leap and then landed on the ground short of Ruth, who scurried backward, eyes glued to the incredible sight before her, and screamed.

The lion writhed and shook, trying to dislodge the bronze figure on its back, but the man clung tightly with one bulging, sinewy arm while repeatedly thrusting his father's hunting knife into the beast's side with the other. Again and again he plunged the blade in, raking the ribs and loins of the great cat, until its yellow-brown fur was caked with blood. The beast growled and roared. Ruth was not certain, but she thought she heard the man growl as well. The lion flopped over and rolled furiously back and forth trying to dislodge its burden. But the man clung fast and continued to thrust steely death, piston-like, with his arm. Never had she seen a sight so savage and violent unfold ten feet in front of her. Its intensity mesmerized her, so that she halted her fearful retreat, enthralled.

At length the roaring of the great cat began to subside. Its thrashing receded into death throes, and it fell to the ground, jerking its last movements, its eyes gone blank.

Tarzan of the Apes rolled off the bloody carcass and stood up, panting. Ruth Cheever stared wide-eyed in wonder at the man who stood before her, blood smeared on his muscular torso, his chest heaving, his black hair hanging over his brow in sweaty strands.

Despite the creature's fierce size, Tarzan's keen eye noticed that it was rather emaciated, evidently starving, which could explain why it had journeyed so far from the veldt. He knew that conditions on the veldt had been harsh this year.

"You are a miracle from the Lord!" she exclaimed, her eyes wide and radiant.

Tarzan, catching his breath and wiping off his knife, said, "I am no miracle."

"You are His agent. The Lord has sent you to rescue me."

The lion writhed and shook, trying to dislodge the bronze figure on its back, but the man clung tightly with one bulging, sinewy arm while repeatedly thrusting a massive dagger into the beast's side ...

Tarzan looked at her. "I came on my own."

Ruth continued, clasping her hands, "He has given you the powers beyond any mortal man."

The ape man shook his head. "I am as mortal a man as any other. My abilities are learned. This place is my boyhood home, and had I not learned these skills, I would not have survived. It is as simple as that."

"You are too modest," Ruth said, with a hint of a smile. "It is clear that God put you here to save me from the lion."

Tarzan replied, with a shadow of disdain crossing his brow, "If God wanted you saved from the lion, why did He put the lion here to attack you?"

Ruth wiped some perspiration off her face and pushed back some hair while she watched Tarzan. She said, "The natives say that your name means Ape Man."

"Close. It means White Skin."

"In what language?"

"Actually, it is an attempt to verbalize my name in the language of the great apes."

Ruth raised an eyebrow, taken somewhat aback. "You can talk to apes? They have a language?"

"It is not a proper language as you would understand the term," Tarzan replied. "It is a series of movements and gestures coupled with vocalizations which I have been able to imitate with some success. But I can communicate things to them. Apes are quite like us in many ways."

"Now you sound like that Granger fellow. Thinking that we came from apes because our bones are similar, or some such."

Tarzan moved the carcass some distance from them and then retrieved his arrows and bow, having cast them aside because using them would not have stopped the cat in time. Wearied, he sat down on a rock a few feet from Ruth. "Granger is a scientist. He is trying to learn the truth through investigation. Why is that such a threat to you?"

"What he is doing is an abomination!" Ruth exclaimed with indignation. "Digging up those bones is the devil's work."

"Why? What are they to you?"

"They threaten to undermine the word of God. He and scientists like him reject the idea of God as the Creator and propose their heresy that man somehow evolved over millions of years."

"Do these bones not prove, or at least strongly indicate, that this idea may be correct?" Tarzan asked.

"We cannot be descended from apes! Apes are simply primitive creatures! They are not like us. They have practically nothing in common with us!"

"I was raised by an ape," Tarzan said. "A great she-ape named Kala. She was the closest I ever had to a mother."

"But you are not an ape!" Ruth sputtered. "Even if you live in the jungle! Isn't it obvious?"

Tarzan stared at her, his brow narrowing, and said, "During my boyhood, I believed that I was an ape. I acted like one. Lived like one. Thought like one. But then I discovered, through long-lost evidence, my own true heritage as an Englishman. But this knowledge did not diminish my jungle origins. I accepted what I was, even embraced it. The truth has given me greater insight into myself and provided me with greater opportunities."

Ruth found herself momentarily caught between her admiration for this paladin of the jungle and her distaste for the things he said.

Tarzan stood up. "You need to return to the village. Are you well enough to walk?"

"Yes, I think so," Ruth answered.

"Why were you out here alone, anyway?" Tarzan asked.

Ruth hesitated. "I…I just wanted to go for a walk."

"You are not in Massachusetts. Did no one tell you that you should not go out into the jungle alone?" He shouldered his quiver and bow. "Come. Follow me back to the Urulu village. Try to keep up."

Tarzan was vexed that he could not continue his pursuit of the killers, but this Cheever woman was obviously ill-equipped to be left on her own. He hoped he could return to the hunt before the trail grew too cold.

Chapter 11

DISCOVERY

When Tarzan and Ruth arrived at the missionary camp, Walter Adamson was in the middle of a service, preaching a sermon he called "The Miracle of Faith" to adult men and women sitting in the wooden benches facing his hand-hewn wooden podium. He was exhorting, "We must remember that God guides all things in our lives. When we make choices, we must ask ourselves if we are serving God or denying him...."

Ruth invited the ape man to stay for some rest and refreshment, but he declined and turned to leave. For her part, Ruth chose not to listen to the rest of the sermon, either, and retired to her tent, feeling that she needed to rest before telling Walter and the others about her ordeal.

But she could not rest. Ruth lay on her cot deeply conflicted, too conflicted to sleep even in her exhausted state. She had, indeed, harbored ill thoughts toward those bones and wished that they were eliminated from the picture. Yet Maximilian had committed theft, and he had done so at her behest. And a web of lies had already commenced to conceal the theft. How could she come here and preach the Commandments to her flock and yet be instrumental in their violation?

She wondered about this man Maximilian and his cohorts. When she first met him, he seemed benevolent and supportive. He seemed confident about jungle living, and he and his men had certainly been very helpful to the mission. She remembered feeling fortunate to have men of their abilities and had wondered more than once how the mission might have gotten along without them. Yet there was something about him that she could not fathom. He had never seemed to her to be particularly religious. He talked about matters of faith and the Gospels hardly at all, she recalled. He and his men rarely participated in the services, preferring to remain on the sidelines and not conspicuously joining in the singing or prayer. Why, then, would such men align themselves with a religious mission?

She had wondered how Adamson had found these men, and now she wondered why. When Walter had introduced them the second month of the mission, she had simply accepted on faith that they were part of the missionary effort. Had she allowed her innate belief in the goodness of people to cloud her judgment? What hidden, darker purpose did Maximilian have in being here that she and Adamson were too blind to recognize?

She had no idea what to do. Should she act on her suspicions? If so, in whom should she confide? Mabuto? Captain Reynolds? Perhaps, it occurred to her, she should be forthright with Tarzan. Perhaps he could be instrumental in setting things aright between the Urulu and the Waziri and Reynolds and Doctor Granger. Perhaps, despite his protestations, he truly was the agent of her deliverance in more ways than one.

And yet, what if she said nothing? She was not directly implicated in the theft. If the bones were discovered, she could safely assert that she had not taken them. No one would suggest that she conducted the raid on Point Station. Perhaps the truth about Maximilian's duplicity would be revealed without her intervention. Perhaps this would be a way for her to be rid of him, a scenario which at this point would be quite welcome.

Tarzan of the Apes traveled through the trees to a small stream which he knew but few others did. There he alighted upon the soft grasses at the bank and commenced to wash his wounds and dirt with the cooling water. He was sore, bruised and tired from his battle with the great cat.

He sought the refuge of a massive tree and settled himself in to ponder what had happened. It was of little consequence to him personally who stole the bones or what their fate would be. But his friend Captain Reynolds was in jeopardy because of the theft, and Reynolds' absence from the station during the raid had been in part Tarzan's doing.

He had his suspicions about why Ruth Cheever had been alone in the jungle and whence she had come. Moreover, he could not let his longtime friends the Waziri be blamed for the killings which he knew they did not commit. He was Tarzan, Lord of the Jungle, and he must not rest until the villains were caught.

He rose and nimbly leaped to a nearby limb, then another, making his way swiftly through the arboreal terraces back toward the place where he had encountered Ruth and the lion, hoping it might provide some answers.

He arrived at the spot in due course and looked around from his lofty perch. The carcass of the lion had already been partially gnawed away, and would no doubt be gone by morning. He observed the matted grass and tangled brush where he had fought the great beast, and he alighted onto the jungle floor nearby. He studied the area. His keen eyesight was able to spot the path along which Ruth had moved, and he could easily distinguish between it and the paths of the jungle scavengers which had stopped to trample upon the ground around the carcass several feet away, leaving scents which were clearly not hers.

He commenced to retrace Ruth's path back away from the area. He noticed immediately that she had not been coming from the direction of the Urulu camp. Her trail revealed a number of things to Tarzan's trained eye. It meandered and zigzagged, suggesting that she had been lost or uncertain of her direction. The trampled grasses and broken twigs at frequent intervals along the way also suggested that she had been rushing headlong, perhaps even oblivious to what lay ahead. *Hardly how one takes a walk,* thought Tarzan.

It was but a matter of minutes for the ape man to retrace the path which to Ruth Cheever had been a torturous journey full of anguish. He came in short order upon the spacious glade. He noted the open area, ridged with palm fronds, which lay bathed in the rays of the afternoon sun filtering lightly through the trees. He observed the small hills and series of rocky outcroppings that encircled him on three sides. He also noticed, off to his left, the unmistakable signs of the same trail that he had been following earlier from Point Station, the trail of the raiders who had stolen the crated skeleton. Their trail and the path Ruth Cheever had run along intersected here. Whether she had come here of her own volition or had been brought here under duress, Tarzan could not tell from the physical evidence. But they had met. She knew who they were. They had, undoubtedly, spoken. What had been said? Had she run from them? If so, why?

As Tarzan inspected further, he saw that the truck trail left this area and headed off in the direction of the Urulu village. *This answers many questions,* he thought. His belief in the Waziris' innocence was confirmed. He also supposed that the members of the Urulu themselves were blameless, since they did not drive vehicles. That left only the members of the white missionary party, and Tarzan was in little doubt as to which of those to suspect.

His eyes panned the area in a wide arc. Downed trees, grassy hillocks, cave-like openings—this spot offered many places of concealment. He began to examine them, one by one, inspecting tree trunks, lifting rocks, studying the turf for signs of recent burial. It was not long before he came upon an opening about three feet wide, partially framed by a rocky brow, an opening which had been covered by recently-hacked branches and stones obviously put there to conceal the space. Tarzan pulled away the stones and branches, scraped away some of the dirt at the mouth of the opening, and peered in. There it was, poking out from the darkness—a corner of the wooden crate which he recognized as the repository of Granger's skeleton.

After verifying the presence of the missing bones, he did not remove it. Where would he take it, if he did? He presumed that only a few people knew of its location, and they had no reason at this point to suspect that its whereabouts had been discovered. Therefore, he began to meticulously replace the stones and branches he had moved.

Reaching for a piece of crinkled brush, he suddenly stopped and cocked his head upward, listening. Rustling in the bushes. He looked quickly around, then, grabbing his bow and rope, crouched low and ambled off to the concealment of large palm fronds several yards away.

Tarzan looked back at the cave mouth to see two men, the young, sandy-haired Bingham and the tall, hatchet-faced Wolfe, emerge from the trail, stop, and look around. They both carried rifles, pointed groundward, in the crooks of their arms. They bent down to look over the hiding place of the crated skeleton and gave the area around it a passing glance.

With their attention thus occupied, Tarzan silently, deftly, climbed the nearest large tree and secured a position about twenty-five feet above the ground, close enough to see and hear them but far enough away to escape easy detection, he judged. He listened, with amusement, to their attempts at investigation.

"Yup, still there. Nobody's found it," Wolfe said.

"But he still wants us to move it anyway?" Bingham asked.

"He showed it to her, but now wants it moved so she can't tell anybody where it is. He's taking no chances. We'll probably move it every other day."

"Till when?"

"Till he tells us different."

Bingham said, "There's some tracks around here. Look at where the grass is just pressed down."

"Nah," Wolfe replied, after a cursory look. "That's just the tracks we made. Us and the woman, back then. Don't look like any animal tracks, either. I tell ya, nobody's been here."

During this exchange, Tarzan had been carefully and silently pulling an arrow from the quiver on his back, nocking it, and taking aim.

"All right. Let's get to it, then. He told us to hide it more securely." Bingham stepped forward toward the opening and began to crouch down to reach toward the concealed crate. In that instant Tarzan's arrow whizzed by his head and lodged with a thud in the dirt a foot away from his boot.

"What the hell!?" Bingham jerked back. He swung his rifle up to wildly fire a shot before dashing back to the cover of the foliage near Wolfe.

"Did you see him?" Bingham asked.

"Nah. Came from somewhere over there." Wolfe gestured broadly.

"Not a great shot," Bingham ventured.

Wolfe turned to him, his dark eyes narrowing. "Or he's exactly on target. As a warning." Bingham, anxiety in his countenance, turned to look back toward the cache of bones and said, "Somebody wants us outta here. Maybe we better go. Maybe we disturbed somebody's hunting. Maybe he doesn't even know why we're here."

Wolfe removed his canvas hat, revealing matted black hair. He stared at the trees a moment, and then wondered, "Who is it? Who would be here? Probably not an Urulu. A Waziri? Some other tribe? Didja get a look?"

Bingham shook his head. "Maybe it's the ape man."

"Max told us to save that guy for him," Wolfe retorted.

Why? Tarzan wondered.

Wolfe gestured his intent to move over behind the cover of a craggy boulder a few feet away. Keeping crouched, they hastily took cover behind it. Just before they stopped, Wolfe partially poked his head and shoulder up from behind the rock's surface. Tarzan unleashed his second arrow, which skidded off the jagged surface and veered away into the underbrush.

A wasted shot, Tarzan lamented. He moved to hurriedly change position to a limb of an adjacent tree as Wolfe fired two shots, the bullets whizzing through the leaves of nearby branches.

"This is nuts," Bingham said. "Let's get outta here. While we can."

"We can't leave now," Wolfe snarled through gritted, yellowed teeth. "We have to take 'im or scare 'im away. I think there's only one." He scanned the trees around them, and added, "And we might have scared 'im already. We have rifles. Let's figure this out."

"How do you mean?"

"We need to find out whether it's the bones he wants, or something else. All we need to do is remove that crate. We use that to smoke him out."

"How?"

"I'll cover you. I'll watch carefully in the direction of those trees. You go out and grab the crate. If he's gone, we'll know. If he shoots, I've got him."

"And I'm dead!"

"I don't think he's that accurate. Not at that distance. All we need to do is watch where the arrow comes from."

"Still, I'm not doing it. You go."

Wolfe frowned. "All right, dammit, I will. You just watch those trees carefully and keep me covered."

"Don't worry. I'll cover ya."

His rifle held up, Wolfe dashed out from behind the rock and across the space toward the cave opening, firing a series of shots into the trees in the general direction of where the first arrow had come, where Tarzan no longer was.

Tarzan unleashed a third arrow. This time it struck true, lodging in Wolfe's shoulder. He shouted in pain.

Tarzan's goal of scaring them off nearly succeeded. But Bingham's eye was quick. He opened fire and sprayed five blasts in the direction the arrow had come from. Mingled with the dying echo of the rifle burst came the sound of rustling leaves and a heavy weight cracking branches as it plummeted down.

Bingham listened. He gestured Wolfe to silence. He rose up a bit and looked intently in the direction of the sound. Nothing further. No movement, no sound, and no arrows.

"Do we have him?" Wolfe asked, grimacing.

Bingham wondered, too. He said, "Let's go see. Now's our chance."

"Hey! Hell with him! Get me back to camp before I bleed to death!"

Chapter 12
INJURY AND INSULTS

Tarzan of the Apes lay on the jungle floor, his mind swirling in foggy consciousness. He was scratched and bruised from his fall. He had hit his head on the tree trunk as he landed, dazing him. His leg throbbed. He looked down to see the blood massing around the bullet wound in his thigh, which had caused him to lose his balance.

He did not know how long he had been here. It could not have been too long, he thought, but he could not be certain. He heard no sign of his quarry. They must have left him for dead, he surmised. Just as well. Had they found him in this condition, they could easily have finished him off.

His first thought, instinctively, was survival. With his knife he cut a length of vine and wrapped it securely around his thigh above the wound, to serve as a tourniquet to stem the bleeding. He considered attempting to remove the bullet with his knife, but it was lodged where he could not get at it.

It was not long before he heard a sound that troubled him. It was the pounding of tribal drums, echoing from one section of the jungle to another, then back. The palpitations were intense, aggressive, as if being pounded out by frenzied drummers. Loosely translated, they said *Waziri steal old bones.* Soon enough, they were answered by fervent denials from the Waziri drums.

This was not good. The Waziri were being blamed for the theft—and undoubtedly, the dead soldiers—yet Tarzan knew that the thieves were men from the Urulu encampment. And white men, too. But why? Why did they try to make it look like a Waziri raid? For that matter, what could Maximilian and his accomplices possibly want with those bones in the first place?

He had to get to the Waziri village. He warily stood up, testing the leg. It still hurt. He gingerly took a few steps and endeavored to accustom himself to the stabbing pain. He gathered his bow, quiver and rope coil and started off, limping, in the direction of the Waziri camp, which he knew was many miles away.

He tried to reach a walking stride, but he was still light-headed. He stumbled and slapped his palm upon a tree to steady himself. He started out again…which way were the Waziri?…he had to get to their village…he thought he heard drums…the tree trunks seemed to spin…he felt moist palm fronds brush against him… and perhaps cracking branches….

Tarzan awoke, thick-headed and groggy, to see the broad grin of M'Bala bearing down on him. "Good morning, my friend," he greeted. "How do you feel?"

The ape man looked around. He was stretched out on a mat in a Waziri hut, his head supported by animal-skin pelts. A small fire burned in the center of the room, and from it wafted some sort of herbal incense he did not recognize. Around him were gathered Uba the tribal medicine healer and his assistants.

"How…." His eyes darted around and back to M'Bala "…how did I get here?"

"A Waziri hunting party found you unconscious and brought you here yesterday."

Uba said, "You are recovering from my sleeping draft. It kept you quiet while I removed the bullet. I have cleaned and sealed the wound. It looks fine. You should be walking soon. The rest will allow you to heal." Tarzan saw the patch on his leg and noted that, although it felt stiff, the leg hurt less. Then he looked left to see another familiar face.

"How are you doing, old boy?" Captain Reynolds asked. "Seems you've had a rather nasty run-in with somebody. Do you remember what happened?"

Tarzan lifted himself up onto one elbow and grasped Reynolds' arm with his other hand. "I think I know who ambushed me," he said. "The same ones who killed your men and stole the bones. And I know where the bones are."

Reynolds said, "I sent men to search the area where the Waziri tell me you were found."

Tarzan told the captain what the men should look for. He described the type of tracks and indentations in the grasses and brush that would be left by a certain vehicle, a vehicle that could identify his attackers—and thus the raiders.

"Excellent," Reynolds replied. "I'll radio that information to them immediately. I am in your debt. I don't need to tell you how keen I am to find those killers." Then he added, "Just as an aside, wouldn't it also be smashing if we could get those damn bones back before Granger brings the entire scientific community down on me?"

He turned to Uba and asked, "How soon can he walk?"

"We must give him some more time. Perhaps tomorrow or the next day."

Tarzan was about to protest that he needed to go immediately, but a stab of pain from his wound persuaded him that perhaps Uba was correct. He settled his head down upon the pelts.

M'Bala said, "A lot has happened since you fell. The drums say that we have stolen the bones."

"I heard them."

"This troubles me." Tarzan knew that M'Bala did not use the word "troubles" lightly. "My people are angry," M'Bala continued. "My warriors say that we cannot allow such lies. They say that the Urulu have spoken these lies."

"But why?"

"Because they think the Waziri are jealous that the Urulu have found the true God."

"What? That does not make sense."

"It is what they say. They have been stirred up by this missionary woman. There is a faction of Urulu warriors who say that we, the Waziri, who have trusted in our gods for a thousand years, must now accept their god. They wish to spread their beliefs to other tribes, too."

Reynolds groused, "It's one thing to come here and preach a little gospel of love and brotherhood, but this has gone a bit far. That Cheever woman is stirring up long-dormant tribal rivalries in the name of religious zeal. That's a bad combination."

"What are you going to do?" Tarzan asked M'Bala.

"We will debate the problem further tonight at the council fire. Perhaps for many nights. But the question is—what are the Urulu going to do?"

Captain William Reynolds found himself in a quandary, as well as distressed at the recent turn of events. Three men dead. But why? For some archaeological relics? Who would want them?

He only had a detail of a dozen men at the station even before the raid. He was always understaffed. The station was not really a full military post, and though he was commissioned, his duties had always been more administrative than military. His job was overseeing his portion of the river traffic, not policing the entire jungle. In the two years he had been there, the only violence in the area had been the occasional scuffle between boatmen on the wharf. He had never even fired his sidearm in the line of duty.

And now this.

What possible reason could someone have to steal the crate and try to clumsily blame the Waziri for murder? Even Tarzan was uncertain as to what to make of that.

He went to the missionary encampment and asked to see

Maximilian and his men. He was told that the four of them were out hunting. Sometimes, Adamson told them, they went for days at a time. Did Adamson or anyone else know in what general direction they went? No one seemed to know. And Adamson did not seem suspicious about that, which struck the captain as odd, too. Reynolds posted a detail at the missionary camp, with orders to bring in Maximilian and his men for questioning when they returned. Two days later, they still had not shown.

He could use the jungle lord's help in tracking them down, but he was on the mend.

And Reynolds' problems were, of course, compounded by the distances involved. It was nearly a day's journey between Point Station and the Urulu village, and another half-day's journey to the Waziri village.

On top of his loss, Reynolds had to deal with the resultant fallout involving disposition of the bodies, notification of families, and requests for replacements, not to mention the morale of the other men at the post and the general questions of Station security that had been raised. He did not even plan to journey to Granger's site and tell him about the theft. That could wait. He had other priorities. Besides, maybe the bones would be found and he would not need to.

Other problems developed, too. The tensions between the Urulu and the Waziri were escalating in ways that made Reynolds uncomfortable. The smoldering resentments, which might have been extinguished by the apprehension of the real killers and the recovery of the relics, were instead further enflamed by an incident that occurred the following week.

It seems that a party of about a dozen Waziri had been out hunting and came across a bushbuck antelope. Among the party were several adolescent boys on their first hunt. One of the boys was directed to try to bring down the animal. He fired his arrow, and the bushbuck immediately turned and ran off into the jungle. The boy was of the opinion that he had hit the animal, and thus the party tracked it in the expectation of finding it hurt or dead.

The injured antelope wandered into sight of an Urulu hunting party, and one of their warriors brought it down with his spear. Shortly after the Urulu began to gut and dress the carcass, the Waziri party showed up and claimed it as theirs. A disagreement ensued.

Part of the dispute was the question of whose territory the animal died in. The area where this incident occurred was near the border between the Waziri's territory and the Urulu's. Traditionally, the outer boundaries between tribal lands were rather nebulous, there having never been any surveys made or fences erected. The precise delineation of the border, a matter of little consequence most of the time, now became salient.

The Waziri said that the kill was the boy's rite of passage. Each adolescent Waziri male must kill a quarry under these particular conditions in order to be regarded as a man by the tribe. Surely, they argued, the Urulu understood the importance of letting the boy have the kill, because they follow a similar tradition. Not any longer, the Urulu said. The Urulu scoffed at this primitive ritual and related with some arrogance that now they had a new rite of passage, called confirmation, which involved making solemn promises to their new God instead of animal sacrifices to the gods of old.

The Waziri pointed to an arrow wound on the bushbuck's haunches which, they maintained, clearly proved the boy shot the animal. The Urulu retorted that it did not matter, since the boy obviously did not kill the beast and thus lost all claim to it.

Insults began to fly:

Is this how the Urulu live—stealing the game of others?

Was this how the Waziri learned to hunt? They would starve if they did not train their boys better than this.

Men from one of the tribes—it is not clear which—moved to pick up the animal and haul it away. By all accounts, a scuffle ensued with much pushing, shoving and name-calling. The incident may have ended in various ways, depending on whose account one heard. The Urulu either picked up the carcass, or wrested it away from the Waziri, and took it. The Waziri let them do it, either because they wisely did not wish to provoke a further incident, or because they were cowards and afraid of a fight.

The council fires burned long and bright that night in the two villages, and many things were said.

At the Urulu fire, the talk was of how the Waziri do not respect the Urulu's territory and have grown so arrogant that they believe they own the jungle.

Some voices said that if the boy was really a good hunter, he would have brought down the animal cleanly instead of letting it run off. He was still a boy and not yet a worthy hunter. They protect and coddle their young. They are weak.

They do not serve God, some said. They laugh at our beliefs, others said. They believe in nothing but themselves.

They need to be taught a lesson, many urged Mabuto.

At the Waziri fire, the talk was of how the Urulu stole the trophy from the boy, humiliating his family and thus, by extension, the entire tribe. The kill was clearly theirs, many voices argued.

Old wounds were brought up. The Urulu did not play fair at the tournament, they charged. Their young hotheads like Gamba are cheats. They blamed us for the theft of the white scientists' bones when we did not take them and did not want them. And when we said that to them, they called us liars.

The drums spread their lies throughout the jungle. They dishonor us, tribal voices said.

They need to be taught a lesson, many urged M'Bala.

In both camps, the arguments, the acrimony, the imagined insults raged on into the night. Both tribes became convinced that their beliefs and customs, indeed their integrity, were not respected by the other. Hot-blooded rhetoric began to fill the air like the smoke from the bonfires, becoming louder and more insistent.

The word was not mentioned at all early in the evening, and only uttered by a few even after some time. But as tempers rose and the rancorous charges and condemnations mounted, the word passed through more lips, first from the indignant younger warriors and later the tribal elders, one after another, until at length, the word became the rallying cry of the night in both camps.

War.

Chapter 13
WAR

All the jungle seems to know when war is imminent. Anyone who bothers to look will notice flocks of birds scattering off away from the clamor. He will notice the usually playful little monkeys screeching and scolding, leaping up and down in anxious frenzy. The great apes, too, fling themselves back and forth across the terraces, grunting uneasy cries of warning, herding their young to higher tiers of safety. Even the big cats, the most fearless of jungle denizens, growl and pace, wondering whether the startled gazelle heading toward them is a boon to be enjoyed or a harbinger of something to be feared.

The drums of war reverberated through the jungle for days. While spears were sharpened and quivers were filled, the drums pounded. While war paint and headdresses were donned and guards posted, they pounded. While the women of the villages prepared to treat the wounded and the elders prayed for victory, the drums pounded.

The drums that had throbbed all through the early morning hours subsided when two parties of warriors made their way to the common meeting ground, a glade framed by towering trees whose foliage allowed the sun to dapple the pale green undercarpet, an ironically peaceful setting for this prelude to battle. For the last stage had come, the final ritual where tribal representatives could meet to posture and bluster in hopes of intimidating the opponents, possibly

215

into surrendering, or whip each other up into a battle frenzy replete
with challenges and bellicose name calling.

Sometimes this ritual meeting resulted in a dispute being settled, and indeed this is what Tarzan and M'Bala hoped might be
the case today. Tarzan, nearly recovered from his injuries, emerged
with M'Bala from the jungle to meet the party from the Urulu,
accompanied by a half dozen tall, well-muscled Waziri warriors in
full battle regalia with spears, shields and sheathed daggers. Their
heads were adorned with white plumes, and their distinctive copper anklets and bracelets gleamed. They were met by a similar
party of Urulu warriors, led by Mabuto. The ebony warriors stared
grimly at each other, forcing themselves to let only their chiefs
speak.

"Why are you doing this?" M'Bala asked in the regional dialect
which they all understood. "This is not necessary."

Mabuto stood tall and glared at M'Bala. "You have wronged
us. You have dishonored our beliefs."

"We did not do these things. And you have falsely accused us.
It is you who have dishonored us. But we do not need to war over
that. And if we do, you will lose."

"You are infidels. The God of heaven will lead us to victory.
This is a holy war!"

"This is not a holy war," Tarzan interjected. "War is not holy."

Among the warriors accompanying Mabuto was the hot-tem-
pered Gamba, who spat out, "We do not need the white ape telling
us what to do!"

One of the Waziri named Asani, who was nearly as impetuous
as Gamba, cried, "We do not need the ape man to defeat you! Give
up now and walk away while you still have your dignity!"

Gamba, muttering the Urulu equivalent of "I'll show you,"
raised his spear to hold it with both hands about three feet apart
and swung the bottom end like a quarter-staff and cracked Asani
hard on the jaw. Asani reeled back. Tarzan leaped in and grasped
the spear. The four hands tugged and wrestled with the spear shaft

for a moment until Tarzan, stronger than Gamba, twisted it and yanked it away from him. The enraged Urulu lunged to attack him, but Tarzan, now holding the spear shaft with both hands, struck him in the gut and smacked him across the jaw with it. Gamba fell, rubbing his jaw and cursing the ape man.

Tarzan drew his knife rapidly, saying, "How many times must I knock you down, Gamba? You are hotheaded and foolish, and you will take your tribe down with you."

"I am Urulu, and they are Waziri, but you have no tribe!" Gamba snarled between clenched teeth.

Mabuto rebuked him to silence, but then, turning to M'Bala, said, "But it is true. The ape man must step aside."

M'Bala turned and said, "My friend, they are right. This cannot be your fight."

Tarzan knew that it was foolish to argue with M'Bala when he was bound by the rules of generations. Tarzan put down the spear, sheathed his knife, and withdrew some distance to the side, away from the tribal delegations.

With trepidation, he watched the two sides part company and return to their respective ranks, far apart, from which they would gather reinforcements and presently mount their attack. The uneasiness and sense of foreboding which he felt watching the final preparations might have distracted his normally acute senses, so that perhaps he did not hear the very slight rustling in the bushes behind him. Nor did he expect the hard blow that struck him from behind without warning, knocking him unconscious.

The front rank of the Waziri force stood in a line fifty strong, spanning from left to right so that an observer would need to turn his head to see them all. They held their tall shields uniformly high in front of them and struck them rhythmically with their spear tips. From their throats a war chant rose in harmonic unison and soared through the air, echoing amid the jungle terraces.

The Urulu prepared for the first attack. Their archers, con-cealed behind trees and rocks, took aim and, at Mabuto's signal, let fly a volley of shafts that soared up and arced, then plummeted down onto the Waziri ranks.

As the last of the arrows landed, the front line of Waziri quickly took several steps forward and crouched down to one knee with their tall shields held in front of them. Behind the protective shield line, a line of Waziri archers emerged from the jungle and took up positions and, as one unit, let fly their volley. Their distance was closer, so that their arrows flew straighter and stronger, and many struck home. They pierced Urulu shields. They lodged in arms and legs. They drew blood.

The Urulu broke rank and sought cover from trees, brush, and rocks. Their archers began to fire at will, individually seeking out targets. The Waziri, too, sought cover.

The Urulu spear men looked around, determined each other's positions, and, crouching, began to advance cautiously, step by step, seeking to regroup and form a line to hold back any encroachment.

Several Waziri, on both flanks of the re-forming Urulu spear line, tried to move in from the cover of trees and foliage. One of the Urulu spear and shield bearers was Gamba, whose position was on the far right of his advancing line. As he crouched and advanced cautiously, he saw a Waziri partially concealed behind huge palm fronds about six feet from him. It was Dajan. Gamba suddenly lurched forward, shouting, trying to startle Dajan, and thrusting his spear point at him. The young Waziri, reacting quickly, de-flected the spear point with his shield. Another Waziri warrior joined the scuffle, but Gamba swung the butt of his spear around and clipped the second warrior across the jaw, sending him reeling.

He pivoted back to face Dajan and feinted a jab high in the air toward his opponent's head. Dajan tried to deflect it by swinging his shield upward. Gamba quickly seized the moment and thrust his spear point deeply into Dajan's side. The young Waziri screamed and folded over in pain. The cocky Gamba took an in-

stant to relish his victory, but that instant was all the other Waziri
warrior needed to thrust his spear into Gamba's neck from the side.
In another instant, two more spears landed in his torso. He cried
out for a moment, then fell.

The Urulu force erupted. Seeing their line begin to fall was
like a spark that ignited their fury. Shouting their war cries, they
charged full tilt.

Tarzan came to his senses and felt leather thongs tightly binding his wrists. His weapons were gone. Dazed, he looked around.
He was standing upright, his arms tethered behind him to one of
the main supporting poles in the Urulu council lodge. He recognized the place because he had been there before. It was a large,
spacious lodge extending many yards before him and behind him,
made of a strong framework of timber poles. Fifty tribesmen could
gather within its walls. Its arched roof rose six feet above where he
stood, supported by a network of log poles that crossed and re-
crossed the space several feet above him. He was about in the middle of the room, facing the wide framed entrance that opened onto
the Urulu village central common ground, near the ceremonial fire
pit. Behind him, on the other end of the structure, was a second
entrance, smaller and covered with a flap of hide.

The structure was empty. No one was around. Other than the
few ceremonial shields and masks hanging on the side walls, and a
few charred, doused torches, no sign remained of its use as a council
chamber. The time for talk and deliberation was over. The war
raged on far from this site, Tarzan surmised.

He tugged at the straps binding him to the pole. They were
tight. He shook bodily and slammed himself against the pole in an
attempt to dislodge it. It stood fast. The construction was solid.
Though the lodge's exterior was thatch and grass, chinked with
mud, it could withstand a storm.

He looked around for something that might help free him, but to no avail. He did not know who had brought him here, or why.

At length, the entrance way darkened and two figures walked in. Maximilian and Wolfe. The tall, hook-nosed Wolfe looked at Tarzan, his dark, yellowed eyes squinting, and scoffed, "Tough guy."

"What is this about? Let me go, Hunter," Tarzan said.

Maximilian strode up to the ape man, his ruddy face and piercing brown eyes scarcely a foot from Tarzan's. "My name is not Hunter," he sneered. "It's a name you well know. It's DeKelm! Do you remember the name Peter DeKelm? Peter DeKelm was my brother! Do you remember him?"

The name sank in. Tarzan remembered him well. It had only been a year. The attack on the Waziri village and others…the slaughter of the Chgala people…the kidnapping of Jack Fredrickson, the son of his good friend…the fiery battle with the Waziri overcoming the mercenary compound….

"I remember your brother," he said. "Why have you come here? What do you want with me?"

"You killed my brother. What do you think I want? I want you dead."

Tarzan said, "I did not kill your brother. The Waziri did."

"So you say. But you called them. If it hadn't been for you, my brother would still be alive. And they will be finished, too," Maximilian said. "If the Urulu don't defeat them, my guns will. And before I take care of you, you will watch them all die!"

The ape man gritted his teeth and yanked at his bonds. Maximilian laughed at the effort. "You won't get free from those straps. Or if you do, you won't get five feet before one of my men takes you down. You might as well relax and enjoy the show!"

He laughed again as they left the lodge.

Chapter 14
DEATH

Point Station was bustling with activity. Captain Reynolds' duties in a situation like this were complicated. He had to secure the Station, first and foremost. But a jungle torn by tribal war was not something he could sit idly by and watch. His duty compelled him to defend the white settlers, tend to the wounded, and do what he could to intervene. Accordingly, he assembled a party of six men equipped with medical and rescue gear—and armaments—and set out for the battle sites.

As the cries and clamor of the battle raged on in the distance, the Americans over in the missionary camp huddled together around their empty fire pit, their eyes darting back and forth, wide with anxiety.

"What can we do, Brother Adamson?" one of the young missionary volunteers said.

"We can pray. Let us kneel and bow our heads and ask God to put a quick end to this hostility." He rose from his chair and proceeded to kneel down in the dirt next to the fire ring. The others followed. Adamson folded his hands, closed his eyes, and began, "O Lord, we beseech you to put an end to this bloody conflict. We ask that you let our warring brothers see the error of the ways and settle their differences so that they may bring peace to this land." They all clasped their hands and prayed silently and fervently.

After a few moments, Ruth Cheever spoke up, "This is not enough!"

"What?" exclaimed Adamson.

"I cannot just stay here like this. I must do something! I must go to help!"

He looked at her, perplexed. "You cannot go out there. There is nothing you can do."

"I can treat the wounded. I can console the children."

She started up. Adamson grasped her arm, pleading, "You will be hurt. Possibly killed!"

"Walter, let me go!" she implored, struggling. "I am partly responsible for this war and I must do something about that!"

Adamson did not know what she meant, but he let her pull away from his grip. He watched her hurriedly gather together a medical kit and various towels and bandages and dash off toward the Urulu village.

"Brother Adamson, aren't we going to stop her?" one of the assistants asked.

"I don't know that we can. She is either a fool or a saint, or perhaps a bit of both."

Ruth jogged down the well-worn path from the missionary camp to the Urulu village, approaching it from the rear. She heard cries of battle and of pain as she neared the Urulu village. There was a great bustle and commotion, and women and children scurried around, some of them crying.

As she approached the center of the compound, near the tribal fire pit, she saw Maximilian, Wolfe, and Bingham standing in a line at the edge of the village grounds, facing the direction of the battle, their rifles held at the ready, pointing to the sky. Between Wolfe and Bingham, Hayes crouched down next to a wooden shipping crate. He had just finished assembling the Thompson submachine gun and snapping the round ammunition magazine onto it.

Ruth stopped and exclaimed, "What are you doing!?"

"Listening for the results of the battle," Maximilian said.

"What is going on?" Ruth said.

"The Waziri may be winning now. But we are going to make sure that they lose!"

"What! Are you going to kill them all!?" she cried, dumbfounded.

"Go back to your camp. Stay out of this!" he ordered and then, ignoring her, continued, "Ready, men? Take out every single Waziri that comes into your sight. We'll wipe out every one of the black bastards! And we'll pile them all up for the ape man to see before we take care of him!"

"You can't do this!" Ruth shouted.

"Are you still here? I told you to get out of here!"

"I've come to treat the wounded…to take care of the children…," Ruth stammered.

"Then do that!" Maximilian snarled. "But stay out of our way or we'll kill you, too!"

Fearful and apprehensive, she left the four men and headed toward a knot of women and children gathering in front of one of the huts some yards away. As she walked, she wondered about Maximilian's reference to the ape man. How would he see the carnage? Was he here?

Ruth stopped to look around the village. No men in sight. Just women and children. The council lodge was deserted. Curious, she approached it just closely enough to peer within. She sneaked a look back at Maximilian and his men to see that their attention was otherwise occupied outside, and she circled around to the rear of the lodge. Opening the flap of the rear entrance, she stepped in and immediately saw Tarzan bound to the pole, struggling with his bonds.

Ruth hesitated but a moment before making her decision. She moved to him and began to undo his bonds.

The ape man looked back to see her at work and whispered, "What are you doing?"

"It seems I am now your guardian angel," she whispered back.

Feeling his bonds loosened, Tarzan said, "Thank you."

"Hunter and his men said that they will kill every Waziri who comes near the village. You must stop him. You must try to stop this war," Ruth whispered emphatically.

"I will do what I can," the ape man said. He looked around and added, "Leave quickly and quietly."

She did. And Tarzan replaced the thongs that had bound him so that, for the moment, he appeared to be still tied in place.

The battle, still a long way from the Urulu village, raged on. At least a hundred warriors thrashed away at each other. The rushing charge of the Urulu had been met with a fierce onslaught from the Waziri, and the opposing forces had fragmented into knots of combatants brutally engaging each other. Some fought in clusters of four or five, fending off opponents with spear and shield. Many clusters broke into individual hand-to-hand combat, some with flailing daggers and some thrashing on the ground with only fists.

Fierce battle cries mingled with shouts of pain. Fast, strong ebony warriors swung sinewy arms right and left, feinting and striking, fists pounding and spear points slashing. Arrows flew from archers who had managed to conceal themselves behind trees or rocks to pick off individual opponents in the fray, only to be taken out by enemy archers, themselves ensconced nearby. Individual warriors, separated from the combat, pursued their enemy into the deeper jungle undergrowth or the concealment of huge trees, or they sneaked up on enemy archers to take them out with spears or knives.

Downed warriors began to litter the ground, some writhing in pain, some bloody and lifeless.

The Urulu fought angrily and proudly, but more Urulu fell than Waziri, and at length, though only gradually, the Waziri began to encroach further into Urulu territory, closer to the village.

Maximilian entered the lodge and set down his rifle, leaning it against the door post. He was followed by Wolfe. "It won't be long now," he said, approaching Tarzan in the center of the lodge. "We're waiting for the first word from the battle site. The way I see it, we'll know with the first warrior returning to this village. If he's Urulu, it means your precious Waziri have lost. If he's Waziri, we'll take him out, and every one that follows him."

Tarzan said to him, "If the Waziri do win, they will march into the village in triumph, not one by one. How do you intend to take them all on with just the four of you?"

Maximilian smiled his smirky grin. "We are hardly four, my ape friend. I have a little equalizer out there that will even the odds." He imitated the rat-a-tat sound of a machine gun. "I can mow down the whole tribe in seconds. Just like you and your precious Waziri mowed down my brother and his men."

With the cunning patience of his jungle breeding, Tarzan had been carefully watching every step these men took. He knew it would be foolhardy to try to take on four men with rifles and a submachine gun. But now they were split up. He needed to wait until they separated themselves from their weapons. Maximilian's rifle was already yards away in the entrance, and the man stood only a few feet from Tarzan. The jungle lord looked wordlessly at them, his expression bland, pretending to be still tightly bound.

It was only a matter of moments until the arrogant Wolfe, certain of the strength of the ape man's bonds, felt confident enough to lean his rifle down against the far wall. With a haughty smile, he took out a cigarette and lit up. Tarzan watched him, his movement revealing nothing. He wished Wolfe would remove his sheathed machete, too.

Wolfe sauntered up to the post, even closer than Maximilian stood, and stared contemptuously into the ape man's gray eyes. With a condescending snicker, he blew a cloud of smoke into Tarzan's face and said, "Ape man. Hah. It was you shot me in the arm, wasn't it?"

It was the last thing he ever said.

Quicker than the eye could follow, Tarzan's unfettered fists lashed out and slammed left and right into Wolfe's face. Wolfe sank to the floor. Maximilian immediately jumped the ape man, and the two of them wrestled fiercely. They fell to the dirt floor and rolled around, grappling, each trying to pommel the other when his arm was free.

The dazed Wolfe shook his head and saw Maximilian and Tarzan thrashing about. They were too close together and rolled too furiously for him to try to shoot one without hitting them both. He pulled out his machete and waited for an opportunity.

At one point, Tarzan slammed Maximilian twice, leaving him dazed. As Tarzan rose from the floor, his quick eye saw Wolfe's arm swing, and he jerked his head out of the way just as the machete blade landed *thunk* in the wood of a nearby support pole, lodging halfway in.

Tarzan instantly lunged for Wolfe, now disarmed, and grabbed him by the throat and shook him fiercely.

Meanwhile, Maximilian staggered up and reached for his rifle, but Tarzan flung Wolfe like a rag doll at him. The two mercenaries tumbled across the floor, though Maximilian again recovered quickly and got up. For a man in his forties, he was brawny and tenacious.

The ape man reckoned he would have to try a different tack. He leaped up to grasp one of the sturdy ceiling cross-poles that stretched above him. He swung out and solidly kicked Maximilian back several feet. The ape man swung his legs back and forth on the beam to build a momentum and then, with simian dexterity true to his name, deftly leaped with one arm to grasp an adjacent ceiling beam, from which he could again kick Maximilian back and down.

Tarzan landed lightly on his feet to see that Wolfe had risen and was plowing toward him. Tarzan whirled and swatted the mercenary aside with a hard left backhand.

At that moment, Tarzan noticed that the doorway to the hut darkened as Bingham stepped into it from the courtyard, wondering at the commotion. Seeing what was happening, he raised his rifle. With lightning-quick reflexes that were second nature to him, Tarzan grabbed the groggy Wolfe and spun him around, putting the man between himself and Bingham, who fired at that same instant. Wolfe caught the bullet and slumped. Tarzan threw the limp body at the shooter, knocking him back, and then he rushed forward and wrenched the rifle away from Bingham.

Stepping away from the doorway and back into the lodge, Tarzan leveled the weapon at Bingham and ordered him to remove the belt with his hunting knife and throw it aside. After the belt was cast off, he motioned to the man to stand up. Bingham began to rise slowly, too slowly for Tarzan, who did not want to take his eyes off Maximilian farther back in the room. Bingham made his move for his knife. Tarzan saw it and swung back around. Bingham quickly grabbed the rifle barrel to force it away. Tarzan struggled with his grip for a moment, then yanked the barrel away and shot his opponent point blank in the chest.

Maximilian, seeing the ape man momentarily distracted, rushed to leap upon him, trying to take him down. Tarzan lost his grip on the rifle in his effort to fend off his attacker's thrashing arms. They rolled to the ground as the mercenary went for the ape man's throat.

Hayes had remained in position many yards away beyond the ceremonial fire pit, near the edge of the village. He had situated himself behind one of several large gnarled trees in the village central grounds, watching and waiting for signs of approaching Waziri.

When he heard the report of Bingham's rifle, he left his post to run to the lodge, Thompson submachine gun in hand. As he passed one of the great trees between him and the lodge entrance, a hand reached out to grab his weapon and attempted to wrest it free from him with both hands. It was Walter Adamson. Hayes yanked the weapon back from his grip, but Adamson grabbed frantically at the barrel again. Their hands both locked on the gun, and they struggled against each other, Hayes cursing the interference.

Stronger than Adamson, Hayes managed to pull the weapon down from shoulder height to waist height, when their wrestling with it turned it at an angle. The gun went off, echoing through the village. Walter Adamson loosened his grip and his face froze in a grimace of shock and pain. Hayes fired again, point blank into Adamson's stomach.

Adamson went limp. Hayes pushed the body away, letting it fall, and continued his run toward the council lodge.

He dashed around the fire pit and headed for the lodge, weaving left around one of the neighboring huts. As he rounded the corner, he heard a voice say, "That's far enough." He swung his Thompson into position to face this new adversary, but before he could fire it, a pistol discharged. Hayes clutched his chest and fell to the ground. Captain Reynolds stepped forward and stood over him, his revolver smoking.

Inside the council hut, Maximilian sunk his fingers, claw-like, deeper and deeper into the ape man's throat. Tarzan tugged at his opponent's arms, one with each hand, but could not completely force them away. Maximilian's eyes blazed with hatred as they stared into the ape man's. Red-faced, teeth clenched, bloody, he trembled with fury.

Tarzan, becoming desperate for breath, let go of Maximilian's arms and began furiously pounding both sides of his opponent's head. The sudden, painful blows were enough to make Maximilian release. Tarzan immediately batted the man's arms away and knocked him backward and off him.

Tarzan rose to his feet, but Maximilian recovered quickly and backed off. Finding himself very near the machete stuck in the pole, he went for it. He yanked it out and, with raw, animal fury, began flailing away at Tarzan. Tarzan backed away, deftly dodging swing after swing. He was nearly backed against the wall, within reach of one of the ceremonial shields the tribe hung there.

Between Maximilian's wild thrashings, he quickly seized the shield from the wall and thrust it out to block the next swipe. The machete connected time and again, and the wooden shield splintered into several shards but still protecting Tarzan from the blows. Holding onto one large jagged section, Tarzan powerfully swung it at Maximilian, knocking the machete to the ground. He tossed the shard aside.

The two men stood, facing off, in wrestlers' stances, staring at each other guardedly.

"You are defeated," Tarzan said. "Surrender while you can."

"I won't give you the satisfaction, you ape," Maximilian snarled, catching his breath.

"I am Tarzan, Lord of the Jungle, and you will die today."

Maximilian feinted to make a grab for the machete on the floor. Tarzan blocked him and landed a blow with his fist hard on Maximilian's jaw. Maximilian spun around and made a run for the rifle he had set down earlier. Tarzan grabbed him and they tumbled to the floor, writhing around in the dirt. Maximilian tried to land blows on Tarzan's head and neck, but the ape man blocked him again and again. They scrabbled brutally. As they locked arms, Maximilian heard a throaty growl like the one he thought he heard in the London alley.

Because Tarzan was shirtless and sweaty, Maximilian managed to wriggle out of his grip at one point and scramble to his feet. He thought he could make it to the doorway, but the ape man was too quick. In an instant, Tarzan's bulging arm encircled Maximilian's neck and trapped it, vise-like, in a headlock the way he had so often trapped the heads of ferocious big cats. Maximilian strained and groaned. His eyes glared with fire and awe at Tarzan's a few inches away, but then began to bulge with growing terror as the jungle lord's grip grew tighter.

The ape man's eyes narrowed and he said, through clenched teeth, "I have but one question for you. Do you have any more brothers?"

With a final mighty wrench, Maximilian's neck snapped. His writhing and flailing subsided, and he slumped lifeless to the earthen floor.

Bloodied and bruised, his arms aching and his head throbbing, Tarzan panted to catch his breath. He stood looking around at the dead adversaries and the disarray in the lodge. Then he looked up and tensed again, realizing that the battle was still raging.

He emerged from the doorway of the structure and, standing in the middle of the village grounds, looked and listened. He saw many of the village women and children crying. Some runners brought in wounded to be tended to. The din and cries of battle were closer. Less than a half mile away. Perhaps it was not too late.

How to undo all of this? How to stop the war?

He saw Reynolds approaching, holding his pistol. Beyond Reynolds, he saw the bodies of Adamson and Hayes.

Reynolds said, "Adamson is dead. Hayes killed him. Hayes is dead, too. What about the other three?"

"They're dead," said Tarzan. "They were going to kill the Waziri, then me."

"The war's still going on. What about that?"

Still panting, Tarzan said, "I've got to try to stop it. I'm going to take a chance. Did your men find the bones where I described?"

"Yes. We have them," said Reynolds.

"Good. Muster as many of your men and medical supplies as you can and help the tribal healers treat the wounded. They will be swamped."

Tarzan turned and rushed back into the lodge. He picked up the lifeless body of Maximilian, flung it over his shoulder, and ran out. He headed for a thicket of trees in the direction of the sounds of battle. With the body of Maximilian slung over his shoulder like a hunting carcass, he seized the strong lower limbs of a jungle giant, lifted himself up, and worked his way from one limb to the next, in the direction of the battle.

He soon arrived at a point where he could look down upon the raging combat from one of the giant trees. Below him, weapons flailed and bodies locked in fierce hand-to-hand combat. The yells of the charging warriors mixed with the cries of the wounded. Both sides had suffered losses, as evidenced by the many fallen bodies littering the sidelines, some lifeless and some groaning in agony. The Waziri were clearly advancing, but the Urulu were putting up a valiant struggle.

Enough, the ape man thought. He stood upon a sturdy limb of the massive tree and stepped forward as far as he could with the weight of his burden. He raised the body of Maximilian over his head and held it aloft. From the ape man's throat there issued a throaty, primitive yell that sailed across the heads of the battling combatants. Some looked up.

He flung the carcass down from the tree. It landed with a thud amid a knot of feuding warriors, who immediately looked up. In an instant their gesture was followed by others nearby, and in a few moments' time most of the antagonists in the area had stopped, some in mid-blow, to see.

Tarzan shouted, "This is the man who is responsible for this war! He has betrayed you! All of you! He has set you against each other! He and his men killed the soldiers at the station, and they did it to sow fear and suspicion among you."

The warriors looked at the bloody, mangled corpse of Maximilian DeKelm that lay in the trampled grasses and then began to look at each other and mutter reactions to the ape man's words.

"He has told lies which made you believe you are each other's enemies," Tarzan continued. "You are not! You must not believe the lies he has spun! There has been enough bloodshed!"

Warriors looked at their opponents. Some glared. Some shook their heads in disbelief. Most looked to their chiefs.

"I have killed him! Let that be the last death today!"

This next moment would not be easy, Tarzan knew. It was not a simple matter to turn off the flood of emotions that had been stirred up by the fevered battle.

Tarzan saw M'Bala emerge from the foliage and step forward. The ape man looked at his old friend, who returned his gaze and then turned away, as if pondering. The proud chieftain raised himself up to his full height, lowered his shield, and issued the order for his men to cease. They stepped back and withdrew, though some still glared at their adversaries.

Mabuto advanced from the ranks of his men and issued a similar command to withdraw.

Tarzan dropped lightly from the tree limb and faced the two chieftains, who approached him with their lieutenants. He began to speak to them about Maximilian's treachery, about who he really had been, and why he had come here, and how he had stolen the bones and engineered some of the hostilities between their two tribes. The tribesmen, especially Mabuto, were slow to accept the idea that one man could be at the root of their hostilities, but Tarzan's reputation for integrity, and the evidence which he told them they would find in the Urulu village and environs, particularly in the testimony of Ruth Cheever, weighed heavily in his favor. Mabuto and M'Bala and their tribal elders withdrew to talk peace. Of course, there would have to be terms and negotiations and probably muttered discontent, but at least no more blood would be shed today.

Chapter 15
FAREWELLS

Walter Adamson was buried in a tribal burial ground adjacent to the Urulu village, a place of sacred honor. Members of both the Urulu and Waziri took time out from their own mourning rites to attend, standing assembled around the grave with Tarzan, Captain Reynolds, and the missionary workers. The wounded, recuperating Dajan was carried to the site at his request. It was a ceremony that crossed cultures, with Ruth Cheever leading "Amazing Grace" and the Urulu singing their mourning chant.

Over his grave, Ruth said, "Walter Adamson was a saint. He did the Lord's work his whole life—honorably, steadfastly, humbly. He was human and made errors in judgment. He was not able to look into the hearts of men, but which of us can? But he was the best kind of person. A good and kindly man. He was a true servant of God and a benefactor to his fellow man. We are all richer for having known him. I will miss him"—she sobbed—"and I will strive to be like him."

She attempted to sing "Farther Along," but found herself choking up too much to get past the first verse. She then moved to conclude with a recitation of The Lord's Prayer, joined by the missionaries and as many of the Urulu as could manage the words. After the "Amen," she dabbed a tear from her eye and took a breath to compose herself as the group began to disperse.

Captain Reynolds walked over to her, expressed his

condolences, and asked, "Will you be returning to America then, Miss Cheever?"

"Yes. I'm taking the boat at the end of the week."

"Does this mean you will abandon your missionary work here?"

"Hardly, Captain. I may return, but perhaps with a new mission."

"How's that?"

"Something you said, Captain. About these tribes needing medical supplies and attention and a hospital. That's what I'd like to pursue. I'm going to go back and get some medical training, and then consider a medical mission. I think I will try to get a hospital built."

"What about your religious missionary work?"

"I have not lost my faith," she said, looking down at the cross at the head of the grave for a moment, "but I have changed my idea of my mission in life. I do not think it is my role to tell people what to believe."

Reynolds put on his hat and said, "I'll have one of my men help you with your things."

She essayed a smile and said, "Good bye, Captain. I hope that next time we meet, no one is fighting."

"It is my sincerest wish, Miss Cheever."

She turned to face Tarzan, grasping his strong hands and gazing up into his gray eyes. "Thank you. I shall never forget you. I don't know how anyone who meets you ever can." The ape man smiled.

Ruth Cheever returned to her tent to finish packing and say goodbye to the children.

Captain William Reynolds returned to Point Station and began his "mopping up" duties, as he put it, hoping that perhaps tomorrow would be quiet.

Franklin Granger resolved to continue to dig for artifacts, convinced that the world was in need of as much scientific evidence as he could manage to find in his lifetime. He personally took the crated bones back to New York, accompanied at all times by no fewer than two of his young, able-bodied research assistants. He purchased a separate ticket for the crate in the airline seat next to him and never took his eyes off it during the entire journey, except to draft his letter of resignation from the university.

And Tarzan of the Apes, the golden African sunlight dappling his bronzed, muscled body as it passed through the leafy terraces, took to the trees and swung off into the deep jungle, far from the reach of man.

1938

*Tarzan the
Conqueror*

Chapter 1
RAID

Nights in the African jungle are never silent. The rustling in the trees and brush, the hoots and calls of nocturnal birds, the growls of predators, and the cries of their prey can produce a layered cacophony that fills the darkness and often challenges the sleep of even acclimated natives. Yet the guards in the Schwarzenstadt Detention Camp No. 1, though they were used to much quieter nights in their European homeland, felt that tonight was a quiet night in the camp.

The Schwarzenstadt camp occupied a space that had been hacked out of the jungle only months before, an installation that until recently had never been seen in this landscape. The perimeter of the camp was delineated by a tall barbed wire fence. In the center of the compound, in the middle of an open yard, stood a flagpole. From it fluttered a large red flag bearing a central white circle, inside of which was a black swastika.

Two guard towers, mounted on steel and wooden gridwork, rose above the fence, one on either side of the entrance gate. An additional pair of towers straddled the rear gate on the other side of the compound. The roofed platform atop each tower housed a machine gun manned by two gray-uniformed soldiers.

On the ground, uniformed sentries armed with rifles and sidearms walked their posts, back and forth, in measured steps. Every guard bore a red arm band with the same swastika symbol.

The camp consisted of a complex of buildings, some of wood and corrugated metal, surrounding a central courtyard. On one end stood the headquarters, the mess hall, and the officers' and soldiers' barracks. Not far from that cluster stood utility buildings and a garage which housed cargo trucks and maintenance vehicles. In front of the garage, facing the courtyard, sat a huge, military-green German tank.

Much of the rest of the camp's space was taken up by three enclosures, again fenced in by wire mesh and barbed wire. Locked inside two of these enclosures, more than a hundred African men and boys lay huddled and cramped on straw mats. Inside the third, at least fifty women and girls were penned up. Some prisoners were asleep, exhausted after a day of constructing buildings or tilling crops. Others dozed fitfully, their bellies rumbling from hunger because all they had had to eat that day was coarse, dry jerky and watery vegetable soup. Some stared vacantly at the night sky, longing for mates and children whom they had not seen in many weeks.

They could see virtually nothing in the darkness of the camp. The sliver of a moon cast only pale illumination, and the only other source of light was the lanterns in the guard towers many yards away or at widely-scattered intervals around the grounds.

All they and the guards could hear were the noises of the jungle. Even if they had strained their ears, they likely would not have heard the faint sounds of a party of fifty Waziri warriors, wearing animal pelts and armed with spears, bows and knives, creeping silently, skillfully, out of the jungle. These warriors paused at its edge, still concealed by trees and great fronds, only yards away from the camp's fence. With them stood one white man, Tarzan of the Apes, similarly armed with bow and knife and quiver of arrows and clothed in a loin cloth of animal skin.

M'Bala, chief of the Waziri, adorned in feathered regalia and tribal markings signifying his status, stepped forward and waved a pointed finger toward the left, and then to the right, signaling warriors to move off in each direction. Silently, efficiently, clusters of archers took up positions near each of the four guard towers, climbing trees under the concealing foliage of the encroaching jungle.

At the same moment, Tarzan scaled a sturdy tree with great agility and then leaped up to a branch to a position close to the top of a section of the fence. He removed a coil of rope from around his shoulder, set it down, and took out a specially-fitted arrow from his quiver. Fastened near its tip was a piece of stone of a particular weight. He attached one end of the rope to the feather end of this arrow and fitted it onto his great bow.

He paused to look around for the signal that the others were ready. At a pre-arranged moment, the archers in tree perches released their shafts. They whizzed upward, impaling the guards in the towers one by one in quick succession. None had a chance to fire his machine gun.

At the moment the tower guards met their silent deaths, Tarzan of the Apes took careful aim and released his arrow. It flew into the tree limbs overhanging the fence high above it. As he expected, the weight at the tip caused the shaft to arc downward much sooner than a typical arrow in flight. During its descent, the rope trailing behind it landed on a limb and thus caused the arrow to catch and wind several times around the limb, effectively anchoring the rope to it. The ape man shouldered his bow, grasped the rope with both hands, tested it, and then launched himself out from his perch and swung across the space above the perimeter fence to land, cat-like, onto the roof of a shed inside the fence.

He crouched low on the rooftop, looking around carefully at the yard below. A sentry approached from around the corner toward him. He drew his great hunting knife from its antelope-hide sheath and waited, tensed, until the sentry passed below. He leaped down to the ground and, with one quick thrust, plunged the blade into the guard's shoulder at the neckline. He hesitated not a moment to grab the slain guard's rifle and hurry over to the main gate where the Waziri party waited. He used the guard's bayonet to pry the lock on the gate and open it up to them.

The Waziri warriors rushed into the camp like a wave, splitting into three forks and heading toward their assigned tasks.

With the formidable advantage of surprise, they encountered little resistance. One group came upon a guard who was impaled with two spears so quickly that he did not know what hit him. A soldier returning from the latrine strolled around the corner toward his dormitory and was startled to find himself standing two feet away from a tall warrior in full battle regalia, his ebony skin glistening in the pale light. Before the soldier could cry out or turn to run, he, too, was silenced with swift death.

While the three waves of Waziri advanced, Tarzan, crouching and staying in the shadows, proceeded to his target. He made his way past two buildings toward the central compound where, from around the corner of the second building, he could see into the area that served as a courtyard and parade ground. It took but a moment to find what he was looking for—the huge tank.

"Halt! Wer bist du?" he heard from behind him. He turned slowly to see a guard hastily unslinging his rifle from his shoulder. *"Was machst du?"*

Tarzan's right side, the side on which his knife was sheathed, was turned toward the building. In the blink of an eye, before the guard could level his rifle, Tarzan drew the knife and powerfully hurled it underhand. It lodged in the guard's abdomen, having been forged with the balance for just such a throw. It did not kill him, but he curled up in pain and groaned, so that Tarzan had a moment to rush forward and knock him down with a roundhouse right to silence him. He retrieved his knife, sheathed it, and moved on to his target, leaving the guard to bleed to death.

Tarzan paused to wait in the shadows, eyeing the tank. By this time, some commotion had arisen in the camp as skirmishes occurred between the invaders and guards. A few guards or errant soldiers managed to utter a shout or two before being silenced by an arrow or well-thrown spear.

Tarzan saw one of the soldiers, alerted to the invasion, head

The soldier tried to fight back, but Tarzan slammed his head against the steel armor of the hatch and threw him aside.

for the tank. Tarzan shed his bow and quiver and waited. As the soldier opened the hatch of the tank, Tarzan headed for him at a run, reaching him before he could climb inside. He yanked the soldier's head up by his hair with his left hand and smashed him in the face with his right. The soldier tried to fight back, but Tarzan slammed his head against the steel armor of the hatch and threw him aside, then he quickly climbed into the tank.

It took him but a few moments to scan the instrument panel and recall the lesson he had received on his recent tour of an Royal Air Force installation. He turned to heft the twenty-pound explosive shell and load it into the chamber and then positioned himself to operate the turret gun. The tank roared to life, and the mighty turret turned. Looking through the targeting device, he set his sights on the main dormitory, which housed most of the soldiers as well as the camp offices. The tank's heavy gun blasted, and the building exploded in a huge fireball that lit up the entire camp. Had the ape man not been encased within the steel walls of the armored tank, he would have heard a chorus of cheers rise up from those imprisoned inside the fences.

At Tarzan's direction, the mighty turret rotated again and fired a blast at the secondary barracks housing the rest of the guards and officers. It, too, exploded in a wall of orange and black, sending flaming timbers cascading to the other buildings and across the yard.

Tarzan opened the tank's hatch and emerged from within in time to hear the second round of cheers that rose to fill the jungle night. He allowed himself a brief smile in acknowledgement.

"Tarzan!" shouted one of the Waziri. Tarzan looked to see him, a few yards away, holding up a hand grenade that he had taken from a guard. He tossed the grenade to Tarzan, who, standing atop the tank, caught it. After collecting his weapons, he unscrewed the cap, pulled the cord, and dropped it inside the tank, and then immediately leaped off and dashed away to a safe distance. He heard the subdued *whoomp* and saw the curl of smoke rise from the tank's interior, telling him that the gauges and controls were quite out of commission.

The Waziri promptly broke open the gates of the enclosures housing the prisoners, and the inmates rushed out, arms raised, cheers bursting from their throats. They charged around the crackling, flaming buildings and toward the central yard. The few remaining soldiers they encountered were quickly overwhelmed and dispatched.

Before long, the inmates stood assembled in the middle of the camp's central yard, smiling, catching their breath, exchanging grins with each other and with their liberators, savoring their new freedom. Around them lay the bodies of the Nazi captors and the charred or still-flaming debris of the concentration camp buildings. The blazing orange light illuminated the jubilation in their faces.

They filed out of the central courtyard and toward the main gate, flanked by Tarzan and the Waziri. As several women in a row passed Tarzan, he asked them each in turn, "Do you have a little daughter named Kima?"

Finally, one woman said, "Yes!"

He smiled. "She is waiting to see you." A cry of praise and gratitude arose from her throat. Nearly driven to tears, she hugged him.

"Come!" Tarzan said to them. "You all have families waiting to see you!"

They pulled down the Nazi flag and tossed it onto the fire. They picked up scattered rifles that had been dropped. From the bodies of the soldiers they removed holstered sidearms, ammunition belts, boots, coats, medals, knives and any other souvenirs they thought might be useful for the trek home or suitable as trophies.

Tarzan took a moment to rifle through the drawers in the commandant's office. Seeing several papers of particular interest, he took them along with him.

The smoke from the burning buildings and the stench from the bodies consumed by the pyre rose and permeated the night for many yards as the party of rescued and rescuers made their way out through the great gate and into the darkness of the African jungle.

At length, with the conflagration far behind them, they stopped to rest. Many took a moment to gaze up at the stars, incredibly bright and crisp in the clear night sky.

"Freedom!" one of the rescued men said. "It feels good." Others assented. M'Bala, proud of his victory, smiled his great toothy smile in gratification.

Yet despite the general mood of joy and triumph at the execution of this escape, Tarzan of the Apes knew that this would not be the end of it. As he looked again more closely at the contents of some of the papers from the office, including geological surveys, he knew this was just the beginning.

Chapter 2

PARLIAMENT

Nine months earlier, John Clayton, Lord Greystoke, had been paying more than usual attention to the debate in the House of Lords. In fact, he took a particular interest in the debate that day. He was listening to the halting, strained voice of the elderly Lord Milbourne, who had raised a topic that had apparently touched a nerve among the frock-coated, immaculately groomed British noblemen in the grand gilded chamber. Milbourne stood frail and hunched over at the speaker's podium, intoning, "My Lords, the world faces a peril greater than it has faced yet in this century. We are seeing the heart of the German people bent to the will of this Nazi party. We have seen a country transformed."

Mumbles and whispers began to circulate through the chamber as several members muttered disagreement.

Seemingly oblivious, Milbourne continued, "This new threat, this man called Hitler and his Nazi party, will bring a regime of terror and domination. We have already seen his annexation of Austria and the humiliation of thousands of Jews and other citizens. We must act. The world must act."

The chorus of mutters continued as a second speaker rose. "My Lords!" called Lord Marbury, a portly, elegantly dressed Peer, his ruddy face framed by great gray mutton chops. His more stentorian tones echoed through the chamber, reaching clearly to the tiered gallery: "We must think long and hard before angering the German people. We have been working hard to change Versailles' reprehensible, onerous strictures. Britain already has an agreement with them to let them rebuild Germany's navy."

The mutterings subsided.

"And, after all," Marbury continued, his eyes sweeping the audience of wealthy, privileged men, "this Hitler fellow can never really be a threat to England. Indeed, he is a potential ally against communism. The notion that we are imperiled is absurd. This business with Austria is merely a political…realignment…a matter of internal German politics…." He paused, to the accompaniment of mumbled assents and a number of "Hear, hears."

"If we interfere, we will risk the censure of the world community," he declaimed, "and suffer the indignity of tarnishing the reputation of the shining star that is our England!"

John Clayton was moved to do something he had hardly ever done. He rose to speak. After being recognized, he said, "My Lords, I must take exception."

"Who is this?" some Lords were heard to mutter. "Have you seen him speak before?"

Clayton continued, "I am appalled at the apparent approval which I hear in the chamber for what Lord Marbury has said. Surely the noble Lords can see the foolhardiness of doing nothing. We know that the Austrian people have been enslaved. We know that Hitler has turned his sights upon Czechoslovakia. People have been detained and imprisoned without cause, tortured and murdered. To deny this or pretend otherwise is blind ignorance."

A chorus of grumbles and harrumphs circulated through the perpendicular rows of red benches and mahogany desks. Heads wagged and turned to peers for confirmation.

"We must have allies," Clayton went on, "for only when we have allies are we truly strong. If we turn our backs on countries which need us, then they will surely turn their backs on us when we need them. We can only sit in silence so long while those in peril cry out before we ourselves become no better than their tormentors."

Pockets of whisperings and mutterings floated through the chamber.

"Who is he?" some said.

"Greystoke, you say?" one gray head asked.

"Barely know the fellow," another commented. "Hardly ever here."

"I hear he's got some connections in Africa," another mumbled to his colleague. "Seems to be down there quite a bit."

"Why doesn't he stay there? The presumption...."

Clayton continued over the swelling buzz of disapproval, "We cannot simply close the walls of our village and hide in our homes and think we are safe."

A few Lords waved for him to sit down. Clayton ended his remarks early as two other Lords rose to speak. The buzz escalated to shouts. He stepped down from the podium, gathered his papers, and strode out of the chamber, uncertain of whether there was even any point in returning the next day.

That evening, Clayton sat in the dining room on the second floor of the Bull and Feathers Public House and halfheartedly poked at the *foie gras* and steak tartare before him. It was not that he was displeased with the taste of the raw beef, and certainly not bored with the company of George Fredrickson, his longtime friend in the Ministry, who sat across from him at the table bedecked in silver and linen. He was still troubled by the events of the day. The jovial, ruddy-faced, balding Fredrickson dug rather more lustily into his platter of roast beef and large mound of potatoes and said, between bites, "So you just walked out? In the middle?"

"Yes," Clayton said. "I didn't think anything more would happen." He looked up absentmindedly, not focusing on the carved walls of dark oak or any of the small oil portraits and landscapes in gilt frames displayed around the elegant room. "I probably shouldn't have said something," he added. "It didn't accomplish anything."

"Well, you don't generally say much in session," Fredrickson said, munching. "Perhaps it's time you did. Someone's got to. Milbourne's in the minority."

"I'm not one for grandstanding."

"You?" Fredrickson said, arching his bushy eyebrows. "Never grandstand?"

"Well, yes, it's true that I will step forward and do what needs to be done, but only as necessary. Believe it or not, I don't always relish conflict." Fredrickson reacted with a bemused smile as Clayton continued, "Speaking of which, what is the government officially doing about this growing Nazi threat?"

Fredrickson's expression turned more grim. "Nothing yet. We're taking it up at the Cabinet meeting next week."

"Next week? And then what do you think will be decided?"

"Can't say. Chamberlain is talking appeasement and nothing else. Evidently they're all just as cautious as your conservative colleagues in the House of Lords. Except for Churchill. But I can tell you that the military is at a heightened state of readiness. We believe they will be ready to scramble to nearly anywhere if called." Fredrickson took a sip of his pint and added, "Which reminds me, how did you enjoy your tour of the RAF base?"

"Very interesting," Clayton replied. "Thanks to your letter of introduction, they showed us all around. They showed us the weapons, the fighters, the bombers—I even got a lesson in how to operate a tank. They showed me how to start it up and even let me fire the cannon."

"Didn't blow anything up, did you?"

"Would I do that?" Clayton said, sipping his tea, and then added, "How's Jack?"

"He's fine. His doctorate studies are coming along splendidly. And I must thank you again for rescuing him two years ago. I am still in your debt. If there is anything I can do for you, you must not hesitate to call."

"Thank you. I hope I'll not need to call in that debt."

"When are you going back?"

"Next month. Not soon enough." Clayton twirled his fork absent-mindedly in the remnants of his beef and added, "Sometimes I think there's really nothing for me in London. I know few people, apart from your family, and don't care to know most of the ones I meet."

"I envy you. I'm stuck here with government problems all year. You can get away and escape all this."

"Yes," Clayton replied, almost as if thinking out loud. "It will be nice to go somewhere where world politics do not intrude."

Chapter 3
ALPINE MEETING

At about the same time as the debate in Parliament, a high-level gathering took place in a chateau nestled in the Bavarian Alps. During most of the morning, one sleek, elongated BMW touring car after another cruised up the winding road and pulled into the wide parking lot in front of the three-story edifice decorated with Bavarian timbers, shuttered windows, and carved balconies. Chauffeurs in military uniforms emerged from the front seats and stiffly opened the rear doors for the passengers.

Inside, a splendid table was set in the main dining hall. The high ceilings and walls were painted in soft beige tones, the arched entry ways edged with gold trim. A huge, sparkling chandelier hung from the center of the hall. At each of the dozen places rested a setting of fine china replete with polished silverware and crystal goblets.

All of the guests were men in uniform, most with splays of medals on their jackets, some with the Iron Cross, and all bearing distinctive red arm bands with a black swastika in a white circle. After removing their coats and milling about in polite banter, they began to file into the dining room and take their seats in the carved oak chairs. Most of them entered and sat down curtly, paying scant attention to the magnificent view outside the huge glass window where the sun glistened off Alpine peaks and dark swatches of pine trees broke up the sparkling whiteness.

One of the officers, Colonel Dieter Fuhrmann, making his first visit to the chateau, gaped at the ornate surroundings a bit more than the others as he took his seat. Fuhrmann was a career soldier in his late forties, six feet tall, still trim of figure, with a firm, angular jaw and slightly receding hair line with just a hint of steely gray around the temples. Never having been at such a high-level meeting before, Fuhrmann was certain that this invitation represented nothing less than a significant step up for his career. Perhaps a new command lay at the end of the road that would begin today. Perhaps even a promotion.

Waiters in starched military uniforms, polished boots, and white gloves glided in unobtrusively through the gilded archway to pour Riesling into the wine goblets. Colonel Fuhrmann, with a wave of his hand, declined the wine and said, "*Haben sie bier?*"

"*Jawohl, mein Oberst,*" answered the waiter and left, to return promptly with a pilsner glass of sparkling lager.

The last one to enter was Heinrich Himmler, who took his place at the head of the table, a gesture which simultaneously brought the rumble of conversation nearly to a halt and signaled the staff to begin serving. Himmler was a small, diffident man with an oval face, wispy mustache, and rounded wire-rimmed spectacles. Apart from the uniform, he looked more like a humble bank clerk than the Nazi Reichsführer-SS and head of the Gestapo.

In almost orchestrated movements, waiters advanced bearing polished sliver trays laden with steaming plates of schnitzel with dill cream sauce, glazed carrots, and buttered spätzle sprinkled with minced parsley.

When the guests had all been served, Himmler rose and lifted his glass, and in turn all the other occupants of the table raised theirs. He toasted, in German, "Gentlemen, to our great effort! Heil Hitler." The toast was met with a chorus of "Heil Hitler!" and they all drank. "Enjoy your lunch," he said, sitting, and began to meticulously consume his.

Fuhrmann thought he was in paradise. Secret orders. This

magnificent chateau with its stunning view. Rubbing shoulders with some of the highest-ranking officers in the Third Reich. Truly this had to be the most significant day of his career. He savored every bite of the meal, every drop of the beer, and every word of the conversation.

When the dessert of Schwarzwalder Kirsch Torte was finished, the dishes were promptly cleared, coffee and cigars were served, and Himmler rose to address the table. "Gentlemen," he began to the silent, attentive group, "nothing said here today leaves this room."

The only notes taken at the meeting were taken by a gaunt, bespectacled clerk who sat at Himmler's left, scribbling in pencil on a yellow legal pad. He would later transcribe and type these notes into the only written record of the proceedings. He would submit a single copy of the typed minutes, together with his hand-written originals, to Himmler, and he would subsequently be shot.

"Some of you," the Reichsführer began, "know of our plans to control and regulate the population of undesirables in Europe, which we have termed The Final Solution. These plans are pro-ceeding apace, and the Führer is pleased with them." He spoke crisply, deliberately. "However, as we look ahead to the coming years, we foresee certain eventualities which are of concern to the Führer and the High Command. One of those is the need for re-sources to clothe and feed our troops and revenue to cover the growing costs of our army, our government, and indeed the growing costs of the work camps themselves, which will continue to drain our resources. It is imperative that we find new resources. And thus today I come to tell you of the new direction we are looking in."

He leaned forward on the table for effect.

"Africa."

He paused for a moment to let the concept sink in. Some of the officers mumbled or wondered aloud at the reason for ventur-ing so far south. Others were silent. Colonel Fuhrmann listened intently.

One general asked, "Are we going to eliminate the African people now as well as the Jews and the Gypsies?"

"That is not the purpose of the plan—though it would be all right with me if we did," Himmler answered. "The jungles and plains and mountains of Africa sit on thirty to forty percent of the world's resources. And their gold and silver and diamonds can provide riches beyond imagination. Hidden far from the armies of Europe. And it is all there essentially for the taking!"

His words were met with raised eyebrows and mumbles of assent around the table.

"Gentlemen, I have proposed, and the Führer has agreed, to an African Initiative," Himmler went on. "Our geologists have predicted a likely place for a remarkably huge deposit of gold in the Bolongo River Basin. We'll build a camp. Several camps. Conscript the natives into a work force to mine it. We'll take control of the river and trade routes, and fund our glorious campaign against all non-Aryan scum and the scheming communists."

One of the men asked, "What about local resistance?"

Himmler smiled smugly. "That is part of the beauty of choosing Africa, my dear colonel. This basin is far from any of the European-held cities, deep in the jungle. I believe there is only one small British outpost, a place called Point Station. And the police in the local towns are a joke, easily bribed and easily cowed. Think of it—thousands of square miles inhabited by only primitive tribes. Genetically inferior blacks. They fight with spears, if they fight at all. Resistance? All that is necessary to overcome their resistance is that our men shoot straight. Do you think the soldiers of the SS-Verfügungstruppe can manage that?" He smiled, and they all dutifully chuckled in response.

Himmler nodded to an aide, who began to distribute manila envelopes to the seated officers. "And now, gentlemen, to the purpose of assembling you here today. Here are your various assignments and responsibilities. Guard these documents carefully. They are the only copies."

He waited a moment until the envelopes had been distributed, and then added, "And to be in charge of this operation, to supervise the construction of the camps and the mobilization of the local populations, the Führer has chosen…" he paused for emphasis… "Colonel Dieter Fuhrmann."

Fuhrmann's eyebrows popped up. No one was more surprised with this announcement than he was. "Me, sir?"

"Yes, Fuhrmann. The Führer has been impressed with your career and has a great deal of confidence in your ability to accomplish this mission. Your sealed orders are in the envelope in front of you. You will begin immediately. An office is being prepared for you in Berlin. You will co-ordinate with Major Schenker on camp design and with Colonel Keller to arrange for the transport of troops and materiel."

Fuhrmann looked at those two men, who smiled in obeisance.

Himmler continued, "You will make and execute plans for the detention and conscription of the locals as a work force for the construction of camps, for the cultivation of food crops, and for the mining of gold and other minerals." He paused, as if reflecting for a moment, in what Fuhrmann thought was a slight flair for the dramatic. The Reichsführer then looked over the entire table, let out a slight chuckle, and added, "The world thinks we have designs on Europe. Wait until they see how we exploit the wealth of ancient Africa to serve the glory of the Greater German Reich, eh?"

The officers around the table smiled and nodded. Many took sips from their glasses.

"And, Fuhrmann," Himmler continued, looking again at the colonel. "This is the assignment of a lifetime. Are you up to the challenge?"

Fuhrmann shifted his posture in his chair to bolt upright and said, "I will not let the Führer down!"

"See that you do not," Himmler said, looking down at his sheaf of papers.

Chapter 4

KIMA

No one has led a more unusual double life than Tarzan of the Apes. Born John Clayton, Lord Greystoke, Peer of the Realm and heir to a seat in the House of Lords, he was entitled (and some of his peers would argue, obligated) to spend his days in Parliament debating taxation and the state of the British economy and hobnobbing with the cream of London society, including ministers of government and even the king.

Yet he was also a creature of the land where he was born and raised, the darkest jungles of Africa. Indeed, it was there he preferred to be, wearing nothing but a loincloth of animal skin, hunting with knife and bow and consorting with primitive tribes who did the same.

His secret, if it could be called that, was known to only a few in London, such as his good friend George Fredrickson. It was the peculiar nature of the House of Lords, where members came and went as they pleased and whose votes and policy statements were merely advisory, that permitted this double life to continue.

In Africa, though he numbered the members of many tribes as his friends and allies, chiefly the Waziri, they knew little of his frock-coated title and cared less. In fact, had he told them about life in London, some would not have believed him. One of the few men in Africa who knew of his British connections was Captain William Reynolds, provost marshal of Point Station.

And so it happened that the same man who spoke out in the

tapestried and carved oak halls of Parliament could be found months later beside a small stream in the primeval regions of central Africa crouched down upon his haunches over the bloody carcass of a wart hog. This proper English Lord, who dined on *boeuf bourguignon* and sipped the finest Burgundy, was now engaged in stripping the flesh off the wart hog and devouring it warm and raw—and savoring every bite.

And he was content. More content than he had ever been in the noisy streets and stone edifices of London. He had slain his quarry with an arrow he had fashioned with his own hand. He had stalked the creature as it came to the stream to drink. He had patiently waited for the right moment...silently sighting down the arrow, knowing that he had but one shot, using instincts bred in him from a lifetime of similar moments. He was enjoying a solitude which he found far preferable to the company of most men, most of the time.

Yet he could hardly be said to be alone.

As he wiped his face of bloody juices, a racket arose in the trees above him. He looked up to see a band of at least a half dozen furry black monkeys leaping up and down on the branches and screeching and chittering in a great frenzy.

Tarzan called to them. Raised by great apes, he spoke the language of the primates—or rather, he was passably conversant with the gestures and vocalizations that they used to communicate with each other. When they heard his call and recognized the gestures he used, they stopped to look, curious. They sniffed. Some began to leap and swing about again, but one of them spoke to him. "Little girl ape! Little girl ape!"

Another began to screech and chant what Tarzan thought was the word for "Fire!"

Other monkeys chimed in, leaping and baring their teeth and shrieking. In the hubbub, Tarzan could not discern all that they said, but he was certain he heard at least one other say the equivalent of "Bang!" This was an utterance seldom heard from the primates. It meant that they had seen gunfire or explosions.

Tarzan gave the gesture and the word for "friend," indicating himself, and bade them come closer. Several alighted from the trees and approached him, cautiously.

He asked them what they had seen. They nodded and jabbered, yes, little girl ape. A child. He asked them how many. One. He asked about blood—injury—and they again jabbered yes. He asked them where. They pointed.

He said, "Show me," and they took off through the branches. Tarzan leaped up to follow them, and it was all he could do to keep up with their speed. Fortunately, they were so noisy as they traveled that he always knew where they were.

They had not gone far when the monkeys halted. Several leaped and swung back and forth among the same few limbs. Some retreated to the upper terraces. Several looked animatedly below to the ground. Tarzan, too, looked down and saw a small African girl seated on a boulder. She was crying. Her hair and garments were disheveled, and blood was caked on her arm.

The ape man alighted some distance from her and walked up to her slowly. In a dialect common to the region, he said, "Hello. What is your name?" She looked up at him wide-eyed, surprised that such a creature could speak her language.

"Kima," she said, hesitantly.

The ape man squatted down closer to her level and smiled. "How old are you?"

"Eight. How did you find me?"

Tarzan pointed up to the surrounding terraces of trees. "They saw you and they told me where you were." The little girl could see, poking through the leaves, two or three monkeys at a time looking down at them. Occasionally, one jumped up and chittered or gesticulated at them.

"Can you talk to them?"

"Yes, a little."

"Who are you?"

"My name is Tarzan."

"You are …a white man…?"

"Yes."

"I have never seen a white man before, except…." She looked down and her face wrinkled, and she began sobbing. "Except for them…the ones who took my mama." She looked up at Tarzan, her round eyes reddened and teary. "They were bad white men!"

"I will not hurt you." Tarzan seated himself on a rock next to her. He waited a moment while she began to dry her tears. "What happened in your village?"

"Men came. They made everyone in the village come with them, except some of the old ones. My people fought them, but it was no good. They had sticks of…of fire…."

"Guns? Spears that shoot flame?" Tarzan essayed. He was unsure whether she knew the word for firearms.

"Yes."

"What did they look like?"

"Tall. Brown hair. Not like ours. Not like yours."

"What did they wear?"

"They wore gray suits. Heavy belts. Heavy boots."

"Did they have any tribal markings?" This was Tarzan's way of asking in her language whether the soldiers bore any insignia.

"Yes. This." She picked up a stick from the ground and, seeking out a patch of dirt, proceeded to draw a circle and, within it, a distinctive series of lines.

A swastika.

"How did you escape?"

"My papa fought them. I think they killed him!" Tears welled in her eyes again, and she sobbed. "My mama told me to run away, run as fast as I could. So I did. I looked back to see and one of the men hit her. I think they took her away, too. I was so scared!" The terror in her wide, dark eyes was palpable.

Tarzan thought for a moment. "Would you like to go for a ride? In the trees?"

"With you?"

"Yes. On my back. It will be like flying."

She smiled faintly, puzzled. "Where?"

"Back to your village. Show me the way. You must show me what happened."

"What if they are still there?"

"Then we will stay high in the trees and be safe from them."

"All right."

Tarzan hoisted her onto his broad back and said, "Hold on." With a running start, he leaped up onto the lower branch of a jungle giant, then leaped to a nearby branch and with great agility proceeded to smoothly swing from one limb to another, his muscles rippling as he glided. The little girl was thrilled. It was indeed almost like flying.

As they coursed through the middle terraces, little Kima found the ride such a diversion that she momentarily forgot her grief and apprehension. In all her life she had never seen a man swing through the trees like a monkey.

At length they neared her village, where the available tree branches thinned out because the area had been cleared over time, and the ape man was compelled to drop to the ground and proceed on foot. Little Kima insisted on holding his hand as they approached the village entrance

What Tarzan saw next saddened him. Most of the village was a shambles. Many huts had been burned and were now only charred remains. Others had been stove in. Fragments of timbers and grasses and mud from their walls and roofs were scattered across the grounds. Signs of a struggle were rampant. Splintered benches and tables, broken pottery, strewn clothing and other possessions littered the area.

More poignantly, perhaps a dozen bodies lay around the central yard. Some had been burned in the fires. Others were slain warriors, who had evidently attempted to resist the invaders. Tarzan could tell from a cursory look at wounds caked with dried, darkened blood that some were marks of sharp blows and some were bullet wounds.

The village was eerily silent. It appeared deserted at first, but as Tarzan approached holding Kima's hand, clearly indicating that he was no threat to her, the hoary gray head of an old woman poked out from one of the few intact huts.

"Who are you?" she said, apprehensive.

"I am Tarzan of the Apes." He halted several paces in front of the hut's doorway.

"I am Koba. I have heard of you. I did not think you existed. I thought it was a story."

"I mean you no harm," he smiled. "Does this girl belong here?"

"Yes."

"What happened here?"

The old woman wheezed, her breathing clearly an effort, and haltingly told the same story Kima did of invasion and kidnapping, but with more detail. Uniformed soldiers had come with many guns and set fire to one hut after another. They took all the able-bodied men and women and most of the children. Some of the villagers ran away, but so far little Kima had been the only one to return.

Koba began to cry. "They took my son and his family. They left me behind, I think, because I was too old."

"There are signs of a battle," Tarzan asked. "Did the villagers resist?"

"Some did, but it was a waste. Those who resisted were struck down. They were no match for the fire and strength of this army."

During their conversation, several other heads poked out of doorways. The few other survivors of the attack gradually revealed themselves and came forward to see this tall, white stranger close at hand: a boy, a crippled old man, one wounded man, and three more withered grandmothers, one carrying a sleeping infant.

"This is what is left of our village, O Tarzan," said Koba.

One of the women said, "If you are indeed this Tarzan, Lord of the Jungle, you can find this army and kill them. You can bring my family back."

Tarzan shook his head. "I cannot fight an army by myself. But I can try to find out where they are. Perhaps there are ways to help. Can I leave the girl here? Are you able to care for her?"

"We have very little food. The nearest village is too far away to hazard a journey."

Tarzan took the afternoon to help repair one of their huts so that it would provide adequate shelter and then slew some game and gutted and butchered it for them. He helped minister to the wounded man and ascertained that he would recover. He told them that he had to move on, but he would try to send help soon. They thanked him.

As he turned to leave, Kima said to him, "Tarzan, can you find my mama?"

"I do not know. I will try."

Chapter 5
THE WAZIRI

Tarzan inspected the trail that led out of Kima's village. It was a simple matter to follow the path of dozens of people being herded through the jungle, and the ape man took to the trees and followed it.

He pursued his quarry for a few hours until darkness prevented further progress. He spent the night ensconced in the limbs of a jungle giant, and rose with the first light to renew his pursuit. The progress of this large group through the dense jungle, a group that included women and children, would undoubtedly have been slow, so that the ape man believed that he would soon catch up with them, even though they had had at least a day's head start.

And, indeed, not long after midday he encountered first the sounds and scents and then the sight of the kidnapped villagers trudging their way through undergrowth. He settled himself in a sturdy tree about thirty yards above them to observe and learn what he could.

A procession of at least fifty natives plodded along, two or three abreast. He saw that all the men, perhaps twenty or thirty, were bound with chains or rope. The women and children walking along with them were not bound, presumably because they were less likely to resist or run if the men could not.

Along both sides of the line of natives, driving them forward, were soldiers wearing camouflage uniforms and armed with rifles and submachine guns. Tarzan counted at least a dozen, all bearing red arm bands with swastikas. They were Nazis, as he had feared. They cursed the villagers to move faster, pushing and shoving any stragglers.

Tarzan considered his options. Clearly, the Nazis did not wish to simply kill the natives, or they would have done so already. He wanted to know where they were being taken and why. He knew that he could not take on this group of soldiers by himself, and he did not wish to try. It would help no one if he got himself killed in the attempt. And he did not want to risk the lives of the captured natives. He would need reinforcements.

It had been many months since Tarzan visited his longtime friends and allies, the Waziri tribe. He would go to them and see what they knew of this development. The ape man made note of the direction the party was heading in and then turned and stealthily left his perch without them realizing he had been watching.

He lighted out westward for nearly a day until he approached the Waziri territory. He followed his usual procedure of approaching their land in the open and giving voice to a particular greeting call, so that the sentries could see him and recognize him. Nothing seemed amiss as Tarzan approached and was welcomed into the Waziri village. He saw the familiar huts and cooking fires redolent of roasting meats and savory stews. He was welcomed with the usual smiles and greetings.

The village seemed as active as ever. Children played with sticks and balls in the central yard. Women were busy weaving and tending cooking fires and carrying baskets in and out of huts. Men and boys tended to their crafts of woodworking, weapons making, metal forging. He noticed that near their forges and work tables there seemed to be an unusually large number of newly-made spears and arrows stacked or lined up.

But it did not seem the same. The place was quiet, almost somber. There was no music—no thumb pianos, no drumming, no singing. It was the quietest he remembered it having ever been, except for the mourning period after the tribal war last year.

M'Bala, chief of the village, came forth when he heard of the ape man's arrival. "My friend!" he said, hand held out in greeting. He looked the same: slight paunch mostly concealed by leopard-skin pelt, elaborate headdress of feathers and bones, lion-tooth necklace, bracelets and anklets of hammered copper. But Tarzan could not help notice that his old friend was not his usual ebullient self. His manner was more somber. He broad grin was missing, though his "It is good to see you" sounded heartfelt.

The chief's hospitality was as cordial as always. Tarzan was bidden to sit at the tribal fire and given drink. M'Bala and the tribal elders joined him cross-legged around the blaze.

"You welcome me, but your village is quiet," Tarzan essayed. "Has something happened?"

"Indeed, my old friend, you come at a bad time. We have had a loss."

"What happened?"

"A hunting party of a dozen men and boys went out this morning. The drums said they were attacked by soldiers. White soldiers. They resisted, and apparently at least three were killed."

"And the rest? What happened to them?"

"Taken away," said Uba, the tribal healer. "And, Tarzan…one of the ones taken was Dajan."

Tarzan paused. He remembered the eager youth whom he had helped instruct in combat for the tournament at Khanja last year, and who had nearly died in the bloody tribal war with the Urulu. He would be about seventeen now. His father, a skilled metal-worker, had fashioned a great hunting knife for the ape-man. He had hoped to see this fine young man grow old.

"Which way did they go?"

"East," said M'Bala. "We do not know where yet. The drums say they are slavers. But they are unlike any slavers we have ever heard of."

"Why?"

"They are an army. They have uniforms. They fly a flag. My

friend, what army from the land of your people would want to come and wage war on us?"

The question gave the ape man pause. He recalled the debate in Parliament and the London newspaper articles and reports from Germany and Austria about Nazi aggression. "I know of only one," he said. "And I hope that is not their purpose, but I fear that it is. I came to tell you that I learned of another village that has been attacked, and nearly all their people have been taken into bondage. I have found them. I do not know if their captors are part of the same group that took your people, but I suspect that they are. Will you go look for them?"

"Yes. I take a party of twenty warriors," M'Bala said. "We leave at dawn. Will you come and help us?"

"Of course."

That night, for the first time that Tarzan could remember, there was no feasting in the Waziri village. The bulk of the afternoon and early evening was spent in preparing provisions for the search party and outfitting it with as many arrows and spears as could be made in the time allowed. Tarzan's hunting knife was honed and cleaned for him, and his quiver was stocked with as many new arrows as it could hold. The evening meal was modest, and the entire village retired early in deference to the search party's need for rest.

✠   ✠   ✠

They set out with the first light.

They traveled east in the hopes of picking up the trail of their hunting party and finding indications of where they had been overtaken. They arrived soon enough in the vicinity of where the hunting party had last been heard from. They found trails left by large numbers of men who made no attempt to conceal their tracks— men who, in their arrogance, felt that no one would follow them or that whoever did was no threat.

Farther along down the trail from the point where they picked it up, Tarzan and the Waziri trackers found indications that the party of slavers had apparently rendezvoused with a second group, probably a separate detachment bringing in captives from another village, and that they had then proceeded together to the southeast. Tarzan and the Waziri pursued the trail in that direction.

The search party walked briskly through the jungle, stopping only occasionally to talk and less often to rest. They made their way nearly in silence, their ears attuned, listening for indications of other parties, for predators, and, of course, for other drums that might guide their quest.

Drums were the medium of jungle communication, a way to convey messages from tribe to tribe in a language older than the oldest of jungle giants. Messages of announcement, of exaltation, of query, or of warning regularly floated on the wind, often picked up by one drummer in one tribe and passed on to the next, so that a message might be circulated over dozens or even hundreds of miles in a single day.

Foreign explorers and scientists visiting the Dark Continent heard drums often enough, but regarded them as no more than primitive rhythmic expressions and rarely suspected that the drum palpitations had any meaning, a secret which the natives were not particularly disposed to reveal.

Thus the Waziri had brought along several drums for this purpose. Tanga, their chief drummer, carried his own kurukutu-type drum, one well suited for this mission because its deep, resonant tones could travel long distances, yet it was still light enough to be carried slung upon his back.

They halted several times during the day to allow Tanga to pound out a message that they were searching for their tribesmen taken by slavers. The Waziri used the drums freely, even if they heard no responses, believing that the white captors would be oblivious to the message, but their captured fellow tribesmen, hearing the sounds of the pursuing party, would be heartened by the realization that their rescue might be near.

On the morning of the third day out, Tarzan stopped abruptly on the trail and raised his hand to gesture the rest to freeze. Off in the distance, just barely, they could hear shouting and the faint rumble of what sounded like machinery. "I will go and look," was all the ape man needed to say. He scaled a nearby tree until he reached the middle terrace and lithely swung from one branch to another so that he was out of sight in a moment.

He traveled toward the sounds. Before long, he could hear a great rumble and the movements and voices of many people. He moved in to seek a vantage point high in the closest tree he could without being detected, and spied down upon the scene below and in front of him.

A large section of the jungle had been cleared away. Tarzan saw a bulldozer in the distance pushing aside still more trees, diesel smoke belching from its stack. Chainsaws buzzed and roared as workers stripped off limbs and carved up the huge trunks into lumber suited to their purposes.

Buildings of wood and corrugated metal had been constructed, and others were being finished. Workers nailed shingles on the roofs of existing buildings, while carpenters hammered and sawed, erecting frameworks for additional ones. He saw trucks rumble back and forth with lumber, fencing and other materials. The trucks and the chain saws were operated by soldiers. Virtually all the rest of the labor was performed by perhaps a hundred men from various local tribes, at work unloading trucks, lifting lumber, pulling limbs, and shoveling dirt.

Tarzan saw uniformed guards standing everywhere, legs apart, holding rifles or Schmeisser MP-28/II submachine guns. They all bore the ubiquitous red arm band with the swastika. When a black worker apparently moved too slowly for one of the guards, the guard might push him or kick him in the rear, often accompanied by a loud curse. Tarzan saw one guard strike a woman with the butt of his rifle. One man a few feet away from her protested, and he, too, was struck by a nearby guard.

Tarzan scrutinized the garments of the captives as best he could from his distance, looking for tribal markings, but in vain. Most of them wore ragged, nondescript cloths pulled over their torsos, or in some cases, simple loin cloths. Many were shoeless.

He tried to scan for familiar faces. Most of the heads were turned downward or away, or simply too far for him to clearly discern their features. He could see that the workers were men and women, young and old. After several minutes of careful observation, he believed he recognized Dajan, a muscled youth working on one of the roofs.

He wondered what the purpose of this installation was. It was not exactly a fort, though it was surrounded by an imposing fence of chain link and barbed wire and was protected by four guard towers. He noticed barracks for quartering the soldiers and fenced-in compounds that seemed to be for housing prisoners. He noticed ground being tilled, apparently for the cultivation of crops.

And then he noticed a collection of drills and mining tools. What would they mine for?

The Lord of the Jungle beheld nothing less than a Nazi concentration camp and mining operation in the final stages of construction.

Tarzan returned to the Waziri to tell them what he had seen and that he had found a suitable vantage point for reconnaissance. He took three strong, able-bodied Waziri warriors back with him. The four of them scaled the mighty tree and nestled in the crooks of its great limbs to study this installation at length. They watched the camp for more than an hour, until darkness had nearly fallen and they had barely enough light to return to their encampment.

That night, around the bonfire in their camp, Tarzan, M'Bala, and the Waziri sub-chiefs planned the strategy that they would use to rescue their imprisoned comrades and liberate Schwarzenstadt.

After a considerable debate about the required size of the raiding party, they decided to send two messengers back to the Waziri village to fetch thirty more warriors, all of whom were eager to join the effort.

During the two days that it took for the additional men to arrive, every Waziri warrior had time to study the installation in detail. They all noted the layout of the buildings and the distances between them. They noted the guard towers and how they were manned. They watched the comings and goings of the soldiers and the inmates. They developed a sense of the daily routines.

It was not a pleasant sight to behold. The Africans were bound and pushed around like animals. Cruel beatings were frequent. On one occasion, Tarzan was perched in his lofty observation post with a Waziri named Batu and three others, when they witnessed one of the Nazis, apparently an officer, approach the work area where a detail of women hoed and weeded the garden area. From their position they could not hear what was being said, but they could see the officer summon one of the guards near the women, to exchange words with him. He then walked up to one of the women, apparently one he had had his eye on, and began to talk to her and stroke her. She pulled away. He ordered her to put down her implement and come with him. She protested, and he clasped his left hand on her arm and pulled her away. When she resisted, he drew his sidearm and placed it at her temple. He began to lead her off to a nearby storage building when one of the men working a few rows down shouted in protest and ran to stop the officer.

"That's my brother Tano!" Batu said, choking to hold his voice in a whisper.

"Silence!" Tarzan whispered in the Waziri tongue.

"The woman is his wife!" Batu said. Batu glared back at the ape man, but then turned his gaze to the scene below in time to see the officer fire point blank at Tano and drop him in his tracks. The woman screamed, and the officer continued to drag her into the building.

Tarzan clamped his hand upon Batu's mouth and glared at him. Batu shuddered. Sweat beaded upon his brow. It took every fiber of his being to resist the urge to fight Tarzan's silencing grip.

Tarzan ordered the four in the reconnaissance party to return to their encampment. When Batu, enraged, related what he had seen to M'Bala, the chief said, "You did the right thing by remaining silent."

"I could have saved him!"

"No. You would not have been able to save him. You would have revealed our presence and endangered the entire mission. And that would have helped nobody."

"I want them," Batu said through clenched teeth. "We must get them."

"We shall," said M'Bala.

When the reinforcements arrived, they were briefed about the plan, and final preparations were made.

Thus it was that Tarzan of the Apes and a Waziri war party came to raid and liberate Schwarzenstadt Detention Camp No. 1.

Chapter 6

DESTINATIONS

N ews of the destruction of the camp and the liberation of the deportees spread like the proverbial wildfire through the jungle, though the German High Command did not hear of it straight away because no Germans survived to send a message.

Eventually, scant details and conflicting reports worked their way north from Africa to Berlin, and Colonel Dieter Fuhrmann was incensed. He was summoned, predictably, to the office of Heinrich Himmler.

An aide ushered Fuhrmann into Himmler's spacious office, clicked his heels smartly, and turned to leave. Himmler was staring at some papers on his desk. Fuhrmann noted that, true to form, Himmler continued to stare down at the papers for several moments, almost as if he did not notice Fuhrmann's presence, though he was fully aware of the colonel having been shown in. Fuhrmann wondered whether this habit was simple rudeness or a deliberate calculation to make the visitor more ill at ease. If the latter, it certainly worked.

Fuhrmann stood on an Oriental rug that covered a portion of a well-buffed oak floor. He observed that the huge polished desk was immaculate, containing no stray papers or pens, not even a stray paper clip. The brass desk lamp, the ceramic ash tray, and the black telephone gleamed as if they had been polished that morning (which they probably had). A large portrait of Adolf Hitler in a massive gold frame hung on the wall, and the only vaguely personal item on Himmler's desk was another framed photo of Hitler, with Himmler, which sat propped up on one corner of the desk, this one a shot taken at the Nuremberg rally two years earlier, and autographed.

Himmler closed the file he was looking through and returned it to a drawer at his right. He removed his eyeglasses and cleaned them with a linen handkerchief. Then he said brusquely, "Sit down, Colonel."

Fuhrmann sat on the plush upholstered seat of a carved walnut chair.

"You've heard the report?"

"Yes, sir," Fuhrmann said.

"An entire camp installation was destroyed. I don't even have the details. Somehow it was blown up. What have you got to say for yourself?"

"As you said, sir, we have few details. I will find out what happened. This is entirely outrageous and unacceptable."

Himmler replaced his eyeglasses on his nose and stared at Fuhrmann. "I have two choices," he said in a low voice, his lips and teeth barely moving apart. "I can tell the Führer that you are incapable of this assignment, in which case God knows what will happen to your career, or you can give me your personal assurance that this was an isolated incident and that any doubts which my colleagues in the High Command might express about your competence are entirely unfounded."

Fuhrmann swallowed. "The latter, of course, sir. This incident will be thoroughly investigated and all necessary and appropriate measures will be taken."

Himmler leaned forward on his elbows. "Our plans for Africa must go forward. And the perpetrators of this raid must be crushed."

"Yes, sir."

"If that is to happen, you can no longer direct the operation from Berlin. I want you in Africa, personally supervising the entire campaign. Establish headquarters in Nyumba. Prepare to leave at once."

"Yes, sir."

Fuhrmann's new orders commissioned him to journey to central Africa to investigate what happened, to ascertain blame, and to seek retribution. He was further presented with an accelerated timetable for the construction of new camps and revised production quotas. He informed his chief aide, Lieutenant Wolfgang Schmidt, to begin packing immediately.

✠   ✠   ✠

At about the same time, Tarzan of the Apes sat in the office of Captain William Reynolds, provost marshal of Point Station, a compound situated deep in the Belgian Congo at one of the major ports along the Bolongo River. Reynolds, his longtime friend, leaned back in his wicker desk chair, his shirt collar open. Reynolds never felt the need to present a formal image to his old friend, and thus the coat of his navy blue uniform hung from the clothes tree in the corner. The ceiling fan whirled unsteadily, swirling up dust out of some of the irregular cracks in the well-worn wooden floor.

Reynolds pushed aside a sheaf of dog-eared reports and stacked them atop a pile of bulging manila folders next to the battered Remington typewriter, to make room for the pot of tea his sergeant had just delivered, it being too early in the day for scotch. He poured his friend a fresh cup and retrieved a rag to wipe out his own favorite and well-used mug and poured some into it as well.

Reynolds' brow was a bit furrowed this morning. Handing the cup to Tarzan, Reynolds said, "I like the way you and your Waziri friends always take action into your own hands first, then tell me about it afterwards. I do love those surprises."

Tarzan smiled and accepted the drink as well as the sarcasm. "You have been around here long enough to know how the tribes think. When they are threatened, they respond. And they have never felt that they had to report to you."

"But what about you, my friend? Weren't you rather in charge?"

"I helped them. Because they asked me to. Some of my friends were behind those fences."

Reynolds sighed. "Well, I'm afraid my duty compels me to report it, old boy. Nazi incursion. Geologic surveys. I at least need to tell Wellington."

"You do? You will go all the way to Nyumba?"

"Yes. I wouldn't mind a trip to Nyumba anyway. A pleasant boat ride down the river, a night or two at the hotel. Their bar actually serves Watney's Red Barrel. Want to come along? I expect Wellington will want to talk to you, too."

Tarzan agreed that it might be a pleasant diversion.

"It's settled, then. We'll leave tomorrow," Reynolds said, and then added, "It may be the last time I'll have an excuse to go to Nyumba. In a week or so I'll have my new phone."

"You'll have a telephone?"

"The line to the Nyumba substation will soon be completed. I'll be linked with the world without waiting for wires or mail delivery by boat. I'll even be able to phone in for a reservation at the hotel."

"So now you've arrived in the Twentieth Century," Tarzan smiled.

"Just barely," Reynolds sniffed. "I'm still waiting for the indoor plumbing!"

And such was the turn of events that led Captain William Reynolds and Tarzan of the Apes to pack and leave on the next riverboat at the same time that Colonel Dieter Fuhrmann made arrangements for himself and his aides to fly to Nyumba.

Chapter 7

NYUMBA

Reynolds and Tarzan arrived first.

Nyumba was a town of about three thousand permanent residents, though its population often swelled to twice that with travelers and visitors. Once a jungle way station before the Great War for safaris entering or emerging from the deep jungle, it had grown to the closest thing to a city for hundreds of square miles around.

The town lay on the far eastern end of the Bolongo River, a great blue highway that stretched many miles west from Nyumba, past Point Station and all the way west until it broke into several tributaries, one of which passed through the Waziri territory. Consequently its docks were bustling with activity during most daylight hours as several stately riverboats loaded and unloaded passengers and cargo, and dozens of smaller passenger craft, from fishing boats to rickety catamarans and canoes, vied for spaces at the wooden piers.

Among the town's lures were a well-traveled main street and many side streets lined with a diverse variety of shops and outdoor trading booths, purveying goods and services rarely found elsewhere in the jungle. It provided the only hospital in fifty miles and the only airstrip in a hundred. It boasted three hotels, only one of which could truly be called a fleabag, and four restaurants, two of which managed to serve up passable European cuisine. It also housed the office of Nigel Wellington, a lower-level British consulate, whom Tarzan and Reynolds had come to call upon.

Tarzan and Reynolds disembarked from the riverboat and strode down the painted gangplank amid the sputtering of old steam engines and the chatter of commands and greetings and shouts in so many languages that they made a veritable din. Carrying their valises, they proceeded across the dusty walkways (they could hardly be called streets) of the wharf area and several blocks down the main street until they reached the Hotel Nyumba.

The lobby of the three-story hotel was as eclectic as the town. Just inside the entranceway, a rather impressive stuffed lioness reared up on a pedestal, prompting admiring comments from many male guests and occasional gasps from female guests. African shields and spears decorated the walls, and guests strode across a Moroccan carpet. Yet European craftsmanship was clearly evident in the richly-carved mahogany registration desk.

To Reynolds' surprise, Tarzan was far from the only guest in a loincloth, a dashiki, or similar jungle garb. This crossroads town was a gathering place for all manner of visitors, and the hotel's clientele was a heterogeneous group, from African businessmen to Moroccan traders to Arab chieftains to Europeans on safari to the occasional visiting dignitary.

After checking in, Reynolds and Tarzan went to their room to freshen up. Reynolds tried his best to brush the dust off his blue uniform. Tarzan changed into khaki trousers and a tailored white shirt (from Savile Row, no less) and leather shoes. He combed his shock of black hair and the two of them, spruced up, ventured forth.

The office of Nigel Wellington, British Consul to the region, was located a few blocks down the street from the hotel, in an old brick building with a bit of lawn and a manicured brick pathway approaching the veranda, and—if one looked through squinted eyes—just enough detail, such as flag and plaque, to suggest the British colonial era.

They were ushered into Consul Wellington's office, a sparse room with a wooden floor and rather weathered wooden desk in the corner, facing the door at an angle. The walls were predictably decorated with a portrait of King George VI and various certificates of achievement and commendations Wellington had earned, mixed in with a few African artifacts.

The two visitors had met the paunchy, ruddy-faced Wellington a few times before. Introductory pleasantries were brief. Tea was offered, but declined. Tarzan wished to come to the point. He told Consul Wellington the tale of how he came to learn of the Nazi camp and its inhabitants, how they were treated, and how they were liberated.

The consul was not entirely impressed.

"You did what!?" he reacted. "You blew it up? You launched a hostile action against a sovereign state?"

Tarzan was a bit taken aback at this reaction. "Rescuing my allies and friends from imprisonment and slavery is not a hostile action. Putting them there is."

"My good man, since when do you have the authority to do that?"

"The Waziri did it. I merely helped them. They are not subject to your rule. It was an African solution to an African problem."

Wellington's manner became more intense. "But you are a British Peer and you led them."

Tarzan calmly but firmly said, "I was not wearing a British uniform or carrying a British flag. I was helping my friends. Had I not been there, they would have done the same thing. I like to think that my contribution saved a few African lives, but the results would have been essentially the same."

"But they're African, and you're not," protested Wellington. "Let them solve their problem if they want to."

Tarzan drew a breath and fixed his gaze upon the consul. "I was born and raised in this land, and I count the people here among my best friends. I have lived with them and fought at their side for years. The fact that I inherited a British title changes none of that. What would you have me do, anyway?"

"Well, report it to us first," Wellington answered.

"And then what would have happened?" Tarzan pressed.

The consul stammered a bit. "Well,...an investigation, of course...lodging an official protest with the higher levels of government, which would have determined the wisest course of action—"

"And meanwhile," Tarzan broke in, "months would go by, and more would die. Listen to yourself. A little girl, eight years old, looked me in the eye and asked me to find her mother, who had been taken away to face an almost certain death had we not intervened. I do not need any more justification than that. The question is, why do you?"

"But, dammit, man, you're a Lord of the Realm! You can't go leading commando raids!"

"Well, if you need more evidence," Tarzan said, handing the sheets of paper that he had confiscated from the camp commandant's desk over to Wellington, "look at these. Geological surveys. They think they have found gold in the Bolongo basin. That's why they're here. Our research is going to support their war effort."

Wellington took the sheets and scanned them. "Hmm. I'll have to get a ruling on this. But you took them from the desk of the camp you raided? So you have no legal right to these? This might prove embarrassing if I have to reveal their source to my superiors."

"Embarrassing!?" Tarzan scowled. "I came here to report an incursion by a foreign power which I thought our government might want to know about. And you seem to be turning it into an attack upon me. I don't know that I care to be a Lord of the Realm if this is the way my country reacts to kidnapping and slavery and torture. I've a mind to just give back my Peerage and live here, thank you very much."

"No need to get excited," Wellington said, raising his hand. "What exactly do you want me or Britain—which, I reiterate, is also your country— to do?"

"Do?" Tarzan replied, somewhat wide-eyed. "The list is endless. Alert the world to the Nazi incursion into Africa. Wake up the sluggish British leadership to the kind of conquerors these men are. Seek alliances with other nations to combat this threat. How about ordering troops in to protect the native peoples which you have an economic as well as a colonial and humanitarian interest in protecting? Those surveys mean the Germans will be back."

Wellington, apparently unruffled at this diatribe, sat back in his chair and puffed on his pipe. "I can see how your actions are justified, from your point of view, at least. I'm just concerned about what my superiors will have problems with. All right, I'll look into it. It may be just the spark we need to start the move to put these Nazi ruffians in their place." He looked down to jot a few notes on his pad and then looked back up. "Are you staying in town?"

"Yes, at the hotel," Reynolds said, "before we head back tomorrow."

"Check with me before you leave and I'll tell you if I've heard anything more."

They left. Out on the street on the way to the hotel, Reynolds said, "Don't mince words, old boy. Tell him what you really think."

"Well, what should I have said?" Tarzan replied.

"The man is a dolt," Reynolds said.

Tarzan explained, "He got this appointment through political friends, of course. I suspect he wants to ride it out for another year until he can retire and get his pension. Meanwhile, we have another bureaucrat sitting on his hands doing nothing. He'll believe what the puppet police tell him, but he won't believe me. Doesn't want to stir anything up. It's the same kind of blind indifference I heard among those gray, overfed Lords in Parliament. They can always find a reason to do nothing. If it doesn't affect them personally, they can put off taking action forever. If these Nazis do try to take over, he'll be on the next plane out, and call it 'security precautions.'"

"Come on, let's have a drink in the bar. Then I'll treat you to supper."

Trying to lighten the mood, Tarzan said, "Do you suppose they serve wart hog?"

The bar and lounge in the hotel was a fairly large room opening off the lobby. Its walls were decorated with trophy heads of lion, rhinoceros and antelope and rimmed by African masks and spears gaily adorned with plumage, an extension of the lobby décor. Yet its furnishings were French Provincial chairs and tables, complemented with more Moroccan rugs, fringed ottomans, and beaded curtains. In a further effort to be multinational, it served everything from French champagne to Spanish sherry to English ale.

Reynolds and Tarzan ordered drinks and settled into chairs at a side table. Tarzan began to feel relaxed for the first time in quite a while. Reynolds was halfway through a tale from his university days as well as halfway through his glass of Watney's when, glancing through the entranceway into the adjoining lobby, he said, "Hello. What have we got here?"

Tarzan looked. Into the lobby strode a party of at least eight Nazi officers and attendant guards carrying luggage. Their bearing was tall and straight, and their gray uniforms, bedecked with brass bars and insignia, stood in stark contrast to the warm browns and yellows of the room.

Tarzan whispered, "Their boots are more polished than yours. I did not think that was possible in this jungle."

Colonel Dieter Fuhrmann stepped forward to the desk and slowly cast his eyes around the area as he removed his leather gloves finger by finger. He turned to the bespectacled clerk behind the desk and said, "*Sprichts du Deutsch?*"

The desk clerk gave a blank stare and a slight shake of the head.

Then he said, "But I suppose you speak English." The clerk nodded with a nervous smile.

"My name is Dieter Fuhrmann. *Colonel* Fuhrmann. You have reservations for me and my party."

While Fuhrmann registered, Tarzan and Reynolds were called

into the dining room for their dinner. They left the lounge area un-obtrusively, hoping not to attract the attention of the soldiers. At the dinner table, Reynolds was the first to voice the obvious question, "What do you think they are doing here?"

"Following up on the camp raid, of course," Tarzan answered. "I knew this was not over. I wish I could just stop them right here."

"They haven't done anything yet. We can't take any action."

"Well, at least we can try to find out what their plans are," said Tarzan.

"What are you suggesting?" asked Reynolds.

"I'm suggesting the time-honored technique of listening outside their window."

Fuhrmann and his men went upstairs to their rooms. As they had hoped, Tarzan and Reynolds managed to finish their dinners and get up to their room without encountering the soldiers coming down to the dining room.

They let time pass, and darkness enveloped the town.

From their second-floor room near the stairs, Tarzan and Reynolds could hear when the Germans returned to their rooms, which were on the third floor and on the opposite end of the building from theirs. Tarzan waited a few moments and then, still in his civilian clothes, opened the latticed door to the balcony.

"I don't think this is a good idea, old boy," muttered Reynolds.

"This is too good an opportunity," Tarzan answered. "I have to find out what I can." He stepped out onto the wooden balcony, which ran around the outside of the second floor of the building on three sides. He looked up to see the balcony of the third floor, which also ran around the building on three sides. In virtually a single movement, he climbed up onto his balcony railing, leaped up to grasp the railing of the third-story balcony above him, and lithely swung himself up and over, to land softly on the wooden floor of the third-story balcony. The planking creaked a little, but Tarzan proceeded with caution around the corner and worked his way toward the windows of the Nazis' rooms.

He paused outside each window in turn, his keenly developed sense of hearing straining to pick up strands of useful conversation. Though the walls of the hotel were thin and voices from the rooms could be heard in the corridor, the wooden doors were too heavy to allow conversations to be followed. Oddly, people said things next to windows that they would not say next to doors.

Outside the third window along, he heard the voice of Fuhrmann and his aide, Wolfgang Schmidt. Tarzan knew enough German to follow the thread. Fuhrmann's voice was agitated. "Spears! They took the camp with spears!" Tarzan heard him say.

"Not entirely," said Schmidt. "The tank cannon was fired at two buildings, and it blew them up."

"Yes, our own tank! More's the point! We had trained guards with machine guns and rifles. We are the German army! They advanced on the camp with nothing but knives and arrows and spears! How did they do it? And who leads such men?"

"Well, sir, on that matter, there is a story bandied about that the leader may have been a white man. The native bearers believe that some white god of the forest lives with the Waziri and makes them invincible."

Fuhrmann muttered some unintelligible response, but Tarzan could listen no longer, because at that point a Nazi guard with a rifle came around the corner of the balcony and saw him listening at the window. Before the guard could raise his rifle to fire, Tarzan clamped his hands on the balcony railing and swung his legs up and out so that his leather shoes slammed the guard hard on the nose, knocking him back and off the balcony to the street below.

Tarzan heard the footsteps of a second guard, summoned by the cry of the first one as he fell. Not wishing to be identified, the ape man leaped up to grasp a drain pipe from the roof overhang and swung nimbly up onto the roof. He scurried up the roof's gentle slope, reaching the peak about the time that the second guard arrived at his listening post. The guard quickly fired at the movement he thought he detected, but the ape man was over the peak

Fuhrmann's voice was agitated. "Spears!
They took the camp with spears!"

of the roof onto the other side before the bullets splintered the tiles.

"Up there! On the roof!" the guard yelled in German, apparently to another guard, and then added, "Go around to the other side!"

The roof was a hodgepodge of gables and angled slopes, the result of many additions to the hotel over the years. Tarzan nestled in a crevice between two intersecting planes of roof surface, hidden from the sight of the first guard. He saw that the second one, however, had moved around to the side of the building that afforded him a glimpse of his hiding place. He could not remain here, lest he be seen, or worse, lest they begin to scale the roof.

If he turned his head, he could just see that the second guard was being joined by a third man, whose rifle was lowered. Tarzan leaped over one of the gables next to him and scurried across the roof toward the far corner of the building.

They fired, but missed. One of the bullets chipped an exhaust chimney a foot away from the ape man. They were shooting at movement or noise, not aiming. So far, the darkness was his ally.

Tarzan noticed the grove of trees that bordered the hotel on one side, about fifteen feet from him. Between him and the nearest strong limbs stretched a flat plane of roof, which was easy enough to run across, but it was partially illuminated by lights drifting from the street, and thus might expose him to their fire.

He would have to chance a zigzag move. He sprinted from the cover of darkness to double back to the nearest gable. They heard the movement, and shouted, but could not see him to shoot.

He heard the footfalls of at least four men tromping around on the balcony, trying to find a vantage point from which to see him. He thought he heard the voice of Colonel Fuhrmann cursing and yelling, "Get up on the roof!"

One of the guards was being hoisted up on the shoulders of another and scrabbling to gain a handhold on the edge of the roof. In a moment he—and his rifle—would be up. Tarzan had no more time. He dashed to the cover of one of the chimneys and turned to see the guard just pulling himself up to the roof. Tarzan took off and ran across the remaining section of roof, palely illuminated for a moment. As he reached the edge of the roof and leaped for the closest overhanging limb, the guard fired three shots that whizzed near his head, tearing leaves and nicking branches.

Tarzan disappeared into the trees and the jungle night.

Colonel Fuhrmann witnessed most of this from his position on the balcony. Still peering over the roof and into the jungle after the ape man disappeared, he said, "Isn't that…one of the men we saw in the lounge today? Not the one with the uniform, but the other one?"

"I don't know, sir," Schmidt said. "Can't tell."

"Who would he be? What does he want with us?" Fuhrmann wondered.

"Another jungle mystery, sir. This is quite the mysterious place."

Irritated, Fuhrmann said, "The Third Reich does not deal in mysteries and jungle legends. It deals in realities. These mysteries have explanations. And I will find them."

Meanwhile, Captain Reynolds, believing that his jungle friend was in no immediate danger and would return in his own good time, sat on the chair next to his bed, removed his shoes, lit a cigar, and relaxed.

It was not long before there came a knock on the door. Reynolds opened the door to see an impeccably dressed Nazi accompanied by two guards.

"Good evening," he said in accented English. "I am Colonel Fuhrmann of ze Waffen SS!. And you are…?"

"Captain William Reynolds."

"British," Fuhrmann mused. "And vhat is your authority here, Captain?"

"Well, none in town," Reynolds answered. "I am provost arshal of Point Station. That's a port down the river from here."

Standing in the doorway, Fuhrmann looked around the room

within. Reynolds' navy blue coat lay folded across the back of the chair next to one of the two beds, and his valise lay open beside it. On the floor, next to the second bed, a mat had been laid out and a blanket arranged atop it. After a moment, he said, "Are you enjoying your stay, Captain?"

"Yes. A bit noisy. Why do you ask?"

"It seems ve had a prowler. Did you see anyone?"

"No. I heard the shots. Too dark to see anything."

"Yes, pity. And vhere is your friend?"

"Who?"

"The other man you are traveling vis. Vhere is he?"

"I do not know. He went out."

"Who is he? One of your men?"

"What is the purpose of this interrogation?" Reynolds asked, a bit of pique showing in his countenance.

Ignoring the question, Fuhrmann went on, "Are you here on some official business?"

"I don't see that that's any of your concern," Reynolds replied. "I do not answer to you. I take my commission from His Majesty the King."

Fuhrmann smiled unctuously. "Just…making conversation. Perhaps ve vill…meet again. Good night, Captain." He turned to leave and Reynolds closed the door.

Tarzan waited in the dark jungle for a prudent amount of time and then returned to his room through the balcony door. Predictably, Reynolds asked, "What have you been up to?"

"I've been for a walk. Nice night."

"You made enough noise," Reynolds replied. "Did you find out anything?"

"Not much. Not enough."

"Did they recognize you?"

"I don't think so."

"While you were gone, I had a visit from the Colonel. Fellow name of Fuhrmann. Pushy bloke. Pompous. Don't care for him."

Meanwhile, Fuhrmann was miffed at the steps he now needed to bother with. He had to explain to the local police, whose palms he had to cross with currency, that some of his men had been drinking and just took to shooting at pigeons and give assurances that it would never happen again. Then he made his way to the lobby, accompanied by Wolfgang Schmidt. He marched up to the desk clerk, who was casually enjoying a cigarette, and said firmly, in English, "I must see ze register book. Today's check-ins."

The clerk said, "I'm sorry, sir, I cannot show the hotel registry to just anyone. I must respect our guests' privacy."

"I am not just anyone," Fuhrmann said as he unsnapped the flap of his hand-tooled leather holster, pulled out the handsome, polished Luger pistol, and poked the barrel under the clerk's chin. "I am Colonel Dieter Fuhrmann of ze Army of ze Zhird Reich, and you vill let me see ze book now."

The clerk, his head pushed upward by the pressure of the gun barrel, but trying to look downward, trembled and began to perspire. "Yes, yes, of course." He clumsily pulled out the registry book and began to open it. "Here you are." Colonel Fuhrmann returned the Luger to its holster so that he could spin the book around and proceed to thumb through its pages with both hands.

"Here it is. John Clayton." He thought for a moment. He turned to Schmidt and ordered, "Get me everything you can on zis Clayton. At once."

Chapter 8
THE RIVER

Tarzan and Reynolds stopped by the consul's office the next morning, but it was a waste of time. Wellington was absent and had left word with his secretary to tell Tarzan that he would "get back" to him.

Their business concluded to the extent that it could be, Tarzan and Reynolds headed down to the docks for the journey back. They boarded the great *Congo Queen*, the largest of the boats that navigated the Bolongo River from Nyumba to points west.

Boarding with them that morning was a varied collection of mostly native travelers along with a scant assortment of European and Arab tradesmen and hunters. Among the crowd at the wharf were two uniformed Nazi soldiers. They stood waiting for some time next to the riverboat line's administrative building, watching the passengers who boarded, before they themselves moved forward and up the gangplank.

Meanwhile, Tarzan and Reynolds settled into deck chairs on the upper deck as the craft pulled out of the dock and commenced to glide down the broad river. The steam engine hissed and rumbled as smoke wafted out of the stack to dissipate into the verdure of the jungle. Reynolds unbuttoned and removed his coat, in deference to the heat of the day that he expected soon enough. Tarzan was dressed in tan field pants and a straw-colored shirt, short-sleeved, open at the collar.

It was not long before the noise and bustle of busy Nyumba

receded into the distance as they penetrated farther into the dense jungle. At times the river was curved and narrow, so that the boat encroached close to the shoreline and the foliage from towering trees formed a shady canopy nearly covering the river like a roof. At other points, when the river was wide and deep and the forest sparser, the sunlight bathed the boat and glistened off the calm waters whose gentle surface was broken only by a few rocks, half-sunken limbs, or the occasional alligator.

Tarzan, ever observant of his surroundings, scanned the crowd and noticed that the two Nazi soldiers had come up from the lower deck and seated themselves at the opposite end from him and Reynolds. The soldiers tried to sit unobtrusively and appear casual, pretending to read a newspaper, but Tarzan noticed that they spent a great deal of the time glancing up and around, especially forward in the direction of Tarzan and Reynolds.

Reynolds, too, spotted them and said, in a low voice to his friend, "Somehow I don't think they are taking a pleasure cruise for the view."

"They're watching us, though they are trying to make it look otherwise," Tarzan said.

"Or they could be on other business," Reynolds ventured. "They're just sitting there."

"If they are following us, do you want them to pursue us all the way to Point Station?" Tarzan asked.

"Well, no…," Reynolds essayed, "but we can't do anything about it, can we? We can't very well just go up and ask them if they're following us."

Tarzan replied, "There is one sure way to see whether they're following us. The first stop is coming up."

Soon the massive riverboat pulled in for a stop at the Bondu crossing, which was little more than a pier jutting out from an open landing at the edge of the jungle. A man and a woman waited at the pier to board.

Tarzan picked up his valise and the hide case that carried his bow and quiver and walked down the white painted stairwell to the lower deck. From the other end of the deck, Private Gustav Müller nudged Private Franz Hauptmann to point out that the tall, dapper white man was walking down the stairway. The two soldiers rose and stepped at a moderate pace toward the stairwell, not wishing to appear to rush.

As they reached the bottom of the stairway, they saw the man step off the boat onto the pier and proceed to stroll nonchalantly down one of the worn paths leading from the landing into the jungle.

Endeavoring to be discreet, they waited a moment, but making certain that they could still see him, before also leaving the boat.

The jungle grew dense with great trees and thick foliage rather soon after they left the river bank. Their quarry walked farther into it at a steady pace. The two soldiers proceeded into the jungle in the same direction as he, but they kept far enough behind to follow him without making it look as if they were. Their quarry never turned and looked back, so that, as far as they could tell, he did not suspect that he was being followed.

They soon reached an entanglement of broad leaves and brush as tall as their heads, and as they pushed their way through it, they realized that their quarry was out of sight. They stopped to look around—no sign, no sound. Where did he go?

"Split up," Hauptmann whispered and pointed. He veered off to the left while Müller headed to the right.

Looking from side to side, Hauptmann advanced cautiously through the dense undergrowth, trying to be careful not to snap a twig or otherwise signal his position.

Hauptmann thought he heard a slight movement behind a mass of huge fronds up ahead. He stopped to look. From behind tall blades of vibrant green and dusky yellow appeared a bronzed head with locks of black hair. In a moment the German focused and saw that it was staring at him with steely gray eyes and holding a drawn bow.

"*Warum folgen Sie mir?*" it said. It spoke German?

Hauptmann raised his rifle and fired a shot, but the figure had already veered to its left and vanished. Hauptmann whirled around, anxious. From out of nowhere the figure appeared again a few feet away, crouched, bow drawn. Hauptmann moved to level his rifle and fire, but took the arrow full in the stomach. He hunched over and fell. With his death throes, he squeezed off a shot harmlessly into the treetops.

Many yards away, Müller heard the shots and ran to their source. He saw his fallen companion and, alarmed, crouched down behind brush and scanned the area. He saw nothing.

Suddenly an arrow whizzed by him and landed at his feet a yard away. He looked up to see many yards away from him, vaguely, the head and torso of a man emerging from the foliage, but many feet above the ground, as if he were floating.

In the trees? Müller wondered. *How did he get there?*

He barely had an instant to leap behind the safety of a large fallen tree trunk before another arrow whizzed by and drove into the earth dangerously close to him. And then another. A hail of arrows rained on him, one after another, in rapid succession, driven into the ground on three sides. Müller could not believe that one man could fire a volley of arrows so fast. Would he never run out?

The private tried to gather his wits. He had seen where this assailant was. The archer had to take at least some time to re-nock each arrow. Müller had a repeating rifle. He could deal with this.

He readied his finger on the rifle trigger. Another arrow sailed by and thunked into the ground. He took a breath and instantly popped up from behind the log and pumped four, five, six shots into the trees where he had seen the strange figure.

Success? Müller could not tell. He heard no sound except the echo of his gunfire, and saw no movement except the breeze rustling the leaves and wafting away the acrid smoke from his barrel. He was overcome with anxiety at the eeriness he felt.

Suddenly, from behind, he was startled to hear, in German, "Put down your weapon."

He turned to look behind him. Standing ten feet away was what appeared to Müller to be a bronze giant, nearly naked, at least seven feet tall. Like a Colossus, the giant stood legs apart, rock solid, with flowing black hair, sunlight glistening off his incredibly large, taut muscles. The giant was drawing a bead on him with an enormous bow as tall as he was and fitted with an arrow that must have been three feet long, its steely tip leveled at Müller's heart.

The Nazi's mouth opened in a near-gasp. He froze for an instant, half turned around, his rifle pointed upward.

"Drop the weapon," the giant repeated.

In another instant, Müller's military training stirred in him. How could he be intimidated by a primitive man with a bow?

He made his move, thinking that he might be able to swing his weapon back up into position and quickly fire first.

He could not.

The arrow lodged deep in Müller's shoulder. He cried out in pain. The jungle giant dashed forward, seized his rifle, and with it he cracked the soldier across the jaw, so that he fell down, dazed. He thought he heard the giant figure say, "Remember what you saw."

Several miles down the river at the next stop, Tarzan met and re-boarded the *Congo Queen*, carrying his valise and the traveling case for his bow, which now also contained the rifles, identification cards, and a few other items he had taken from Müller and Hauptmann. He walked up to the upper deck and rejoined Reynolds, who was halfway through a glass of sherry. Seeing that his friend was now in his loincloth, Reynolds commented, "You got off the boat to change? They have a loo downstairs, you know."

Tarzan told Reynolds what had happened in the jungle, to which Reynolds reacted with chagrin. "You just took them out and left them there? You killed them?"

"I killed one who fired at me. I left the other injured, but alive."

"You might have killed him, too. What if some big cat gets him?"

"I did not make them go walking in the jungle. It's dangerous. They should have known better."

"Worse," Reynolds continued, "what if he manages to get back to Nyumba and tells that colonel?"

"In that case, it would be amusing to see his embarrassment as he tries to explain what happened," Tarzan replied with a glimmer of a smile.

"I don't know about this, old boy," Reynolds said, shaking his head. "You cannot fight your own private little war. For one thing, it will not remain little for very long. Who knows how many troops they can send here?"

"I did not seek this fight," Tarzan said. "You know me well enough to know that I do not seek any battles, but they find me nonetheless. This one I cannot ignore."

"So you're just going to take them on?"

"I will see what their next move is. I do not know what they are doing here or what their ultimate plans are, but I am quite certain that it does not bode well for my friends in the tribes. They will resist with every fiber of their being, and I share in their resolve. It would be comforting to know I could count on your help…?" He looked at his comrade, his eyebrow arched.

Reynolds took a slow breath and stared for a moment into the blue-green water churned up by the riverboat's prow and said, "My friend, you must realize that my capacity to act in situations like this is limited. My authority is only provisional. I am here mostly to regulate river traffic and cargo coming into Point Station. I am not the law here. Point Station is not a stronghold. My men have only rifles and sidearms. I cannot go taking on an army, and if I provoke an international incident, my government will yank me and my men quicker than a bad tooth." He looked at his friend, his expression more somber than Tarzan had recalled it ever being, and added, "This is a job for diplomats, and then maybe armies. Not us."

"Perhaps I know a diplomat who can provide us with an army," Tarzan mused.

✠   ✠   ✠

Days passed.

Colonel Fuhrmann commandeered the entire third floor of the Hotel Nyumba to house his staff and establish his headquarters. He appropriated the room with the most scenic view for his office and ordered the manager's carved oak desk brought up for his use.

He was proceeding with plans to order more telephone and telegraph lines to be installed and more troops to be shipped in when Wolfgang Schmidt walked in from the adjoining room, which had been converted to his anteroom. Though the thin, be-spectacled Schmidt, forty-one, with receding, wispy hair, had learned to become sensitive to his commander's temperaments, he was a bit surprised to find Fuhrmann in a reflective mood.

On his desk Fuhrmann held a small, hinged oblong case coated in black velvet, its edges lined with brass. He opened it to reveal a distinctive shiny medal attached to a ribbon of striped red, white and black. "Do you know what this is, Schmidt?" he said.

"Of course, sir. The Iron Cross."

"My father won this. In the war. He lost his life fighting for the fatherland, trying to make our homeland a better place for my family to live in. He won this Iron Cross for me, Schmidt. And I intend to honor his memory."

"Yes, sir," Schmidt said.

"Did you know the Führer plans to reinstate the medal to re-ward those who distinguish themselves in furthering the goals of the Reich?" Fuhrmann continued. "I intend to win this medal, Schmidt. This African initiative can be a glorious achievement for the Reich. You could win one, too. The Führer himself would per-sonally decorate us."

"That would indeed be an honor," said Schmidt.

He snapped the box closed and set it down. "Now, any sign of the missing man?" he asked.

"No, sir. He seems to have vanished."

"People don't just vanish," Fuhrmann said, with a note of condescension.

"Actually, sir, they do. People disappear in this land without a trace. Animal predators and such."

"And how is the one we found at the river bank—Müller, was it?"

"He's recovering, sir, but he seems delirious, probably from the fever. Keeps rambling on about being shot by some jungle god or giant. Claims he's ten feet tall—and white. He's spooking some of the men."

Fuhrmann frowned. "Tell the doctor to keep him isolated. When his fever breaks, we'll have to send him home, though I don't much care to send back anybody who's telling tales like that. Makes us look bad. I cannot afford to lose more men in this African campaign, or Himmler will replace me. And you. I need good news."

"I have something that may please you, sir." He set a manila folder on Fuhrmann's desk. "I think you'll find this interesting."

Fuhrmann looked. "What is it?"

"The dossier on John Clayton. Known in these parts as Tarzan of the Apes."

Fuhrmann opened the folder and began to peruse its contents, leafing through the first pages. "What's this? Born here? Raised in the wild?"

"Yes, sir. Expert hunter. Strong as a lion, agile as a chimpanzee. Speaks many languages. He can even talk to animals, they say. Altogether a remarkable character."

Fuhrmann leafed through more pages. "A British Peer of the Realm? Member of the House of Lords?"

"Yes, sir," Schmidt said. "By inheritance—his father was Lord Greystoke. And it appears that earlier this year he gave a speech in

Parliament denouncing German imperialism and calling for Britain to oppose the Führer's crusade."

"He gives speeches in Parliament and runs around the jungle, too?"

"Apparently some of the Lords think he is just a landowner with some kind of holdings in Africa which he goes to visit every year, and he evidently does little to dispel that notion."

"So this is our white god of the forest?" Fuhrmann studied the pages for a moment, stroking his chin. "This is the kind of man I want on my side."

"I don't think that'll ever happen, sir. If we run into him, we'd best kill him immediately."

"Oh, no," Fuhrmann said, looking straight up at Schmidt. "I don't want him killed. I want him broken. His role in frustrating our efforts has earned him a special place in my plans." He closed the folder and continued, "Provide his description to all of the men, and issue orders that he is not to be killed, but brought to me. The sooner the better. Is that clear?"

"*Jawohl, mein Oberst!*" Schmidt said, clicking his heels together and extending his right hand briskly, palm out, before turning on his heel to leave.

Chapter 9
GUERRILLAS AND APES

Dieter Fuhrmann wasted little time in re-establishing the Nazi presence in the region. He bolstered his troop level to more than two hundred. He ordered the construction of barracks near the edge of town to house the garrison assigned to Nyumba. Within a matter of weeks, soldiers in Nazi uniforms could be seen regularly strolling the streets of the town in twos and threes, laughing and talking loudly in their unfamiliar language. Though the locals gave them wide berth, arrogant soldiers often started altercations with them, fueled by the Bitburger and Pschorr Brau now available in the hotel bar.

The local African police, who were outnumbered (and outgunned), could do little and let minor incidents pass. They were bribed to look the other way at German indiscretions. More serious complaints or disturbances of the peace were referred to Fuhrmann, who invariably promised that he would "look into" the matter, but little else. Consequently, tensions arose.

Fuhrmann immediately set about to build another concentration camp, to be called Schwarzenstadt Number 2 and located to the northwest of Nyumba, unlike the first camp. He planned other changes, too. Fuhrmann reasoned that it had been a mistake to house the man in charge of the entire region in the camp itself. He decided that he would appoint a commandant of the camp to report to him, but that he should maintain his headquarters in Nyumba, which was, of course, not likely to be attacked in the manner that Schwarzenstadt Number 1 had been.

Raids on African villages were begun to provide manpower for the construction and operation of the camp. He first conducted raids within about a day's march of the camp, and subsequently branched outward.

✠   ✠   ✠

The Africans, too, wasted little time in planning counter measures. Upon learning of Tarzan's report, the four tribes who had had members imprisoned at Schwarzenstadt Number 1 sent delegations to an intertribal council held in the Waziri village.

When word of the council spread, they were soon joined by delegations from three more, making it an almost unprecedented gathering of tribes, some of whom had warred with each other in the past, but who now agreed to work together to combat this common enemy. As the bonfire burned on, a great many voices spoke. Disagreements about tactics and strategy went on into the night, but all agreed that the Nazis were a threat to the entire jungle and needed to be resisted on a massive scale.

An intelligence network was set up that would rival that of any army in the field.

Whenever the Nazis sent a work party or a raiding party out into the jungle, they were watched. Tribal spies knew the numbers of troops normally sent out on raiding parties and how they were armed. They knew their established routes and how far they could walk before wanting to rest.

Schwarzenstadt Number 2 was discovered and its progress noted on a daily basis. The spies knew the numbers of troops committed to it, its captive population, and its fortifications. The drums conveyed information to the other tribes between council meetings, which were held almost weekly. As a result of these meetings and the intelligence reports, the tribes began to form a realistic picture of how they might best and most effectively engage their enemy.

And then they began to strike.

Their first target was a detachment that captured a group of Chgala men and women from their village. Tribal spies knew that the Nazis had taken natives from this area before and knew what path they would take to march them to the river.

Only a few hours elapsed between the news of the capture of the Chgala and the mobilization of their rescue party, so that a detachment of warriors from four tribes, traveling with Tarzan through the jungle much more rapidly than the marching prisoners, was able to catch up with them before they reached the river.

The Nazi soldiers herded the Chgala along a barely-worn path that wound through undergrowth and massive trees draped with rope-like hanging vines. Unused to life in the primeval jungle, the soldiers, mostly new recruits in their teens and early twenties, did not ever feel the need to look up into the trees or vigilantly watch the underbrush. Thus they were oblivious to any unusual movements or warning signs of activity which they might have done well to heed. Instead, the uniformed Nazis passed the time along the trail thinking that this was just another routine maneuver, and they could not wait to get this march over with so they could return to the relative comfort of their barracks.

All that changed in an instant when they reached a particular point in the trail.

From out of the trees a volley of arrows sailed down and landed one after another in the ground near the soldiers' feet. The astonished soldiers looked up to see about a dozen black men—and one white man—swinging down from the trees on vines and clutching spears and knives. The instant they landed, the warriors surrounded the group and poised their spears, ready to throw. Off in the distance from both sides of the road, archers simultaneously emerged from the brush, bows drawn and aimed.

The white man, naked but for a loincloth, spoke: "You are surrounded. Drop your weapons."

Soldiers looked at each other. One said, "What? He speaks German?"

Tarzan said, "You are alive only because I say so. We could have killed you all, but we did not. Now drop your weapons."

He gave them a moment to gaze around at their situation and convince themselves that, yes, he spoke the truth. They dropped their weapons.

"Now take off your clothes," he said.

They looked at each other. Some said, "What?" Several began to respond, then apparently thought better of it.

"You heard me," the ape man repeated. He stepped forward to face the lieutenant in charge of the detachment. He drew his knife and sliced one shiny button from his coat, then another, and another, until it fell open. "Go on," he continued. "Drop them on the ground. Now."

The lieutenant nervously removed his coat, saying, "Do as he says."

"Boots, too," Tarzan said.

All the soldiers proceeded to remove their uniforms and cast them onto the ground, until they stood in their undershorts staring at the black tribesmen, who began to grin. The tribesmen proceeded to collect the clothing, breaking out in laughter and song as they gleefully tossed it all on a pile. The lieutenant in charge clenched his jaw as he watched, and a chorus of chuckles spread through the raiding party.

Barely restraining a smile, Tarzan stepped up to the lieutenant, his gray eyes penetrating, and said, "Go back to your colonel and tell him how easy it was to defeat you. Then go home. Get out of Africa. If you do not, you will die here."

The tribesmen gathered up all the uniforms and boots as well as the rifles, sidearms and insignia that the Nazi soldiers had worn so proudly moments before. They waited until the Nazi troops turned and began to walk back whence they had come. Unaccustomed as they were to walking in their stockinged feet upon the

The astonished soldiers looked up to see about a dozen black men—and one white man—swinging down from the trees on vines and clutching spears and knives.

uneven jungle floor that the natives trod upon their whole lives, they could only take a few steps at a time before crying "Ow, ow" at a protruding tree root or uneven dirt clump poking their feet.

Their discomfort was the source of much amusement to the Africans. Still laughing, they disappeared into the jungle with their bounty and the newly freed captives, leaving the Nazi soldiers to stumble their way back to Nyumba unarmed and unclothed, their fate at the mercy of the jungle and the wrath of Colonel Fuhrmann.

✠   ✠   ✠

The wrath of Colonel Fuhrmann was very much on the mind of Wolfgang Schmidt as well. In the succeeding days, another raid was made on an overnight camp the Nazis had set up en route to a targeted village. Schmidt did not look forward to the staff meeting where he had to deliver such bad news. He knew that Fuhrmann would be in no mood to hear of another setback, yet it was his duty to keep the colonel informed of all developments. This was the part about being the colonel's aide that he did not relish (though at least his position meant that he did not have to stand guard in some swampy, insect-infested jungle hell hole.)

Fuhrmann began the staff meeting by saying, "Tell me some good news."

"Uh, yes, sir," Schmidt began, addressing the half dozen uniformed men sitting around the conference table. "Construction is underway on our second camp, to the southeast. The fence is being finished even today, and will be ready for new inhabitants by the end of the week."

"At last?" Fuhrmann replied. "That is good news."

"But what shall we call it, sir?" one of the lieutenants asked. "We've already named Schwarzenstadt Number Two. We shouldn't really continue to call them the same name, should we?"

Wolfgang Schmidt said, "How about Dunkelberg?"

Fuhrmann's lip curled upward in a smirk. "Amusing. I like it."

Schmidt made a note of it. While he had the colonel in something of a good mood, he ventured to bring up the next item, which would, were the colonel in a darker mood, only serve to exacerbate it.

"We have a report of a field camp being attacked, sir."

"Attacked? By whom?"

"Well, that's just the thing, sir. Attacked by apes."

"Apes?"

"Yes, sir, great apes, gorillas, whatever they were. It seems they came charging in out of the blue and went wild, knocking over tents, throwing our men around, bashing heads in."

"I've never heard of such a thing."

"That's what's so puzzling, sir. Ordinarily, the great apes, despite their size, are shy and withdrawn, easily scared off, preferring to live far from any human settlements. It's almost as if…"

"As if what, Schmidt?"

"Well, sir, it's almost as if someone organized them, directed them."

"Impossible. Who could do that?"

"I don't know, sir. It's not like waging a campaign in Europe. Death comes out of nowhere in this jungle. It takes forms we never expected. It is hurting the men's morale."

"Bah! They are soldiers of the Third Reich, and they will do their duty! Increase the guards around every installation!" The spittle flew from his clenched teeth. "Be more vigilant!"

Chapter 10
RIVER RAID

Captain William Reynolds was also uncharacteristically in a dark mood after Tarzan, on his next visit, told him about the raids. Though all of the raids had been conducted far from Reynolds' jurisdiction, he was nevertheless uneasy about the reports he had been hearing.

Reynolds did not offer his friend the customary refreshment of any kind. He stood, stack of papers in hand, and addressed the ape man from across the room.

"Do you really think you and the tribesman can wage a war against the German army? They have tanks and trucks," Reynolds said, alternately looking at the ape man and at the reports he held.

"They cannot chase us with their tanks and trucks," Tarzan assured him. "The jungle is too thick. They blunder their way through like great water buffalo."

"Still they have superior firepower. They have rifles and machine guns."

"Yes, they are dangerous. But you see, this is not a battle of numbers, but of wits. We have the tactical advantage. They do not know the jungle. They are not schooled in jungle fighting techniques. They have been trained to fight in fields or trenches, as in the Great War. We can sneak up on them silently, but they cannot do the same. We can vanish into the thick of the jungle where they cannot find us, even if we are twenty feet from them."

Reynolds looked up at him. "But my God, man, you've declared war on them and they won't stop. How long can you keep this up?"

"You beg the question, my friend. If we intended to give up, we would not have begun this campaign at all. The die is cast. My tribal brothers will live free, or they will die. It is that simple."

Reynolds sat in his chair and tossed the stack of reports on the desk, so that they no longer distracted him and he could look Tarzan in the eye. "I admire your courage, old boy, but I don't care to go to your funeral. I still say they will continue to send fresh troops and eventually outnumber you."

"I have considered that, and that is where you can help."

"Me? How?"

"May I use your new phone?" Reynolds looked at the newly installed telephone on the corner of his desk. The tall, black cylinder stood on its pedestal, the black mouthpiece flaring out on top, the metal hook on the side cradling the cylindrical earpiece.

"My phone? You want to call somebody?"

"London. I have an idea."

Reynolds pursed his lips for a moment, then picked up the black flared earpiece with his left hand and spun the crank with his right. He connected with a voice and asked for the overseas operator. He paused to wait, looking at Tarzan and saying, "This takes a while." He reached one connection, asked for the next, and after waiting some moments, handed the receiver to Tarzan and pushed the pedestal toward him, saying, "Here you go, old boy. You've got the London operator. Give her the number."

Tarzan took the earpiece and spoke the number into the mouth-piece. After another wait, it connected, and he heard a familiar, though distorted, voice. He spoke, pausing for responses:

"George? This is John Clayton. Yes, I'm calling from Africa. I'm having a little trouble hearing you, too. By the way, thank you for arranging that tour of the military installation and the tank lesson. It came in handy. Do you remember when I helped rescue your son Jack, and you said if I ever needed anything, I should just ask? Well, my old friend, I'd like to take you up on that offer. It seems that we've got a bit of a situation down here. Let me tell you what we need…."

Reynolds listened to the request Tarzan made of his friend in London, and responded with a low whistle. When Tarzan finished the conversation and hung up the phone, Reynolds said, "Can he actually do that?"

"He isn't sure. He will try to find out and get back to me."

"What happens in the meantime?"

"We hold out."

✠   ✠   ✠

Two days later, in the middle of a sweltering afternoon, one of the larger river boats that plied the Bolongo, a cargo carrier, slowed to a stop at a landing along the river. Like several other stops on its route, this landing was hardly a port, little more than a wide path leading up to the shore. Roads diverged from it off into the jungle, where they soon became mere trails. Wooden pilings green with moss poked up from the waterline, old but sturdy barricades against which the massive boat came to rest.

When the engines shut off, a squad of Nazi soldiers, at least twenty, mustered out from the two decks and began to unload cargo: wooden crates, boxes and bags of food, camping supplies— and weapons. After an assemblage had been stacked on the river bank, they turned their attention to unloading the main cargo, a troop transport truck. A heavy steel ramp was extended from the cargo bay area down to the shore, and the truck was maneuvered up onto the ramp.

A half-dozen soldiers strained at the large mooring ropes on either side of the ramp, trying to hold the boat steady enough in the current to allow the large, khaki-colored truck to steer down it and onto the shore without drifting.

"*Pass auf! Langsam! Unveränderlich!*" shouted the captain in charge.

Privates Hans Bauer and Josef Ritter, their hands red and sore from their grip on the rope, had had enough of the captain's bellowing for one day. They *were* being careful. They were holding the ropes as steady as they could with a four-ton cargo truck lumbering down the ramp.

"*Schnell!*" the captain now yelled.

Make up your mind—fast or careful, Ritter thought as he waved the driver slowly backward down the ramp. *We're unloading a truck down a ramp. It's not that hard, if only you would let us do it.*

The bulky vehicle made its way down the steel ramp and came to rest a few yards in from the shoreline. The driver shut its engine off, and the soldiers proceeded to finish the rest of the unloading.

"That's only the beginning," Ritter muttered to his friend next to him. "Now we have to go God-knows-where in this heat, and…." He stopped. "Hans?"

Private Hans Bauer grasped his neck, winced in pain, and fell. Ritter, stunned, looked to his aid. He noticed a small thin shaft of wood like a long sliver, rimmed with delicate feathers, protruding from the flesh. In the moment it took the private to grasp what had happened to his comrade, the victim stiffened and then fell limp.

The hasty jungle training they had received before being shipped here did not mention anything about a Wahali blowgun dart, whose sting was lethal to a leopard at thirty yards.

"Captain!" Ritter cried, but his cry was cut off by an arrow that flew out of nowhere and lodged in his sternum.

"Ambush!" the captain shouted. "Take cover!"

A volley of arrows flew in unison at their position from three sides and landed nearly in a line not far from their feet.

The soldiers sought cover around the truck or behind rocks at the shore and leveled their weapons but realized that they could see no target to shoot at.

"You are surrounded! Drop your weapons!" a voice called, in German from the forest. "Surrender!"

The captain peered out into the wilderness bordering the river and saw nothing but jungle growth. He faced massive trees hung with clinging vines and layers of leaves and blades in multiple hues of green. But he could see no enemy.

He crouched in the silence for a moment, waiting for some bit of movement.

"Now!" the disembodied voice called again from, apparently, nowhere.

The soldiers looked ahead and around, tense, waiting for an order.

The captain thought he glimpsed a feathered headdress behind a large palm leaf about forty feet away. He quickly turned to the soldier nearest him, who held a submachine gun, and grabbed the weapon from him and sprayed a burst of fire in that direction.

Two tiny blowgun darts, launched from positions much closer to him than he imagined, caught him in the neck and leg. He winced, dropped the weapon, and fell.

The soldiers panicked and began firing their weapons. Their first volley was answered with a hail of deadly, well-aimed arrows that flew out from unseen archers, as if propelled by the leaves and branches themselves.

In addition to arrows and an occasional spear, the sharp crack of rifle fire burst forth from at least three positions in the jungle foliage.

"They have guns!" one private shouted, but it was the last thing he said.

Soldiers who sought cover on one side of the truck or the other found none; deadly missiles whizzed in from all sides. A few soldiers tried to trace the trajectories of arrows and pump bullets at their source, but apparently hit nothing. Their opponents moved like wraiths from position to position after firing, invisible in the thick overgrowth.

All who tried to climb into the back of the truck for protection were cut down.

Those who tried to run back to the boat did not make it.

In a minute, it was finished. The shouting, the rifle cracks, and the machine gun clatter were suddenly no more than faint echoes hovering in the air like the wisps of acrid gunpowder smoke.

Twenty African warriors emerged from the thick foliage and walked cautiously toward the landing, making certain that the bodies littering the ground were all still.

M'Bala, walking up with Tarzan, said, "Gather the weapons and the uniforms!" The warriors descended upon the fallen soldiers and began to briskly strip the corpses and seize their weapons.

"They should not have tried to resist," the ape man said.

"Perhaps," said M'Bala, "but now we have sent a stronger message than last time."

Tarzan walked over to the edge of the shore where he could be seen by the pilot and the mate, still in the wheelhouse of the boat. They held their hands in the air, and he realized that they were not Nazis but merely employees pressed into service. "Take your boat back," he called up to them. "Tell Colonel Fuhrmann that the more troops he sends, the more they will meet with death. Tell him that we say to leave Africa alone and go home!"

The ape man turned aside as one tribesman approached to show him an open wooden crate he had pulled from the back of the truck.

"What are these, Tarzan?" he asked.

"Mortars. The shells are in that box over there."

"Are they of use to us?"

The ape man arched his eyebrows. "Oh, yes."

M'Bala came up to him, his beaming face relishing the victory. "It seems we have a truck. Can you drive it, my friend?"

"I think so," Tarzan said.

"Then it may come in handy. Let's go for a ride!"

✠   ✠   ✠

Colonel Dieter Fuhrmann slammed his fist down on his green

felt desk blotter. "They slaughtered a squad! And they stole a truck!" he shouted. "What the hell do they want with a truck!? There are only six roads in the entire jungle besides the ones we had to build! They're just looting to spite us."

He plopped down in his carved, leather-backed chair and continued, "These raids are starting to annoy me, Schmidt. And especially that white man Clayton or Tartan or whatever they call him."

"Tarzan, sir," said Schmidt. "Do you wish to rescind your order that he be taken alive?"

"No, not yet. But I'm about ready to order every third captured raider publicly executed, as an example. It seems that in Europe we can take over Austria and never lose a man. But here..." his voice trailed off as he shook his head in disgust. "We cannot see them in the woods. And they know where we are and what we are doing almost as soon as we do. How do they do that?"

"We'll just need more men if we want to maintain our productivity, sir," Schmidt said.

Fuhrmann turned to him, his expression stern. "Don't you think I know that? But they're not going to send me any more. That's the real problem. I'm not getting the support from Berlin that I need."

"No more, sir?" Schmidt said.

Fuhrmann continued, "I've succeeded in getting fifty more troops sent here to man the new camps, but that's it. Berlin has said that they will not approve more unless I show more results. These raids have to stop."

He rose and walked to the window and stood, hands clasped behind him, staring out at the street below. "Typical bureaucrats. They describe their ideas in such glorious terms and have such grand plans, and then we hardly get moving before they want to cut back on budget and resources. How do they expect anything to get done? They don't understand that I am just getting started here, and that these things take time. We haven't even begun to look for gold or diamonds yet."

He turned from the window to walk back to his desk, still standing, and said, "So… how are the men reacting, Schmidt? Are they beginning to be disheartened by these setbacks?"

"Well, yes, sir," Schmidt hesitated. "Some are reluctant to go out on missions."

Fuhrmann toyed absent-mindedly with the brass paperweight on his desk, then looked up and said, "We need some victories. We will have to be more clever. Assemble the senior staff for a meeting at one o'clock."

Chapter 11
RETALIATION

After a series of raids, Tarzan and the native tribesmen had amassed a considerable cache of captured Nazi weapons, including two mortars, several submachine guns, hand grenades, many pistols, dozens of high-powered rifles, and plenty of ammunition. Since he had had some experience with firearms, Tarzan thought it would be useful to teach the tribesmen the rudiments of how to use them. He set up a series of lessons with delegations from various tribes to share with them what knowledge he had of how to load and fire these weapons.

The tribesmen proved willing pupils. Their facility with the European weapons grew quickly, which only strengthened their resolve to pursue their resistance efforts against the invaders who had provided them.

The riverboat raid, in particular, had emboldened them. Now they had a truck, and while it was true that only Tarzan knew how to drive it and they really had no idea what they were going to do with it, it nevertheless came to symbolize for many tribesmen the idea that they could take anything they wanted.

A certain newfound bravado crept into their talk. They were no longer content to simply target small raiding parties in the jungle. Many voices at council meetings began to call for a plan to attack and destroy one of the camps. Other voices, Tarzan included, disagreed, citing the danger and calling for patience. "It's our fight," some said. "This is how we want to pursue it. We can't let our people stay in these camps week after week when we know we can save them."

"We must be certain we can save them," Tarzan said. "We must be sure of ourselves and our plan. Conditions in the camps are bad, but the inmates will not be killed. These soldiers would not take them and build camps to house them if all they wanted to do was kill them. They need them alive to work."

Tensions were inflamed—and Tarzan's view was further challenged—when the drums brought word of an atrocity committed against the Wahali. A company of Nazi soldiers had raided a Wahali village and took over two dozen men and boys off to Schwarzenstadt, about two days' march away.

It seems that en route, a disturbance ensued, and some of the Wahali villagers rose up against their captors. The outburst was quickly put down, and the offending villagers were lined up and shot. Their bodies were left to rot in the brush while the rest were forced to march on.

The Wahali council members appealed to the tribal council for justice—to rescue the remaining tribesmen and avenge those killed. "They have not reached the camp yet. They are still out there as we speak," some said. "We know their route. They are using the same trail they have used for other raids."

Another added, "They have built a road to march along, and drive supplies along, to get to the camp. Soon they will be near it, and they will surely follow it."

"We could use the truck!" someone said. He described a spot along the trail which they all knew, where it would be possible to meet up with them when they reached it.

A plan was quickly formulated. M'Bala said to Tarzan, "It could work. But it will need you, my friend."

M'Bala perceived that the ape man had misgivings. Yet he acknowledged that it was important to respond promptly to the slaughter of the Wahali men. The Nazis would probably not expect the swift retaliation that they had in mind, and the tribesmen, to their credit, were taking a novel approach. With some reluctance, Tarzan consented to their plan.

Lieutenant Wilhelm Stammler slapped another mosquito as his sergeant and five other soldiers tramped and shuffled through the jungle, escorting the remaining dozen Wahali villagers, out of what had been once a party of twenty before their foolish attempt at resistance. Stammler knew that these Wahali would give him no more trouble now after their comrades' recalcitrance had been put down. In fact, shooting a few upstarts had worked so well that he thought he might recommend it as a regular part of the process of rounding up these primitive blacks. The Wahali, bound together with rope, required little goading from Stammler's men and shuffled along sullenly but steadily.

When the soldiers were not poking at the tribesmen to keep moving, they frequently looked up at the terraces of the trees and off toward the vegetation in the distance. The recently-hacked path that they followed would soon meet up with a wider road, which the weary soldiers welcomed.

When they reached the road, Stammler ordered them to halt and rest. The Wahali were a bit puzzled at the break, but sat to rest nonetheless. The soldiers paused to light up smokes, though remaining vigilant, never taking their eyes entirely off their charges and continuing to scan the surrounding jungle from time to time.

After a brief respite, Lieutenant Stammler ordered them up and said, "All right. We need this road in better shape! Let's start clearing this!" Though the Wahali did not understand his words, the soldiers made it clear that their job was to clear rocks and debris from the roadway.

The natives were puzzled. Road clearing? Is this what they had been captured for? They also noticed that the Nazis looked up and around at the trees and off into the nearby vegetation rather often.

But they followed their orders without comment, afraid to do otherwise.

Before long, the group was surprised to see a khaki cargo truck rumbling up toward them from the road ahead. The lieutenant and his sergeant looked at each other and turned to meet the vehicle. It was one of their cargo trucks, with a large canvas tarpaulin supported by metal bars over the cargo area and Nazi insignia emblazoned on the side.

The lieutenant walked up to greet the driver as the truck pulled to a stop. The driver was tall, rather bronzed in skin tone, wearing a brown soldier's uniform, and black hair poked out from under his helmet.

"We're here to pick up the prisoners," the driver said.

Stammler pulled out his Luger sidearm from its holster, leveled it at Tarzan behind the wheel, and said, "We know what you are here for. Get out slowly."

As if on cue, at least twenty Nazi soldiers emerged out of the brush from the bordering jungle. From every direction, Nazi rifle barrels bore down on the truck. Five guards cocked their rifles and surrounded the back of the truck in a semicircle. One shouted, "Come out slowly! Hands up!" Another carefully grabbed the canvas covering the cargo area of the truck and flipped it up and over, revealing ten armed ebony warriors huddled inside.

It was a trap.

Stammler said, "You took the bait, eh? We've been expecting you."

While this had been transpiring, the ape man's hand had been slowly moving toward the door handle. Now he quickly jerked the handle upward and forcibly swung the door open, knocking Stammler down.

He bolted out of the truck cab and made a run for it, but a soldier landed upon his back and tried to wrestle him down. Tarzan slammed his elbow into the man's midsection. When he loosened his grip, Tarzan hoisted the soldier up and heaved him off. Another man landed on top of him. "Alive!" he heard Stammler shout. He reached around with his left and pounded the second attacker's face until he let go and the ape man could break free, but he did not get very far. Three other soldiers chased him. Sharp blows on the head sent him tumbling to the ground. His head throbbed and his senses reeled in dizzying eddies. He thought he heard bursts of submachine gun fire and screams from the truck before he passed into oblivion.

Chapter 12

THE CAMP

Tarzan found himself a prisoner in a camp which he later learned had been named Schwarzenstadt No. 2. He did not know how he got here; it had been late at night and he had been unconscious.

Morning light began to spill over into the camp. He saw that he was chained in a line with about a dozen other men in one of two fenced-in holding areas similar to the ones in Schwarzenstadt No. 1. His knife was gone. Not long after he awoke, guards came in to unchain the prisoners and lead them out to a meager breakfast on long, crude tables in the mess area. Every move was watched hawk-like by a great many uniformed Nazi guards with rifles or machine guns.

Breakfast was a sort of gruel, insufficiently cooked and bland, served from a large kettle. Water was rationed with a gourd. When the men finished breakfast and began to file out as directed, a sergeant poked Tarzan with his rifle barrel and said, "You. Step aside."

He gestured for Tarzan to move over to a cluster of three other guards. The sergeant said, "Do you speak German? We know that you do." With curdling sarcasm, he continued, "We hope you had a pleasant sleep. Welcome to our camp. This is your number. Wear this at all times." He handed Tarzan a smock made out of scratchy cloth, which Tarzan put on over his head and shoulders. On the front and back were crudely written the number 720. All the inmates were wearing such numbered garments.

The sergeant continued, "You are alive because we have orders to keep you alive to serve the Reich. But you do not want to try anything. Guards watch your every move. If you try to escape, we will to shoot you. And if you encourage anyone else to try anything, we will shoot them. Clear?"

The ape man nodded slightly, his expression grim.

"Now get to work with the others."

There was a great deal of work for the inmates to do. The camp was in the final stages of construction, with several buildings already finished and in use, such as the office, troop dormitories, and storage buildings built of wood, a vehicle garage of corrugated sheet metal, and fenced-in areas where the prisoners were herded. Much of the work force seemed to involve the actual construction of the camp, which at this point included landscaping or finishing details on the existing buildings, such as painting.

Some fields had been carved out of the jungle and tilled and planted with crops, presumably for food or export, and other fields were being prepared and needed to be cleared of trees, rocks and choking vegetation. The work was done by hand, and implements such as shovels, hoes or machetes were carefully rationed. Few machines were available, apart from the commandant's car and the supply trucks that came and went.

The Lord of the Jungle had little choice but to perform the tasks as ordered.

He did not know most of the men in the camp. He recognized a few Urulu and Chgala that he did not know well. He searched the rows of faces in vain for any of the ones who had participated in the raids with him, but saw none. He tried to strike up conversations with several of the men when a passing moment presented itself, though opportunities to speak to fellow inmates were rare and strictly regulated. He tried several regional dialects. Most of the men either shook their heads no or looked the other way and said nothing. Perhaps they did not know, or perhaps they were too intimidated by the guards to risk any talk.

He was not the only white man in the camp. Several lighter-skinned men, possibly from Northern Africa, somehow had been sentenced here. In fact, one distinctly European-looking man was rumored to be a Nazi soldier himself. Some said he was being punished for attempting to steal supplies, a demonstration of the Nazi ruthlessness. Others were convinced that he was a planted spy, even more of a reason to be taciturn.

Tarzan's days consisted of labor in the fields, chiefly lifting and hauling felled tree limbs to the lumber saw or heaving rocks out of the way to clear space for a road or street or tilled row in the garden. The Nazis clearly took advantage of his strength to assign him a great many tasks involving lifting heavy objects such as limbs and lumber and rolls of fencing. He suspected that they were also attempting to ensure that he was quite tired at the end of the day and was thus less inclined to try escaping. To some degree, they succeeded, but he never ceased to think about escape.

This went on for weeks. Tarzan mentally kept track of each passing day.

At least two guards were assigned to the ape man at all times. They focused on him to the exclusion of the other activity in the camp, and they stood far enough apart so that he would never be able to make a move for one before the other could react to stop him. This struck Tarzan as a rather inefficient use of manpower, but he realized that they were trying to make a point to the other inmates.

Some of the guards apparently did not realize or remember that Tarzan knew some German, and thus when they conversed within earshot of the workers, he was able to learn many things. One of the things he learned was that there was at least one other camp in operation, called Dunkelberg. He wondered where it was and who was interned there. He wondered whether any Waziri were at the other camp.

New inmates arrived almost weekly. Tarzan endeavored to get close enough to them during meals or in the evening to learn something about what had been going on outside the camp. His ever-present guards, however, rarely allowed him more than a passing word.

He recognized at least three arrivals as ones who had participated in some of the raids with him—a Waziri and two Wahali. He was surprised that he had not seen more familiar faces arrive in the camp. Perhaps it meant that their guerilla raids were continuing successfully and few warriors had been captured. He tried to find out, but these men were usually on the other side of the compound or kept in separate areas, so that he rarely had a chance to even exchange glances with them. He believed that they recognized him.

As it turned out, his opportunity to talk with these men was cut short.

About a week after the three had arrived, they were assigned to a detail of men, including Tarzan, who had been put to work digging a rather large trench on the far end of one of the fields. As usual, Tarzan was not allowed to exchange words with them. They dug with shovels into the rootbound earth most of the morning, until they had created a hole at least six feet deep, three feet wide, and a good ten feet long. For what purpose such a trench might be needed, no one could guess.

The mystery was explained soon enough when the camp commandant and two aides pulled up in a vehicle. The commandant got out and spoke to the overseeing guard, who then called out six men, including the three Tarzan had recognized. These men were ordered—indeed, pushed—to line up at the edge of the trench, facing the hole. The rest of the workers were herded off to the side in a cluster, carefully watched by a semicircle of guards.

The commandant with his two aides, both armed with machine guns, stepped over to the six prisoners in line. He stood about six feet behind the first man and said, "You participated in the raid at the river." He took out his sidearm and aimed it straight at the back of the man's head. A tongue of yellow flame spat from the barrel, and a sharp crack echoed through the jungle. The black man's head recoiled, blood-spattered, and he crumpled at the knees and fell forward into the trench.

The commandant proceeded to the next man, to whom he made the same accusation and then shot him in the head. He went down the line and, one by one, accused each prisoner of participating in some raid, and then executed him. They all tumbled into the grave which they had just helped dig.

The bile rose in Tarzan's throat and his jaw clenched. The witnesses to this cold-blooded horror made no cry out, lest they be next.

Tarzan was certain that he did not recognize three of those victims as members of any raiding party, and he had been a part of them all. Was he wrong, or were the Nazis wrong? Had they just picked three men at random for show? And why did they not kill him, too?

When the commandant's car roared off, the remaining work detail was ordered to fill up the mass grave with dirt. The men worked grimly, stoically.

An old man next to Tarzan broke the silence to say, "Why didn't you do something?"

"What would you have me do?"

"You could stop them. You could save them."

"You wish me to commit suicide?"

"You two! Shut up!" a guard shouted.

They returned to work, silently.

Tarzan understood the impetus behind the old man's question, but he resented the implication that he alone was responsible for "doing something." Every day he gave consideration to what he could do, and how. There was little else to think about. Tarzan had decided that the only hope for saving these people—all of them— was to destroy the entire camp system. That would require more than just individual acts of rebellion, more than he could manage just now.

He could only hope that that was the wisest course.

One day the camp was being prepared for a visit. Much of the day was devoted to tidying up the grounds, apparently to make the camp look more finished and less like a work in progress. Many of the field workers, including Tarzan, were driven at a particularly back-breaking pace. Clearly it was important that they be seen doing a great deal of work. All the inmates suspected that the visitor must be some sort of dignitary, but through eavesdropping, Tarzan knew the visitor's identity before the others did.

It was Colonel Fuhrmann.

In mid-afternoon, a brown troop transport truck entered through the main gate and rumbled on up to the parade grounds, where it parked. Colonel Fuhrmann got out from the passenger side. From the rear emerged several SS guards, who grouped themselves in a formation around the colonel as he proceeded to the administrative office to be greeted by the commandant. They were too far away for Tarzan to hear what they were saying, but soon enough they all made their way past the camp buildings and out to the fields. All the field workers were ordered to stop working, to lay down their implements, and to stand at attention, as if they were soldiers at an inspection.

Today, five men pointed rifles at Tarzan while he stood. They had him covered, and he could not make a move.

With his party, Colonel Fuhrmann strode slowly along the first line of workers, his hands clasped behind him, his head moving slightly up and down, inspecting the men and their work. He walked up to the ape man and stood feet apart in virtually a swagger, and stared him in the eye. "So," he said in his accented English, "You are zhe ape man?" He spoke in low tones in a snakelike sneer, his mouth barely opening.

He looked slowly up and down at Tarzan's muscled but bruised body, caked with dirt and sweat, and muttered, "Not very impressive."

He again looked the ape man in the eye and said, "Ve haf an expression: *alles ist kaput*. Do you know vhat it means? Our soldiers said it at the end of the last var, vhen defeat was imminent and surrender vas our only option. After zhat, many German officers resolved that ve would never haf to say it again. Vell, now I tell it to you, Mr. Ape Man. Tell your ignorant black savage friends zhat *alles ist kaput*. Zheir puny little revolt is over. Zhey will all be rounded up and put into camps, just like you. Zhe only reason ve haf not gotten zhem all yet is zhat ve haf other priorities. But ve will soon find all your little villages, and all your rebellious friends vill be serving zhe Reich in camps like zhis one."

"You cannot enslave an entire race," Tarzan said. "Leopold tried."

"Oh?" A ghost of a smirk crossed Fuhrmann's face. "You haf no idea vhat ve can do. Ve *can* eliminate an entire race if ve choose. Leopold vas an ill-equipped barbarian compared to our Reich."

"What makes you think we will not escape?"

Fuhrmann smiled sardonically. "I know you better zhan you zhink you know yourself, my friend. You vill not make a stupid move, because you know zhat if you do, you vill die. And you do not vish to die. No, not you. Zhat vould be too easy."

Fuhrmann stood in close, very close, eye to eye with Tarzan. "You vant to stay alive in zhis camp, don't you? You vant to live to prove me wrong. Vis every fiber of your being you vant to resist my domination. And zhat is my greatest asset, you see. Because every day you live, every moment, you vill be serving zhe Reich. Delicious irony, don't you zhink?"

The ape man's expression remained stolid, and Fuhrmann moved along, chuckling to himself.

Chapter 13
LIBERATION AND LOSS

C onditions in the camp were bleak. The men and women worked all day from sunup to sundown or later. The guards shouted and cursed at them regularly, often prodding them with a gun barrel or striking them with the stock. The threat of punishment or even death for lethargy or recalcitrance — real or imagined—hung over them at all times, like a wraith.

Many of the men became sick from the poor sanitation and meager food, which was apt to be spoiled meat or rotten vegetables. Food was withheld as a punishment, yet inmates were chastised or beaten for sluggish performance when they were weak from hunger.

Tarzan was unlike the other men in this place. He had grown up with apes, and thus his diet had often consisted of grubs rooted out of the ground or insects scraped from under rotting logs. Indeed, some of the jungle fare he considered delicacies would make his European peers cringe. His palate was then perhaps less repulsed by the camp fare than those of his fellow inmates. But he hungered, too.

Most of the other detainees spent their days and nights bemoaning their fate, longing to get out, feeling sullen and abject that they could not. The ape man also yearned to be free, but years of jungle living had taught him extraordinary patience. He had long ago learned that even if he had to go hungry for days, sooner or later the right animal would cross his path at the right moment, and that when it did, he needed to be ready to react instantly.

It was no different in this place. Unlike most of his impatient fellow prisoners, he knew that he needed to bide his time, remain observant about his surroundings, and be ready to seize a moment when it came. And thus, as he passed the days toiling in the fields or in the yard or in transit, he appeared to be stolid and focused on the assigned work, yet he was ever vigilant, watching out of the corner of his eye, listening.

He learned the routines of the camp. He noted where guards usually stationed themselves. He observed what they tended to focus on and what sorts of things distracted them. Whenever he could, he studied the fences and gates, looking for weak spots, mentally measuring distances and calculating his odds.

And, indeed, when his opportunity did come, it would have passed in a moment had he not been alert and able to seize it. It happened simply enough, but quite unexpectedly, a series of events which could not have been foreseen but which provided just the momentary disruption in the routine that the ape man could seize upon.

A detail of about two dozen inmates, Tarzan among them, was toiling away in a newly tilled field on the far side of the camp. The heat was intense, and the work was back-breaking—chopping out stumps, pulling out roots, lifting rocks. Sweat rolled off everyone.

The cargo truck that had brought their gear to the work site sat parked a few yards from them at the end of the tilled rows, its front end facing them. A guard stood near it, rifle at the ready.

A dozen yards or so behind the parked truck stood the eastern gate of the camp. It was fashioned like the rest of the perimeter fence, of strong wire mesh framed with metal pipe and topped by rolls of barbed wire. This gate was guarded by one guard tower, which today was manned only by one guard instead of the usual two, since the second one, Tarzan had overheard, was ill.

About midafternoon, a rumble arose from the road outside the gate, and inmates and guards alike turned to see a supply truck approaching from the access road. One of the guards—not one immediately guarding Tarzan—walked to the gate to unlock it and converse with the driver. The supply truck was directed to back in to make unloading easier. It stopped a few yards inside the gate and not far behind the first truck, so that their back ends faced each other. Two uniformed German soldiers got out of the truck's cab, went around to the rear, and began unloading crates and a hand dolly.

Tarzan, like the other men, tried to sneak glances as best he could without incurring the wrath of the overseeing guards. He did not care what they were unloading, but he was keenly interested in the position of the second truck relative to the guard tower.

In four trips, the two soldiers from the truck wheeled their cargo boxes over to the supply garage south of the work area. After they had emptied the back of the truck, they proceeded to get back into the cab to leave, when one of the guards called to them. Tarzan's knowledge of German served him well enough to learn that the impatient driver was being told to go to the commandant and get receipts signed before leaving. The two got out of the cab and left to walk to the commandant's office with the paperwork.

The keys were in the ignition.

None of these details would have mattered were it not for what happened next.

As the two delivery men left the area, one of the men working in the field was overcome by the heat. Standing upright, he dropped his arms, letting his shovel fall, turned his head upward, and collapsed onto the ground. The man working next to him called out to the nearest guard and crouched down to help the stricken worker. The guard pushed the man away with his rifle butt and commanded him to stay back.

"He has heatstroke! He needs water! Help him!" the friend cried.

"Back to work!"

"He is my friend!" the man said, and angrily lunged at the guard. The guard cracked him across the jaw with the butt of his rifle, and when the man fell back, the workers erupted, shouting and raising their arms in protest.

One worker lunged forward at the nearest guard. The guard pushed him back, raised his rifle, and fired into his face, splattering gore out the back of his head.

Another prisoner leaped upon the back of the guard who had fired, but the other two guards rushed in to his aid, slamming heads and shoving prisoners away. A melee ensued. Two more shots were fired.

Tarzan knew his chance had arrived. In a moment the uproar would be brought under control, and then it would be too late. All of the guards in the field, including one guarding Tarzan, rushed to help their comrades and break up the scuffle. That left one remaining guard watching Tarzan, standing about ten feet from him, and he was also distracted by the uproar.

The ape man rushed this guard and slammed him in the face, grabbing his gun. He ran the short distance toward the second truck, the one that had been backed in. As he passed the first truck, he shot out the front tire on his side and then the rear one. He continued to run until he reached the cab of the second truck.

By the time the guard in the tower noticed him, he was shielded by the truck body, whose position was such that it concealed him and prevented a clean shot from the tower. He climbed in and started the engine. Depressing the clutch and shifting into gear, he picked up speed as the truck lurched toward the entrance. He crashed through the gate and drove on down the road into the jungle.

It happened so fast that the other guards scarcely had a moment to think. One and then another turned to hastily aim and fire at the departing truck, but then found themselves compelled to turn back and hold off the other inmates, lest any of them, too, made a move.

The guards cursed. Several of the captive men yelled and whooped at the joy of seeing someone escape, but became quickly subdued when the rifles and the glares of the guards were turned upon them.

Tarzan hardly looked back at the receding camp from the dusty, littered cab of the supply truck. He tried to work up as much speed as he could from the vehicle already battered from jungle use, though the twisting, uneven route required him to shift gears often. He rumbled for miles down the dirt road, the truck jerking and rattling as the tires bounced over bumps and in and out of the ruts in the road that the Nazis had crudely carved out of the wilderness to suit their needs.

They did not seem to be following him, though he felt certain that they would try. He realized that sooner or later he might encounter another vehicle on this road, and it could only be one bearing more soldiers. He did not want to risk running into that. He debated whether to abandon the truck and take to the trees or try to save the truck for possible use later. He was also unsure of where he was. He needed to risk a stop to get his bearings. He pulled over, shut off the engine, and climbed a tree to afford a broader view of his environs.

He saw that the sun was setting to his right, which meant that he was headed south. He surmised that this road would most likely have been constructed to link the camp with the river, since most of their supplies were shipped down the river from Nyumba. That meant that if he headed in a southwestern direction, he should soon enough begin to recognize the territory around Point Station. He resolved to leave the road and drive as far as he could in that direction. It was his hope to encounter one of the service roads that eventually would connect him with Point Station.

Before he left, he inventoried the cab and the cargo box of the truck to see what he might have to work with. He found no knife, no weapons. His only weapon was the rifle he had taken. He missed his bow and knife, which were apparently lost forever. Under the seat he found a dirty gray metal box with a hinged lid. He opened it to find an assortment of tools—screwdrivers, pliers, fuses and the like. In the back, he found a tire iron and some flares. At least he could change a tire.

He discovered what appeared to be the remnants of a hunting trail that veered off from the dirt road, and he resolved to proceed that way. He started the truck again and steered around trees and over roots and through the less dense sections of the jungle terrain as best he could, until he began to recognize the area and was quite certain he was nearing Point Station. It was not long before he did indeed come across a service road, and he continued along that.

He amused himself by imagining Captain Reynolds' face when he pulled up in a Nazi truck. As he began to smile while rehearsing a sardonic line or two he might use on his old friend, the engine sputtered and died.

He was able to steer the vehicle just off to the side of the road with its last bit of momentum. He looked at the fuel gauge and saw the little red needle pointing to *E*. He expected as much. He abandoned the truck to take to the trees the rest of the way to the Station. He looked forward to seeing a friendly face and at least a temporary respite from the nightmare he had been living.

But that was not to be. He emerged from the jungle to see that Point Station had been laid waste.

The office building and barracks had been blown apart and reduced to charred splinters. He saw ash and debris scattered over the grounds, as well as many spent shell casings.

Stunned, Tarzan walked slowly across the main yard, rifle cradled in his hands, looking back and forth. He saw bodies spread across the ground. At least a dozen, which would have been the full complement of the station. Nothing moved. No moan or other sound indicated that someone might still be alive.

The body of Captain Reynolds lay sprawled on the ground in front of the ruins of his office. A swath of bloody wounds ran in a line across his abdomen, staining his jacket. He had been cut down by machine gun fire.

Tarzan stood legs apart and looked down at the body of his old friend. A whirlwind of emotions welled up inside him—shock, then grief, then anger. His fists tightened. He took a deep breath and his mighty throat let out a tremendous cry of pain and rage that nearly shook the leaves on the trees in its vehemence.

His mind reeled with a wave of guilt and rationalization. He should have been here to help...no, he would have been killed, too...but perhaps he would have seen it coming...no, they obviously were surprised. The raiding party may have pulled up in a riverboat. Reynolds, ever gregarious and conciliatory, may have even invited them for tea. Despite his uniform and occasional sidearm, he was an administrator, not a soldier. Reynolds was not their enemy. There was no point to this attack.

Tarzan looked around the rest of the place, steeling himself for whatever else he might find. The door of the rear storage shed, the place where his British clothing and personal items were stored, had been blasted with a grenade or two. Debris and fragments of storage containers and shrapnel from the metal walls lay scattered for yards. He did not even look to ascertain the condition of his personal effects. At that moment he was not sure whether he would ever need them to journey back to England.

The Lord of the Jungle suddenly felt alone. Even though most of his formative years in the jungle had been solitary, he had had a welcome friend in Reynolds, perhaps his best one, with the possible exception of M'Bala.

He did not know what to do. The families of the men would have to be notified. How? Wellington, he supposed. But at the moment he had no idea how to go about that.

His senses were deadened, his resolve drained. Mechanically, methodically, he picked up the body of each dead man in turn and carried or dragged it to the one utility hut that remained standing. After stacking the corpses inside, he repaired and reinforced the rickety door and secured the latch. At least they would not be devoured by hyenas in the night.

Weary from his gruesome task, weak with hunger, the ape man sat down on the weathered gray planks of the Point Station pier and stared absently at the gently flowing current of the Bolongo

River. No river traffic at all today. It was eerie. He wondered whether the Nazis had begun to control the river traffic from Nyumba. Or perhaps people just feared to be out on the river these days.

Several small, colorful birds landed one by one on the well-trodden earth of the Point Station main yard, each cocking its little head and pecking away for a moment at whatever attracted its curiosity and then fluttering off again.

Tiny red and brown monkeys chittered from the trees and cavorted about, springing from limb to limb. One ventured down and into the yard to investigate, its large brown eyes darting around and its tiny nostrils flaring. It apparently smelled something it did not like and scampered away.

Tarzan watched them for some moments. This is how people should live, he thought. Free.

He yearned to be free and unencumbered. He was seized by a sudden urge to head toward the deep jungle, away from all of this, far from the company of any men. He could do it. He could live the rest of his life like that. To hell with the Nazis. To hell with London and European politics.

But what of his friends? Could he just abandon them? They would never know, he considered. They would believe he had died at the hands of the Nazis. Perhaps they already believed him dead.

He hesitated. If he took off now, he realized, he would be abandoning the noble efforts the native tribesmen had already made in their quest for freedom. He would be betraying the grand words he had spoken to Reynolds about resistance and determination.

He resolved to at least find out how his friends the Waziri fared. Had their village been found? Was it, too, in ruins? What else had happened while he was gone? He needed to know whether the resistance movement he had helped give birth to was still alive or whether it, too, had been cut down.

The ape man shed the cumbersome cloth smock from the camp and retrieved a hunting knife and sheath from one of the corpses, who had no further use for it. He slung the captured Nazi rifle over his head and shoulder and took to the trees. He could have taken one of Point Station's utility canoes and paddled upriver toward the tributary of the Bolongo which eventually led to the Waziri village, but he reasoned that he might be spotted on the river, and no one could keep up with him in the trees.

This day-long journey took him deep into territory farther away from Nyumba and, as far as he knew, farther away from the established Nazi camps. He believed, therefore, that perhaps there was a chance that the Nazis had not advanced this far yet.

A chance. Perhaps.

Chapter 14
RIVER LESSONS

The Waziri village was still there, and the villagers rushed out to greet him, exuberant at his return.

Most welcoming of all was the great piano-key grin with which M'Bala greeted the sight of his lost ally. Tarzan suspected that M'Bala had not grinned so broadly in some time.

Tarzan was promptly bidden to sit while the great fire was stoked with logs. The ape man would have preferred to rest, but there was much to talk about and the villagers were eager to hear what had happened to him and share their news with him as well.

Tarzan gratefully accepted food and drink as M'Bala began, "Many things have happened while you were gone, Tarzan. More people have been taken to the camps, but the soldiers have been met with more resistance, too. As you see, they have not found our village yet, but we fear it is only a matter of time. They have focused their movements to the northwest and the southwest of Nyumba. We only recently learned that they have begun a second camp to the southwest. In the meantime, we have constructed a rendezvous area deep in the jungle, far from where they patrol. Six tribes have joined our effort."

M'Bala bit into a huge joint of roasted meat and, chewing, continued, "They have made fewer raids lately. We believe that they are concentrating their resources on camp construction and operation for the moment, and will need more reinforcements before they can launch many additional raids."

"Perhaps that means that now is the time to move," said Asani, one of the younger warriors. "The tribes are eager. The drums could call a council in a day."

M'Bala looked at him, and back at Tarzan. "We have been debating that. Many voices said that we should wait until you returned before making a major attack. No one wished to believe that you were dead, certainly not without proof."

"Now that you have returned, you can lead us!" a tribesman said.

M'Bala ventured further motivation to the ape man. "You wish to take revenge for the death of your friend, do you not?"

"It has crossed my mind," Tarzan allowed.

Many of the tribesmen in attendance voiced their determination: "Let us move."

"This oppression has gone on long enough."

"What are we waiting for?"

Tarzan found inspiration in their zeal. After a moment, he said, "Then we must move, and we must move quickly."

"What shall we do?" asked one tribesman. "Resume raids?"

"We need to move to the next level," Tarzan said. He explained the call he made earlier to George Fredrickson, saying that Fredrickson expected to contact him again with details. "Since then, I have been out of touch, of course. I should attempt to reach him, but I can no longer use the Point Station telephone. I need to find another phone or a different way to contact London, and quickly."

"Where else is there such a phone?" asked M'Bala.

"Only in Nyumba. I daresay we cannot get into the hotel. Perhaps I can use the one in the consul's office. I need to tell him about Point Station anyway."

"But if you go there, you will be recognized."

"That's the problem."

The ape man thought for a moment and then said, "Do you still have all those uniforms and clothing we took in the first raid?"

"Yes. Why?"

"Well, one of those officers' uniforms might fit me. My German is a little rusty, but passable. Posing as a Nazi officer, I might be able to mingle with the crowds in the streets of Nyumba, find out the current status of things there, and make my way unobtrusively to the consul's office. There I could use his phone to contact London."

"That sounds risky. We tried wearing uniforms once before. It was a trap, remember? It did not succeed."

"That failed, I believe, because they recognized the truck, not me. But, yes, it is risky. Everything we do is risky. But we must hit them when and where they don't expect it, and with more than they expect."

"Do you want several of us to go with you?"

"Thank you, but dressed as what? Black Nazi soldiers? The idea is to not draw attention to my presence."

"You should not go alone. How about a manservant?"

Tarzan said, "Even better—how about a young man as a servant? Less conspicuous."

"Very well. But who?"

"I was thinking of Dajan."

M'Bala looked down the row of seated warriors to see the youth who had heard his name and whose large eyes brightened eagerly, in gratification that the ape man should think highly of him. The chief of the Waziri smiled. "A good choice."

The journey down the river in a Waziri canoe took the better part of two days. Tarzan sat in the front and Dajan in the rear, their provisions and belongings bundled in the center under pelts to provide some protection against possible splashing. They set out west from the narrow straights of the tributary bordering the Waziri land and progressed onto the broad, wide Bolongo.

With the exception of one large falls and one set of rapids they encountered, the river was tranquil for most of the way, their progress aided by the smooth glide of the downriver current. Their journey was peaceful, ironic in light of the purpose of their mission.

Lush, verdant green bordered most of the river, the trees often towering so high as to shade the river like a canopy. The water swirled and eddied around the rocks that lined many sections of the river, occasionally interrupted by stretches of marsh grass or muddy shores where animals came to drink. They saw few crocodiles or other beasts on this outing. Once they believed a great cat came to the river, but their approach appeared to scare it away.

"I've been thinking," the ape man said at length, breaking the silence. "It might add to the illusion if you knew a little German. It would be reasonable to assume that your master would have taught you some."

"What should I know?" said the black-skinned youth, eager to learn from this great warrior who had long been a mentor to his tribe.

"Well, *Ja* is 'yes,' and *nein* is 'no.'"

"*Ja. Nein,*" Dajan repeated. "I think I can get that."

"How about the German for 'I don't understand.' *Ich verstehe nicht.*"

Dajan stammered, "Ick vurste nik...."

"*Ich,*" Tarzan said. "Let the air out. *Ichhh,*" he stressed, exaggerating the sound. Dajan repeated the phrase with more precision.

Tarzan continued, "How about 'I don't know?' *Ich weiss nicht.*"

Dajan struggled with that phrase for a few passes, until he became comfortable with it.

"And how do I address you?" he asked.

"Always *Meinherr.* It means 'sir.'"

Dajan proved to be an apt and eager pupil. He asked for more. They continued the lesson for another mile of river, until Tarzan was compelled to say, "Slow down. It will not be credible if you speak the language too well!"

* * *

At the end of the first day, they stopped at a suitable spot and concealed the canoe along the shoreline. After taking a brief supper from the provisions they had brought along, they ensconced themselves high in the crooks of sturdy trees and settled in to sleep.

Early the next morning as they prepared to leave, Tarzan said, "Time to put on our costumes." He unpacked the clothing they had brought and donned his Nazi military uniform, complete with belts, boots and visored cap. Dajan struggled a little with the unfamiliar shirt and pants which they hoped would suffice to suggest the clothing of a manservant. It amused Tarzan to have to show him how the buttons were fastened.

They launched the canoe and set out on the river for the remainder of the journey, just as morning mist was lifting off the water's cool surface.

Such a canoe trip down the river allows a traveler long stretches of thought, and the ape man was no exception. As he steadily paddled, with only flitting birds overhead to disturb his thoughts, Tarzan considered the lot of his companion, this tall, vigorous seventeen-year-old who not that long ago had passed into manhood by Waziri ritual. Already he had seen his share of strife. He had been nearly killed last year in a tribal war fomented by greedy, vengeful white men, and this year he had been imprisoned in a concentration camp. It was for him and other young ones like him that the tribes resisted their conquerors. It was for him that the events Tarzan was about to set in motion must be undertaken.

Soon they passed the ruins of Point Station, and Tarzan told Dajan what had happened there. He spoke of his friendship with Captain Reynolds and his grief at the waste and loss he had witnessed.

They were silent for some time after that. Insects hummed and birds cawed and screeched in the distance.

At length, Dajan spoke up, "This clothing feels funny. Do white people wear such things all the time?"

"Yes, all the time, except for sleeping," answered Tarzan. "Remember, it is often not very warm where they live."

"I don't like the shoes. They pinch."

"They do take some getting used to."

They journeyed further on, the lapping of the waves against the paddles the only sounds they made.

"Tarzan, do you like being white?" Dajan asked, out of nowhere.

"What sort of question is that? Do you not like being black?"

"Well..." the youth thought for a moment, "when I am with my family and my friends and my tribe, I do not think about it. Only when I am with others who might treat me differently because they are not black, am I reminded of the difference."

"Exactly," said the ape man.

"Tarzan, why do white men hate us?"

"They do not all hate you. Captain Reynolds and his men do not hate you. You have met white traders and missionaries who did not hate you."

"But many do."

"To them, you are different. And men fear and hate what they don't understand. I cannot explain it, but it seems to be true."

"I saw terrible things when I was in that camp. Why do these Nazi men want to enslave us? What drives them?"

"Greed and power. It may be that they want the riches that Africa provides. They intend to grow more food than they need here, and mine gold and diamonds, which they will send back to their country. And they want the cheap labor to provide it."

"I don't understand why men do this. Do they not have hearts? Can they not see how much misery and suffering they cause?"

"They think you are inferior, and thus they think that you are easily conquered, and expendable."

"We will show them otherwise!" Dajan declared, proudly.

"It seems we will have to," Tarzan answered, his gaze lost in the depths of the murky river water.

Chapter 15
MESSAGE

Tarzan and Dajan arrived at Nyumba in the early after-noon. Tarzan had hoped to reach the consul's office before he left for tea time, a ritual still clung to even in this re-mote region. They tied up their canoe at one of the less conspicuous mooring spots just up the river from the main wharf area and pro-ceeded to walk across the wharf docks and out onto the hot, dusty streets of Nyumba. The Lord of the Jungle walked tall and straight, saluting passing Nazis but avoiding their eye contact, lest they look too closely. Dajan tried to act the part of a serving boy on his first visit to the city, a role which was not particularly challenging for him to play. As it turned out, the sight of a Nazi lieutenant accom-panied by an African manservant was not that conspicuous, since Africans had evidently been pressed into service as landscapers, bearers and valets on a large scale.

Tarzan was taken aback at the changes that had been made in Nyumba since he had last been there. The Nazi presence in the town had dramatically increased. Fuhrmann and his men had moved in quickly. Clusters of soldiers walked everywhere. Guards patrolled outside several buildings, as if the Nazis had comman-deered them. As they passed the hotel, Tarzan saw that it was crowded with Nazi guards, and uniformed soldiers passed in and out of it regularly. A large red and white banner bearing a black swastika had been hung from the front balcony, announcing where the colonel had established his headquarters. Indeed, Colonel

Fuhrmann was still in the process of ordering furniture, wall hangings and fixtures to make his office the most impressive in town.

"They are everywhere," Dajan said softly.

"Shh," Tarzan whispered in reply. "Do not speak Waziri if there is a chance you can be overheard. I'm not supposed to understand it, remember?"

"*Jawohl, Meinherr,*" Dajan whispered. The ape man smiled.

Tarzan made mental notes of the approximate number of Nazis he saw and several prominent buildings which seemed to be under their current control. He would have liked to reconnoiter much longer, but he feared that he risked exposure if he appeared to wander aimlessly. Nazis always seemed to be occupied with some task.

Consequently, he turned and headed toward Consul Wellington's office. As they approached it, Tarzan turned and led Dajan to the back of the building and around to the other side, keeping under the cover of the bushes and landscaping.

"What are you doing?" Dajan asked, confident that no one would overhear them here.

"I do not have time to ask for an appointment. I believe, however, that I can get in without one. Through here." He stopped outside the large widow framed by curtains and opening into the consul's office, a window which Tarzan had noticed the last time he was here. Through it, he could see that Nigel Wellington sat at his desk and, at the moment, alone.

Tarzan told Dajan that he would meet him in the front. He then hoisted himself up and crawled through the open window. Wellington looked up from his paperwork and uttered, "I say…?" before the ape man stood and removed his hat, letting his distinctive shock of black hair fall loose.

"Greystoke! What…what are you doing here in that uniform?"

"Hoping that I will not be recognized. I do not have much time, consul. Have you heard anything from London about the fact that Germany has essentially invaded this region?"

"Well, that's putting it rather bluntly. The home office is still working on it, and they will get back to me—"

"I expected as much," Tarzan said with disdain.

"The situation is complex," Wellington said, shaking his head slightly and wagging a finger. "The relations between Britain and Germany are delicate right now—"

"There is nothing delicate about it," Tarzan said sternly, his steely gray eyes narrowing. "These men are butchers. I was in one of their slave camps. And Point Station has been attacked. The entire garrison has been slaughtered."

"My God…!"

"You need to send a detail over there. The bodies need to be picked up, families notified, and so on."

"Right away. Anything else?"

"And I need to contact London. I need to use your phone."

"My phone?"

"Yes. Can you get me the London operator? It's crucial."

"Well, all right," Wellington acquiesced. In deference to the English Lord's bold manner, he presumed that this was more than a social call. He picked up the handset of the black desk phone and instructed his secretary to put him through to London straight away. When the line was established, Tarzan took the phone and made the connection to George Fredrickson.

"George, yes, this is Clayton again," he said, pausing to hear the responses on the other end. "Yes, it's been a long time, and a lot of things have happened that I didn't expect. Yes, that's what I'm calling about. You did? You have? The sooner the better. When?" He listened for a moment. "Excellent. All right, yes… many thanks." He hung up.

"What did you just do?"

"Something that you have been unwilling or unable to do. Called in troops."

"Lord Clayton, I know you are a Peer and as such are entitled to a certain amount of latitude, but do you expect me to just sit idly by while you charge in here and—"

"No. If I were you, sir, I would arrange to be far away from here in about three days. Thank you for the use of your phone."

Before the befuddled Wellington could say any more, Tarzan turned and strode out through the reception area and then out the front door and across the shaded veranda into the sunlight, where he joined Dajan. Together they left across the manicured yard.

They crossed the main street and made their way down two blocks crowded with foot traffic, heading toward the wharf. As they neared the river, Tarzan said to Dajan, "Time to go home."

"I do not sink so," a voice said in accented English. They heard the soft click of a rifle bolt behind them, and then the click of several more. Tarzan and Dajan turned slowly around to see four Nazi soldiers spread apart in a semicircle, pointing rifle barrels at their heads.

"Come vis us," one said. "Ze colonel vould like to speak vis you."

Chapter 16
RENDEZVOUS

"What are you doing? Put that gun down," Tarzan said in his most officious German.

"Zhis way, toward zhe headquarters," said the lieutenant, the commander of the group, gesturing with his rifle.

"You do not know what you are doing. You will regret this," Tarzan said.

"I zhink not. March!"

The lieutenant led the group down the street, followed by Dajan and Tarzan and the remaining three in line behind them. Tarzan noticed that Dajan, to his credit, accepted his circumstance without becoming timorous or apprehensive. He walked ahead tall and cool-headed, attentive to his surroundings, as Tarzan had coached him.

After a block, the lieutenant turned to the right to proceed down a side street packed with street booths and carts lining both sides, with merchants hawking their weavings and produce and grains at the passers by. The pedestrian traffic thickened as browsing and haggling shoppers crowded the booths, making walking down the narrow center more of a struggle. As they navigated through the increasingly cramped block, the lieutenant barked orders for the browsers to move aside.

Tarzan saw that the block ahead was more open and less crowded. He caught Dajan's eye, and with a subtle look from the ape man, the boy knew that he needed to be alert. A few steps ahead were several booths that they would pass very close to. The first one was a miller who had bins of grain and flour on display. In a movement so quick that Dajan would have missed it had he not been watching for it, Tarzan seized an open sack of grain and threw it into the eyes of the three soldiers behind him. They reeled back.

As the lieutenant in the lead turned to see what had happened, Dajan seized a crock of grain and smacked him across the temple with it. The German fell back onto the counter, his weight breaking the top and collapsing it, sending him flailing to the ground.

Meanwhile, Tarzan seized the rifle from the first of the three soldiers blinded by the grain, kicked him away, and used the butt to knock down the second one, who had begun to rise. The second one tumbled backwards into the third soldier, who tumbled into a garment booth, and the two of them became entangled in dashikis and swirls of cloth.

In the confusion, Tarzan and Dajan took off. They rounded the corner and headed down the short side street to the river bank. By the time the dazed soldiers regained their composure and gave chase, the ape man and the boy had nearly reached the river, and it was only a matter of moments before they found their canoe.

As they began to untie their rope, one soldier came into view from around the corner of a wharf building and yelled, "*Halt!*" He raised his rifle. Tarzan leveled the rifle he still held and fired first. The soldier fell. People on the wharf shouted and scattered. Dajan quickly untied the canoe and they scrambled in, seized the paddles, and hastily set off.

They paddled vigorously to gain a brisk speed and put as much distance between them and Nyumba's wharf as they could. After a few minutes, they looked back to see that several soldiers had boarded a motorized launch and had just started out from the wharf after them.

"Tarzan!" Dajan cried. "They are coming after us! We cannot outrun them!"

Tarzan quickly surveyed the banks on both sides of the river. He had the advantage of knowing the river better than they did, and thus he knew where it bent up ahead, and how. "Paddle quickly to try to get around those rocks up ahead," he said. The water churned with their paddles as they pounded forward toward a cluster of boulders bordering the river on the left.

In a few moments they reached the boulders. They left the water and carried the canoe ashore to conceal it behind the boulders and under brush. Tarzan said, "Take your bow and quiver." Tarzan seized the captured rifle, and they hurried off into the jungle.

Not long afterward, the launch bearing three Nazi soldiers rounded the river bend and slowed suddenly as the occupants looked ahead across the broad bosom of the river and saw—nothing. No canoe. No sign of their quarry.

They hastily surveyed the shore and saw no beached canoe. They decided to put ashore a bit further down from the boulders and look more carefully. Two of the soldiers clambered out onto the shore and searched for several minutes. But they only looked around, not up. Little did they know that their quarry peered down upon them from lofty perches, following their every move with sighted rifle and drawn bow.

After an interval, they abandoned hope of success and reluctantly returned to the launch and headed back to Nyumba, dreading the task of having to recount their failure to Colonel Fuhrmann.

Tarzan and Dajan climbed down from their trees and returned to their concealed canoe. "Are they stupid?" Dajan said. "They did not even think to look up."

"We were lucky."

"If they had seen us, we could have killed them easily enough."

"Be glad that we did not have to," replied Tarzan. "There will be more than enough killing if our plan succeeds."

Before re-launching, the ape man and the youth took the opportunity to shed their costumes and return to their more comfortable loincloths. Tarzan also retrieved the small drum that had
been secured inside the canoe and began to pound out a message.
He paused and listened for a response. He repeated the cadence,
and this time he heard a response a few moments later.

"They will be ready to meet us," Dajan smiled, interpreting the
message.

"Let's go," the ape man said.

The drums told the two that they did not need to journey the
entire way home. As they had planned, war parties from the Waziri
and the other six tribes were even now gathering at a rendezvous
point about halfway between their location and the Waziri village,
awaiting the ape man's arrival.

They took the canoe as far as they could and, after several hours,
left the river to venture inland. They sought and quickly found the
trail markings left there to guide them, including piles of stones
and strands of grasses knotted together in a particular way.

By the time Tarzan and Dajan reached the rendezvous point,
darkness had begun to fall. They were met by the sentries, who recognized them and guided them into the meeting area.

They were amazed to see that the numbers of tribesmen had
swelled to several hundred. It was almost as if a new village had
grown overnight in this remote sector of the jungle far from the
river, and far from any observed Nazi movement.

Several camps had been set up, and fires roasted the flesh of
recent kills. The sounds of drums and chanting wafted through the
air, apparently in the confidence that this location was so deep in
the jungle that the Nazis wouldn't find it. Even if they did, its
perimeter was well patrolled.

Tarzan admired the large meeting place had been carved out
of the wilderness over the past few weeks. Rows of logs had been

terraced into a hillock for seating, like a natural amphitheater, before the council fire pit. The massive council fire roared, flames licking around the logs, and each newly added log sent showers of sparks cascading upward toward the towering limbs overhead. Great torches flanked each row of log seats, illuminating the night.

Tarzan and Dajan approached the Waziri area and were greeted by M'Bala and some of his tribal council. The ape man recounted to them what had happened in Nyumba, and the Waziri chief said that he was pleased that Dajan had done well.

The ape man was impressed with the sheer size of their assembled armory. In addition to their own weapons, the tribesmen had brought along their entire cache of captured Nazi firearms, including rifles, pistols, submachine guns, mortars and hand grenades, and every man who would carry a firearm had had practice in using it. Warriors who did not carry firearms bore a full complement of native weapons including spears, bows, knives and blowguns, all quite deadly in their experienced hands.

"Here, Tarzan," M'Bala said as he handed the ape man a hunting knife holstered in a sheath and belt. Use it until this is over, when we can make you a proper new one. Do you want to take a bow?"

"Under the circumstances, I think I'll take one of these." He picked up a Schmeisser MP-28/II submachine gun, checking to see that it had a full 32-round magazine box.

Around the bonfire that night, all the warriors sat in council in the meeting area. The latest intelligence that anyone had was shared with the others, including Tarzan's report and as well as reports about the status of the two camps currently in operation. Spurred by Tarzan's return and the information he provided, the warriors settled upon their plan and finalized their strategies.

During the course of the evening, many men stood in the center near the fire pit and spoke to the rows of listeners. One after another told his story about what the Nazis had done and why he had committed to this course of action.

A member of little Kima's tribe, freed in the Schwarzenstadt raid, told of the devastation of his village.

One man rose and said, "These white soldiers have taken my brother!"

Another said, "When they came to my village, my father resisted and was slaughtered."

Yet another said, "My mother and sister are dead at the hands of these butchers!"

The rumbling of muttered assents grew to a chorus of shouts and cheers, amid raised arms and brandished weapons.

Tarzan drew inspiration from what he beheld. Among the ardent, determined faces, he saw the men of many tribes he had worked with: the diminutive Wahali, experts at camouflage, whose lean, wiry bodies could conceal themselves behind rocks or inside hollowed tree trunks, and whose blowguns brought instant death; the proud, often arrogant Urulu, who only last year had fomented a religious war but who, once they embraced a cause, pursued it with a fervid passion; and the Waziri, the proud giants of the forest, their white plumes undulating on their heads and their distinctive copper bracelets circling their sinewy wrists and ankles, men who could run ten miles and fight a battle at the end of it.

The ape man also saw many others who had rarely traded or even spoken with each other, yet they had joined together in this effort. Though their villages may have been days' marches from one another, and their customs quite dissimilar, together they constituted nothing less than the heart, the driving force of the entire jungle.

At one point near the end, the Lord of the Jungle was moved to rise and speak to them, the amber firelight flickering off his face and muscled torso:

"What you have decided to do here is dangerous and difficult, but it is a great thing. You have organized in a way tribes never have before. Even those who have recently been enemies"—he looked at some of the Waziri and Urulu—"now fight on the same side. If you are successful, what you do will be heard of in far off lands. You will give inspiration to other people who have been oppressed to fight back. You will show them that it can be done."

He looked around at the stern faces, some of whom he had never seen before but who had all agreed to dedicate their lives to this effort.

"Let us make our final preparations."

The evening ended with the camps breaking into their tribal rituals. Each tribe followed its customs to prepare psychologically as well as physically for the task ahead. Some tribes had brought along African death masks to exorcise hatred. Some donned amulets for luck or brewed potions for fortitude. Most of the camps broke out in chants and songs to bolster their spirit and heighten their resolve. Members of tribes were even seen joining in each other's dancing and drumming.

Tarzan had never witnessed anything like it. Often-fractious tribes had united behind this cause, an impressive display of will and courage. He could only hope that their will would be triumphant.

The next day at dawn, the camps disbanded, and the warriors split up and set out in three directions. One group of at least seventy-five set off to the southeast toward Schwarzenstadt No. 2. Another group of about fifty set off to the northwest toward Dunkelberg. The remaining group, numbering over a hundred, including Tarzan and Dajan and M'Bala, headed for Nyumba.

✠   ✠   ✠

In his third-floor office in the hotel, Colonel Fuhrmann was not having a good morning. He had just sat down to his breakfast tray of omelet, grilled ham, salted rye roll and Viennese coffee and had taken a few bites when he promptly stopped, dropped his fork, and sent for the cook. A young, fresh-faced corporal in a white coat and apron arrived in the doorway a moment later, nervously wiping his hands on a towel, and said, "Yes, sir?"

With his fork Fuhrmann picked up a piece of meat, pink with

brown griddle marks, and held it in midair. "What is this?"

"Ham, sir," the cook answered.

"Is it Westphalian ham?"

"No, sir."

"Did I not specifically order Westphalian ham?"

With some trepidation, the corporal replied, "Yes, sir."

"Then why don't I have it?" the colonel asked, his tone beginning to drip with umbrage.

"Well, uh, sir, the quartermaster didn't send us any."

"And why not? Is it too much to ask for a little bit of home in
this mosquito-infested jungle!?" Fuhrmann returned the meat to
his plate, his voice becoming louder in irritation. "Tell him that
when I order something, I expect it to be carried out. If this is too
much for him to handle, ask him how he would like latrine duty
in one of the camps! How will we ever get anywhere if no one can
follow simple orders!?" He shouted this last phrase through
clenched teeth and slammed his fist on the desk hard enough so
that the silverware jumped.

The young cook scurried out.

"Now, Schmidt," Fuhrmann said, continuing with his breakfast
and turning to look across his desk where his aide was seated.
"About this ape man's escape…how exactly did this happen?"

Schmidt did not look forward to this conversation. He did not
foresee that the dark mood with which the colonel had begun the
day would brighten with anything that he had to report.

"We are investigating the incident, sir. We have conflicting accounts."

"We always do, don't we? Everyone covers his ass."

"We pursued him. We found the truck abandoned. It had run
out of fuel."

"Where?"

"North of the river. A few miles from Point Station."

"Then he probably went there. I hope he enjoyed what he
found."

"Do you still want him taken alive?"

"Oh, I want him dead, all right, but I want the pleasure for my-self. What progress has there been in tracking him?"

"Well, sir," Schmidt hesitated, reluctant to say what he had to say next, "we think he came back into town. Disguised in a uni-form."

"What!?" Fuhrmann shouted, bits of egg spurting from his mouth. "Then why isn't he in custody?"

"We had him, sir, but he…slipped away."

The colonel was livid, the veins throbbing in his neck. He slammed his fist down upon the oak desk for the second time that morning. "Why can't all our forces stop one man!?" He turned back to his disappointing breakfast and added, "At least the blacks haven't conducted any raids for a while. We seem to have them under control."

Little did Fuhrmann know that a great deal more trouble lay in store for him that day.

Chapter 17

THE AIRFIELD

Nyumba's airstrip was situated on the northeastern section of the town, where the jungle thinned into a broad plain consisting mainly of grasses and scrub trees. The landing strip had been graded a few years earlier when air travel had become available and increasingly convenient for well-to-do visitors with more money than time. Since then, several hangars and a control tower had been built on the edge of town bordering the airfield.

The afternoon sky was cloudless. There had been no air traffic at all that day, and the airfield had been quiet.

In the cramped space of the small control tower, Fuhrmann's agent, Lieutenant Volkmann, trained his binoculars on a tiny speck that had appeared in the sky from the northeast. He strained for a moment to see what it was. As it grew larger, he realized that it was approaching the airstrip. In another moment, he could discern a second speck following the first.

"Do you see that?" he said to the African controller manning the console.

The controller looked through his set of binoculars and confirmed, "Yes. I see it."

"Do we have contact with it?"

"No, sir. No identification, no request for landing."

Volkmann continued to look, waiting for the specks to grow larger…and soon the first speck became recognizable as the figure of an approaching Armstrong Whitworth AW 27 Ensign British military cargo plane.

Volkmann was not the only one who studied the specks in the sky. At that same moment, Tarzan of the Apes, perched in a tree near the jungle outskirts of Nyumba, peered through a pair of captured binoculars and saw them, too, and turned to M'Bala to say, "They are coming."

Lieutenant Volkmann picked up his phone and called Colonel Fuhrmann. "Colonel," he said. "We have spotted two approaching planes. We have received no notice about them, and they don't respond to our hails. They seem to be coming in for a landing."

"What are they?"

"They appear to be British transports."

"Try to contact them and ask them what they want. Keep me informed."

Fuhrmann pressed down on the receiver hook and ordered his aide to connect him to the office of Harold Wellington at the British consulate. "Wellington!" he barked when the consul answered. "What is going on?"

"What do you mean?" he heard on the other end of the line.

"There are two British transport planes approaching the airstrip as we speak. What are they carrying?"

"Well, uh… I'm not sure…I've received no word…," Wellington stammered.

Fuhrmann slammed down the receiver. "Bumbling idiot! He doesn't know anything!" he declared, and then ordered, "Send a platoon out there. Fully armed. Get a machine gun crew on top of a hangar. If British troops get off those planes and fire one shot, stop them in their tracks!"

Fuhrmann's lieutenants rounded up most of the Nazi troops

on duty in the town, rousted out the ones who were off duty, and ordered them all out to the airfield. Within minutes, coats were hastily donned, gunbelts were buckled, weapons were grabbed, and dozens of pairs of boots hit the streets at a run amid puzzled queries and shouts of fevered urgency.

The Africans in the town took notice of the sudden activity. When they saw armed Nazi soldiers running through the streets or staff cars full of soldiers careening past, they promptly made way. Most took shelter in their homes. Dozens of street vendors hastily closed up their stalls. Some natives looked to the sky and pointed as the approaching aircraft became visible.

Soldiers arriving at the airfield scrambled to take up defensive positions behind and around the hangars. A two-man team climbed to the roof of the main hangar and set up a machine gun nest, in addition to the two that were already in place and manned elsewhere. Magazines were loaded, safety catches were clicked off, and weapons were cradled in position. The soldiers listened to the rumbling sounds of the approaching aircraft and waited.

Thus occupied watching the skies, and loudly inquiring of each other what was going on, the usual Nazi patrols in the town were not in a position to notice that at the same time, from the deep jungle to the west and south, over a hundred African warriors stealthily advanced upon the town. Fully armed with knives, spears and bows in addition to a great many machine guns, rifles and pistols, this ebony army grouped themselves in clusters of at least six and cautiously worked their way from the bordering jungle paths and the wharf out onto the side streets, toward the center of town or the airfield.

Among them, Tarzan and five Waziri warriors crawled nearly on their bellies along the rocky outcroppings lining the shore of the river, toward the higher ground of the wharf area. They kept low, concealed in the shadows cast by the abundant foliage, even in the mid-afternoon sun.

Up the slope of the bank and several yards ahead they could see the rear of one of the rickety storage buildings on the outskirts of the airfield. From the street beyond it, they heard footsteps approaching. In another moment there arrived seven or eight Nazi soldiers to begin fortifying a position at the side of the building.

The one in charge was Lieutenant Wilhelm Stammler.

Tarzan and the Waziri men looked at each other, their expressions indicating surprise that any soldiers arrived so quickly. They hunkered down in the underbrush to avoid being detected by the detachment that worked mere yards ahead of them. In the effort, one of the Waziri snapped a branch.

"*Was ist das?*" Stammler said.

A burst from Tarzan's submachine gun would have alerted other soldiers to their presence prematurely. And they had to act too quickly even to nock their arrows.

Pulling out his hunting knife, Tarzan bolted forward and thrust the blade full and hard underhanded into Stammler's stomach. Upon seeing this, the soldier a few steps to his left came at him, but the ape man turned swiftly and plunged his knife piston-like into the oncoming man's midsection. As he withdrew his knife hand, another soldier caught him from behind by surprise, grabbing his wrist, and wrested the knife out of his hand. The ape man wheeled around to catch him with a left cross followed by a solid knee into the abdomen. As the assailant doubled over, Tarzan firmly seized his chin and the back of his head and wrenched his head sideways, snapping his neck.

Tarzan bent to retrieve his knife and spotted another soldier coming at him. He whirled, and in one smooth, rapid motion he plunged the blade into the man's stomach and using his forward momentum, hoisted him upward and flung him into two other soldiers, knocking them down.

At the same time, the five Waziri attacked and made short work of dispatching the remaining soldiers.

One of the warriors said, "Close. Do you think they heard us?"

"I hope not," the ape man said. "Gather your weapons. The planes are landing."

The first of the two great gray aircraft, RAF tri-color circle insignia emblazoned on its side, touched down at the far end of the runway and rumbled toward the cluster of hangars and the control tower, its wheels kicking up clouds of dust and gravel from the crudely-paved runway as it bounced along. In a few minutes, it rolled to a stop about a hundred yards from the hangars. Even before its engines shut off, its rear cargo hatch popped open and swung outward on its bottom hinges until the top arced down and rested on the ground to form a ramp. From the bowels of the cargo bay, a dozen British soldiers hustled down the ramp. Holding rifles and machine guns at the ready, they looked swiftly around in the African sun to get their bearings and assess their situation before moving aside for the remaining two dozen men in the platoon to exit the plane.

"*Soldaten!*" someone shouted.

The sharp crack of a rifle split the air.

An instant later, tongues of flame and puffs of smoke spat from gun barrels on both sides of the airfield.

The British soldiers already out of the plane hit the dirt to assume the prone position and expertly commenced to fire. The remainder of the unit followed suit.

The second plane rumbled down the runway under a hail of bullets and taxied to a stop a short distance from the first and slightly behind it. It, too, opened its cargo hatch and spilled out almost forty men, who hit the ground, rifles blazing.

Bullets flew across the hundred yards of airfield between the hangars and the two planes, turning the airfield into a deadly no-man's land.

From the roof of the hangar, the machine gun clattered. The nest had been set up on the roof at such an angle that the British troops could not get clear shots at it from their positions, and thus were not able to take it out. Moreover, the machine gun's position, high and off to the side of the airfield a considerable distance from where the two cargo planes had stopped, was too far away for it to hit its targets with deadly accuracy. But the Nazis manning it pumped a continuous spray of bullets, churning up dirt along the airstrip so that the British soldiers were prevented from advancing. For the moment, the British were pinned down.

But only for the moment.

Suddenly the machine gun nest on the roof exploded, propelling the gunner and loader nearly aloft and sending shrapnel flying. The British soldiers gaped, puzzled as to who blew it up, since none of them had. A moment later, several Waziri warriors emerged from around the rear of the hangar, cheering. It became clear that they had pitched a hand grenade onto the roof.

The soldiers in the other two nests, surprised at the sudden explosion, hastily looked around. One of them saw running warriors emerging from the edge of the jungle. Before he could say anything or swing his machine gun around, two more grenades were lobbed at his nest. The explosion rocked the area, spewing smoke and fragments into the morning air. The third nest went up a moment later. Smoke began to cloud the sky over the airfield.

The emboldened British troops began to spread out and work their way toward the town.

The rest of the Nazi soldiers in the area were taken aback, not expecting forces from the rear. From their building corners and other places of concealment, they turned to face their new African enemy.

But they now found themselves in a crossfire. British troops fired at them from the runway. African resistance fighters emerged spraying arrows, spears, and rifle fire at them from the hangars and surrounding outbuildings and from the jungle foliage that rimmed the airfield. Pandemonium reigned.

A great many of the Nazi soldiers in the vicinity of the hangars were cut down in the first volleys. Those who were not, scattered. Some ran across the graveled airfield yard toward the town, only to be picked off by British fire. Some turned and headed toward the river, where they ran into African forces. Those who chanced to be spared and managed to escape from the embattled airfield ran for the streets of the town. Some tried to make a stand, thinking they could resist. They were wrong.

✠   ✠   ✠

Twenty miles away to the southeast, a party of African warriors raided and liberated—for the second time— a Nazi concentration camp named Schwarzenstadt.

Spies had reported for some time on the operation of this camp, and thus the raiders knew, among many other things, where the fuel tanks were located and how thick their metal walls were and when they were last filled. Tarzan had also given them detailed information about the camp's layout.

From the outskirts of the fence beyond the camp's perimeter, warriors drew back their taut bowstrings nocked with special arrows, while a tribesman touched a lighted torch to them one by one. The first flaming arrow whizzed through the squares of the chain-link fence toward the fuel tank, but bonked harmlessly against it and fell to the ground. The second and the third arrows, however, penetrated the metal of the tank and set off one and then another thunderous fireball, rattling the foundations of the camp with a prodigious roar.

Panic ensued as the flames spread upward and across to nearby buildings. Prisoners screamed. Soldiers broke ranks and ran to see what had happened, only to be met by a deadly barrage of arrows and blowgun darts.

In another moment, a mortar fired its deadly missile toward one guard tower, and while the guards of the second tower at the entrance gaped and took a moment to overcome their shock and gather their wits to retaliate, a second grenade blasted apart their tower, too.

While this was going on, a contingent attacking from the opposite side of the camp tossed a hand grenade at the single guard tower and the rear gate, the one Tarzan had escaped from, while another blasted a hole in the fence.

The guard towers thus demolished and the gates rent open, the liberating force of natives from four tribes rushed in shouting battle cries and brandishing weapons. It was a rout.

For the second time, flames from a Schwarzenstadt concentration camp blazed upward and filled the African sky, their roar drowned out, once again, by jubilant cries of freedom.

✠   ✠   ✠

Some twenty-five miles in the opposite direction. the drums had already spread the news of the attacks upon Nyumba and Schwarzenstadt. Detainees toiling in Dunkelberg, the newer, smaller camp, heard the drums and quickly passed word that a rescue party was coming. The Nazi guards, oblivious to the drums' import, paid little heed to the guttural chatting of the inmates and just ordered them to shut up from time to time.

When the raiding party arrived, the first arrow landed in the back of a Nazi guard supervising a work detail just inside the perimeter fence. The half dozen prisoners who saw the guard fall shouted "Rescue!" in their dialect and immediately turned on three other guards in the work area and struck them down. A fourth guard turned to stop one of them, but was cut down by an arrow.

In a moment, the remaining population of detainees rose up and seized every guard in the camp, knocking them down, beating their heads, sometimes cutting their throats.

Guards manning the machine guns in the towers managed to fire off a few bursts at the melee below them before they met swift death in a hail of arrows.

The camp was already nearly overtaken when the rescue party crashed through the gate and invaded, shouting and waving spears and bows and captured Nazi rifles. The guards and officers who tried to resist and make a fight of it were either cut down by their own prisoners or by the advancing rescuers. Some guards who chose to turn tail and run for their lives never made it, either.

The commanding officer of the camp was rousted from his tent office and impaled upon a spear, to the giddy cheers of the inmates.

The entire operation took less than fifteen minutes.

Chapter 18
FERTIG

In his office, Colonel Dieter Fuhrmann heard the noise and the gunfire and from the window. His first response was to try to raise the airport from the phone in Schmidt's outer office.

"Volkmann!" he shouted into the receiver. "What is going on there? Volkmann!?" He cursed the silence.

A moment later, a young blonde radio dispatcher interrupted nim, "Colonel! A radio report just came in from Dunkelberg. It seems, sir..." he hesitated, not wanting to infuriate the Colonel.

"Well...what!?" Fuhrmann said, impatiently.

"Well, sir, they said that there has been a riot. A camp revolt. They're asking for reinforcements, sir."

"A revolt? What happened?"

"They were attacked...by Africans, apparently...an invading force. And then the prisoners rose up and turned on the guards."

"And then what!?"

"And then they asked for more troops...and then the radio went dead, sir."

Fuhrmann cursed loudly.

"Post six guards at the front. Don't let them get in!"

The African warriors who descended upon Nyumba fought with a ferocity that intimidated even the Nazi battle troops. Nearly every tribesman knew a friend or family member enslaved or killed by the aggressors, and thus for most of them, this mission meant nothing less than personal vengeance.

The Nazi soldiers, often raw recruits, were new to this land and unnerved by the surprise appearance of fierce African warriors. Most of these Germans were familiar only with the downtrodden prisoners in the camps or the grinning, obsequious merchants or compliant servants in the town. The sight of great numbers of tall, muscled warriors in battle regalia bearing down on them was fearsome indeed.

Some Nazis turned tail and ran, but were chased down by warriors who could run faster and farther. Even the burliest of the German soldiers were little match for the hardy blacks, who were bred by years of jungle survival, not sixteen weeks of boot camp.

Skirmishes with gunfire, and sometimes even hand-to-hand, broke out along the streets and alleyways of the town. One group of four soldiers running from the airfield toward the barracks rounded a corner to come up face to face with six warriors. One soldier discharged his weapon directly at the oncoming blacks, and felled one, but before the rest could muster an attack, the Africans furiously leaped upon them and made short, bloody work of them.

At the airfield, Tarzan saw that the situation was well in hand. He believed his assistance was not particularly needed, so that he felt free to turn his attention to another priority—Fuhrmann. No one had seen the arrogant commander at the field or in the town. Tarzan ran around to the back of the now-secure hangar complex and dashed across the open spaces between utility buildings until he reached the cluster of buildings that began the town proper. He nimbly scaled the wall of the first building until he reached the roof. The roofs of a long row of buildings were connected or closely adjoined, so that he could move easily and quickly across them to progress toward the center of town.

He had traversed about a block's worth of rooftops when he was compelled to stop in mid-stride because he saw below him a cluster of Nazi soldiers waiting in the alleyway to ambush a party of African warriors advancing down the main street. He promptly unslung his submachine gun and fired into them. The suddenness and surprise direction of the ape man's fire stirred up the party like a hornet's nest, but before they could turn to ascertain who had shot at them from above, the noise attracted the warriors, who stormed into the alley and decimated the soldiers.

Tarzan leaped down from the one-story roof to see whether any of the Africans had been injured. This particular party of African raiders carried several captured high-powered rifles, hand grenades, and one of the mortars. Tarzan could see that they did their firearms training proud when, a few moments later, a staff car bearing four heavily-armed soldiers as reinforcements came charging down the street from the direction of the barracks toward the airfield. It swerved right to come to a stop, but before it did, two Waziri in the group directed their mortar at it and fired. The explosion rocked the vehicle off its wheels and overturned it, spilling its contents into the street. Arrows and spears finished off the occupants in short order, almost before the upturned wheels on the vehicle had stopped spinning.

The warriors carrying the mortar then proceeded with Tarzan and a group of about twenty other warriors to the newly constructed barracks about two blocks away. They hastily moved into position and fired a deadly missile, which blew a great gap in the wall near the main entrance, igniting blazes and churning up smoke and debris.

The few soldiers who were still in the barracks and survived the blast ran out of the building, only to be cut down by a barrage of arrows and bullets from the warriors in the street. Screams and shouts of the burned and wounded filled the air like the cries of injured animals.

As the smoke roiled out, some of the Wahali warriors from the group noticed the utility garage in the rear, where they found several troop transport trucks parked, the vehicles which had carried troops to their villages or carried their loved ones away from them. They took great relish in heaving their remaining hand grenades into the garage to blast those vehicles to smithereens.

The assault on Nyumba had stained with blood virtually every Nazi uniform in town. Clusters of warriors emerged from engagements and skirmishes behind buildings or from corners to gather in the street. The African warriors were at the point where they looked around for any other enemy to engage, since they could see none attacking.

What they did see approaching along the main street from the airfield was a crisply-dressed, clean shaven British officer with an escort of troops. The officer strolled up smartly and said, "Captain Trevor Jones, commander of this little detachment. You must be the Tarzan I was told to look for."

"I am Tarzan," said the nearly naked white man standing among a cluster of blacks. They shook hands. "Thank you for coming. Your men have done well."

"Your African friends seem to have done quite all right on their own."

"They are fighting for their families and their homeland."

"I'm glad I didn't have to go up against them!" He surveyed some of the nearby destruction, including the blazing barracks and the smoking vehicle carcass. "Well, we seem to have just about cleaned them out," he continued. "Are there any other troops about?"

Tarzan explained, "There are two concentration camps in the jungle which by now have been attacked, successfully I hope. We should check on those. As far as the troops in town, there is at least one man unaccounted for. The commander, Colonel Fuhrmann."

"Where is he?"

"We haven't seen him. I suspect he's at his headquarters at the hotel, on the other side of town."

"Would you like us to find him?"

"If you don't mind, I think I'd like to do it."

Captain Jones nodded. "I understand. We've got medics for your wounded. We'll mop up here. I'll just send a few backup troops to tag along at the rear, in case things get sticky."

Tarzan selected a group of about eight warriors, including Dajan, who had been nearby, and they cautiously marched to the wharf and advanced toward the hotel from the smaller side streets, clinging to the shadows and doorways to conceal their movement, since they could not be sure of the fortifications of the hotel.

The din of gunfire and battle cries could still be heard in the distance as Tarzan and the Africans approached the hotel from an angling side street. They could see two guards, rifles at the ready, standing at the main entrance, one on either side of the door, and at least four others crouched behind the veranda railings or shrubbery, looking off into the distance toward the barracks and airfield.

They surreptitiously positioned themselves across the street from the hotel, behind the corners of buildings and behind several empty street vendor booths and overturned carts abandoned in earlier chaos. So far, they were unnoticed.

Tarzan said to the Africans, "You will have to take out the guards. I'm going around to the side. Let's use arrows first, because shots would alert any troops inside." He turned to Dajan and said, "Would you like to try first?"

"Me?" said the young Waziri, gratified to be selected.

"It's time you try," said the ape man.

Dajan drew back his bow carefully, his hand trembling slightly with the significance of the moment. He released. The arrow sailed over the front lawn and bounced off one of the large white pillars supporting the roof, next to the guard he had aimed at.

Embarrassed, Dajan cursed in Waziri.

The next arrow, from a more seasoned archer, struck home. Stirred to action, the Nazi guards shouted and returned fire. The attack would not be silent. The Africans quickly switched to their rifles, and a gun battle ensued.

With the security forces of the Nazi headquarters thus occupied, Tarzan cradled his submachine gun and disappeared behind
the building near them and worked his way back around the wharf
area, from which point he could take to the trees and advance on
the hotel from the jungle growth bordering its northwest side. He
moved swiftly, so that in a few minutes he reached the overhanging
limbs adjoining the hotel property, the place where he had leaped
from the soldiers' rifle fire the last time.

Tarzan leaped from the tree limb and landed lightly on the
gently sloping roof. Keeping low to avoid stray bullets, he made his
way up the roof slope, over the peak and down the adjacent slope
until he arrived next to the gable that marked the area near
Fuhrmann's offices. From this position he could see the last few
skirmishes playing out further down on the main street and a few
of the side streets. Shots were fired sporadically. What appeared to
be the last holdouts of the Nazi forces were rounded up as Africans
and British troops combed the streets.

He could see all the way down the main street where flames
and smoke curled up from the garage and the barracks. In the distance further to the east, the smoke from the explosions and gunfire
at the airfield hung in the sky like a wispy shroud.

He looked over the edge of the roof and down into the street
below to see that the troops guarding the building were quite occupied with the African ground force and that British soldiers were
holding positions further back, ready to support them.

He noticed that, in the turmoil, no guards were on the balcony,
and no one seemed to be looking three stories up. He was about to
move forward when two soldiers ran out of the building from the
side door below him. They rushed, guns blazing, to the cover of
landscape shrubbery and the few trees that grew in the hotel's east
side yard and exchanged fire with the warriors assaulting from the
front.

Tarzan's movement on the rooftop above caught the eye of one
of these soldiers, who turned and fired upward at him. The bullets

only shattered roof tiles on the gable near Tarzan, but pinned him down so that he could not move.

The soldier shifted to a slightly more advantageous position. He cracked off one more round, and then, gasping, eyes agape, he suddenly stiffened and dropped his rifle.

Dajan's arrow, sure and true, had stopped him.

The second soldier, caught off guard momentarily by this, left himself exposed enough so that rifle fire from the Waziri cut him down as well.

Dajan waved up to Tarzan that all was clear, smiling. The ape man let a smile cross his face and acknowledged the wave, then turned his attention back to the purpose at hand.

He secured the submachine gun sling on his shoulder and swung down from the roof overhang to land on the third-floor balcony. He carefully moved along the row of windows and balcony doors until he arrived at his destination—Fuhrmann's outer office. Keeping to the side of the door frame, he peered in to see Wolfgang Schmidt seated at his desk and one guard at the door. Drawing a breath, he charged in through the double doors. The guard leveled his rifle to shoot, but Tarzan fired a burst from his machine gun to drop the guard. Schmidt was reaching for a pistol in his desk drawer, but Tarzan caught the move and said, "Do not even think about it." Schmidt quickly snapped his arms into the air and stood up.

"Where is Fuhrmann?" the ape man asked.

Schmidt gestured toward the inner office door, which was closed. Tarzan walked over to the door and, standing to the side of the door frame, tried the knob. It was locked.

"Fuhrmann!" he yelled. "Give it up! *Es ist fertig! Alles ist kaput!*"

He heard a shot. He exchanged glances with Schmidt, whose expression was also puzzled.

The ape man slammed against the door and broke into the office.

The sharp, sulfurous smell of pistol smoke hung in the air. Fuhrmann lay at his desk, his head slumped down, his right hand on the desktop still grasping his Luger. A large bullet hole gaped in his temple, and dark blood pooled from his head, spreading in little rivulets through the fiber of the desk blotter.

Chapter 19

E P I L O G U E

When word leaked out about the insurrection in the African river town and its surrounding region, Nazi propaganda did its best to portray the events as a minor and ill-executed revolt, quickly put down by crack SS troops in the area. Die-hard rumors, however, continued to surface that "something more" had gone on down there.

In succeeding weeks, Nazi Germany invaded Czechoslovakia and then went on in September of 1939 to invade Poland, precipitating World War Two. Priorities shifted. The personnel and resources necessary to commit to an African initiative became an unbearable extravagance under the increasing burden of maintaining more and more European concentration camps and, ultimately, fighting a European war on two fronts.

The only complete and detailed written account of the events in and around Nyumba in late 1938 was the official report, begun by Colonel Fuhrmann and finished by Wolfgang Schmidt, submitted to the German High Command. It was delivered in a sealed brown envelope to the office of Heinrich Himmler. When his chief of staff presented him with the envelope, Himmler said, "You are certain that this is the only copy?"

"Yes, sir. As instructed."

"And no one else has seen it?"

"Of course not, sir."

Himmler dismissed the aide and perused the document at

some length. He had had scant time lately to pay attention to distant African issues, his mind reeling with the myriad challenges of new European initiatives and the Final Solution.

He read over its conclusions again:

"...primitive native population thought to be docile but consistently proving belligerent...particularly vigorous and resourceful native resistance forces...some led by the previously described native white man whose identity is uncertain...continuation of the project seems futile...recommendation to abandon any central African initiative..."

Himmler realized that he could not show this to the Führer. He could not show this to anyone.

A revolt that consistently overpowered the forces of the SS and the Reich? Primitive black men? A white ape man? He shook his head, almost involuntarily. No.

He knew what he had to do. He took out his cigarette lighter, flipped open the silver-plated top, and spun the little ridged wheel with his thumb to strike a flame. He touched the flame to the corner of the report, held it momentarily while the flame spread, and then dropped it into the ceramic ash tray on his desk and watched while the pages burned to black flakes.

Himmler's face was expressionless, and history does not record what his thoughts might have been, as he destroyed forever any historical evidence linking the Third Reich, the African resistance, and Tarzan of the Apes.

Acknowledgements

My thanks to my wife Amy for all your support. My deepest thanks and appreciation also go to my loyal readers Chris Schoggen and Dan Roskom, who tirelessly pored over my manuscripts and offered advice on matters large and small, and particularly to Lin Courchane, who urged me to submit these stories for publication. Their optimism and encouragement were tremendously gratifying.

I grew up on the Tarzan movies and, to a lesser extent, the comics. But I became hooked on the real Tarzan in high school after picking up a new Ace paperback edition of *Tarzan and the Lost Empire* for fifty cents, the one with the Frank Frazetta cover of our hero, monkey on his back, hanging from a limb on a cliff and looking down upon the Roman city. I went on to collect the entire series of Ace and Ballantine paperback reissues of Burroughs' tales (and still have them).

I discovered that Burroughs' stories were quite unlike the family-friendly Tarzan of the movies, with inarticulate Johnny Weismuller as the hulking hero living for some reason in the jungle with a classy, aristocratic Jane. No, Burroughs' hero was a British lord who spoke educated English and had a fascinating backstory. I was impressed with the far superior level of development and action found in these tales.

I attempted writing my first Tarzan tale in 2005 (*Tarzan and the "Fountain of Youth"*) as something of a lark, and then followed it, to date, with six more Tarzan tales. Friends encouraged me to try to get the stories published. I am grateful to Jim Sullos of ERB, Inc., for giving me the chance.

Here are my first three. In these stories, I have tried to craft realistic, page-turning adventure tales featuring classic Tarzan elements while at the same time taking the character in directions that have never been done in Tarzan stories before.

I invite you to share your thoughts and comments with me at zachekbooks@gmail.com.

Thomas Zachek
Menomonee Falls, Wisconsin

TARZAN

Return to Pal~ul~don

The Wild Adventures of Edgar Rice Burroughs

TARZAN

Return to Pal~ul~don

by Will Murray

CPSIA information can be obtained
at www.ICGtesting.com
Printed in the USA
LVOW11*1231160717

541555LV00006B/24/P